Praise for *The Origins of Iris*

'An empathic, brave exploration of serious themes'
Daily Mail

'Extraordinarily raw, gripping and totally unforgettable'
Peterborough Telegraph

'A beautiful reflection on the great conundrum of choices
made and abandoned, loves pursued and betrayed'
Sophie Ward

'Evocative and unexpected, tender and fierce, *The Origins of Iris*
is unlike any other thriller I've read in years . . . Outstanding'
Sarah Hilary

'This novel is like a dream, from the haunting narrative
to the beautiful prose to the way Iris and her wilderness
kept making their way into my subconscious at night.
It is everything I could want from a book'
Anna Bailey

'Compelling, original and highly readable'
Kate Hamer

'Atmospheric, thought-provoking, complex.
A haunting exploration of one woman's
journey into the dark heart of herself'
Tamar Cohen

'A tale of wonder, heartbreak and mystery,
beautifully told. Loved every word'
Emma Haughton

'Evocative, transportive writing telling a story of
regrets, choices, loss, and love in many forms.
This is a lyrical, dark, and beautiful book'
Amanda Jennings

Also by Beth Lewis

The Wolf Road
Bitter Sun

the origins of iris

BETH LEWIS

HODDER*studio*

First published in Great Britain in 2021 by Hodder Studio
An Imprint of Hodder & Stoughton
An Hachette UK company

This paperback edition published in 2022

1 3 5 7 9 10 8 6 4 2

A CIP catalogue record for this title is available from the British Library

Paperback ISBN 9781529357714
eBook ISBN 9781529357691

Typeset in Plantin Light by Hewer Text UK Ltd, Edinburgh
Printed and bound by in Great Britain by Clays Ltd, Elcograf S.p.A.

Hodder & Stoughton policy is to use papers that are natural, renewable
and recyclable products and made from wood grown in sustainable
forests. The logging and manufacturing processes are expected to
conform to the environmental regulations of the country of origin.

Hodder & Stoughton Ltd
Carmelite House
50 Victoria Embankment
London EC4Y 0DZ

www.hodder.co.uk

For all the many possible yous

Between every two pine trees there is a door leading to a new way of life.

John Muir

Into the Woods

A telescope was the only thing of value I took when I walked out of my life. Aged thirty years and fifty-nine days, I boarded a bus and rode through three states to a small town in the Catskills. I could have driven a car. I could have flown in one of those tiny-engined planes. I could have taken a direct bus route, with four hours' travel time, instead of the eight-stop, twenty-eight-hour journey I'd chosen. Any other mode of transport would have been quicker, more convenient and much more comfortable than this bus.

But this bus would be the hardest route for Claude, or the police, to track.

I watched grey freeway after grey interstate pass by the window, and two hours into my journey, my brain went through a panic cycle. I regretted every decision I'd ever made.

I should go home. I can still make it back before Claude even realises I am gone.

No way I'm going back. See that smug look on Claude's face I know so well?

Couldn't make it a day on your own, Iris, what were you thinking?
Bitch.

But after a few minutes of indignation, the panic started again.

I settled down into my window seat in the mostly empty bus. Midweek, mid-morning, not many long-haul travellers hoboing it on the NYC–Philly line. I had my pick of seats, so I went two from the back, my childhood bus position. A minor but satisfying fuck-you to front-seat Claude.

Beside me, a small daypack filled with essentials – magazines, snacks, a sweater, bus timetables. Below my seat, in the luggage compartment, the telescope, a tent, a sleeping bag, enough freeze-dried meals to stock the International Space Station for a year, and all the brand-new hiking gear I'd bought on my flight from the city. I'd stuffed everything into Claude's Harvard duffel. She loved that bag. So I took it.

That morning, I'd withdrawn every cent in my account in crisp greens, slid the thin wad into a pouch and wrapped it round my waist. I could have emptied the joint saver and lived like a queen, but I wouldn't take another penny from her. I tightened the straps on the pouch too much so they'd dig in and I'd remember it was there.

Another hour on the bus. The sound of a radio floated up the aisle. A passenger near the front, no thought to headphones or common courtesy, cranked up the volume as the bus picked up speed. Crackly headlines matched the rhythm of the engine: the president did something stupid, a terrorist incident in Europe, a selfless hero saved a dog stranded on the freeway, a three-point-five earthquake recorded in the Adirondacks, seismologists baffled, and on and on until the headlines began to repeat and the listener switched off the radio.

I was drifting in and out of sickly travel sleep when:

'Apple?'

I nearly jumped out of my skin.

Nobody talks on buses. Klaxons and wide eyes.

A man across the aisle was offering me a Golden Delicious. He had a bag of them on the seat beside him.

I took it. Smiled my best 'this is weird but I'm going with it' smile and held the fruit like it was a grenade. The man nodded, seemed happy to help out a destitute-looking lone female, and went back to his own company. A moment later, a thunderous apple crunch and the man smiled at me again.

I stared at the gift. Can't roofie an apple, can you? But still, I'd wait for the man to disembark before I ate it.

Trust no one. If I'd learnt anything these last six years, it was that. I wasn't going to get anywhere in the forest by relying on the kindness and good nature of strangers. I'd seen *Deliverance*.

I'd chosen the forest because my wife would never expect it. I'd asked myself, where is the last place Claude would think to look? Iris hates dirt. That's what she'd think. Iris doesn't have a practical bone in her body. Iris can't take care of herself even with a fully working kitchen and stocked refrigerator. There is no alcohol in the forest, why would Iris go there?

After a few days and no sign of me, she'd report me missing, call my mother and my sister. They'd look for me in motels and hotels, quaint B&Bs, then the houses of my one ex and my one old friend, even in my office, under my desk, wrapped in a nest of shredded paper and coffee filters.

But they would never find me.

As the city tapered away to small towns and longer stretches of countryside, I imagined my family poring over the last few months of my life, my financial records – one credit card, a checking account teetering on red, the joint account that was all Claude and no me. They'd find a recent statement, within it a clue, a golden nugget, something I'd kept from the woman I was meant to love. Here, look, Miss, Mrs, Ms? She spent two hundred bucks on a tent, was she planning a trip? And they'd look confused because, a tent? Iris in a tent? There must be some mistake. I thought of them digging into my life and finding all those secrets you only find after someone dies. Was it the same as death, to abandon life?

To say I was ill prepared, impulsive, idiotic would be accurate. All words beginning with I. Like Iris.

Along with the hiking gear, tent and telescope, I'd brought a stack of notebooks to record all this. The insanity of it, the wonder, the secrets of life and happiness I hoped to find between the spruces. Or I'd starve to death or fall off a mountain and those notebooks would be the only thing left of me. In any case, keeping a journal can be cathartic, healing, blah blah blah. Maybe I'd send them to Claude, to explain everything I'd done and why. She told me everything, after all. Until she didn't.

I took a notebook from my bag and opened it to a blank page. Anything I wrote would be muddled, broken up into memories of

her and me, who I was and who I never wanted to be, the things
I'd let her do, the person I'd let myself become. Was that a way to
find peace? Was it a way to admit what had happened?

On an empty page, I dug the pen into the fibres and dragged
the ink.

Claude

But the rest of the words wouldn't come. I couldn't write
them. I couldn't bring myself to see them there on the page in
black and white. Then it would be real. Then it would all have
been real.

I closed the book, shoved it in my bag and stared out the
window, let the rhythms of the bus rock me to sleep.

Twenty-six hours after I left my apartment, I arrived in Albany
and changed to a local service. The bus, which should have been
decommissioned in the eighties, had hard seats, a misfiring engine,
and few riders. An elderly man with a walking stick up front, a
woman and her burbling baby in the middle, and in my spot, two
from the back, a woman in a red hiking jacket, same brand as
mine, hood pulled up, covering her face, slumped and snoring
against the window. I took a seat behind the driver and tried to get
comfortable.

A few more hours and I'd be at the edge of the forest, at an
unmaintained trailhead. The trail petered out after eight or ten
miles and the wilderness took over. I'd found it in one of those
magazine lists of forgotten tourist attractions.

At this last leg, the reality of my situation finally sank in and I
began to shake.

I should go home. God, she'll be so angry. I should apologise. I
should beg for her forgiveness.

Her forgiveness? What about yours?

She should be begging after all she did. You got out of there just
in time, for both of you.

The panic eased, the defiance rose again.

I relaxed in my seat. I'd have to convince myself every day, and already I was exhausted.

I stepped off the bus in a small town near Catskill. Barely on the map. I hefted Claude's duffel onto my back, walked to the trailhead, and stopped at the sight of the trees crowding over the narrow pathway, dripping lichen and broken branches, hiding darkness behind a bright, verdant mask.

The trail was still marked despite years of disuse. A blue and white plaque half-swallowed in a hornbeam, the screws a permanent wound in the bark, easy to miss unless you were looking. In a few more years, the tree would win and all trace of this trail would be gone. The sight of nature taking over, disappearing evidence of human destruction just with sun, water and time, unrooted my legs, unclenched the knot in my stomach. I had plenty of wounds, like nails driven into my bark, still open and stinging, threatening to scar, but, like the trees, I finally had sun, water and the time to heal.

I hadn't set foot in the forest since my father died. I'd tried, and I'd turned away from the memories, but this time was different. I wasn't afraid. There were no giants barring my way. The forest welcomed me because I was ready now and the trees knew. They passed on the message, under rivers and over mountains. Iris is here, they said, she's come home at last.

The smell of leaves and dirt enveloped me as I stepped into the wilderness. Sounds of civilisation hushed, replaced with the gentle rhythms of nature. The darkness receded to a thick green glow and the ground softened under my feet.

I'd come to the forest to rediscover the part of me I'd left there as a child. The girl I was on those trips with my father to camp and stargaze with no light pollution to dull the majesty. The person I was before he died and took all that wonder with him. The person I was before Claude.

It's New Age bullshit, really, *finding myself*, spoken in stretched, languorous vowels, in a private school, magazine-intern accent. Like some yoga retreat and colonic would fix me and my marriage.

The forest, the trees, the stars, the isolation, they might not fix me, but distance, perspective, remembering where I came from, who I was, they would. They had to.

I wanted pure connection to nobody but the earth, the past, the sky. I wanted to find the version of me I knew was in there, somewhere, hiding in the mosses.

The universe certainly has a sense of humour.

Before

My name is Iris, but I look like a Jane. Or a Kate. Or a Maud. The same four-letter structure but none of the exotics. I'm plain. That's my identifier. Oh her . . . yes, the tall plain one. Her name is *Iris*?

I was born into a family that desperately wanted children, then as soon as they got them, desperately didn't. I have an older sister, Helen, who doesn't fit her name either and started going by her middle name, Veronica, during college, but it never caught on at home. My mother is Josephine, never Jo, always Josie to my father, Mitchell. Mitch. Everyone had another name. Growing up, it felt like nobody in my family was quite who they said they were.

My mother, who wasn't too enamoured with two-year-old Helen, thought a second child would be more successful. *I'm a second child*, she had said, *and I turned out far better than my older brother*. So they had me. And her disappointment and distance grew. She just wasn't cut out for it, my mother told her friends, a cackle of waspish women from the neighbourhood. Of them all, my mother was the only one who worked, so there was a certain judgemental pity associated with our family. We didn't have money. We flew economy. Tater Tots were a staple but we weren't allowed to tell anyone that. My father gambled, my mother shopped, my sister shoplifted, and I rebelled by having no discernible vice. Insufferable, Helen called me, a goody-goody, a square.

Then I realised I was gay as a tennis player, told them at a family dinner while holding the hand of a girl with a tattoo on her neck, and was never called square again.

It's not like they were terrible. My father, when I was young at least, was a joyful man, a jolly Santa-dress-up type with a soft, well-kept beard. As the years dragged on, the weight of life and responsibilities he never wanted (kids, a mortgage, my mother) weighed him down, pulled on his shoulders and the corners of his mouth, turned his beard grey and prickly.

But I'll always thank him for bringing wonder into my life.

One night, when I was eight, I couldn't sleep. It was after midnight, the wind was up, throwing a tree branch against the side of the house. Every gust was a howl, every rattle of the window someone trying to get in, every dull bang of the branch a stranger knocking at the door.

In between bangs, I heard the television. I crept downstairs – a dangerous activity past lights-out – and found my father in his den, watching Carl Sagan.

He spotted me, frowned, and set his beer out of sight. 'Hey there, Rissy, bad dream?'

Iris. Ris. Rissy. I hated it, except that night when the sound of the pet name from my father's lips was the comfort I needed.

I nodded. Didn't want to admit I was scared of the wind. That was babyish and I was eight years old, thank you very much, practically a grown-up.

He waved me over, snuggled me on his lap in the recliner and hiked up the volume on the TV set, though not enough to wake Mother.

'Ain't that something?' he asked, after we'd been watching a few minutes. 'So much out there we don't know anything about. All those planets and stars, more than we can ever count.' He sighed and I wasn't sure why.

'Are there people on other planets?' I asked, my head pressed against his chest.

'I'm ninety-nine per cent sure of it. Because if there isn't anyone out there but us, and this planet is all there is, then that's the loneliest thing I can imagine. I don't feel lonely when I look up at the stars, do you?' He didn't wait for an answer. 'I feel part of something big, something old. I'd give my right leg to be up in those stars, see another planet, walk on another world. Wouldn't that be something, Rissy-pie?'

I nodded into his chest. That would be something all right.

'Sometimes,' my father said, and his voice sounded strange, far away almost, 'I wonder if on one of those planets there's another me and another you and we're living different lives. We've got a different house. Maybe we live in the woods and I'm a park ranger and you're a wild thing, swinging in the trees.' He squeezed me tight. 'Maybe that me up there made a different choice. What would our lives be if we turned left instead of right? Or didn't get married to the first person who asked, or just tried that little bit harder?'

'Maybe I don't have to go to school on the other planet.'

He laughed softly. 'Maybe not.'

He held me close and let out another long, gentle sigh. A sad sound I'd never heard from my father before. We stared at the TV, at the thin man in a blue turtleneck sweater talking about the size of the universe and all it contained. I stopped hearing the wind, the banging branch, heard only my father's heartbeat and Carl Sagan's voice. We fell asleep together, and in the morning, my father hustled me upstairs before my mother woke to find us.

For my birthday that year he bought me a telescope with a note signed from him and Carl (faked, but at nine, I thought my dad was best friends with the man from the TV).

I hope this shows you other worlds, the note said.

That's when my obsession with the stars began, and it carried on, simmering in the background, until it became both help and hindrance, until my failure to make it the focus of my life grew into reckless regret and settling for the wrong thing. As the years passed, I began to make some of my father's mistakes, setting me on a course that would see us share a similar fate. The first step on that path was Claude.

I was twenty-four and green as lime the first time I laid eyes on Claude. I was too tall, too thin. A breeze would sway me. I'd graduated in the top half of my class, though nearer the middle than I liked to admit. Dream job? NASA. I was under no illusions about my scientific aptitude (my mother: 'You're a dreamer, Iris, not a doer'), but I knew how to talk about space, the stars, the cosmos, the possibilities, to translate some of science to lay-speak, even inspire a bit of awe.

Turns out nobody would pay me for that.

Someone, however, would pay me to enter lines of invoice data for a materials company that supplied NASA.

I was NASA-adjacent, despite being in an office block in the outskirts of NYC instead of Space HQ in Washington or Kennedy in Florida. Good enough, I thought, fresh out of the classroom. I had an income when dozens of my classmates had to move back in with their parents between unpaid internships and spiralling debt. A year of data entry, then I'll move closer to my dream. Head down to Washington, get one of those NASA baseball caps.

A year turned to two, then I was offered a better-paid version of the same job for a company producing pipe insulation for the space shuttle.

A shimmy closer and a hell of a raise. A twenty-something win.

I was out in the Village for some farewell drinks with colleagues in an upmarket steel-and-wood bar, all natural materials and charred panelling and bartenders with moustaches in tweedy waistcoats and linen shirts, when I saw her.

She sat alone at the bar, legs crossed, foot kicking the metal siding to the beat of the music. It was the rhythmic knock, the petty irritation of it, that drew me. I whipped around, scowling and tutting, louder than I thought because I was five shots deep with three more on the table.

The woman raised an eyebrow at me, and if I could have died in that moment, I would have. She wasn't effortlessly stylish or strikingly beautiful or supremely confident or stop-me-in-my-tracks-I-must-meet-her magnetic. She was a slice of all four. My opposite. The North Pole to my South. Long, rich brown hair to my mousy shoulder-length. Rosy, clear skin to my washed-out white. Dresses and heels to my fitted Ts and flats. I got the impression, months later, on our first date, that it was mostly a front. A shiny mahogany veneer over the scarred, pitted, worn wooden heart of her.

She held my eyes for what felt like forever. My cheeks turned red.

Then she turned away and kicked the bar harder.

My friend Ellis pulled me back into the conversation, forced a drink into my hand, and the woman faded from my immediate thoughts but never left them. I found myself searching for her for the rest of the evening, catching glimpses, seeing her raise a hand to order another drink, stand to double-kiss a man who joined her. I felt a jealous stab when she touched the man's arm, laughing, a stomach-drop when I couldn't find her, then a bright surge when she returned from the restroom.

Ellis nudged my shoulder. 'You should speak to her.'

'Don't know what you mean,' I think I said. At this point the evening was a fuzz of tequila and beer.

He handed me two shots. 'Go up there and say, "What's up, beautiful, wanna get wasted?" and give her these.'

I laughed at the slur in his words, and even in my three-sheets state, I had enough self-awareness to know this was a terrible idea.

I would do what I always did. Laugh it off. Watch from afar. Let her leave. Pine over her for weeks. Go out, see another woman, repeat all steps, and eventually die alone. The Iris way, which was why, except for some fumblings in college, a few terrible one-nighters, I was in a Gobi-sized dry spell.

I looked again, and a sharp, cold spike ran me through. Her spot at the bar was empty. I watched the bartender clear away the two empty glasses and sweep up a few folded notes in one smooth movement. Gone. Just like that.

I'm going to die alone.

Movement at the door caught my eye. There she was, shrugging on her jacket. The man, a step ahead, opened the door for her.

She turned. Saw me staring. Stared back.

I tried to do something, anything, move, speak, run over, ask for her number, her *name*, shove the man – boyfriend? Husband? – out the way, but I didn't. Then she was out the door and gone from my life before she'd even entered it.

This feeling was not new to me, and yet there was something about this woman I couldn't articulate, like she'd shot out a hook and caught me.

I went back to my table with a pitcher of beer and tried to forget about her, but quickly found I couldn't. There was a connection. A gravity. Passing asteroids drawn together on a collision course.

And what a collision it was.

After

Balsam fir. Sugar maple. Trembling aspen. Northern red oak.
My father taught me to name the trees. Along with the stars, the
woods lit up his heart and gave him peace. He wasn't a happy
man, always looking for a way out, a different life. For a while,
he tried to convince my mother to move to a cabin upstate, live
off the land. The following year, he wanted to pack up and move
across the country to Napa, California, to make wine. The
summer after that, he put down an offer on a ranch in Montana
but didn't tell anyone about his idea to raise horses. He was
outbid on the land and my mother didn't hide her relief or her
anger at him for being so reckless in the first place. That broke
his heart.

For my father, it was anything but the suburbs. The homoge-
nous, identikit life. The Saturday lawn mow, wave to Bill across
the street, same conversations. How about them Giants? Where
you headed on vacation this summer?

He soothed himself with trips to nature. He was a junkie, and
the woods, the beach, the mountains were his fix. They became
mine too, for a while, until he died when I was sixteen.

It was my fault. If only I'd gone with him that day, if I'd not
been so selfish, he would still be alive. From then on, I couldn't
stand the emptiness of nature without him. When Claude
suggested a vacation to the Rockies, I baulked, told her I hated
the mountains, the forest, dirt of all kinds. The wilderness became
hostile to me, a place of memories I'd locked away and an environment I couldn't navigate without my father's guiding hands.
Only the stars gave comfort. He told me once the night sky was
full of ghosts, old distant light from dead stars, visible to us for

thousands of years but no less beautiful for the death of their source.

He was one of them. A dead star. But I still saw his light.

Walking did this to me. Made me reflect and reminisce. Like a trance. For the first time in years, I felt a spark of my old self. The Iris my father knew.

I walked into the woods with the vaguest idea of where I was headed. This section of the nine-hundred-kilometre-long trail, abandoned a decade ago in favour of pumping funds into the more photogenic and accessible Appalachian, wound through the Catskill Mountains and forests, up to the Finger Lakes, then south-west to the Allegheny National Forest in Pennsylvania. The article I'd read devoted all of two short paragraphs to the shame of forgetting such a beautiful hike. It spoke of campgrounds long since demolished or stripped of value, and hiker huts sprinkled every thirty kilometres or so.

I had it in my head to go to one of those huts, make it my own. I'd live my father's dream. Escape the city. Escape Claude. Forget Iris, become Jane.

That first day off the bus, I was still in blissful ignorance that this would be easy. That this was a clever plan of mine to simultaneously rid myself of Claude, be closer to my father and solve all my problems.

In truth, and I'm not too big to admit it, this whole adventure was an extreme overreaction to a marriage turned rotten.

I walked for about five hours along the ghost of a trail, still visible if you knew where to look – the occasional intact waymarker, painted post, rusted plaque. I stopped sometimes to sip at my water bottle and eat a handful of peanuts, to take a breath and calm the doubts.

As I got deeper into the forest, further from civilisation, I felt it. What my father had talked about when I was a kid. The deep sense of rightness and peace that came from the hush between trees. Sunlight struggled through the canopy, throwing shifting spotlights on the forest floor. Brittle brown leaves cracked under my boots, birdsong filled the air, endless and joyful and everywhere. Spindly aspen trunks strobed the landscape like a living barcode. Ferns brushed my bare legs. If warmth and calm had a smell, it would be the forest in summer.

The first hut I found was a ruin. The roof collapsed and rotten, the walls disintegrated to soft splinters, the stink of animal mess and decay. Nothing left to even camp beneath for the night. But that was okay, I told myself, there would be another one. A better one. Besides, I still had daylight. I would be fine.

Just fine.

So I kept walking, but no hut appeared between the trees. The sun was slipping, and night edged closer as I came to a relatively flat spot, thick with leaf litter and mosses. The trees made a tight horseshoe clearing, fringed with ferns and high bracken, a natural shelter from the wind. As good a place as any to camp.

I went about clearing fallen branches and the bigger rocks, then pulled out my tent. I'd never put up a tent. Never even packed a backpack. My father always made camp while I played as a kid.

Cross-legged on the ground, I read the instructions twice.

Lay flysheet down. Peg out groundsheet. Assemble tension poles. Insert into pole sleeves.

I sat in the middle of a mess of pegs, fluorescent ropes and reams of bright nylon with no clue what I was doing.

Claude's voice purred in my head. *Oh darling, really?* This *is your big plan?*

Fuck her and her underestimation of me. Cue montage music and Rocky punching the bag.

I put up the stupid tent.

But I didn't have a mallet and the ground was hard. I ended up hammering in pegs with a rock. Bent two. Broke one. The tent sagged on one side, but I didn't care, because I'd done it.

Well into darkness, three-dollar head torch lighting my way, I slung my gear into the tent, unrolled the sleeping bag and climbed in. I ate the bus apple, the rest of the peanuts, too tired to mess about with the stove and astrofood, then zipped the sleeping bag up to my chin.

Day one. Probably lost. Barely made camp before dark. Not the best start, Jane.

Claude's tittering laugh flitted through my head and I felt the red heat of shame fill my cheeks. She was laughing at me, like she always did, for not being strong enough.

The sun rose on the first day of my new life at 4.58 a.m. exactly, and I hadn't slept a wink.

I saw the sun creep grey light up the side of my tent and almost wept with exhaustion. After thirty hours on buses, five hours of hiking, a dozen new aches in my side and back from the hard ground, I was on the edge of giving up, heading back to my apartment and grovelling to Claude, forgiving her everything, begging her to forgive me.

They say everything becomes clear in the cold light of day. I sat outside my tent, elbows on my knees, and took stock.

In my panic and desperation to leave, I'd grabbed everything in the apartment I could think of before heading to the outdoor store. I just needed to get out before she got home that evening, and well . . . I pulled over my bag, emptied it and laid everything out in front of me.

Three uneven changes of clothes. Half of them unsuitable for the environment.

Not enough underwear.

Three pairs of socks. One with polar bears stitched into the toes.

Two one-litre water bottles – one almost empty.

A road map of the Catskills I picked up at the Albany bus depot.

Money pouch.

New boots.

Notebooks. An assortment of pens grabbed from a drawer.

One pack of tissues.

Watch. One of Claude's. All rose gold and diamond chips. Not waterproof.

Tiny single-burner gas stove with a spare bottle. Still in its box.

One pot.

A multi tool I'd mistaken for useful but was in fact just a folding fork, spoon, blunt knife, and toothpick.

Emergency whistle, because it was at the till and the cashier said it deterred bears.

The whole freeze-dried, pre-packaged food shelf from the outdoor store, swept into my cart in one dramatic gesture and later shoved into my bag at the bus depot.

Extra batteries for my torch? No.

Bug spray? Of course not, and the mosquitoes knew it.

First aid kit? Shut up.

Compass?

But I did have a telescope.

I looked at everything I had, spilled out onto the ground like I'd upended a trash can. Most of it just as useful. What was I doing out here? Where was I going?

'I can't do this.'

The bright bloom of rage and defiance that had carried me to this point had wilted to a drooping bud.

'*I can't do this!*' I shouted, but the forest wasn't listening. It smothered my negativity in moss and fern and projected nothing back to me.

I shook my head, sighing, then felt the smile. Tickling the edges of my mouth. Then I was laughing. Laughing hard at the sheer absurdity of what I'd got myself into.

Why would anyone walk away from their life to a situation so far removed from their everyday?

Heartbreak. Loss. Fear.

If I hadn't made that rash, dangerous decision to leave, I would have withered to nothing. I would have died, like my father. Unhappy and beaten down flat.

'Besides,' I said to the trees like they were old friends, 'can you imagine Claude's face if I stumbled back home after two days lost in the woods?'

'*Iris, sweetheart,*' I said in her voice, '*why did you think you could do that? You hate the woods!*' Oh do I, Claude? Do I really?

I looked around at the trees, then at my mishmash of gear and unsuitable clothing and pile of cardboard food, and groaned.

'Yes. Maybe I do.'

Then Claude would tilt her head to one side, shake it sadly and hold out her arms for me to collapse into like a child. And I would, because I always did. I got upset, she held me, told me without ever actually saying it, to stop trying so hard. I shuddered and shook away the image.

I shoved everything back into my pack, wrapped the telescope in a T-shirt, took down the tent, swilled a glug of water around my fuzzy teeth and finished off another bag of nuts.

I pushed my tired legs until the muscles warmed, tenderised, found their deep, true strength. Then every step was easier. The heat of the day got up, prickled my skin in uneven dapples, irregular clearings of full-blast light into dark green shadows and cool air. I lost the trail twice, had to backtrack, but it didn't deter me. I hadn't been alone or in control in six years. I'd started to believe I couldn't be, but I'd survived my first day and night with nobody else, no phone, no email, no constant news stream, nobody on the other end of a text message in the middle of the night.

I was alone. At least twenty kilometres from anyone else.

The trees stared back at me, silent sentinels.

I kept walking, watching the sky turn from blue to overcast grey, concentrating on each step and the way the straps of the duffel and daypack cut into my shoulders, the burn in my thighs, and the rocks I had to avoid, and the dry creeks I had to scramble down and up again and the trickle of water left in my first bottle. If I concentrated on all those things, I wouldn't have time to panic or regret or feel how bone-deep tired I was or remember that night in the bar I first saw Claude or the next time I ran into her and fell head over heels or the first kiss or our first night together or the six years of firsts and seconds and hundredths. And now here I was, running away, cursing her name, painting her a monster in my own mind because it was easier than missing her.

Before

I was running late. Sprinting down Fifth in a classic New York downpour. November rain drenched me, my carefully picked-out shirt, my forty-dollar blow-dry and style, my new suede boots. It was a special occasion. Ten minutes after leaving my apartment, the rain began. A further twenty minutes of trying to get a cab proved fruitless, and by then all was lost. I committed to the soaking, deciding the sympathy I'd get when I finally reached the restaurant would be worth it.

The little Italian place, tucked away in a forgotten alley, was a beacon. Light spilled from the windows, shimmering in the rain, splitting into a dozen colours like an Afremov painting. Outside, bleak and dark and cold. Inside, an island of warmth and cheer and her.

I found her at a table in the back after the waiter had helped peel off my coat and hung it to drip. The restaurant was a sauna compared to outside, and immediately my cheeks reddened and my scalp itched with damp. My hair was flat. My boots ruined. My shirt – white, what an idiot – had a grey triangle of rain at the neck dipping all the way to my waist.

Bella stood up to greet me, shaking her head.

'I'm so sorry,' I said, out of breath, flashing hot and cold, wanting to collapse.

She kissed me hello and smiled.

'I love the look,' she said. 'Bathroom is that way.'

I stuck my head under the hand-dryer and patted my clothes with paper towels. I washed the remnants of my scant make-up from my face and scraped my hair back. I'd had it cut short the week before, just long enough to tuck behind my ears, and

bleached it white-blonde. I loved it. After the initial cringing shock
from Bella and my friends, they'd come to terms with it. Even
slicked back ragged like this, it looked good, like a more sedate
Blade Runner Pris without the fringe.

I returned to the table, where Bella had ordered a bottle of red
and I couldn't have been more grateful.

'You're a train wreck, you know that?' she said, smiling, cheeks
rosy in the low light.

'I don't know what you mean,' I said, and took a long draw on
the wine.

We ordered huge amounts of pasta and toasted our three-
month anniversary. We'd met at a public lecture on comets and
their trajectories at Columbia University. She was doing a post-
grad in art history and her thesis talked about the placement of
stars in seventeenth- and eighteenth-century works of art.
She'd sat next to me at the lecture and shouted down a whiny
boy behind who couldn't see the slides over my 'giant head'. We
talked about Edmund Halley and how he used art to predict
the trajectory of a comet, how art and science were two sides of
the same coin, how they fed and tugged at each other, each
nudging the other to go further. We went for burgers after. We
exchanged numbers. She called to invite me to breakfast the
next morning.

Bella was a good four inches shorter than me, with red hair and
a smile that reached all the way to her eyes. The way she talked
about her favourite artists – Bernini, Caravaggio, Frans Hals,
Lieve Verschuier – was like listening to a chef speak of their favourite dish. Every word was drenched in love.

'What are you doing this weekend?' I asked as the food arrived.
A mountain of thickly sauced spaghetti, sides of dough balls,
olives, a tricolore salad, another bottle of wine.

'The Met. Then thesis. The usual. You?'

'Ellis wants to drown his sorrows,' I said, taking a too-big
mouthful of pasta. 'His girlfriend dumped him last night.'

Bella didn't look up from her plate. She wasn't Ellis's biggest
fan. 'What did he do?'

'Nothing. She cheated,' I said, and Bella winced. 'She wasn't over her ex, they got drunk, hooked up. Tale as old as time.'

'Such a cliché.'

Then she reached across the table and took my hand, squeezed it. 'Don't take this the wrong way, but I'm so glad you don't have a significant ex.'

I smiled and made the same joke I'd made the morning after we first stumbled into bed.

'You got me fresh out the box.'

We ate, we drank, we laughed. We talked about art and movies and her thesis and avoided all mention of my job because it was awful. We split the bill despite me saying it was my treat. Bella wouldn't have it. I knew she wouldn't.

The rain had stopped by the time we left the restaurant. My job paid enough to allow me to live alone, while Bella was in student digs – five to an apartment, labels on everything, quiet after eleven, and *no 'partners'*, inverted commas and all – so we took a cab back to my place.

I lived in a cosy apartment. That's what the listing said. Everyone knows 'cosy' is real-estate speak for fucking tiny. My bedroom, into which I'd shoehorned a too-big-for-the-space double bed and a wardrobe that wouldn't open fully because it hit the mattress, was my sanctuary. The telescope my dad had given me was positioned at the window, a smallish white tube about two feet long on a tripod, pointing to Venus. The week after I moved into the bleak box in the middle of a bleak tower, I spent a day in the library printing a huge vista of Hubble photographs of the Milky Way. I stuck them on the ceiling like wallpaper, plastering a galaxy above my head. Then, balancing on the bed, I painted over the brightest stars and constellations – Sirius, the Pleiades, Rigel, Canopus, Cassiopeia – in luminous paint so even in the middle of the city, with the worst light pollution in the world, I would have stars.

Bella and I fell into bed and did what those in three-month-old relationships do, several times. In the night, I heard her murmuring when she thought I was asleep. She stroked my hair and whispered *I could love you* into the dark silence, as if trying out the shape of the words, making sure they fit her mouth. I kept my eyes closed and my breath even, because those words hit me like a one-two punch in the chest. First, a swelling of similar feeling, then a deep sinking terror when that feeling burst. A soap bubble of love.

I left her the next morning to go to work and we made loose plans to see each other the following week.

On Saturday evening, I met a tearful Ellis in the Village and we went to our usual haunt. The steel-and-wood bar with waistcoated servers where I'd had my leaving drinks four months before. Ellis spilled his woes over neat whisky, and what Bella had said resurfaced in my mind. *I'm so glad you don't have a significant ex.* She was right. There was no one in my past to tempt me away from my present and from her, and yet there was something. The gravity and pull that kept me coming back to this bar every other week, sometimes with friends but often alone. This place, which was overpriced and pretentious and inconvenient to my home and work by thirty blocks. But something in me thought if I come back, maybe I'll see that woman who was kicking the bar. Maybe if I saw her, I'd realise my memory of her had morphed into a fantasy the reality couldn't possibly match, she wouldn't be as beautiful and magnetic as she was in my mind, and the spell would be broken. I could fall for Bella as fully as she'd fallen for me and I would be ready to reply when she eventually spoke those words out loud.

That's what I told myself.

'Are you listening?' Ellis shook my arm.

'No. Not a word,' I said.

'I'm heartbroken, Iris, heartbroken, and you're not even listening! I'm never going to stop loving her. I'm never getting over this. She was the *one* and now she's with that *moron* who works at Goldman bloody Sachs.'

He slumped down onto the table and I slumped with him. 'Shut up. You were together for six months.'

'Love is love, Iris, it knows no time limits, and when you know, God, you know. Hits you like a freight train. Bam! Right in the chest,' he said, and sighed, always the theatrics with Ellis.

A slightly overweight, baby-faced man in his late twenties, he was a chronic underachiever, with a constant stream of four-five-six-month-long relationships, who could match me drink for drink and could always be relied upon to join me for a Spielberg or Kubrick marathon. My best friend.

While he wallowed, my attention drifted around the bar, seeking out the woman. Would I even recognise her? Had this little ritual become an excuse over the last three months for not committing to Bella?

'She's not here,' Ellis said.

'Hmm?'

'You know who I'm talking about. Don't think I don't know why we come to this shitty place all the time. It's been months. Get over it,' he said, and leant closer, dropped his voice. 'Bella's great.'

Band-Aid ripped off a stinging wound. Those last words delivered with a pointed spear to my chest. I forced a smile.

'Another drink?'

'Make it a double. No, a triple. Nothing is enough to drown these sorrows.'

I went to the bar, ordered, waited, all the while searching faces, watching the door in case she walked in, turning at a laugh I thought might be hers. It was more habit now than hope.

But I caught myself. Had I really become this desperate?

Yes, I had, and Ellis, intentionally or not, had shone an unflattering, stalkerish light on it all.

I shook my head, laughed, and got a startled look from the bartender as he set down the pitcher and two glasses.

I carried the drinks back to the table and listened for another hour as Ellis told every story he had of his beloved. How they'd met (online). How they'd ended up dating (she'd cancelled four times before they finally went out). How funny she was (she wasn't) and how much she'd opened up about herself and her past (she talked about her ex a *lot*). I consoled him and didn't call him an idiot too much and told him he'd find someone new, plenty more fish, big wide world out there, the usual.

At around midnight, I put him in a cab and gave the driver a fifty to make sure he got home safe. As I was closing the door, Ellis grabbed my arm.

'Bella . . . she's a good one. Don't let her go, you hear me?'

'I hear you.'

I watched him drive away, waving out the window, shouting, 'Don't let her go!'

I stood on the sidewalk. Cold November air sobering me up better than coffee. I checked my phone to find a message from Bella a few hours old.

Double bill at the Ockey on Weds. 2001 and Close Encounters. WE'RE GOING, SPACE NERD.

I smiled, face lit up white from the phone in the yellow glow of the street lamps. Bella was a good one. A surge of bright, hot yearning blasted through me and all I wanted was to be in that cinema with her, holding her hand, sharing popcorn, stealing a kiss or two. I didn't want to be with anyone else.

I texted back:

I'm in!

Then, that surge still singing in my veins, emboldened by alcohol, I typed a second message.

I could love you too, you know.

I lingered a moment, hoping and fearing she both would and wouldn't message back, before realising this was the path to madness and pocketing my phone. Glowing with the almost drug-like euphoria that came from making a decision, I couldn't imagine sitting still in the back of a cab. I needed to walk. Stride out the alcohol and the nerves so only joy remained, distilled and undeniable.

I turned uptown, oblivious and dream-like, checked my phone again to see no message – it was late, Bella would be asleep – and ran straight into a woman. Hard enough to knock me down, hard enough for her to drop her bag and send the contents skittering across the sidewalk.

'Shit! I'm sorry.' I scrambled, picked myself up, grabbed my phone before someone else did.

'Jesus! Can you watch where you're going?' the woman said, strong French accent but perfect English. She knelt to gather her bag and I knelt to help, and then I saw her face and didn't believe it. I handed her a lipstick and she looked at me and I saw her eyes and there was no doubt.

The woman from the bar.

'Do I know you?' she asked after a moment of my slack-jawed staring, but I couldn't answer.

I picked up a few coins. Passed them to her. Her fingers brushed mine and something in me clenched, like all the air had been forced from the world and left me gasping.

'I don't ... Maybe? You look familiar.' I had no idea how I sounded, what tone I took, or if those were the actual words I said. An evening of shots and beer had mushed my senses and clouded my vision, and yet she was clear.

'I think I'd remember,' she said, and almost smiled. She put the last object – a pack of mints – back in her bag and we stood up together.

'Well,' she said, 'I'd say it was a pleasure running into you ...'

I stood there, dumb and awkward, and smiled and kind of laughed, and when I didn't say anything back, she half nodded and walked past me.

What are you *doing*? my brain screamed at me as I watched her get five feet, eight feet, ten feet away.

'Wait!'

She turned, eyebrow raised like that night in the bar, and the clench came again, stronger and fiercer than before. This was it. My chance.

Take it. Goddam take it.

'Wait,' I said again, and cast around for a reason to give her. 'You forgot this.'

I held up a pack of gum I'd just pulled from my pocket.

Her eyes narrowed at me. She smiled and waited as I jogged over to her.

'Here.'

She took the gum. She looked at it. She knew very well it wasn't hers.

'Can't believe I missed this,' she said, and her tone shifted. No more impatience, no more irritation. She looked up at me through her eyelashes, and I was snared. The heat in her voice, the way her lips formed the words, the tilt of her head and the under-the-surface smile dimpling her cheeks, and her eyes. Jesus Christ, her eyes. A light brown that was almost gold. Like the dark heart of the sun.

'Thank you,' she said with an arched eyebrow. I'd been staring, gawking, not saying a word.

'Sorry, again,' I said finally, 'for barging into you like that. I wasn't paying attention, you know.' I was mumbling and hated myself for my nerves. I'd blown it already, I knew it, so I threw the Hail Mary, because why not?

'Would you let me buy you a drink? To apologise properly.' I held my breath.

A long moment of hesitation, then: 'Sure.'

'There's a bar half a block that way?'

She looked where I was pointing, back to the steel-and-wood hipster hole, and frowned. 'Oh. Do you mind if we don't? That place is not my favourite. It tries far too hard. I know somewhere else.'

We walked three blocks downtown in a strange silence. I had no idea what I was doing or thinking or feeling in those ten or so minutes. They're a blur. A time outside of time. There was minimal chit-chat – 'just a little further' – as if we were both waiting until there was a table between us before we could speak. The one thing I did pick up on, without a hint of doubt inside me; she was nervous too.

She led me into a narrow-fronted building. The long bar was made of dark wood panelling. The small square tables the same, the chairs covered in cracked burgundy leather. And the wine. Every inch of wall, behind the bar, above the tables, was mounted with bottles. A line of champagne bottles in ascending size sat on the counter, and the name of the bar, Balthazar's, was etched in faded gold and red paint on a pitted mirror above the door. This was old New York. Even this late, the place was almost full. The room buzzed with low, intimate conversation, none of it loud enough to overhear. Scents of cigarette smoke on clothing, strong perfumes and the tannin smell of good wine.

While I was looking around, the woman had gone to the bar and ordered two glasses of white. She appeared with them beside me.

'Oh,' she said. 'I'm sorry, I assumed you drink this? I always think everyone drinks wine. I can get you something else?'

'No, no, this is perfect,' I said, taking the glass. I didn't much care for white wine, but right then I'd have taken paint thinner if she'd offered it.

'Though,' I said, 'I was meant to be buying you a drink.'

She smiled, and her eyes turned cat-like. 'You can get the next one.'

Heat rose in my cheeks and I was glad of the dim light to hide it. We found a table in the back and sat quietly. I sipped my wine and she sipped hers and I had no idea what to say.

'I do know you,' she said after a minute or two, her voice as low and intimate as the surroundings. 'Your hair is different but I remember.'

'You do?'

'That awful bar. About, what? Three, four months ago?'

'Guilty.'

She smiled.

'You were staring at me. All night.'

I looked down at the table, scratched at the grain.

'I'm sorry, I'm not usually like that. I was pretty drunk.'

She shrugged, sipped. 'I was staring at you too.'

I looked up then. Like a door had swung open inside the fuzzy darkness of my head and let in cold, clear light.

'You were?'

'Yes. I thought you looked interesting. And very tall.'

I laughed. 'What about the man you were with?'

'Virgil. An old friend from Montréal. Awful name, right?'

I melted a little at the way she said Montréal.

'I thought you two were . . .'

'Most people do, but no, he's, shall we say, not my type.'

Her eyes held mine. There was something raw about her, primal, a jaguar in the jungle. She seemed so sure of herself now; every word spoken perfectly, without hesitation or doubt, every swipe of her hand through her long, dark hair, the way she gripped the stem of the wine glass.

'I even went back to that bar once, to see if you would be there,' she said, and for the first time, she looked off balance.

'You did? When?'

'Maybe two weeks later. I was in the neighbourhood. I thought, why not? But of course you weren't there.'

I raced through my mental calendar. Two weeks after my leaving drinks.

The lecture at Columbia.

The night I'd met Bella.

Fuck. Bella.

'Uh . . .' I couldn't form words. Here I was, out with my obsession, finally, after months of looking, the same night I'd told Bella I loved her.

The guilt crashed into me. What are you *doing*?

'I'm sorry, such a pathetic thing to do. Forget it,' the woman said, shaking her head and backing away, crestfallen and, I realised, embarrassed.

Instinct took over, the guilt evaporated. I reached out and grabbed her hand, pulled her back to the table.

'No. Sorry. I was just surprised because . . . actually, I did the same thing. A couple of times.' I relaxed my grip but she didn't take her hand away. 'I can't really explain why.'

'Who can explain attraction?' she said, dropping her voice even lower.

Her thumb ran down mine and electricity shot through my body. The tiniest touch. The biggest jolt. I'd never felt that with Bella. Bella was great. Bella was easy. Safe.

But this? This was the freight train. This was the lightning strike. The air thickened around us, the world outside our table dropped away until we were encased in an orb of candlelight. Even the sound muted. I had no periphery. It was all her. The wine. Her hand in mine, delicious and painful and exciting. I was afraid of this woman. Afraid of how she made me feel after only a fleeting glance in a bar, after less than half an hour in her company.

I should have felt guilty, but I didn't. Shame and guilt were insignificant in the face of what was happening to me in that dark, smoky wine bar.

'I'm Claude,' she said, a purr of a word.

'Iris.'

'Funny,' she said. 'You don't look like an Iris.'

After

I came upon the next, mercifully intact, hiker's hut around noon.
My back hurt. My legs hurt. My throat hurt from too little water
and my stomach hurt from terrible food choices. I dropped the
duffel and stared at my new, rent-free home. Four stacked-log
walls, wide slanted roof, door, window, narrow porch with a picnic
table outside and an uneven ring of flat stones circling a fire pit.

'Home sweet . . .' I sighed, trying to calm the fear bubbling up
in my chest. The oh fuck, the journey is over, life begins, here I
am, you made your bed now get eaten by bears in it.

I left Claude's duffel on the ground and went to the cabin.

The door was latched shut, the window had a spidery crack in
the bottom corner, and the porch was covered in leaves and a few
toppled logs from a low stack against the front wall.

Inside, a forgotten relic of a hiking heyday. A fan of dust and
leaves blown under the door. A cold black stove. A dusty radio.
Two wide cabinets, a dull steel sink with no running water, a
countertop, a square table, pinboard with maps, brochures and
postcards tacked all over, a shelf of ragged paperbacks, three
chairs and a fourth broken. A sagging couch. And a ladder.

I smiled.

A platform at the top of the ladder held a bed. Double mattress,
balled-up sheet, a shelf, and all the dust I could eat.

'Hi,' I said to the cabin from the platform. 'I'll be your new
tenant for a while.'

As I started airing out the place, letting the light in, the cabin
seemed to relax its stiff shoulders, breathe out along with me.

I set up my gas stove and single pan by the pit and rehydrated
one of the astro meals. Glutinous beef stroganoff containing

nothing resembling either beef or mushrooms, eaten with a flimsy folding spoon. The height of survival chic. The dense, powdery mix coated my teeth and I wished I'd paid more attention in the store.

Inside, there were tools for the stove, a broom and mop for cleaning, mismatched utensils – mostly fork-knife and spoon-fork gadgets left by hikers – a pan with a broken handle, two enamel plates and a metal cup with *GO TIGERS* printed on the side. There was an old cooler, and a metal box containing an emergency radio, a flare gun, a bear whistle, six candles, an oil lantern and a tube of waterproof matches.

Despite a good airing, the cabin smelled strange. Not just musty and years-abandoned, but almost . . . alive. Like every backpacker who passed through left a piece of themselves in the grain of the wood. The smell of decades of trail food cooking on single-burner gas or over wood in the black-top stove. Of spilt energy drinks and milestone beer, of morning sachet coffee and creamer, of sweat, of laughter, of conversation and meet-and-greets and *see you at the next checkpoint*. They'd left postcards and phone numbers and physical remnants, *JOSH + JAY SUMMER 2002* carved into the walls, pits in the floorboards from hiking poles. There was a transient energy embedded in the fabric of the place. A cabin full of ghosts.

Add the ones I'd brought along with me and the place started to feel crowded. I sat on the platform with my legs dangling into nothing, thinking of nothing. Below me, a phantom Claude strode into the hut, fresh out of work. Her Manolos stabbed into the wood; she swiped a finger over the table, looking around with a mix of worry and disgust, then up at me watching her.

'This is it?'

I nodded.

'You left our apartment for this? It's smaller than the bathroom.'

'Exactly.'

Her features softened, pretension and annoyance melting away to reveal the woman I fell for. Those brown eyes found mine, eyebrows creased. She stepped to the bottom of the ladder, gripped the rail. The hook dug deeper.

'Come home . . .'

I clapped my hands together. The sharp sound snapped me back to the empty cabin.

Staying still was a mistake. Resting. Reflecting. Thinking of her. All a mistake. I had to keep busy. Keep my mind and body occupied at all times.

I dragged the mattress down from the platform – the mezzanine, if you want to get fancy, and I did – and manoeuvred it outside, leant it against the wall of the cabin beside a woodpile and a rusty axe. I beat the crap out of it with a stick and tried to ignore the stains. Clouds of dust belched out of the old fabric with every hit, and I kept going, my arm aching, until my strikes came away clean. Then turned it around and did the same to the other side.

While the mattress and cabin were airing, I explored the immediate area. A clearing to the east, full of wild flowers and meadow grass, a high ridge to the north-west where the faint trail carried on up and over, and a few hundred yards to the north, a fast-flowing stream and a huge sense of relief.

My father taught me about wild water. *Streams and rivers are like people, Rissy,* he said. *You want the ones that move quick and strong, the ones that push over rocks, not the ones dammed up by them. If you find water standing still, it's no good. Standing still will make you sick.*

I went down to the stream, tasted the water. Fresh and clean, with a herbaceous hint of fallen leaves. I washed my hands and face, filled up the water bottle, drank it down and refilled it, then gave the sheet a good seeing-to. I scraped it on rocks like in the movies, expecting a bright white result, and got a soggy grey mess. But I was keeping busy. Making progress.

I went to the clearing and draped the sheet over a fat bush to dry, even though it was overcast and I hadn't seen the sun for hours. But the evening was young and the air warm and I didn't know what else to do with it. Then back to the cabin. I hefted the mattress inside and managed to get it back up onto the mezzanine without breaking my neck. I unpacked my clothes, folded them and set them on the shelf beside my new bed. Laid out the sleeping bag on the mattress. Resisted the urge to lie down.

The energy I'd gained from the rehydrated beef goop didn't last long. I inhaled a granola bar while checking through the cupboards. Behind the couch, under a loose floorboard, I found a pack of instant noodles with a seven-year-old use-by date, a handful of coins, a torn park permit and an empty plastic soda bottle.

I set up my telescope at the broken window. Adjusted it. Checked the lens. Cleaned it. Adjusted it more. Tried to ignore the growing ache in my bones.

The light waned as I beat the couch cushions.

Head torch guiding the way, I set my food on the kitchen shelves, staring at the packets with a mix of disgust and hope that at least some of them tasted better than the beef. I tucked the stove and gas canister beneath the countertop, then stood in the middle of the dim cabin, muscles buzzing with exhaustion. Nothing left to tidy. Panic fizzed up my throat. When I ran out of things to do, then what? I'd have to live. Thrive. Here. There must be something . . .

The sheet. It would still be wet, but I could light a fire to dry it.

I grabbed a few logs from outside, brought them in and opened the door of the stove.

Something moved. Claws and fur and teeth.

I screamed. It screamed.

A blur of black and grey leapt out of the stove at me. It thudded against my stomach, dug sharp needle claws through my shirt, into my skin, and I screamed again.

The raccoon scratched, tried to climb me, while I flailed, backing away from the creature like a cat trying to back out of its collar.

I hooked a hand under its body and flung it away. It landed by the open door and hissed at me, bared dagger teeth. I balled my fists, waved my arms in the air, shouted. Didn't think about rabies or plague or whatever raccoons have. This was my space. My home.

The raccoon didn't move. Hissed back.

'Get out!'

It tried to get back to the stove, but I jumped in its path.

'Go away!'

What would Claude think if she could see me dancing with an angry raccoon?

Oh Iris, if you can't handle a raccoon, what happens when a bear comes along? Such a silly thing, you are.

Hot rage.

I ran at the rodent – were they actually rodents? Or, like, dogs? – arms wide, banshee-screaming, kicking out at the air in front of me.

I chased it out the front door and to the base of a nearby tree. It scooted up the trunk to a high branch, where it looked down on me and growled.

'Yeah and fuck you too,' I shouted.

I went back inside the cabin, dropped down onto the couch and breathed. My hands shook. My lungs shook. But I'd be damned if a raccoon would scare me away. This was life now, there was no going back, nothing to go back to, so I'd have to figure it out. I'd be cold. I'd be hungry. I'd get hurt. I'd be bored. And after a life of relative privilege and comfort, of bagels and pizza and wine and movies and books on demand, those were foreign, fearsome concepts. But it was just the woods. I could hike into the nearest town when I needed supplies. If I ran out of money, I could find temporary work waiting tables in towns along the route. I could move on, further and further from the city, as soon as I felt like it. I could survive. I would survive.

I sniffed away the fear, went to the stove and pulled out the raccoon's nest. Leaves, twigs, fluff from the couch cushions. I threw it all outside at the base of the tree.

'Here's your stuff, you little shit,' I shouted to the now pacing animal.

It hissed back.

I opened up the vents in the stove, shoved in the logs and struck a match.

The flame guttered against the bark and went out.

I'd never made a fire. Course I hadn't. My father always did that. I sat back on my heels and rubbed my face. I considered using the camping stove, stuck in there and angled to catch the wood, but decided an exploding gas canister wasn't worth the risk.

I went outside, grabbed some of the raccoon nest and used it and one of the postcards as kindling.

The second match caught the paper, struggled against the twigs, but with some gentle encouragement crackled to life. I fed it more kindling until it was big enough to handle a log or two.

Smoke puffed up the chimney – the raccoon highway – and a strong flame breathed out heat. I closed the stove door and went to get the sheet.

Sundown was maybe ten minutes away, and because of the clouds and dense trees, the forest had taken on an eerie premature darkness.

But when I got to the clearing, the hairs on the back of my neck stood on end, as if an electric shock passed through me the moment I stepped away from the trees.

The sheet was there, covering the bush as I'd left it, but I stopped short. My legs wouldn't move me.

Something was different.

An uncanny sense of wrongness needled at me, wormed its way in at my edges. I told myself everything was as it should be. The sheet. The bush. The ring of trees. And yet my primal brain was screaming.

Then I saw it.

The light.

There were no clouds above the clearing, like the hand of the universe had taken a cookie cutter to the sky. As a consequence, the ground, the bush, the sheet were bright, lit up by the rising moon.

I stepped closer. The sheet was dry and stiff, as if baked in full hot sun. But there had not been full hot sun all day.

The electricity hummed through me again, raised the hairs on my arms. I felt like I was being watched from all sides. A hundred eyes on me because they knew I'd stepped into something, some-where *else*.

'What . . .?' I whispered, and the feeling grew so strong I could almost hear the buzz.

I looked up to the twilight sky, where the early night stars, as familiar to me as my own name, should just be crowning. Mars should be visible to the west. Venus low to the south. Serpentine Draco and Ursa Major to the north.

There were stars.

There were a lot of stars. Clear and bright in the sky.

I should have felt the calming influence of their constant, unchanging nature in a world of flux and uncertainty. I should have heard my father's voice teaching me the names of the constellations, telling me their stories, like I did every time I looked up.

But I didn't.

Instead, terror gripped me inside and out. Cold, hard, unyielding terror that I didn't, *couldn't*, understand. It was as if my eyes were no longer connected to my brain. I could see stars but did not recognise them.

They were not my stars.

Before

When I was ten years old, my family went on vacation to Banff, in Alberta, Canada. This was the first time me and my sister had been out of the US and was not our usual vacation. Mother liked beaches and heat and bars open from noon and restaurants on the sand. She liked frilly sweet drinks and parasols and putting Helen and me in a kids' club for the day so she could really unwind.

My father didn't.

Our vacations were to Florida. The Keys, Miami – even Disney World once, but only for half a day because my dad hated the crowds.

Banff was different. It had taken my dad six months to convince her to go. An extra job to save enough to pay for it, and only when he showed her a brochure for the super-luxury Clearmont Hotel beside a lake with a giant spa did she say yes. Technically we were staying at a nearby place that had an agreement to use the Clearmont's spa at a discount, but Dad only let that slip after we arrived.

We flew into Calgary. First time Helen and me had been on a plane. We loved it. Scared at first, then exhilarated, watching the earth fall away until only the biggest landmarks – the mountains, the Great Lakes – were discernible and humanity, civilisation, traffic diminished to nothing more consequential than ants.

When we touched down, picked up a hire car and sped away into the rolling giant landscape of the Rockies, my father's tense shoulders and set frown fell away. He sat taller in the driver's seat, he tapped out music on the steering wheel, he looked a decade younger.

'The air up in the mountains, you girls won't believe it,' he said, grinning from the front seat as we eased our way through Calgary traffic.

'Yes,' my mother said, arms crossed, eyes narrowed. 'It's cold. I hope you packed sweaters.'

But even her icy tone didn't dampen my father's happiness.

'You'll see. We'll go swimming, hiking, even see about getting you girls on horseback.'

Helen squealed and clapped and said, 'I love horses, Daddy!'

'And we'll go stargazing too. It's a dark spot here. You can see all the way to the edge of the galaxy.'

He met my eyes in the rear-view and winked. I couldn't keep the grin from my face. We'd done a few excursions into the woods, mainly in New York State, once in Massachusetts, but they were only day hikes or one-nighters, always in areas with plenty of other people because we couldn't go much further out in a single day or weekend. This vacation, however, would be total immersion. This would be nightly stars and running through the trees and swimming in lakes and feeling the world itself in the grit between my toes and the wind rushing through my hair and the cold air dimpling my skin.

We arrived at the hotel, which wasn't a hotel but a sprawling complex of cabins, and after signing in and a fraught few minutes of whispered argument between our parents, we pulled up outside our home for the next ten days.

A log cabin, beautifully constructed and kept, modernised throughout, high-end kitchen, bathroom, living room covered in bearskin rugs and two huge soft leather couches. Cable TV. Double-fronted refrigerator. For them, a king-sized bed with white cotton sheets and marshmallow duvet. For us, two single beds and a view out into the forest.

Even my mother didn't hate it for long, though she tried.

The cabin, nestled in the trees, sat a dozen or so feet from the lake shore. Milky turquoise water that changed colour through the day in the glare of the sun. I'd never seen anything like it. On the other side, mountains speared the sky, tipped white with snow, laden with glaciers. Forests fringed the mountains, tumbling down to the water's edge. Blue sky so clear and pure I couldn't stop staring at it.

My father stood with me on the pebble beach, strewn all over with bleached logs, bright water lapping at the stones. Helen clambered over the logs, ran screaming back and forth from the tiny surf, skipped stones, while my mother, hidden away inside the cabin, unpacked and, she said, brought order to the chaos.

'You like it here, Rissy?' my father asked, not taking his eyes from the view.

'It's so pretty.'

'How about that air? Don't get air like this in New York.'

I sucked in a deep breath, filled my lungs. 'It's like it's from a different planet.'

He laughed and grabbed me into a hug.

The next ten days progressed in a blur of activity and nature but followed a similar pattern. While my mother and Helen did 'restful' things – shopping in Banff, the spa, afternoon naps, brunch and lunch and early dinner in various restaurants and diners – my father and I struck out into the wilderness.

The first few days were short hikes, ten or twelve kilometres, then a visit to a hot spring which even my mother said she'd enjoy. Then longer walks, twenty kilometres, twenty-five even. We set out earlier, stayed out later. At night, we sat outside by the lake, wrapped up to stave off cold and the biting insects, and stared at the stars. He pointed out ones I didn't know. Talked about the size of the galaxy. Then the size of the universe. And how small we were. How impermanent. It riled him sometimes, he said, that he would never make a meaningful contribution to the universe. Never see commercial space travel. Never walk on Mars. Never know if life really, truly existed out there in the cosmos.

'That's why I find the city life so hard, Rissy,' he said. 'All the pressure and stress of work to pay a mortgage, support a family; it's working to afford to work. Buying junk because society says you need the latest car or TV or whatever. Then working harder, longer to afford it again and again, keep upgrading until you reach the top. But that's the lie, Ris, there is no top, no finish line.' He sighed and rubbed the back of his neck. 'The cycle never ends. It's all more, more, more. We're all trapped inside the wheel, stuck in a loop, repeating the same day over and over. Same train in the morning. Same sandwich shop at lunch. Same bar for a drink after work. Same conversations.'

He turned to me and said, in such a serious tone I couldn't ignore him, 'You have to be brave, Iris. You have to be brave enough to live the life you truly want, not the one society and other people expect of you, you understand?'

I wasn't sure I did, but I nodded anyway.

'That's the mistake I made,' he said, deflated, and turned away.

I wasn't sure, as a ten-year-old, how I was meant to respond, so I reached out and held his hand. He squeezed my fingers and gave a small laugh.

'Sorry, sweetie, you don't want to hear all my grumblings.'

'Yes I do.'

He looked at me and smiled. 'You're a good girl. I wish I could make the world better for you.'

I felt a cold squirm in my chest. I didn't know how to stop him being sad, what to say to make him smile and reassure me the future was sparkling bright and exciting while the picture he painted was bleak, concrete-grey and endless.

I looked away from him, up to the stars.

'Maybe there's a better world up there. Maybe I'll go work for NASA so I can find it first.'

He laughed. 'You do that. I hope I'm still around to see it.'

He patted my shoulder and went indoors. I stayed and watched the sky. A shooting star streaked across the darkness, then another soon after. The cold squirm didn't go away; it chewed on the last few words my father had spoken and turned them to acid in my stomach.

The next morning, the day before we were due to leave, my mother took Helen in the car to Calgary.

'We need souvenirs, Mitch,' she said to my father. 'And there's nothing but kitschy trinkets around here. Besides, Helen and I would like to spend some mother–daughter time together.'

As if they hadn't already spent every day together. I rolled my eyes as Helen jumped in excitement. I wanted to go with them. My legs and back ached from hiking, my shins were bitten up by mosquitoes and scratched and grazed from branches and tumbles. I wouldn't have minded a cold milkshake and a hamburger instead of trail mix and protein bars.

'That's okay,' my dad said. 'Me and Rissy will head on up to Lake Louise. There's a trail there I've been wanting to check out.'

And just like that, I was whisked away in a cab to another hike while my sister got to wear nice clothes and sit in cafés and be spoiled by Mom.

The trail started in a quiet area near Lake Louise, away from the tourists and the well-trodden 'baby trails', as my dad called them. This one started easy but got hard and steep quickly. Dad strode on ahead, powerful legs carrying him up the rocky slope like a mountain goat, daypack bouncing on his back. I dragged my feet. I couldn't tell him I was bored. This meant a lot to him. But shit, I was bored.

'Come on, Iris,' he called from far ahead. 'Push through, the view's worth it, I promise.'

Like the view of Mount Louis was worth it. And the view through the Stewart Canyon and Aylmer Pass. And then another view of another mountain. Another canyon. Another river and lake and sweeping forest vista and *yawn*.

Yes it was pretty. Majestic and breathtaking and awe-inspiring and all those key phrases, but my ten-year-old brain, after a week of it, whined 'seen one, seen 'em all'.

This view, when we finally did get there, was not what I'd expected.

We'd climbed about five hundred metres, skirted the mountain until I wasn't sure what side we were on or where the lake was in relation to us. The trail itself was barely there, a faint line through the rock and ferns, overgrown and invisible in places, yet my father somehow knew where to step.

We crested a forested ridge and descended a gentle slope to the treeline and the 'view'.

'Well, Rissy, what do you think?' he said.

'Uh . . .'

A lake. Perfectly circular, about half a mile wide, with mountains rising on all sides like giants.

'It's a meteor crater,' he said, and my eyes widened. I saw it now. The unnatural mountain slopes, not made by glaciers like everything else in the Rockies, but by something alien. The lake itself was glass-clear, showing a carpet of sandy pulverised rock and dozens of thin grey fish. The water darkened near the centre and I wondered how deep it went, how hard the meteor had hit. The trees all around were slightly shorter than their cousins on the other side of the mountain, but brighter green, the leaves bigger, the grass and ferns more lush, sustained by the lake, protected by the mountains. A little Eden.

'This place was made by something not of this earth,' he said, dropping his pack and spinning around, arms out. 'How amazing is that?'

'It's pretty amazing,' I said, but I couldn't help thinking of the walk back down. My knees ached at the thought. Everyone thinks going up a mountain is the hard part, that walking back down is quick and easy, but when a trail is rocky, going down is ten times worse.

My father darted around, talking about the plants, the lake, how the water got here – a rich mix of rain, meltwater and groundwater – how there were dozens of underwater fissures feeding minerals and fresh water so it would never stagnate or dry up. How an explorer had seeded the lake with fish fifty years ago, fully intending to set up a homestead here, but had died before he could.

'We should do it instead,' my father said, finally breathing out his mania, turning to me wild-eyed, hair sticking up all over.

I laughed. 'I don't think Mom and Helen would like it here.'

'Course not, course not, but you and me. Just you and me. There are enough trees to build a cabin. Enough fish to eat. Wouldn't that be something, Iris? You and me, living the dream.'

I laughed again, but his tone had taken on an edge I didn't like.

'It's getting late,' I said. 'We should head back. We've got to pack and stuff.'

He looked down and huffed a fake laugh. I knew the sound of it, from years of his humouring my mother.

'You're right, I know. We're going home tomorrow.'

The way he said 'home'. Like a prisoner going back to his cell.

He bent to pick up the bag, but stopped, put his hand on his knee instead and shook his head.

'We should stay here,' he said, and looked up at me. 'You're like me, Iris. That life in New York isn't real. It's the trap, don't you see? Right now, we're out of it, we escaped, and Mom and Helen, they want us to go back in. You get that, don't you? They want us trapped.'

I'd never heard him talk like this. The calm, even tone of absolute certainty. He wasn't a dreamer any more, staring up at the stars and wishing to be among them. He was the astronaut who didn't want to come back down to earth.

I backed away a step.

'I don't think that's true,' I said in a tiny voice. The mountains suddenly seemed too big, looming over me like a wave ready to break.

The light waned. Mid afternoon. We'd be walking back in the dark if we didn't leave soon.

'Please, Daddy, we need to go.'

'I can't go back,' he said slowly. 'I won't. But you can. The trail is right there. You remember the way.'

My mouth fell open.

He turned his back on me.

'Dad!' I shouted, but he didn't turn.

He walked away, around the lake, to an open expanse of grass. He dragged a fallen tree into the centre, then a few more until he had a square.

'This is where our cabin will be,' he shouted. 'I'll build it myself. Every log and stone.'

I looked around to find the way we'd come into the clearing, but I couldn't see it. I didn't know the way back. The trail was barely a trail and I didn't have a torch, hadn't been paying enough attention to landmarks, though he always tried to instil that in me. I didn't know what else to do, so I went over to him. Watched.

'Daddy, please,' I tried, but he just shook his head, waved a hand around his ear like I was a fly to be swatted.

'The porch will be here,' he said, setting the outline with some short branches. 'And your bedroom here. Mine there.' He grinned at me. 'You see? It'll be perfect.'

'Daddy . . .'

'I'll put the chimney here, haul up a stove from town. Over there,' he pointed to a patch of grass, 'we'll grow vegetables – yams and carrots, some cabbages too.'

'But—'

'No, Iris,' he snapped. 'No buts. No whining. No "please, Daddy". This is our home now. This . . . magical place . . . it's ours.' He grew angrier, his words snagged, his thoughts muddled. 'This is *real*. This is the only thing that is real!' He paced, a prowling lion at the edge of a cage. 'We can be happy here. I can be . . . Don't you see? I have to do this! Damn it, Josie, don't you want me to be happy?'

He surged towards me and I stumbled back, fell over a log. My elbow cracked on a rock and I cried out. My mother's name hung in the air between us.

He stood over me. Fists clenched. Breathing heavy. He looked at me as if I was her and he was finally able to unleash all the anger he had kept inside.

Tears stung my eyes, but I couldn't move. I'd never been afraid of my father before.

Then just as quickly as the rage had come, it vanished. The mist in his eyes cleared. He blinked and saw me, not her, lying on the ground, fear seizing every muscle.

'Iris. Oh Ris. I'm . . .' He reached for me, but I flinched away.

He dropped to the ground beside me and covered his face with both hands and wept. I let him. He cried for ages. The afternoon sun fell away and chill air sank into the crater.

When he finally looked up, his eyes were bloodshot and full of regret.

'Let's go home,' he said, his voice cracked.

I nodded, and he stood. He almost offered to help me up but thought better of it.

We walked back down the mountain in silence and returned to the cabin far past dark.

After

I carried the sheet back from the clearing and stood in the middle of the cabin for half an hour, maybe longer, trying to understand what I'd seen.

Ursa Major should have been in the north. The Frying Pan, the Dipper, the Plough, whatever, it should have been there. So distinct, so instantly recognisable, that constellation was the first my father pointed out to me. Every culture has a story about it, from adulterous Roman gods to Finnish bear spirits. It's in a Van Gogh painting. It's in Homer. It's in Shakespeare. But it wasn't in the sky.

There were clouds. Maybe that was it? Really well-placed clouds that obscured specific stars. Sure thing, Jane.

So what, then?

The wrong stars. Too random in their placement, too equal in size, brightness, colour, no sweep of the galaxy behind them, no shapes to inspire stories and myths, just black and white, flashing and strobing in impossible rhythms. Fundamentally, primally, cosmically wrong.

Don't be ridiculous. You're tired, hungry, going insane.

I pressed my eyes shut. Held them closed for ten seconds. When I opened them, the cabin came into focus. Felt solid and real and right.

The night hit hard and fast. The greying twilight disappeared to pure darkness. I lit a lantern, fed the stove and ate a granola bar while staring into the flames.

The wrong stars? Impossible. You're seeing things.

Despite my own human failings, my crazy, impulsive decisions, my years of uncertainty about my own perceptions, even, I still knew that it was impossible to see stars that didn't exist. So I hadn't seen them. That's that, as Claude would say. For all Claude's faults, her rational mind always put my flighty panics at ease. She could logic away a unicorn sighting in ten words or less. Impossible. Different stars were impossible.

And yet ... and yet ... they weren't entirely unfamiliar. That pattern. Those pinpricks of light, I'd seen them before. In a place, a time I'd hidden in the black pit of memory, echoing walls, hard bathroom tiles, recessed spotlights slowly fading to darkness.

I lay on the mattress wrapped in my sleeping bag, feeling warm and snug for the first time since leaving my home. This wasn't so bad. I had a roof, I had a bed. I had air and water and fire and some food. The stars were still the stars. They were my comfort, my connection to family, to the universe, to my own sense of self. I'd chosen to turn my back on the life I'd built, walked away from a wife, friends, a job I hadn't given notice to, future plans I hadn't cancelled, a sister I barely spoke to, a mother I never wanted to speak to again, and I'd told no one. Maybe the stars changed along with me. They'd become something new, as I had.

Or maybe I was going mad like my father.

I often thought of other worlds, other lives, escape routes from my own bad choices. I pictured lives for people I knew: maybe if Ellis had asked that girl out, maybe if my father hadn't married my mother, maybe if I'd had the guts to move to Washington or Florida, to Space HQ. A whole universe of maybes. I imagined versions of me, my family, my friends. All on different paths because they'd made different choices. Was there another Claude tormenting another Iris? Was there an Iris who had never even met Claude? Was my father there? Was there a world where I'd saved him?

The last time I saw him, he was smiling. That's something at least. I was sixteen. My sister had just graduated high school and had already started packing for college. That weekend she was staying at a friend's place and my mother was on a weekend away with some women from the neighbourhood, so it was just me and my dad at home.

'How about we drive on up to the woods this weekend, hey, Rissy?' he said, leaning against my bedroom door. 'That old spot, you know the one, with that big oak tree. You used to climb it. We can camp out, burn some hot dogs. How about it? It'll be just like old times.'

But I was sixteen, it was November and I had an overwhelming, end-of-the-world crush on a girl in my class and she was having a party this weekend. I just *had* to go because that party was where she'd realise she loved me back and we'd have this epic, life-changing romance and run away together.

'I'm busy,' I said, lying on my bed, flipping through magazines, planning out the perfect hairstyle, the perfect sexy-not-slutty outfit. 'Sorry.'

'Come on,' he tried, desperation in his voice. 'It'll be fun. You can invite some friends.'

I rolled my eyes. 'No way. It's *freezing*. They don't want to go *camping*, that's for kids. I'm going to a party, okay?'

He'd grown thin, gaunt almost, and stopped trimming his beard. His clothes were crumpled, and leant more to plaid shirts, which Mother hated. She was spending more and more time away from him, Helen was getting ready to leave home, and I had my own adolescent drama to deal with.

He was lonely. I wish I'd seen it then.

'Well all right then, Ris,' he said. 'I'll see you for dinner.'

We ate that night at the same table, but I was deep in magazines while he seemed just as distracted. I finished, jumped up, put my plate in the sink and went to rush upstairs.

'I've got homework,' I called mid run.

'Iris.'

I stopped, his tone strange and distant.

He smiled at me from the table, meal untouched. 'Sweet dreams, Rissy. I love you.'

'Love you too, Dad,' I said and hurried up the stairs.

I stayed in my room for the rest of the evening. I came down in the morning, poured cereal, snuck a cup of coffee from yesterday's jug – I wasn't supposed to have it – and flicked on Saturday

TV. Three inane cartoons later, my dad hadn't come down. He was an early riser and it was close to eleven. I went up to my parents' room.

I knocked, but there was no response.

'Dad?'

I opened the door. The room was empty, cold from an open window, bed made but not neatly, a depression in the edge of the duvet where he might have sat for a while.

I looked out the window. His car was gone.

I went to the phone, dialled his cell. I heard it ringing upstairs.

He's just gone to the store, I told myself, and slumped back down on the couch. Just to the store.

But something felt wrong.

An hour later, he wasn't back.

Gone to the store and then maybe lunch or a drink. He liked to drink early in those days. I flicked through channels on the TV but couldn't focus.

His cell phone began to ring. He must have realised, thought he'd lost it, was calling from a payphone to see who had found it.

I raced up the stairs two at a time and caught the call.

'Dad? Is that you? Where are you?'

An automated voice crackled down the line, '*Are you satisfied with your long-distance provider?*'

I swore and hung up. Checked his phone. A missed call from home – me – and nothing else. I checked his messages – his password was Carl Sagan's birthday – but there were none.

None at all. But I'd messaged him the day before. My throat tightened.

He'd deleted them. I checked his call list. Deleted. His contacts. Deleted.

On purpose? Maybe he'd broken his phone . . . sure. Broken his phone. That made sense. Pressed the wrong button somewhere, restored to factory settings . . . that was plausible. He didn't like technology and could barely use it at the best of times.

I went back downstairs, sat back on the couch, cell phone in hand, and tried not to worry.

By mid afternoon, there was still no sign. Maybe he stopped off at the bowling alley or dropped in on one of his friends, though I couldn't think of a single person he'd call a friend. The party started at eight and I needed a ride.

I made some food, couldn't eat it. He's got lost. Got stuck. Car broke down. Gone to work.

At six, I was angry because he knew he was meant to take me to the party. He knew how important it was. No trip to the shops takes this long. How could he be so selfish? How could he do this to me?

At seven thirty, I was afraid. I called my mother, but she didn't answer. I called Helen, but she told me to stop being a baby and Dad was probably out having fun, stop bothering her.

By nine, I'd forgotten about the party and the girl I liked. I'd checked every room, the garage, the garden, even knocked at the neighbours on either side. I'd checked his closet. All his clothes were still there. His boots, his camping gear, his hunting knife and fire kit. He wouldn't leave those. He loved them.

He wouldn't leave me. He loved me. He's coming back. He has to.

At ten, I replayed yesterday's conversations. The look in his eyes, the tone of his voice, the strange sadness in his whole body when he told me he loved me. I found the number for his office. I called and got their answerphone. I left a message. I tried to keep the tremble from my voice and sound grown up. I didn't want to embarrass him in front of his colleagues by sounding like a kid.

I tried to call my mum again. She didn't answer again. I began to pace the living room – that's what they did in the movies, right? Paced until news came, and it always did.

Except it didn't.

At eleven, I called the police. They called my mother, and finally she answered, finally she listened.

She and Helen came home the next morning to a frantic day of calls and canvassing and car rides to his usual haunts – the bar, the bowling alley, the park – but all responses were the same. Haven't seen him, sorry.

The police questioned me for an hour. My mother for longer. A dough-faced cop made me repeat every word Dad and I had exchanged in the last two days, but I wasn't paying attention to most of them and forgot things and couldn't believe I'd been so stupid.

'Did he give you any reason to think he would leave? Did you two argue?'

'No!' I cried and cried.

'Did he give any indication about where he might go?'

'No!'

'Are you sure? You mentioned he wanted to go to the woods. Which woods? The ones at the park?'

My insides ran cold.

'Not the park,' I said. 'About an hour out of town. He asked me to go with him,' I gripped my mother's arm. 'What if something happened to him and I wasn't there to help?'

'Don't worry, Iris,' she said with all the warmth of a snow bank. 'Mitchell' – she full-named him; she *never* full-named him – 'is probably sleeping it off in the back of his car.'

I pulled away, disgust all over my face. 'What does that mean?'

Dough-cop coughed. 'Can you show us the woods on a map?'

When my dad didn't turn up on Sunday, he was officially declared missing and the police decided to search the woods. Monday morning, they set up a search party. Twenty people, give or take, plus a few of Dad's work colleagues and a gaggle of my mother's soccer-mom friends. Those women, in their spindly heels and tight jeans and loose blouses, came with Tupperware boxes of muffins and Thermos flasks of steaming coffee. They set up a table at the edge of the forest, gossiped, rubbernecked.

Don't worry, Josephine dear, they all said, overlapping each other like squawking gulls, he'll be just fine, he's outdoorsy, they'll find him whittling spoons by a campfire or, you know, something. My mother stayed with them, fanning her false tears instead of searching for my father.

Me, Helen and a cop who looked too young to shave, formed a group. We had sticks to bat the undergrowth, a clutch of flags to plant in case we found anything. Nobody would tell me what we might find and I was too scared to ask.

I knew these woods. I'd been here a dozen times, but not for a while, and my brain wasn't firing right. The paths were foreign, overgrown, but I stumbled on, Helen silent beside me, the cop whistling somewhere further off. The sun was too bright, the forest too loud, the air too cold. Everything was heightened and painful, like my nerves had been stripped, my skin peeled back to expose raw pink meat.

My feet took me where my mind wouldn't. Up the hill, along the ridge, past a stand of aspen and down to a flat spot, and the oak tree.

I saw his tent first. Then I saw him.

Heard the creak of the rope on the branch.

The soft ruffling of the wind on his empty tent.

I don't remember much of that day. My mother told me later the police thought he'd died on Saturday night. He'd hung there for two days before we found him. My mother said, so bitterly I never forgave her, that my father had finally found a way to stay in the woods forever.

Before

It had been a week since the smoky wine bar and I had almost convinced myself it had been a dream. Claude had asked for my number, I'd given it, carefully etching the digits on a bar napkin. But nothing. No call. No text.

Music throbbed around me, a heavy beat, a favourite song, but I wasn't dancing. I was hiding in the backyard while the house party raged, pretending to smoke, watching the cigarette burn down, bright orange cap to grey-black tower, to collapse. That was how I felt.

I didn't really smoke. Not unless I wanted to pick a fight. My mother found a pack of Virginia Slims in my closet when I was thirteen. They weren't mine, I said. Likely story, she said, and launched into a lecture on how I was a stupid, selfish girl who would die at thirty if I carried on this way. I'd never even taken a draw on a cigarette when she told me I'd have lungs full of black tar and no boy would ever love me because I stank and my teeth would rot out of my head. They aren't mine, I shouted. That's what they all say, she shouted back. She didn't trust me. That's what hurt the most. So the next day at school, I went behind the bleachers with the boy who'd given me the Slims for safe keeping and smoked until I threw up. After that, I kept a pack hidden somewhere in my room at all times, moving it around so she'd never find it. A habit I'd never broken. The current pack was inside a shoebox in a kitchen cupboard, tucked beneath a stack of old phone bills. I only lit one up when I wanted to rage at someone or at myself.

Bella hated smoking. She'd smell it on my clothes and make that face. Through the kitchen window, I could see her dancing with the hosts, Elena and Francesco. She was Bella's thesis supervisor, he the devoted, beautiful husband. They threw these parties twice a year, invite-only bacchanals, evenings of debauchery and marijuana and discussions of Sartre and Nietzsche and cubism between open-shirted artistic types and fire-eyed English majors. There were rumours Elena and Francesco regularly invited students into their bed. Watching them dance like that, I wondered if Bella was one of them. But as the idea came out, I lunged to pull it back and checked myself. My brain wanted to pick a fight with Bella because another woman hadn't called. How fucked up was that?

I stubbed out the cigarette and wrapped my arms around my chest against the November cold, watched my breath make clouds in the darkness. I closed my eyes and pictured that low-lit, wine-scented bar, the woman across from me, the reflection of smoke swirling in her eyes.

'Who are you, Iris?' she asked, her French accent shaping the common words into uncommon delights.

'I'm . . .' How could I answer that question? In factual terms – last name, date of birth – or in ethereal ones – a lost girl, a dreamer, a nobody? 'I'm . . . just me.'

Claude smiled, ran her finger around the rim of her wine glass. 'Sorry. That was a strange question. I mean, what do you do?'

My footing evened. 'I work for a company supplying parts to NASA.'

Her eyebrows shot up, along with, I hoped, her estimation of me. NASA was the golden word that turned people from polite but uninterested to intrigued. It had worked with Bella. It had worked with Claude.

Guilt stung my insides.

'Very impressive,' Claude said. 'NASA. You like space?'

'Oh yeah, Carl Sagan is my hero. I love the stars. Ever since I was a kid and my dad bought me a telescope.' I felt it bubbling up my throat, the rambling, child-like obsession, and I couldn't stop it. 'It's so massive, you know? So many possibilities for other worlds and other life. Like, what would a person from Europa look like? Or from a planet orbiting one of the *trillion* stars in the Andromeda galaxy? And there are so many more planets, so many more stars, so much to explore.'

I looked at her, waiting for that burst of excitement back, because how could anyone not be in awe like I was? But Claude's eyes were fixed on mine, eyebrows up, head back, like she'd stepped into strong winds.

'Sorry,' I said. 'Get me talking about space and I'm a kid again.'

The surprise on her face broke into a smile. 'Never apologise for your passion. Passion is to be cherished and fed, never hidden.'

'What are you doing out here?' Bella's voice behind me. I turned as she reached me, back door to the house swinging gently closed. Her cheeks were flushed, her breath short, tiny specks of sweat on her forehead glittered in the light from the kitchen.

I forced myself to smile. 'Just getting some fresh air. It can get a bit much in there.'

She screwed up her face, dismissed me with a hand wave. 'Oh they're just having a good time. They're asking after you.' She grabbed my arm. 'Come dance with me.'

She was drunk. The flush in her cheeks didn't go down with the cold, and I couldn't bring myself to look at her.

'I'm going to go home,' I said. Her face fell. 'I'm not feeling great, and this is more your crowd than mine.'

The playful drunkenness evaporated and her grip on my arm softened. 'I'll get our coats and call a cab.'

'No, you stay, I'll be fine.'

'Hey,' she fixed my gaze with hers, 'you're more important than them. Let me look after you.'

My body washed with guilt, surging from my feet, then up, hot and stinging, into my face. I wrapped my arms around Bella and sobbed out great clouds of smoky air.

We didn't talk about it. She didn't ask. But she took me home and asked if I wanted her to stay. I did. We climbed into the cold bed and warmed it with kicking feet. She held me, kissed me.

'I love you,' she said into my hair.

'I love you too,' I said into her chest, and I meant it. I was being such an idiot, throwing away something amazing, some*one* amazing, for a flirtation, a woman I barely knew who hadn't even fucking called.

Fuck her.

I had this. I had Bella.

I came back to the table with two more glasses of white wine. Claude took a sip and I noticed a tiny shake in her hand.

'What about you?' I asked. 'What's your story?'

'I grew up in Paris, moved to Québec, then Montréal, now here. I work in finance.' She dropped her eyes, smiled. 'It's not glamorous like NASA, but I like math, numbers work for me. I try to see patterns in the world and apply formulae and get a high return. It doesn't sound exciting, I can see that in your face,' I laughed, shook my head, 'but it's exciting for me, to identify a sector where there will be a boom or bust before anyone else, then calculate the risk, the reward. It's like chess.'

Her eyes lit up with the same enthusiasm I had when I talked about stars, but she quickly retreated into herself, dismissed it despite her earlier assertions about passion.

'My friend Virgil calls me a math geek.'

I laughed. 'If you're a geek, what does that make me?'

She lowered her eyes, then looked up at me through long black lashes. 'Beautiful.'

The blush rose high and hot in my cheeks.

'That's not fair,' I said. 'We were talking about math and you throw that out. That's a third- or fourth-drink move.'

She laughed and raised her hands in surrender. '*Oui, oui,* you are right. Forgive me. Let's talk more about work.'

There had been a change in her tone after that point in the evening. She'd tried to steer the conversation to romantic territory and I'd yanked away the reins, driving us back to cold, sterile topics. Did she think I wasn't interested? Was that why she hadn't called?

I rolled over, out of Bella's arms, onto the cold side of the bed.

But I *wasn't* interested, not really. I enjoyed the attention, I'd admit that, but it wasn't serious. So why couldn't I sleep? Why couldn't I stop thinking about how I'd fucked things up because I'd been caught off guard? Why did I care so much?

Because of the lightning strike. The freight train.

I buried my face in my pillow.

'You're different to other people I've met in this city,' Claude said. 'People here, they drone on through life in grey suits, but you, I think you have a sharper edge.'

'Is that a good thing?'

'I don't see how it can be bad. I find myself wanting to know more about you. Like why you have bleached white hair and how you end up in a supply company and not NASA itself.'

My throat tightened. Admitting to liking space was one thing, but telling her I cut my hair like a character in an eighties sci-fi movie and that I wasn't all that smart was a whole 'nother ball game, as my dad would say.

'If I told you' – oh God, don't say it – 'I'd have to kill you.'

I hated myself immediately. I couldn't have come up with a worse line and she knew it.

She coughed, awkwardly, and took a too-long sip of her wine so she wouldn't have to speak. I wanted to drown myself in my half-empty glass but instead I finished it off in one mouthful and added 'potential alcoholic' to my growing list of embarrassments.

'Would you like another?' I asked, brightly, pretending I'd never said it.

She took a moment, slender fingers playing with the stem of the glass. 'I better not. Early conference call tomorrow.'

And there it was, the brush-off, and I deserved it.

She didn't finish her glass, instead left it on the table as we stood and struggled into our coats.

'Sorry,' I mumbled. 'I say stupid things when I'm nervous.'

We stood opposite each other beside the table.

'I make you nervous?'

I nodded.

'I'm sorry too. I can be . . . intense? More so when I'm nervous too.' She laughed, and even in the low light I saw the red in her cheeks.

'Maybe next time we'll get our nerves under control.'

'Mmm, yes.' She looked me in the eye. Heels brought her close to my height, and I'd never realised until then how levelling that was in more ways than one. 'Give me your phone number.' She pulled a pen from her bag and took a napkin from the table, handed them both to me.

I scribbled out the digits and my name and handed it back. She folded the napkin and slid it down the side of her bag without looking.

We walked out of the bar together and stood for a tense moment on the sidewalk.

She was going uptown, I was going down.

'This was fun . . .'

Before I could make more of an idiot of myself, she nodded and said, 'Goodbye.' Then she turned on her heel and walked away. I stood there, stuck on the spot, while I watched her disappear up the street and hail a cab.

She'd asked for my number as a pre-emptive strike. I understood that now, ten days on and still no call.

I didn't have her last name or where she worked. I couldn't look her up or drop by her office (not that I would. Crazy people do that. The same crazy people who revisit bars for months on the off chance).

I tapped away at my computer in my windowless mid-floor office – I was a team leader now, so I got a coffin instead of a cubicle – inputting orders, approving deadlines, signing off invoices for my juniors.

I checked my phone.

She wasn't going to call.

I checked it again.

She really wasn't going to call.

My phone rang.

I snatched it up, fumbled it over and saw Bella's name. My insides deflated, an iron weight sunk through me, chest to feet. I stared at the picture she'd added to her contact in my phone, a grinning selfie of us both at the Guggenheim a few weeks after we met.

I let it ring. A few minutes later, I had a voicemail.

'Hey,' she said, slow and careful, not the bouncy tone I was used to. 'I . . . haven't heard from you since the party and I wanted to make sure you're okay. I mean . . . you've been acting strange . . . I wanted you to know I'm here for you, if you want to talk. Whatever you need. I miss you, okay? And I love you . . . so you know, call me?'

I listened to it three times and cried into my desk.

I called her back, asked her to meet me for a drink after work.

Over two beers and a bowl of peanuts, I told her everything, from my leaving drinks to Claude's clipped 'goodbye' at the end of the night.

She was quiet for a long time. I started panic-eating the peanuts so the only sound between us was a muffled crunch. When the bowl was empty, she spoke.

'You're an asshole.'

'Yes.'

'You went out with another woman.'

'Yes.'

'Are you going to see her again?'

'No. We didn't even exchange numbers.'

The lie burned in my throat, but I had to claw back some ground.

'I guess . . .' I said, 'I guess I needed to be sure. We're getting serious and, well . . . No significant ex, remember? This grown-up relationship stuff is a new frontier for me and I've been too scared to boldly go. Until now.'

Bella looked up from the table.

'Until now?'

'Going for that drink put everything in perspective. We have something great and I don't want to lose that.'

'God, Iris. You're a nightmare, you know that?'

'Does that mean you forgive me?'

She shook her head. The anger fell away from her eyes but left a residue of hurt. 'It's not like anything happened between you two.'

Just a freight train to the heart. Just electricity and unrivalled attraction.

'Nothing happened.'

Bella went to the bathroom while I ordered more drinks. When she came back, a frown creased her forehead, like she'd made a decision she wasn't too happy about.

'I wanted to talk to you about this tomorrow,' she said, 'but this is as good a time as any.'

I waited. She took a breath.

'I'm submitting my thesis next week. My classes are done and my lease is up at the end of the month. I need to move out. Erin is getting a place in Brooklyn with Tove, and I know Brooklyn is a bit far—'

'Move in with me.' I blurted it out. My subconscious took over my mouth, knew what I had to say before my fear could mess it up, knew what to say to keep her. Because I loved her. I really loved her.

A surge of white-hot affection married with cold, sharp terror and guilt. I said it again, made it real, forced the affection to win out.

'Move in with me.'

'Are . . .' She leant over the table, scrutinised me. 'Are you sure? Like, ten minutes ago you said you were scared of this grown-up crap.'

'I'm sure.'

She asked again.

I reached across the table and took both her hands in mine. 'I'm *sure.*'

Bella laughed. 'All right then. Let's do it.'

'Yeah?'

'Yeah!'

I laughed, she laughed.

'Are we really doing this? Moving in together after four months?' she asked.

'Looks like it. Cliché or what?'

'I better pack.'

She stood up and I stood up and we kissed and she called me crazy, and I think I was.

We parted. She would call me tomorrow, we'd celebrate, talk logistics, figure out where she'd put her stuff in my apartment.

This was it. This was life. And it was a good one, all things considered.

After

I woke to the sound of scratching. Tiny claws on metal. I bolted up. The fire had gone out. The chimney pipe rattled. The bastard raccoon was trying to get back in. I surged up from the bed, slid down the ladder and banged on the pipe with my one pot. The scratching disappeared up the pipe, then across the roof, and gone.

I opened the front door and stood on the porch. There, in the high branches of a tree, the raccoon's black mask.

'Is it going to be like this every day, huh?' I shouted. 'This is my place now. You're evicted. Get over it.'

The beast stared at me, eyes glinting green in the sunlight.

Beautiful sunlight. The forest bathed in yellow gold stretched out before me. I breathed it in. The air was cool and damp. A thousand scents mingled to a sweet perfume and my ears picked out tiny sounds: a mouse rustling through leaf litter, a bird singing in the branches, the gentle babble of the stream, the pissed-off raccoon growling. The forest was quiet without ever being quiet. Still without ever being still.

I relit the stove and set a pot of stream water to boil.

In a notebook, I wrote down everything that had happened since I set foot on the bus three days before. Had it only been three days? By now, I'd be reported missing. The police would question Claude, they'd visit my office, speak to my boss who would angrily huff that I hadn't been there for days and if I ever came back I'd be fired. They'd speak to Ellis, though I hadn't seen him for almost six months. They'd interview my mother, my sister, they'd find out about my father, they'd do their duty and discover I emptied my bank account, they'd find a bag and clothes missing, maybe they'd trace me on CCTV going from the apartment to the outdoor store to the bus depot, duffel in hand. They'd conclude I'd run away. No foul play. Case closed.

Claude would get over it. Eventually.

The water bubbled away. I rifled through the stack of space meals, made up a vaguely breakfast-sounding one – freeze-dried egg hash, whatever that meant, not as bad as the beef but still a gluey mess – then poured the rest of the water into the GO TIGERS cup and blew to cool it. I had no tea or coffee, but there's nothing like a hot cup of anything to soothe the soul and make a new place feel like home. But it wasn't home yet, not without a few creature comforts.

In the back of the notebook, I wrote a list.

1. Alcohol. Chocolate. REAL FOOD.
2. Knife.
3. New sheets, blanket, pillow!
4. Anti-raccoon pellets?

The map tacked up on the cabin noticeboard marked the nearest town, Mennier, as a twelve-kilometre trek away. If I left early enough, I could be there and back before dark. I took two hundred dollars from my pouch and hid the rest under the mattress, then emptied out my daypack except for map, water bottle and granola bar. I thought about clambering up onto the roof to block the chimney, but I didn't want to risk breaking my neck in my first week, so resigned myself to the idea of another fight with the raccoon when I got back.

Mennier was a town left to quietly degrade after the trail closed and the tourist trade dwindled. There was a campground a kilometre or so out of town, a drug store, a small supermarket, one outdoor and camping store with three more on the same street shuttered and dark. A diner, a bar, a spread of houses reaching the treeline, a garage with a tow truck outside, and not much else. Remnants of the rich tourist past were everywhere. A sign hung at the edge of town, gaudily painted with a mountain view and a scrolled *Welcome to Mennier! Gateway to the Catskills*. I passed a boarded-up motel with A-frame tipi-like huts, former glory faded into graffiti, and padlocked doors. Kitschy stores selling souvenirs, 'native' jewellery, key rings with your name on them, hastily cast resin ornaments of mountains and bears. All boarded up except for one narrow store that looked like it doubled as a head shop.

But it wasn't destitute. The stores that remained were well kept, one with a freshly painted sign, another with top-of-the-line electronics and an elaborate window display. Like the town had over-inflated during the tourist years and had now shrunk back down to its true size. There was an atmosphere too, a warmth in the air that had nothing to do with the weather.

I found the supermarket on the other side of town. I couldn't remember the last time I'd gone to a supermarket. Claude liked to order in, and when the mood to cook struck, she always had groceries delivered or went to Dean & DeLuca. I certainly wasn't trusted to shop, not after the disaster of her birthday one year. Claude was particular. You got *which* brand of caviar? For Christ's sake, Iris! I said *this* one!

I'm exaggerating. She hated caviar and never made me buy it, but she was a bitch about labels. *It must be those olives or frankly, Iris, what is the point?*

I pushed the cart between the five aisles, loading it up with rice, pasta, cured meats that wouldn't go bad for a while, a dozen tins of vegetables and soups, a small sack of flour, packs of dry yeast – I had an idea to bake my own bread on a wood stove, just call me Mrs Wilder – cans of coffee, colossal bars of chocolate, and two – no, three – bottles of rum. Big, useful hunting-style knives were kept in locked glass cabinets and needed ID and a conversation to obtain. I settled for a stubby vegetable peeler concealed in plastic that would barely scratch the raccoon, let alone give me a chance against a bear or an intruder.

At the end of one aisle hung a small collection of gardening equipment and rows of seeds. If I could grow things out there, I could stay indefinitely. I brushed my fingers along the edges of the packets, fanned them like pages in a book, but didn't take any. I had enough to carry, I reasoned, and my shoulders already ached at the prospect.

Two checkouts away, a woman unloaded her groceries onto the belt while her husband, I assumed, waited at the end, arms folded, foot tapping. They bought boxes of diapers and sacks of frozen kids' food, and the woman, hands trembling, handed over coupon after coupon. He kept looking at her, scowling with every coupon beep. He didn't help pack. When she'd paid and packed, he grabbed her arm, laden with bags, and tugged her roughly away from the checkout.

He said something harsh. I felt venom in the air, the threat of violence. She mumbled apologies. The supermarket staff averted their eyes. I did too. Pretended I didn't see. I pushed down the familiarity. The rising fear and shame. My breath caught halfway to my chest, ballooned in my throat until I couldn't breathe or speak or think of anything but hands around my neck.

'Miss?'

The checkout lady. Bright round face, not quite smiling, not quite not. 'You okay there?'

I forced a smile. 'Yes. Sorry.'

I unloaded my cart onto the empty belt. The unhappy couple were outside, halfway across the parking lot. The tightness in my chest eased. The tension flowed away like blood washed down the sink.

The air was thin again, breathable.

The woman at the checkout eyed me every time she passed an item through the till, watching as I loaded it into my bag.

'You hiking the old trail, miss?' she asked.

I flinched at the question.

'No. Just . . . shopping,' I said, then saw myself as she must see me. Dirty, alone, clad in heavy hiking boots and bright, water-proof jacket, and packing a suspiciously large amount of dry goods into a backpack.

I smiled. 'Road trip. Me and my husband. He's gassing up the Jeep. We're going cross country. Camping.'

The woman nodded slowly. The stream of produce passing over the checkout didn't falter: beep – swipe – pack – beep – swipe – pack.

'Sounds like a good time. You got enough here to last you to California, that's for sure. Looks like you're laying in for winter.'

I smiled, but my insides sank. She was right. I had to carry all this twelve kilometres. It was rapidly becoming clear my pack wouldn't hold everything, but I needed it all. Even the chocolate. Especially the alcohol. So I kept smiling. Fake Iris had a Jeep and a husband; she wouldn't worry herself about carrying bags.

The woman swiped the first bottle of rum and looked me up and down a second time. 'ID?'

My throat clenched. My hand went to my back pocket and took out a thin wallet containing my credit card and driver's licence.

'Here you go,' I said, forcing a smile.

Her brow furrowed and she scrutinised me a third time against the picture on my card. Taken years ago, hair cut short, bleached white, my Pris cut. My pre-Claude cut on my pre-Claude self. Now, my hair was past my shoulders, natural, boring brown.

My hand, holding a bag of cashews, shook.

Then the woman smiled, a small crack of it in the corner of her mouth. 'Good to meet you, Iris. From New York, eh? Funny route west you and your husband are taking to bring you through Mennier.' (Pronounced 'Men-yer', none of that French twang. I'd lived with Claude too long.)

I forced a smile, took back the ID and shoved it in my pack.

She passed me the rum and it was all I could do not to rip it open right there and fortify myself.

I paid in cash, loaded up as much as I could in my pack, carried the rest in bags, and left quickly. A lumbering turtle, top-heavy and arms straining. The woman called after me, 'You need any help, sugar?' but I was gone, the doors hissing closed against the final syllable.

I looked for the angry man and his long-suffering wife as I crossed the parking lot, listening for shouts or the dull slap of a fist, my body in a constant flinch, but they were gone. Back to their home. Behind closed doors. Where anything might happen.

I fast-walked through town, laden like a camel, watching for friendly locals and fellow hikers. I had a vision of that checkout woman picking up a phone, frowning, and dialling Claude's number, 'We got her.' And then helicopters, searchlights. I'd be dragged back. Made to answer for what I'd done.

As soon as I entered the trees, the forest soothed me. The more distance I had from Mennier, the quicker the fear fell away, dropping off me with every step like snow off stamped boots. There was no way the checkout woman would know where I was or what I was doing or why. But it needled me that anyone here knew my real name. I wanted to be Jane of the forest, not Iris of NYC. But what did it matter, really? I wouldn't need to resupply for a while, and when I did, maybe I'd hike to a different town – there was one twenty-five kilometres or so away. Or maybe the checkout woman wouldn't be there next time. Maybe she'd already forgotten me. Who cares? I didn't. Not any more. Claude would never find me. I covered my tracks. I'd taken circuitous routes. I'd left no clue as to where I was headed. And if, by some terrible twist of karma or kismet, she did find me, out here in the back of nowhere, I wouldn't go without a fight.

By the time I got back to the cabin, I'd forgotten about the supermarket. I was more concerned with the ache in my shoulders and the strain in my arms and legs. Whose bright fucking idea was it to buy so much rice? And flour? I didn't need flour. And cans. Why were cans so fucking heavy? And why hadn't I drunk one of the bottles of rum on the way? That would have made the hike more bearable.

I dumped everything inside the front door and collapsed on the couch in a puff of dust.

All of me hurt, from dull throbbing in my back to sharp, stinging blisters on my toes.

But at least there was no sign of the raccoon.

I relit the fire, went down to the stream and filled a pot, put that on to boil, then found a flavour of space food I hadn't tried yet. Spicy chicken. In dust form. Delicious.

Get used to it, Jane. This is your new normal.

After I'd rested and eaten a hot meal, I felt more human.

I put away the groceries, neat, tidy, everything in its place, and stood back to admire the order of it. Rows of cans. Packs of dry goods. Meat separate. Then the sweet things, sugar, chocolate and rum. Glorious rum.

I poured two fingers into the GO TIGERS mug and kicked off my boots. I sat back on the couch and watched the jumping flames in the stove. The sounds of the fire and the wind, the smell of woodsmoke and trees, the caramel taste of rum. The bone-deep exhaustion that comes from a long day of physical activity.

I sipped, savoured the burn in my throat, a celebration of a job well done. I had food, I had water, I had heat. From now on, this was going to be easy.

Before

Bella moved in on December 1st and for three weeks, it was bliss. My place became ours. My routine adjusted to fit hers and hers to mine. We cooked for each other. We stayed up watching movies. On the first Saturday, she ran down to the corner and brought back coffee and pastries before I woke up. We ate in bed. She loved the stars above our heads as much as I did. We talked about repainting the living room, about making it more 'ours'. We considered a cat but decided it was one cliché too far.

'This is what contentment feels like,' I said to her as we lazed in bed one Sunday afternoon.

She made a soft 'mmm' sound and held me closer.

We parted for Christmas with our families with a plan to meet back in the city for New Year. Still too early in the relationship to ignore family holidays and hibernate together in the tiny apartment. She went west to Michigan, I went upstate to spend the holiday with my mother and her husband – who, despite them being married for years, I still called Mr Fischer to piss him off – plus Helen, her husband, John, and their one-year-old daughter, Minnie. I still hadn't forgiven Helen for calling her that.

The day progressed as usual. Gifts, eggnog, the annual walk around Barrent Park, a tradition my father had started and my mother needed guilting into keeping. Then back to the house for games and dinner prep, which, with a mixture of nog and beer and drinking since dawn, descended into snide remarks about when I would settle down, when I would grow up, when I would bring Bella to meet the family, when I would get a better job, and when, dear Lord, I would dye my hair back. I shot equally snide comments back. Second kid on the way yet, Helen? Going to name it Mickey? How's the home-making going, Mom? You must be thrilled Mr Fischer here is rich enough for you not to work, it's what you always wanted. Come on now, Iris. Fuck off now, Fischer. And so on until the inevitable explosion.

But the explosion didn't come this year. The fuse was pinched before it reached the keg. After turkey and before apple pie, my phone rang. I didn't hear it at first. Christmas songs blared, Fischer and Helen shouted a version of 'Jingle Bell Rock' while the baby screamed. It took me a while to find my phone, tucked in the inside pocket of my coat, hanging on the rack in the hall. Four missed calls from an unknown number, the fifth still ringing. I answered, shouted hello. They turned up the music for 'Holly Jolly Christmas' and Mother joined in the chorus. I had to press my finger to my other ear to hear anything.

'Hello?' I shouted again.

Something faint on the other end. I pushed through the kitchen, out the back door. Snow fell in a thick curtain, but I barely felt the cold. Too much food, too much of Fischer's mulled whisky.

'Hello?' I said, quieter, ears ringing.

'*Bon Noël*, Iris.'

Her voice made me shiver.

'Claude?'

'I held off calling you as long as I could.'

Her voice was low, sad almost, with the soft warmth of wine about the edges.

'Iris?'

I dragged myself together, stamped the cold from my feet. 'I'm here.'

'I want to see you,' she said, and my heart broke open, flooded with red heat. 'Will you meet me?'

I paused.

'Yes.'

I made excuses and apologies to my mother and boarded the morning train back to the city. She wasn't upset and didn't ask me to stay. Helen scowled and told me I was selfish. When Bella called in the afternoon to ask how my hangover was, I didn't tell her I'd left early, that I was in our apartment, that I was pulling out every piece of clothing in our closet deciding what to wear. See you in four days, I said. I can't wait, she replied.

There was no guilt. Not this time.

These were stolen days. A time between reality and fantasy, where the city streets were dark, snow-strewn and empty of people, where stores and bars were closed for the holidays and all life had moved behind doors and windows, morphed into interior existences with no knowledge or care of what was going on elsewhere. I was outside of time and family and Bella.

I met Claude for the second time six weeks after the first. She gave me an address in the Upper West Side, a block from Central Park, not an area I'd ever had need to visit. When I arrived, she was standing on the street without a coat or bag. She wore slim dark blue jeans and an oversized knitted sweater with brown boots. Her hair was up, the ponytail bouncing as she stepped side to side to keep warm. She didn't look like the same hyper-stylish woman I'd gone to the wine bar with, yet she moved with the same ease, clothes hung from her frame perfectly, suggesting curves without giving them away. She was relaxed and all the more attractive for it. I was horribly overdressed in a red satin top and tight black pants and a string of necklaces I'd agonised over for close to an hour, and make-up done just so, with a perfect cat eye and just the right amount of smoke and . . . well, fuck.

'*Bonjour,*' she said, jogging a few steps out into the snow to greet me.

She kissed me on both cheeks, hands on my shoulders. The brush of her lips was agony; the smell of her was pure, unbridled want.

'We're not going far,' she said, a tremble in her voice from the cold.

'Where exactly *are* we going?'

She smiled, a more relaxed grin than the last time. She turned and gestured like a magician's assistant to the building behind her. A pre-war beauty, red brick, ornate detailing, a marquee outside and a doorman standing just inside the glass doors in top hat and dark green overcoat.

'Ta-dah.'

I stared up at the building with my mouth open. This was rich. This was million-dollar bathrooms and original features and views across the city. A side of New York that existed only in movies and over-the-top TV shows.

'You . . . live here?'

Claude stepped close to me as snow began to fall around us. She was shivering, her teeth chattering.

'Will you have a drink with me?'

There was a moment of perfect silence; the city held its breath, stopped its heart as I nodded.

She took my hand and led me inside.

After

I was at war.

It was little things at first. A packet of nuts ripped open, half eaten. A new hole in a couch cushion. Postcards missing from the noticeboard. A vanished spoon.

The raccoon was trying to drive me out, waging a subtle war of attrition meant to break my resolve. I never actually saw the little fucker doing anything, but when I rushed outside, brandishing a log or the club-like branch I'd brought inside for protection, I saw it sitting in the same tree, far out of reach, staring down at me. Laughing its rodenty laugh. One time, at the base of the tree, I found a granola bar wrapper, and two days later, the spoon, covered in shit.

I threw rocks at it.

They missed.

I screamed and shouted and waved my arms.

It screeched back.

And on we went. An incident every day or two. Minor stuff, it kept me busy and oddly entertained, but also on edge. When would the bastard strike? Had it already and I didn't notice? Did I move that plate, or did the raccoon? On and on, checking under my bed for droppings, checking my food for teeth marks, circling the cabin searching for how it got in with the door and windows closed, keeping the fire lit so it couldn't climb down the chimney, keeping watch on the porch in case it moved from its tree. It became easy to forget there was a world outside this strange new routine.

I fell hard into the rhythms of the forest. The dawn chorus more effective than an alarm, the sun hitting the roof, warming the room, shining blocks of brightness through the windows. I had expected languorous days staring into the wilderness, writing screeds of Waldeny prose, being wistful. But that idea died on the vine. I was always doing something. Sweeping out the cabin. Fetching water. Washing pots in a freezing stream. Washing myself in a freezing stream. Tending the fire. Chasing away the raccoon.

I was only responsible for myself. My body. Feeding it. Resting it. Keeping it warm. Keeping it dry. And that was it. There was no rent to pay, no bills, no social obligations, no commuting, no travel cards or credit cards or ID cards or gym cards or loyalty cards. No one asking. No one expecting. No one waiting. No one calling or knocking or popping over. No one but me.

But I wasn't alone.

Claude was always somewhere. I heard her heels on the hardwood floors, felt her breath on the back of my neck, smelled her perfume on the breeze. Sometimes she'd show herself, leaning against a tree in that red dress she knew drove me crazy, looking at me like I was an absurd child.

I tried not to think of her. Tried not to miss her.

'I miss you too,' she'd whisper beside me when my thoughts drifted to those early stolen days. 'I need to see you.'

More than once I saw movement in the trees around the cabin, heard footsteps crunching dried leaves. I followed, called her name, but there was nothing there.

'Chasing ghosts, Iris?' she said when I came back to the cabin, breathless. She sat on the couch, legs crossed, smiling.

'Why won't you leave me alone?'

She stood up, took my hands. I could have sworn I felt her. 'Oh my love, we're not done with each other yet.'

I closed my eyes and counted my breaths until she was gone.

On those haunted days, I'd wait for the sun to go down, then wrap up, pull my hat down over my ears and go out to the clearing.

One night, maybe a week into my new life, I needed the solitude more than ever. I lay on the ground, on a mattress of brown leaves, and looked up into the clear sky. The stars – the *right* stars again – like nocturnal sentinels staring back at me from a million worlds away.

The moment I saw those stars, I calmed. All at once, my shoulders lowered, my back loosened, something in my stomach unclenched. Claude retreated, and the memory of the wrong stars lost its sharpness. I'd been imagining it. Hallucinating a fundamental shift in nature after I'd made a fundamental shift in life. These were my stars. My comforter stretched taut above me like a giant blanket fort. I watched them move each night, mentally charted their path, made note of each constellation, drew up star maps back at the cabin, ripped the pages from my notebooks and tacked them to the walls around my bed. I made a nest of me, myself and I, and revelled in it.

That night, after a dull, routine day capped by phantom Claude's sniping, the stars seemed distant. The forest around me was quiet, no night-time insect chirping, no rodents raiding the undergrowth, no owls or bats. The trees too were still.

The stars blurred. My eyelids began to droop.

Then they sprang open at a sound.

I don't know how long I'd slept, but my arms and legs were heavy with cold.

I heard it again. The crunch of dry leaves.

My head screamed, *Bear!*

I lay still, patted my pockets, looking for anything I could use.

Another crunch. Slow. Tentative. It couldn't be a bear. Then again. Footsteps. Unmistakable.

I sat up and the sound stopped. The forest was deathly still. The fauna invisible and silent. Only my breath. Only my heartbeat.

And another footstep.

Claude? Had she found me already? The police closing in, guns drawn?

I wouldn't blame them. I'd be looking for me too. She must have called them. She must have called everyone. Had she figured out I'd taken a bus? Had she bribed the cashier to tell them where I'd gone? I couldn't breathe. My face and hands and neck felt hot and I wanted to run. But if I ran, she'd see me. Find me quicker. I felt her all around me, her laugh between the trees, her perfume on the wind, her footsteps . . .

The brush of nylon on foliage. Crunching leaves. A flash of torchlight.

I scrambled up, got a face full of blinding light, then the torch went dark. The footsteps stopped. Silence returned.

'Who's there?' I shouted into the trees.

My eyes readjusted to the dark. The outline of a figure emerged from the gloom between a pair of pines at the edge of the clearing.

My heartbeat thudded in my ears. She's here. What is she going to do to me?

'Who is that?' I said, but again, no response. I swallowed hard and balled my fists. 'Claude?'

The figure took a step closer and I took a step back. Blood surged through me banishing any trace of cold. My hands turned to fists. My legs braced. Ready to run. Ready to fight.

'Don't come any closer. I have a weapon.'

The figure lifted an arm. Took another step, into the clearing, into the moonlight.

It was a woman, but it wasn't Claude. I saw her clothes first. Same boots as me. Same jacket, though I couldn't tell the colour. The moonlight turned everything black, but somehow I knew it would be red.

Another step. Her hair was short and light.

Another. Her face became clearer. But I couldn't look. She was speaking, but made no sound. She was reaching for me, coming closer, moving faster.

Then she was gone.

My ears popped and I stumbled. The clearing was empty. The sounds of the forest returned, the volume dialling up one notch at a time until my ears ached.

'Hello?' I called. My voice shook, my hands too. I knew I wouldn't get a response, but speaking was a comfort.

That woman was not my wife. That woman was someone – some*thing* – else. I'd seen her face but I couldn't believe it. Wouldn't.

I wandered back to the cabin in a daze, guided by candles I'd left burning in the window. The picture of the woman was stark and bright in my mind. My boots. My jacket. My five-years-ago haircut.

My face.

I shook my head. Not my face. Couldn't be my face. Just another hallucination. Or a dream. Yes, a dream. I'd fallen asleep, hadn't I? Drifted off in the clearing, heard a noise – probably the bastard raccoon – and imagined footsteps, imagined me. Then I woke up and she was gone.

My breath came easier, lungs loosened as I walked.

I would get back into the cabin, stoke the fire, pour myself a large measure of Mennier's second-cheapest rum, and devour a rehydrated packet of mush. Just like the pilgrims.

'That's right, Iris, make jokes,' Claude purred in my ear as I stepped up onto the porch. 'Explain it all away, easier than facing the truth, isn't it, *ma chérie*?'

I pushed past her, went inside, and got blind drunk.

Before

I left Bella in February. I told her why. I told her everything. She yelled at me for lying to her about the phone numbers, about Christmas. It took a day and a night to end things. We talked and cried and fought and slept together, but it was dead time. The last gasps of a relationship that would never have worked.

'I would have made you miserable,' I said.

'You already have.'

I packed a suitcase in the morning. She watched, red-eyed, from the bed as I took down the telescope, folded the tripod and put them in my case.

'You're really doing this?'

I was running on no sleep, no food, just sorrow and guilt – a terrible, irritable fuel. 'I'm sorry.'

'This is so fucking ridiculous,' she said, shaking her head. 'You're throwing us away over a woman you've known for a month.'

'I can't explain it. I know it doesn't make sense, but . . . this, us, you know it wasn't working.'

'Funny,' Bella said. 'I thought we were in love.'

I closed my eyes. I'd thought so too. Until I felt the real thing.

'I have to go,' I said.

She sprang forward, slapped her hand on top of the suitcase. 'Don't.' She grabbed my face and kissed me. Gently, then more urgently, her grip around my neck tightened. I pushed her away and she sank onto the bed.

My heart ached. I zipped up the case.

'I'll call you,' I said, and she looked up. 'To arrange picking up the rest of my stuff.'

As soon as I heard the door lock click behind me, the relief came. Every step away from Bella and my tiny apartment was lighter than the last; the hurt lessened and the excitement grew. It had been quick, from Christmas to moving in with Claude. Maybe too quick, but it felt right.

I called Claude when I was outside, suitcase wheeling along beside me.

'I'm all yours,' I said.

'Oh my God, are you okay?' she said. In the background, the sounds of shouting and movement in her office.

'Not really. But I will be when I see you,' I said.

'Go home. I've left a key with Dante at the front desk, he knows to expect you. I've made room for you in the closet. I will be back before seven and we will celebrate.'

I hung up, smiling. The mid-morning sun glared down at me, flashing in my eyes with every passing car and high-rise glass tower, accusing me.

As I turned to head uptown, a woman slammed into my shoulder. She was rushing, with a bag from the bakery across the street. The one Bella liked, I thought with a stab of guilt. She didn't stop, or turn, just shouted an apology as she ran to my building.

Not your building any more.

I didn't recognise her, and yet ... I did. She was almost too familiar. Same height as me, same hair colour. We even wore the same T-shirt.

My phone rang. Ellis. I winced.

I looked again, but the woman was gone. I must have caught sight of myself in a shop window, or a mirror; happens all the time. I shook away the weird, déjà vu like feeling and braced myself for the call.

'Yeah?' I said.

'What have you done, Iris?'

'Ell, don't—'

'Bella called me. She said you quit her for some Upper West Sider with a fancy apartment you've known for a week? You kidding me?'

I pulled my suitcase out of the stream of pedestrians and leant against a wall.

'It's more complicated than that,' I said, pressing my palm against my eyes.

'What's complicated? You threw over the perfect woman. You know what I'd do for that?'

'Claude is the freight train, Ellis.'

He went quiet, I could hear him breathing, maybe pacing his office. Finally, a nasal sigh and he said. 'For real?'

'Big time.'

'You're *sure* it's not just some crush? Because you and Bella . . . you guys were the goal.'

'I'm sure. Bella and I weren't right for each other. We just looked like that from the outside. Relationships . . . they're never as simple or perfect as they seem. But Claude . . .' I paused, felt the surge of love, felt my smile grow. 'She's it, Ell. I swear.'

After a moment of silence, he gave in.

'She better treat you right,' he said, his tone softened. 'Or she'll have to answer to me.'

I laughed. 'I'll tell her that.'

Ellis sighed again. 'Real love, hey? Lucky bitch.'

We agreed to get a drink the following night, talk it through. We hung up on happy terms, but I didn't see Ellis again for a month. Too wrapped up in Claude, in my new life and new routine, the rest of the world fell away.

I went to Claude's apartment, the first time I'd been there alone, my new key clutched in my hand. It was barely midday; I had seven hours before she would be back. I went about the rooms, breathing them in as if they were mine.

I replayed that first night, the December evening she'd led me into her building, when her hand played against mine in the elevator, when she held my eyes across her marble kitchen island as she poured a glass of red wine. She'd taken a sip, licked her lips and walked around the island to me.

She'd slid between me and the countertop, glass in one hand, fingers of the other running up the side of my arm. I was alight. I could barely breathe. This isn't happening. This definitely shouldn't be happening. But I was weak and she was irresistible.

She'd kissed me. The single most perfect kiss of my life. Something in me exploded into fireworks and agony and tastes of wine and her and pure, primal desire.

'I thought I would get that out of the way early,' she'd whispered. 'So there is no confusion.'

'I'm not confused,' I murmured, and kissed her back.

We'd spent the next four days and nights tangled in Egyptian cotton sheets. The stolen days went on forever. A dream-like affair in the time between one year ending and another beginning.

The next six weeks had been stolen too. The occasional lunch. Sporadic evenings. A personal day taken together and a drive away from the city. A 2 a.m. sneak out and a cab uptown. Calls in the hallway, sprints downstairs for privacy.

I'd become a cheater. Something I never thought I'd be. For a while, I didn't know who I was. The guilt came in waves, a crest and break when I crept home to Bella, kissed her and pretended it was perfect, then a calm sea as soon as I set eyes on Claude.

Now I was in her – our – apartment and we wouldn't have to hide any more. No more sneaking, no more coded texts or secret calls or clock-watching. We could have all of each other all of the time. I held out my arms and spun around the glossy parquet floor. I ran from the master bedroom to the second bedroom to the office to the living room. I lay fully clothed in the free-standing roll-top bath. I breathed in high New York air from the private terrace. I set up my telescope at the bedroom window. I made coffee in the stupidly complicated espresso machine that didn't look like it had ever been used.

I waited for Claude.

Seven o'clock came and went. I kicked my feet and watched my phone.

At 8.15, I heard her key in the door. She bustled in, talking on her cell, saw me and jumped, as if she forgotten I'd be there.

She hung up, tossed her phone on the counter and wrapped her arms around me.

'I'm so happy you're here,' she said.

Any lingering doubts I had evaporated.

'Me too.'

'I hope it wasn't too awful.'

I shrugged. 'It was.'

I held her close, felt the weight of her against me, the smell of her breath and skin. It all felt right.

'But it doesn't matter. This is what I want,' I said.

She smiled, asked me to order Chinese and slipped away to get changed. She returned as I hung up the receiver, menu in hand, wearing loose cotton pyjamas and slippers, her face clean, scrubbed of make-up, hair in a ponytail, as natural and relaxed as I'd ever seen her. Almost a different person. She paused in the doorway to the bedroom and watched me.

'This is me without the styling. Me in my home,' she said, carefully.

'I like it.'

She gave a half-smile. 'Are you sure?'

I threw the takeaway menu on the counter, walked over to her and put my hands on her hips.

'We have about twenty minutes until the food arrives,' I said.

'You will be fine with waking up next to my messy hair and the black bags under my eyes?' She smiled, kissed me.

'Nineteen minutes,' I said, and pushed her into the bedroom. She let me, hands in my hair.

We found the Chinese outside the front door an hour later.

Eight months after I moved in, Claude and I were engaged.

She threw a party, invited all her colleagues, a few of my friends, Ellis, my sister. She booked out a restaurant, gave a speech, told the tale of how she'd proposed – the Staten Island ferry, the applause of strangers, the romance of a public declaration – she fed everyone five-star food and bespoke cocktails, and we danced until midnight. Even Helen looked happy for me.

Ellis seemed determined not to have fun. I'd been neglecting him, only hanging out a handful of times in the past eight months.

'Is this bougie bullshit everything you hoped?' he asked.

'I won't lie, it's pretty great.'

I loved Claude with a ferocity and selfishness I couldn't bear. I was protective of our relationship. I was territorial if we went out, laughing inside at the men who tried to pick her up, throwing shade at the women who looked twice. I was ensnared and I knew it, and part of me liked it, but another part, the independent, self-sufficient part, worried about who I was becoming. With Bella I'd been 95 per cent happy, and now, with Claude, I was nudging 99.9. Was this the life I always wanted? I looked around at my friends, my family, until my eyes settled on Claude. Yes, I thought, it was.

Claude worked late and long and loved her job. I worked only as much as the clock told me to. She would come home buzzing with energy at a deal done or a stock position exploited. I would listen and smile and congratulate. We would talk and laugh into the night, until she fell asleep on my shoulder or I dragged her to bed.

Where she came home smiling, I would drag my feet into our apartment and need an hour or more to delouse myself. I tried to speak to her about it once. On one of the rare evenings she was home before seven, she asked how my day was, and I launched into a moaning diatribe. Boss is awful. The work is dull. I'm trapped. I hate it. Blah blah blah.

'Stop, stop,' she said, waving her hand at me. 'You hate your job, I get it. So quit. Do something you love.'

'I love space. I love astronomy,' I snapped back. 'But without a million advanced degrees and years of experience, there are no jobs for me.'

We were on the couch, her with a glass of wine, me with a bottle of beer, her legs thrown over mine, me absently massaging her calf with my free hand.

She brought the glass to her lips but didn't drink. 'What about the Planetarium?'

'What about it?'

'Why not get a job there?'

I laughed. 'Like it's that easy. I've tried before, never got anywhere near the front door.'

She lowered her glass. 'One of my clients is a donor to the museum. I could make a call.'

I sat up. 'You'd do that?'

'Why not? Just a phone call.'

The next day, she made the call. Two days later, I phoned in sick and went to the Hayden Planetarium to meet with Neil, the director of programming. I'd spent many a Saturday afternoon staring up at the domed ceiling, craning my neck in the padded seats, losing myself to the booming music, the speaker spinning tales of the cosmos.

In the afternoon, Neil offered me four days a week. Two giving talks to school groups, two working with him to plan events and attract speakers. A literal dream, handed to me on a platter. All because of Claude.

But of course, there was a snag. The salary was a fraction of what I currently made. It wouldn't even have been enough to cover half my rent in my old 'cosy' apartment.

'Doesn't matter,' Claude said when I told her that evening. 'I make enough for us both. You don't even need to work if you don't want.'

'Yes, I do. Besides, I can't let you cover for me like that.'

She grabbed me and kissed me and said, 'Today is the first day you have come home excited and I love to see that. You *have* to let me do it. Besides, it's not like you're a . . . what is the word? Free? Free something?'

'Freeloader.'

'Yes. You are not a freeloader. This job, it is your dream, isn't it?' I nodded.

'So take it. Money is temporary, it comes and goes and doesn't really matter. Happiness can't be bought.'

'But—'

'No. No but. Call Neil and accept, then call your awful boss and quit. We are getting married. We are partners. Let me take care of you.'

I met her eyes. I was going to marry this woman. Me. Iris. The too-tall, awkward underachiever. How had I got so lucky?

'Okay,' I said. 'I'll do it.'

'Good. Now you'll come home happy. No reason to complain, huh?' She laughed and I laughed but there was a tiny something in the back of her voice that didn't sound like a joke. I dismissed the thought as quickly as it came, put it down to several glasses of wine and a nuance lost in translation.

I handed in my resignation the next day. Ellis all but put on a parade. I celebrated with my friends and with Claude – though they didn't mix well, they all tried, for me – and started a new chapter in my life.

The hook she'd cast sunk deeper, grew over with scar tissue and new muscle, became a part of me. Something I could never live without and I had no idea how I had lived before her. She'd given me my dream and the push I needed to go after it and she'd done it just for me. Because she Loved me – capital L – and I Loved her. I could never repay her for that, so I made myself the best girlfriend, best fiancée, best wife she could wish for.

And for three years, we were unstoppable. A paradigm of a loving marriage. The envy of friends and co-workers and my sister. For three years, I had joy. We had our disagreements, a few heated words, but they never lasted long and never ran deep. No grudges were held, because after she looked at me with those bright hazel eyes, after she took my hand in hers and kissed it, whispering her sorrys and sweetness, all anger melted away and the reason for the argument faded.

They say love is blind. Blind to white lies and small failings. Blind to pain. Blind to cruelty. They are right. I was blind to it all.

A new Claude emerged and my wife became someone else. Or maybe she'd been someone else all along and the real Claude had finally broken free.

After

Living in the city, I'd built myself armour. Everyone does it. I'd filled my gaps with clay, painted over the cracks, put on the mask we all wear to survive. The brave face, the forced small talk about weekends – what did you do last, what will you do next – the smiling through boredom, and pretending enthusiasm when the boss asks, how are you liking the role? I'd put six inches of insulation between me and the world, but in the woods, the air and rain and tree roots and falling leaves peeled back the layers of metal, wore down the rock.

Exposed. Pink-skinned and naked, a newborn in a new world. It's what nature does. Erodes. Changes. Grows. I was adjusting to it, seeing my internal earthquakes and transformations take form in the world around me. That's what Claude would say. I was projecting. Therapy speak. I had to work through it.

That's all this was. The clearing. The woman who looked like me. The stars. I was projecting.

'But what if it's more than that?'

Claude stepped out from behind a pine tree. She wore the dress I'd bought her last birthday, with her credit card, after she told me which one she wanted. It hugged her. Suited her, matched her skin tone and eyes, just like she'd said it would. She was beautiful. She'd always been beautiful.

'Still living in the woods, I see.'

I sat outside the cabin and watched her pick her high-heeled way over to me.

'Have I already gone mad?' I asked. 'Or am I still going mad?'

'You have always been mad, my love.'

My hallucination wiped dust from the step before she sat beside me. Close enough that I could feel her brush against my arm. She turned to me, knees touching mine, and ran the back of her hand down my cheek. The touch brought an all-too-familiar pain, one I loved and hated.

'But . . .' she said, her voice impossibly close, inside my ears, in my head, a soft, purring attack, 'considering what you did to get here, the insanity appears to fit the crime.'

'What do you mean?'

She laughed and kissed my cheek. My stomach clenched and the hook in my heart wanted to drag me back to the city. To that kiss.

I closed my eyes. When I opened them, she was gone and I was alone again.

Days had passed since I'd seen the woman in the clearing. I saw no more red flashes in the trees, heard no more footsteps in the night. The days blurred into each other and I lost track.

I'd bled once since being out here, but I'd always been irregular; months passed sometimes before I noticed I hadn't cramped up. Not needing to worry about accidental pregnancy, I didn't pay much attention to my cycle. I just dealt with it as it came and it had only come once. So three weeks? I should have counted days, done a Shawshank and marked the walls.

It wasn't just my emotional state that was dropping away; my body showed the signs too. In my old life I'd had a soft layer of fat and skin that spoke of three meals a day and regular visits to the Italian on West 87th or the diner on 11th with the best cinnamon toast in the city, of bars and work functions and nights out with friends, of high-end whisky and wine with Claude and beers and wings with Ellis, of irregular but earnest gym workouts and a quick metabolism. The forest took away all of that. Stripped me back to sinew. My pants hung looser, the bones in my chest, my collars, my shoulders all gained definition. I could have drawn on my own skeleton in magic marker and named my parts.

My food supply was healthy and I rationed down to the last oat. I didn't want to take another trip into the real world until I absolutely had to. I had enough to last five or six weeks if I was careful.

I filled my notebooks, yet that one page remained empty but for Claude's name.

The air had grown warmer, the light yellow-greens of new growth darkened. I struck out from the cabin every day, exploring the area, keeping busy. I found a vantage, a narrow overhang of rock with views over the forest to the mountains and a drop that could break bones. I found a narrow waterfall and a plunge pool no bigger than a hot tub. I found a lake where fat silver fish fed in the shallows with no fear of a hook. I swam naked in the freezing waters every chance I got.

I gave myself over to it. Let the forest carry me. Ignored the reasons I was there, ignored the niggling demons from my past, from Claude and my father, and lived on the surface. I'd come here to heal but I let the wound fester.

I had broken my life. Snapped it clean in two. Into a then and now, a before and after. All because I'd loved the wrong woman. When I was a kid, with the world showing me pictures and movies and TV shows of men and women falling in love, getting married, having children, I'd resigned myself to an alternative existence. Society told me the greatest love stories – Romeo and Juliet, Han and Leia, Aragorn and Arwen – were between men and women, not men and men, and certainly not women and women. There were no epic, I'd-do-anything-for-you lady-and-lady stories. So I grew up expecting a nice life, a nice relationship, but never capital-L Love. I never expected anyone to cross oceans for me. Or me for them.

Then I met Claude and I understood the hype. Perhaps I held onto it so tight I eventually broke it. I still loved Claude, deeply, painfully. I missed her too, felt the excuses bubbling up my throat. Was it really so bad, what she'd done? Was it just the price of true love? Just look at Cathy and Heathcliff. Passion and violence. Twin flames burning on the same fuel.

Besides, hadn't I done worse, by the end?

After a morning spent tidying the cabin, I hiked up to the over-hang with a measure of rum in one of the water bottles and a packet of pretzels in my pocket. I sat against a tree and watched the world. Far down the valley, a town went about its day, smoke curled from chimneys; a road scarred the landscape, but it was quiet, no rush of motors or honk of horns. Humans fit snug against the curves and snags of the mountains, sheltered by the puffy green canopy, the town little more than a tiny blot on the expanse.

Something moved behind me, rustling the brush.

I hugged the bottle to my chest, because that's what's important when a bear attacks, right, Jane? Keep the alcohol safe.

The rustling neared and a pair of small black eyes stared out at me from the middle of a bush.

My nemesis.

It stepped out, tentative, creeping, and sniffed the air. It didn't attack or scream or bite me; just watched, expectantly, as I sipped my drink. I dug into my pocket and the animal flinched back a few steps.

I threw it a pretzel.

It sniffed, then grabbed and devoured it. It licked its paws then sidled closer, sniffing around for more. I threw it another and it edged closer still. Repeat until the creature, the bane of my existence for weeks, took the pretzel right out of my hand.

'Monty,' I said and it – he – looked up at me. 'That's what I'll call you. Don't make me regret it.'

I offered him another pretzel and settled against my tree.

'We had a dog called Monty when I was a kid,' I said, as if the raccoon gave a shit. 'A chihuahua. My mother wanted a dog she could carry round in her bag, like the other women in the neighbourhood. The *rich* women. Monty shit all over the house and chewed my sister's hair when she slept.' I looked down at the raccoon. 'You remind me of him.'

The raccoon pawed at my pocket, dug his nose right in there and pulled out the bag of pretzels. He sat a foot away and ate them all. When the bag and my bottle were empty, I headed back to the cabin with Monty trailing behind.

War over. Ceasefire reached. Monty lived in the tree outside the cabin and I threw out the occasional handful of nuts, the last bite of a protein bar, raisins, hand-fed him every now and then, even managed to stroke his back once before he bolted up the tree, hissing.

Every morning, half an hour or so after dawn, as I stoked the fire and set a pan of water to boil, he scratched at the door. Suddenly I had a creature needing me, wanting me, or at least the contents of my kitchen. That was new. The loneliness receded. The rationing didn't seem so important. I had plenty, and I needed the companionship more than I needed a bag of peanuts. I found myself talking to him, telling him about my day, asking him questions about his. Crazy-looking on the outside, but it felt normal. The most normal thing I'd done since entering the forest. The other strange events – the stars, the woman – had faded to dream-like memories, easy now to dismiss as my own troubles manifest. I was getting the hang of things, and that bastard raccoon was my bellwether.

I kept my mind occupied as well as my body. I read the books left in the cabin. Teen vampires. Donna Tartt. A guidebook to the Himalayas. A schlocky romance. *Anne of Green Gables*. A locked-room mystery. A sprawling fantasy. *Walden*. *Wild*. A half-dozen more.

I lived deliberately, as Thoreau did. Or at least I tried.

I thrived. And with my new happiness, my validated decision, came more and more memories of Claude. The good ones. The ones that made me question whether this had been a mistake and I should go home, work things out, now I'd proved I could survive without her. I'd found myself. I'd won, hadn't I?

'Do you remember,' Claude whispered into my ear, 'the first time I told you I loved you?'

I closed my eyes against her. 'Sunday morning in summer. I brought you coffee and a croissant.'

'The sun lit up our bedroom. The doors to the terrace were open and the air was warm. The pastry flaked on my lip and you kissed it off.'

'I remember.'

'We had so many Sundays like that, didn't we?'

My heart split open, a pomegranate spilling blood-red seeds. Sundays spent lounging in white cotton sheets. Fridays at the theatre or cinema or a new restaurant. Mondays where we lingered at the doorstep, unwilling to end the weekend, just one more kiss, one more moment.

I'd been so happy.

Before

Claude dragged crimson over her top lip. She blotted it with a tissue and checked her teeth. I watched from the bathroom door, fingers playing with my wedding band. She wore a sheer green satin gown and four-inch heels, which made her taller than me in my almost-flats. She'd chosen my shoes. And the simple but expensive black dress I wore. My long brown hair – Claude had asked me to dye out the bleach and grow it long for the wedding, and she loved it so much I'd kept it – was twisted up and held with a clip while her ebony waves fell loose over her shoulders. My make-up was subdued, hers glossy and rich. My jewellery unassuming but tasteful, hers exquisite. It was all part of the plan. This evening was important. I couldn't risk overshadowing her – not that I ever could – yet I still had to make a favourable impression.

Her hand shook as she swept thick mascara onto her lashes. I stepped behind her, kissed her exposed shoulder.

'You'll be fine. You got this,' I said.

She pursed her lips, frowned for a second, then relaxed into a tired smile. 'I can't be confident. Not until I have the handshake.'

'You'll get it. Sophia and Lloyd think you're brilliant.'

She raised a single eyebrow. 'I am brilliant. But they are traditionalists. Sophia the worst. She climbed through a skylight in the glass ceiling and closed it behind her. And Lloyd, well, he sees my breasts before my brain.' She sighed. 'They cannot deny the quality of my work but they can deny the quality of my life.'

'What do you mean?'

She turned to face me, leaning on the edge of the basin.

'Don't be naive. I am better than any senior VP. I am better than my apparent superiors. They know it. I already have to fight harder, tooth and claw, to get where I am because I am a woman. I fight even harder because I love a woman instead of a bald man in a blue suit like I'm supposed to. But after Beltran, they cannot delay me without their prejudices showing.'

The Beltran trade. Claude's crowning glory in an already impressive career. She'd spotted the gap in the energies market, she bullied her way through it and netted nearly seven hundred million for her two bosses. It was the biggest single trade in the bank's history. I didn't understand it, her job, how it all worked, but I nodded along, I said the right things, because that's what a good wife does. I was rubbish at a lot of things, but marriage wasn't one of them.

'They give me partnership or they lose me, they know that.' She turned back to the mirror, ran the corner of her nail across her top lip, wiped the crumb of lipstick onto the tissue, then widened her eyes to check the liner. 'Tonight is the final test.'

'You'll wow them, you always do.'

She met my eyes in the mirror. '*I* don't have to.'

I swallowed the nerves but couldn't drown them completely. In three years, I'd been to a handful of Claude's work functions, but none this extravagant. None where I was the subject of their judgement. I'd faded into the background before, a side note to Claude; now I would be front and centre and I was expected to perform.

In the car – a black Lincoln sent by the bank – Claude sat tight against her door, hands clasped in her lap, staring out of the window at the passing night. She'd been distant for the past few months. I put it down to work, the stress of the promotion, the importance of the trade, but when I tried to hold her hand, give comfort, she moved away, tucked closer into the door and wouldn't look at me.

Stress. Nerves. Nothing more.

I looked at my wife, my Claude, at the clench in her jaw, the veins pulsing at her neck, the worry coiled in every inch of her.

Her fingers played over each other, scratching her skin, cracking her knuckles. She steadied her breathing as we approached the party. As the car pulled into the queue for drop-off, she turned to me, her tense expression broke into a beaming smile and she slid across the seat.

She pressed against my side. I felt the curve of her beneath the thin fabric, the sudden closeness, separated by two layers of silk. She kissed me deeply, her hand found my thigh, then crept beneath my dress. Then higher. Until.

Until . . .

A burst of red heat and I gasped. She pulled back and smiled that sleek, jaguar smile.

'Ready?' she murmured.

I shuddered out a breath, and, after taking a moment to compose myself, nodded.

We entered the party arm in arm. Up the stone steps of the hotel, through the plush, gilded lobby, into the elevators with a clutch of other guests. I barely noticed any of it. The grand foyer, the scrolling and detail in the elevator. My eyes were firmly locked on Claude, my senses still in the car.

Claude's company had booked out the roof and top two floors of one of Manhattan's oldest hotels. Terrace for the party, rooms for the staff, including a suite for Claude and me. Technically, it was to celebrate the company's fiftieth birthday, but in Claude's eyes, it was all for her. For Beltran. For seven hundred million. *I paid for this party*, she said, and I couldn't argue.

I'd never been to an event like this. I was used to the occasional after-work drinks in a slick bar with Claude's colleagues; before Claude, my work functions were pitchers and wings at the cheapest place we could find. This was another level. This was a soirée in the truest sense. A sea of dinner suits and cummerbunds and the joker in a purple bow tie, the women in red-carpet-worthy gowns and so much jewellery they sparkled under the lights. Crisp white-uniformed staff pivoted between guests with silver trays of champagne or canapés or buckets of fresh oysters. A stage occupied by a string quartet, a piano behind waiting for the next performer, fairy lights strung here and there, an ice sculpture and an endless supply of food and drink. It was a movie scene. Dazzling, jaw-dropping expense, luxury and excess, and it swept me up.

Claude had planned me carefully; I blended in enough to look like I belonged but not enough to fade into the background. I was the jewel on her arm, but I had to be the right kind of jewel. I was grateful now I'd seen the company she kept. High society. Stupid money. Hamptons houses and private jets. I was the girl from the Tater Tot family, from the cheap end of the neighbourhood. If my mother could see me now, breathing the same rarefied air as these people, she might finally be proud of me. My father would be horrified.

I needed a drink.

As if a mind-reader, a waiter appeared with a tray of champagne. I asked if he had Macallan, because it was the most expensive whisky I could think of, and hell, why not? Two minutes later, he handed me a heavy tumbler of golden liquid over fat chunks of ice. Claude sipped her champagne, delicate fingers grasping the stalk of the glass.

'Take it easy,' she said, keeping a smile I knew she didn't feel.

'Dutch courage.'

A tight sigh. But she put the smile back, took my hand and led me through the growing masses of the city's elite. Part of me wished I were here with Ellis. He'd have a cutting take on every fat cat here and I'd be in stitches all night.

Claude's two bosses stood on a dais on the far side of the terrace, champagne flutes in hand, talking to a group of Japanese men. Claude kept her eyes on them and redirected us to the centre of the terrace.

'Ms Marceau,' came a woman's voice from the crowd.

Claude turned, saw the source, whispered to me, '*Merde.*'

A man and a woman appeared beside us. He in a standard dinner suit, probably a rental, with a glow on his cheeks suggesting the glass in his hand was not his first, nor his second. She wore a dark purple two-piece dress, which showed a slice of her midriff and I wasn't sure was completely appropriate for this shindig. The way she looked at Claude, a mix of fear and worship, put me on edge.

'Iris,' Claude said with a laugh in her voice I barely recognised, 'this is Nazia and Daniel. They work in my department.'

'Pleased to meet you,' I said, like I'd been coached, and extended my hand. They shook it in turn. I'd heard about these two. The letch and the leech, Claude called them. Daniel was a trust-fund kid with a senior VP for a father, and Nazia a brilliant analyst with designs on Claude's job.

'Can't believe we're finally meeting the power behind the throne, eh?' said Daniel, draining his champagne and grabbing another glass from a passing tray.

I fixed a wide smile on my face. 'Oh, I wouldn't say that.'

Daniel eyed me shoes to hair, lingering at my waist and chest, and made no move to hide it. Claude saw, and I could tell by the look in her eye she found it amusing.

'What do you do, Iris? Are you with a fund in the city?' Nazia asked, leaning in so she wouldn't have to shout.

'I'm deputy head of programming at the Hayden Planetarium.'

Eyebrows up, surprise in their eyes, the usual response and I loved it. Suck on that, rich kids, I've got depth.

'That sounds lovely,' Nazia cooed. 'It must be so interesting and diverse. I went there once as a kid, all those stars and, you know, things. So fascinating.'

'Huh,' barked Daniel, plucking another glass from a nearby waiter. 'What's that net you?'

'Excuse me?'

'Take-home? Can't be in the six figs. You lucked out marrying the Queen here.' He laughed as Claude's expression soured.

'How much do you net, Daniel?' I asked, the Macallan working through me, lighting me up.

'Four hundred thou last year, plus another six in bonuses. Cool mil, you know.'

Nazia rolled her eyes.

'All that money,' I said, and he edged closer. 'And yet you have trouble doing up your fly.'

Nazia burst out laughing and Daniel fumbled at his crotch as Claude and I glided away.

When we were out of sight and earshot, Claude tightened her grip on my hand and whispered to me, still smiling, always smiling, 'Don't do that again.'

I kept my voice low, nodded and smiled to someone as we passed by. 'He's disgusting.'

'Yes,' she said, 'but his father and Lloyd play golf on weekends.'

Boys' club. Fucking boys' clubs. Sometimes I wondered why Claude put up with that kind of crap.

'Sorry,' I said.

She sighed again, sipping her drink. I pulled her to a stop. Made her look at me.

'Claude. I'm sorry.'

'Fine, fine.'

I slid my hands around her waist, put on my best smile. 'Don't tell me you've never wanted to say something to him.'

Her expression softened. 'I have.' Then softened further. 'He's an asshole.'

We laughed. She kissed my cheek and squeezed my hand. The tension in her shoulders fell away for a moment, but quickly returned when a tall man in a suit brushed past and didn't apologise or acknowledge her. The sickly smell of overly sweet cologne trailed behind him.

'Who is that?' I asked, so startling was her reaction to him.

'My competition,' she sneered. 'Sophia wants him for partner instead of me.'

'Shall I throw him off the roof? I could, you know.'

My levity fell like a tear on lava. Claude rounded on me.

'You think this is funny?' I shook my head, because Jesus, that look could stop traffic. 'I need you to be an adult, for just one evening.'

'I'll be good,' I said. 'I promise.'

Her iron gaze melted. She closed her eyes for a moment, and when she opened them, she was Claude again. She kissed me and said, 'I'm sorry. I spoke too harshly.'

I smiled and gave a dismissive head shake that said, don't worry about it, and she didn't.

The evening went along smoothly, but I couldn't relax. Despite Claude's smiles and kisses, she was a knot of tension underneath. We went from person to person, cluster to cluster. I kept quiet, kept nodding along and saying the right things and making sure Claude looked good and I looked like the adoring spouse I was. When she wasn't watching, I got another drink. And another. It was the only way I could get the viciousness of her words out of my head. Be an adult. Don't embarrass me. Well, you know what adults do, Claude? They drink.

Finally, when Claude deemed it time, she made her move on the dais, where the two head honchos had been receiving guests like royalty all evening. I was in bad shape but hiding it rather well. Lloyd spotted her and waved, but as he was about to help her up the steps, the Competition swooped. He grabbed Lloyd's outstretched hand for his own. A smile flickered over Sophia's haughty face. Lloyd, not wanting to be rude, went with it, throwing a consolatory look over his shoulder to Claude. She demurred and went to usher me away in a smooth, practised movement.

But I wasn't having any of it. My drunk self was affronted more than I ever had been in my life. That besuited, coiffed, overprivileged MAN. I didn't even know his name, but I hated him. Fiery, protective, you-don't-fuck-with-my-wife hate. Who was this guy? What deals had he done? Not Beltran, that's for sure. Look at him, talking to Lloyd like they were old buddies from the club, eyeing Sophia like they were old buddies from the bedroom.

Fuck that. Fuck him.

I surged forward, Macallan-filled blood burning in my cheeks. 'Excuse me!'

'Iris . . .' Claude tried, hand on arm, but it was too late, the leash was off.

'No, babe. It's okay. Excuse me, sir, sir.' Up the steps, I tapped him on the back.

He turned.

'Hi, yes, hello,' I said, beaming smile against his confusion.

He was exactly as you'd expect. Slick dark hair, handsome, cheeks like he'd never grown facial hair in his life. He looked about twenty-two.

'Do we know each other?' he said in a crisp, alcohol-free voice.

Claude hissed behind me, '*Iris.*'

'Hi, no, we don't. But you just snuck in there, knocked us out of the way just now. Sure you didn't mean it, but, uh, yeah, mind if we just cut in?'

Competition, startled, looked from me to Claude to Lloyd and Sophia, both of whom seemed just as surprised.

'Uh . . .' He stammered, laughed, waited for me to give, but I wasn't going to. No, sir. Not to some jumped-up baby-faced Ivy Leaguer.

Claude stepped up beside me. 'Iris, no need to interrupt. We'll see you later.'

She grabbed me a little too tight around the arm and pulled, but I held firm. Just for a second. And it was enough.

Lloyd saved me with his big, rich voice. 'So this must be the Iris I've heard so much about. A firecracker and no mistake.' He stepped past Baby Face, stretched out his hand to me. 'Delighted to meet you finally. Claude speaks so highly of her wife.'

The Competition took the hint and fucked off, and I stood taller. Claude joined me, annoyed. I felt it in the air around her, tense and hard like ice, but she would thank me in the end, I knew it.

'Charmed,' I purred.

Sophia smiled over her glass. 'You must be very proud of Claude. She's rather a star at the firm at the moment.'

'I am. Very proud.' My victory had gone to my head. 'I work at the Planetarium, so I know a star when I see one.'

In my head, it sounded funnier, and they, to their credit, gave a polite titter.

'You're lucky to have her,' I said, and slid my hand around her waist, pulling her to me. 'And so am I.'

'Naturally!' Lloyd boomed. A greying man, fifty or so, and despite the occasional glance to the chests of all the women present, he seemed kind. I couldn't be a hypocrite, I'd stared at women. Women are beautiful, and sometimes your eyes just stray and ... well, I'm only human, leave me alone. But I was more subtle about it than Lascivious Lloyd, even with a few drinks in me.

'What a delight you are, Iris. You say you're at the Planetarium? I golf with Hawthorne, you know him?' I didn't, but I'd seen his name on a building. 'He's a card. He said his granddaughter demands he take her to see the Story of the Universe at the Hayden every month!'

I felt a buzz of pride in my chest. 'That's my favourite too.' Because it was the first I'd programmed myself, all mine. It replaced a worn-out, dense history of the cosmos that had been running since the early nineties. The Story of the Universe was a simple tale of Big Bang to Now for kids, both entertaining and challenging enough to get them interested in learning more. A delicate balance, but if I do say so myself, I'd nailed it. Hook 'em early, Neil said, then we get the parents' ticket sales, then theirs, and then they bring their own kids, and we keep the lights on for another generation. We're a generational business, Iris, so think like that. Think big.

Lloyd raised his glass to me. 'Old Haw said he's sunk more in tickets to that show than he's given to the building it's in.'

'That's the plan,' I said, and waved over a waiter, taking the champagne because now I was drunk enough to like it.

Claude leant in. 'Haven't you had enough?'

But I shushed her and drank deep. I felt her resentment beside me, the colossal argument we'd have later, but I didn't care. Right then, I couldn't have given a whole shit if she was mad, because I was having fun. And this big-shot banker was impressed with my work. Nobody had ever been impressed with my work before, not even Claude, and that made me drunker than any whisky ever could.

'Tell me, Iris,' Sophia began, a snake where Lloyd was a bear. 'How did you and Claude meet? Was it at one of your places?'

Claude turned shark then. Eyes narrowed. 'Our places?'

'Oh, you know, gay places. Bars. Or was it over the internet? You know my nephew met his boyfriend that way. Do you know him? Emmett?'

Claude laughed off the whiff of prejudice. 'Actually, Iris ran into me on the street. Knocked me down. She asked me for a drink to apologise. Then we didn't see each other for many months.'

'I was seeing someone,' I added. 'But I couldn't get Claude out of my mind.'

'I was the same, but at that time I was concentrating on my career. The Korean deal, you remember?' she said, and Lloyd gave a small nod. She knew how to give enough to seem open but not vulnerable. 'But eventually, when I wrapped up the deal, I realised I was still thinking about this woman. I called her. The last four years have been wonderful.'

'How ... lovely.' I heard Sophia's bitter tone. She didn't know where to place the romance in a tale of two women: the pursuer, the pursued, the great declarations and proposals, who knelt, who got the ring. It wasn't in her experience. And that's why Claude wasn't already a partner. I imagined Sophia saying to Lloyd, *I just don't get Marceau, she's good but is she really Tillman and Gaines partner material?*

'It *was* lovely,' I said. 'It is. We were married last year.'

Sophia let out a high-pitched laugh. '*Married.* How wonderful you people can do that now.'

'You people?' I shot back.

'I wonder, is it quite the same as a normal marriage?'

Claude's jaw clenched. 'Identical.'

'Except maybe we don't take our vows for granted like you people do.' I smiled. Claude's nails dug into my hand.

Sophia's eyes widened. 'Ex*cuse* me?'

'I just mean when you have to fight for something extra hard, you appreciate it all the more,' I said. 'Like the right to marry. Or, I don't know, a promotion. Things we deserve but have been denied for so long because of who we love. Thank the good Lord the world is seeing sense and discrimination like that is now *illegal*. Am I right?'

I grinned, drove it home to an uncomfortable Sophia and an awkward Lloyd. Silence for several seconds while Sophia tried to lower her eyebrows and Lloyd coughed into his tumbler.

'Well,' Claude said brightly. 'If you'll excuse us. Sophia, Lloyd, enjoy your evening.'

She pulled me away before I could ask if they were Republicans.

I had made a mistake. I didn't really realise it at the time, but Claude did. She barely spoke directly to me for the rest of the night. She kept a smile plastered to her face, a rictus of disappointment, and she only addressed me to introduce me to another colleague, another important person I had to make nice with.

The party grew louder, the music turned from plinking strings to a full band. Drums and guitars and the sweet voice of a woman I vaguely recognised who'd had a hit album a few years ago.

I drank their champagne and their whisky and their wine. I ate their tiny bites of perfection – their caviar popped on my tongue, their chocolate melted on my fingers – and I danced to the beat of their expensive music. Claude worked the guests, did her thing, while I did mine. These people were not my people and Claude was half in their world, half in mine. Never had I seen it more starkly than that night. Why did she love me? How could she want me when she also wanted them?

I danced away the confusion until she was beside me, guiding me off the floor to the edge of the terrace, to the elevators and down two floors to our suite. Three rooms. Fresh flowers. A fruit basket. A golden key card. A vast bed of puffy white sheets. And quiet. So quiet. Except for the ringing and the buzzing and the swirling, moving, throbbing all around me. Then I was on the bed and I was laughing and Claude wasn't. She pulled off my shoes and the room went black and I don't remember much else except for her words in the dark.

How could you?

I didn't want to wake up, because I knew what was waiting. Knew it in my sleep. I had royally fucked up, though in my still-drunk state, I wasn't sure how. I sensed morning, woke up ears first and kept my eyes closed, alone in the giant bed. I heard Claude in the bathroom, shower blasting, humming softly. If I keep my eyes closed, I thought, and stay asleep, she will forget about last night and everything will be fine. I won't be in trouble.

In trouble, huh. Like I was a child. I sighed into the pillow. That's what it's become. Four years together and I was worried she would tell me off.

But she didn't say a word.

We ate breakfast in silence.

We dressed, packed. Nothing.

I tried. I said I was sorry. I said, I know I drank too much, I was nervous. I really am sorry.

Nothing. She didn't even acknowledge me.

We left the hotel, her smiling and breezy, laughing with a few colleagues in the lobby, holding my hand as if nothing was wrong. All the while, I was a mess of anxiety and guilt.

She didn't speak to me during the cab ride home.

Nor in the elevator up to our apartment, or the walk down the hallway.

As soon as our front door closed, as soon as the outside was shut away and we were alone, with no chance of anyone overhearing, she turned to me.

She met my eyes. She curled her lip.

And she slapped me.

A single crashing blow across my cheek.

My ears popped. I stumbled against the couch and slid to the floor. My hand clutched my cheek. I couldn't understand what she'd just done.

She stood over me, trembling. Hands in tight fists. Eyes on fire. Glaring down at me while I stared up at her in shock, in fear, in utter, heartbreaking disbelief.

'You embarrassed me,' she said through clenched teeth.

'I'm sorry.' My voice was small. She didn't hear.

She pointed a dagger-like finger. 'Don't ever do that to me again.'

She held firm, looked me right in the eye, waiting. I nodded. Small, then frantic. Yes. I won't do it again. I promise. I promise.

In a moment, she transformed back to my Claude as if she'd flipped a switch. The aggressive hunch, the sneering curl in her lip, the fire in her eyes. All gone. All back to normal.

'Coffee?' she asked, floating into the kitchen while I sat paralysed on the floor, hand still at my cheek.

She looked back at me. 'Iris?'

I nodded. Not because I wanted coffee, but because I was too afraid not to.

She made it, handed me the cup, still on the floor, then took the overnight bag into the bedroom to unpack. I could barely breathe.

'I'm going out,' she called to me. 'I have some things to do at the office. I'll be back for dinner. Maybe I'll pick up Thai on the way home. That sound good?'

I drew my knees up. Go. Just go.

'Iris?'

'Sounds great.' I closed my eyes, trying to hold in the tears.

She grabbed her bag, keys and jacket, then looked at me strangely and stopped. She knelt, reached her hand out to my face. I tried my best not to flinch, but I did. I couldn't stand her touching me. Not while my cheek burned red and my jaw ached from the force. She hadn't held back.

'Oh, *ma chérie*.' But she didn't apologise. She looked at me like I had tripped over and cracked my knee. Then she took my hand and kissed it and whirled away, out the door.

Finally, silence. Solitude.

I cried into my fists for what felt like hours.

When I had nothing left to cry, when the pain had dulled, when I had picked myself off the floor and fallen into the shower, I started making excuses. And once I'd started, I couldn't stop.

After

Funny, isn't it, how one moment can change the entire course of a person's life. In my life before, that moment had been Claude's office party. Her first slap changed everything.

But in my new life, everything changed when the raccoon disappeared.

I woke with the sun, thick with unhad sleep and a worry in my chest I couldn't shake.

I climbed down from my mezzanine, bones clicking, muscles straining, and stoked the fire. I topped it up with two skinny logs, the last two in the pile, and added 'collect wood' to my mental chore list. I filled the pan, blackened from overuse, and set it on the stovetop to boil.

The morning was quiet. Distant birdsong, muffled, as if they sang through glass.

The cabin was quiet too. The raccoon wasn't scratching at the door. Wasn't hissing or growling to be let in and fed. Wasn't pissing me off.

I opened the door. 'Monty?'

Not on the porch or steps. Not in his tree.

'Monty? Where are you, you little shit?'

The forest didn't answer. He didn't appear and the birds didn't sing any clearer.

I ate, wrote in my notebook. Maybe an hour passed and Monty didn't show.

I collected firewood, chopped as much as I could with the blunt axe. Noon came and went and still no raccoon.

I imagined awful scenarios where he'd been eaten by a bear or bitten by a snake or, worse, found another, better chump to feed him.

The next day, he still hadn't come back.

I walked far out into the forest and called his name. I dropped pieces of food to lure him back. Nothing worked. The loneliness crept up on me. I didn't notice it at first, stealing an inch here and there, until it had consumed me, covered me up and I couldn't move for the weight of it.

I began sleeping far past dawn, the birds having lost their power over me, and staying up into the early hours, staring at the ceiling, worrying over a raccoon.

Then the rain began.

Heavy and hard, like golf balls on the roof.

I stared out of the window, felt like I was trapped in one of those tiny plastic houses inside a snow globe. A world of water outside. I'd drown if I took a step beyond the porch.

The cabin sprang three leaks. The rain invaded, brought with it the smell of damp and a chill that wouldn't go no matter how hot I burned the stove.

Then I ran out of wood and couldn't, wouldn't, go outside to cut more. Not that it would burn if I did. I resorted to the single-burner camping stove to boil water once a day for a meal I barely ate. The gas wouldn't last long.

Monty still didn't come back.

For days, rain. Rain, rain, rain. The hammering on the roof and windows worked its way into my skull, a nail gun on rapid fire in my brain. No respite. No headphones to drown out the drone. No one to curl up and listen with, laugh with and tune it out with.

Just me and never-ending rain.

'This is quite the sorry state you've got yourself into,' Phantom Claude said on the third day. She sat on the back of the couch in a red cocktail dress, legs crossed, dagger-heels kicking the fabric. I walked past without looking, felt her eyes, felt that constant, infuriating, amused smile of hers, tried so hard to ignore it where once I'd loved it. I picked up one of the pots I'd positioned to catch a leak and emptied it out the door.

On my way back to the window, she grabbed my arm and I flinched, the pot clattered to the floor. Phantom turned physical.

Her grip softened, her fingers teased the inside of my wrist. 'Iris, please. Come home.'

'What home?'

'Our home. The one we made.'

I wouldn't look at her, though I wanted to. 'That wasn't real.'

She pulled me close and I let her. I felt her all around me, her breath, her heat; the smell of her overrode my senses.

'I miss you. That's real,' she murmured, lips on my cheek. 'I need you. That's real. I love you.'

'Is that real too?'

She just smiled. I shook my head and pulled away. She was gone and I was alone with the rain. I opened the second bottle of rum.

That evening, I burned a book for heat.

In the night, the wind began to howl, the chimney rattled so fiercely I thought it would snap. I soaked my boots running outside to relieve myself and had no way to dry them or my feet.

In the morning, feet soft and pale and threatening trench foot, mind blown by lack of sleep, body racked by freezing cold, the smell of damp constant and engulfing, the gas canister ran out halfway through making oatmeal. I stared at the pan of cold mush, balanced just so on the tiny burner. I picked up both, wrenched open the cabin door and threw them into the rain.

I had to leave.

I was done. The sun had abandoned me. The raccoon had abandoned me. I was alone and I had no heat source and I was trapped by the weather. This whole grand plan had been a mistake, I wasn't too big to admit it. This new life? I wouldn't find it in the woods. I wasn't like my father.

I'd go to Ellis. I'd ask him if I could stay. I'd tell him not to talk to Claude, not to tell her where I was if she ever contacted him.

Why? he'd ask. What happened?

And I'd stall. I'd swallow back words I couldn't say out loud. Nothing, I'd end up saying, we just had a fight. I'd figure out a new job, probably grovel for my old one. I'd go back to the same old routine.

I'd go back to Claude. I knew I would. If I left the woods now, if I returned to the city, I'd go back to her eventually.

I slumped down on the couch, half-packed bag on the floor.

I could go somewhere else. Anywhere but here. Somewhere warm, where it didn't rain. I still had some money. I'd board a bus, any bus, and figure it out at the other end.

I packed what I could carry, what I might need, enough food to get me to Mennier, and zipped my coat to my chin, drew the hood tight to my face. I put as much as I could fit in the plastic bags from the supermarket and stuffed them into the duffel. As long as I kept some clothes dry, I'd survive.

I had to survive, to show Claude I could.

Within a minute of stepping outside, I was soaked to the skin. The coat I'd thought was waterproof was, in fact, not, and my boots, which *were* waterproof, still couldn't handle being totally submerged in the lake-like puddle that had appeared at the bottom of the steps.

The forest was waterlogged, leaves swimming, rivers of mud slaking down the tiniest incline, cutting canyons into the dirt. The birds and animals were silent, hunkering in their nests and nooks, waiting for the sun.

I put my head down and walked. I slipped, I sank, mud sucked and splashed, my legs spattered with wet leaves and pine needles. I fought through it. I stole breaths between raindrops, stopped to rest against trees.

I flitted between regret and resolve. I wanted the comfort of the cabin, the triumphant feeling of living on my own, of succeeding, of proving Claude, my mother, my sister all wrong. And then my stomach would flip and my lungs would strain and my brain would misfire from sleep deprivation but I would think of cheeseburgers and cold beer and strong, hot coffee and I'd walk faster.

It was during one of these delirious bouts of food fantasy, only an hour or so out from the cabin, when I lost my footing on a ridge.

I slid on my back. Rocks scraped against my spine. I dropped the duffel and heard it tumble below me. Sounds of panic and pain I didn't recognise escaped my throat; not screams, not shouts, not 'Help!' but primal animal noises I couldn't bite back. I spun and rolled and cracked my elbow, my side, my thigh, my head. I tasted blood. My ears rang and pulsed in and out in horrible concert. My vision flashed grey and white and brown and black and I didn't know sky from soil, rain from blood. I thought I'd fall forever, off a cliff, into a ravine, snap my back on a boulder.

I tried to grab the slope. Fingers dug into mud and I brought fistfuls down with me. I had no energy to fight, to stop myself. I was falling, spinning, end of Iris, end of Jane.

Then I stopped.

Rain beat down on my back, finding every injury, every bruise and scrape. Water filled my mouth, muddy, dirty, taste of rot, on my tongue, swirling around my teeth, inching up my nose.

I breathed and it was in my lungs and I coughed and it wouldn't go away and I tried to breathe again and it was inside me again and I might die, I might die, but I had to live, I had to move and breathe and *live*.

I reared up out of the water, coughed my lungs clear, despite every inch of me, every tiny piece, feeling broken and stiff. I rolled my jaw and pain shot up the left side of my face and my hands went there and came back red. My head was too big, brain bulging and pressing my eyes out of their sockets. I rolled over and my back screamed, hot and wet on the inside. I reached, felt the rip in my coat, the ragged skin underneath.

I lay for a while telling myself to breathe, gently feeling my way around my body for broken bones. My bag lay half submerged in the pool that almost killed me. But I wasn't dead, that was the important thing, and nothing seemed to be broken, though my right ankle swelled against my boot, wouldn't roll or flex. A sprain? A spiral fracture held together with shoelaces? The bone sheared and spearing my sock, quietly soaking the cotton with my blood? I couldn't bring myself to check.

I looked up at the slope, maybe thirty feet of almost-cliff, studded with sharp rocks and gnarls of tree root. To my left, it curved around in the wrong direction, cutting off my path to town, taking me God knows where. To my right, back towards the cabin, it seemed to keep a steady line.

I hauled myself to the closest tree, used it as a support to stand. I tentatively put weight on my ankle. For half a second I thought, this is going to be okay, it doesn't even hurt that much. Then the pain came as an explosion. I felt a crunchy sort of movement. I imagined the splintered edges of my bones grinding against each other and nearly threw up.

I couldn't walk four hours to the road.

I would have to go back.

The tears came then. From pain, yes, but from failure too. Claude tried to tell me for years to stop trying so hard, accept my failings, but stubborn old me wouldn't. Stubborn old me kept striving, and now here I was in the middle of the woods, with a possibly broken ankle, a scrape on my back I was glad I couldn't see, a soaked bag, soaked clothes, soaked hair and no way to get dry.

And it was still fucking raining.

'What do you want from me?' I shouted, but the forest didn't answer. It wanted blood and sweat and time, and I'd given it everything. But still it wouldn't let me go.

I couldn't stay here. The puddle at my feet was fast becoming a lake, and I would get pneumonia or leeches or drown in my sleep.

I pulled the duffel from the mud, slung it across my back. I spotted a long, stout stick nearby and hobbled over to grab it. The stick sank into the ground and the rain kept falling.

The wind picked up, slicing the rain into my face and neck, putting a chill through me I thought would never leave.

It took me two hours, maybe more, to get back to the cabin. Each step brought pain and pain and more pain, the straps of the duffel bag felt like sandpaper against a fresh wound. Blood mixed with rain and ran in rivers down every inch of me. My ankle throbbed. My toes were numb. My head felt like a live grenade.

I was afraid.

I'd only been this afraid once before. When I thought I was going to die. When I hoped, for a fleeting moment, that I would.

Pain I can take. But fear is unbearable.

I stumbled into the cabin. Just as I'd left it. Damp smell overwhelming. Almost no drier than outside. I slammed the door, muffled the rain. One of the pots I'd used to catch a leak was overflowing.

The pain had turned from sharp to dull. I edged the duffel off my back and dumped it, held onto the stick as I peeled off my jacket.

The jacket had a jagged tear in the centre, fibres ripped and concertinaed by a rock. The sight of the damage, of what that meant for the skin of my back, brought tears to my eyes, made my lungs constrict.

'Fuck,' I breathed. Speaking helped. Made me realise I was still alive and I could still swear, and FUCK, swearing felt good.

'Jesus Christ. Jesus fuck. What have I done . . . Oh God.' Panic welled alongside pain and my breath got shorter, stiffer.

'No.' I closed my eyes and pulled in air, slowly, steadily. 'Shake it off.'

I hobbled to the stove. Half knelt with my bad ankle stretched out behind me. I grabbed a nearby book, ripped out the pages – sorry, travel guide – and restarted the fire. Fed it anything I could. Stayed there until it was blazing. I lit candles. Light and heat inched back to the cabin, but it wouldn't last long.

I dragged myself to the couch, stared down at my foot. It looked so normal, bundled up in a sturdy boot.

'Come on. It might not be that bad. Doesn't hurt so much any more.'

Yeah, Jane, because all your nerves have died and your foot will come off with your boot.

I took a deep breath and tugged my pant leg up to my shin.

My sock dug into my leg more than usual. I swallowed and reached for my laces.

As soon as I loosened them, I felt a rushing sensation in my foot. Like the tight boot had acted as a dam and suddenly the dam had broken.

Dizziness hit me. Nausea hit me.

I pushed through it. Had a job to do. I needed to know right now if I'd broken my ankle.

I tossed my boot to one side and gently pulled off the sock, and . . . well, shit.

My ankle wasn't an ankle anymore. It was a balloon. A balloon that some clown was still inflating. It grew and swelled as I watched. Dark red bruises surfaced around what used to be my bone. A purple line formed along the bottom edge of my foot. But there was no blood. No bone piercing the skin. I felt around, found my bones, found their edges, pressed on through the pain. Nothing seemed broken. That was something, at least.

'Fuck.' I sat back against the couch and immediately shot forward, wincing. I closed my eyes.

The deep terror, the I Might Die Here, returned with a vengeance.

I felt it again, the overwhelming primal fear. Pain clawed at every inch of my body. I flexed my spine and felt my skin tear afresh. I curled up on the couch and let sleep, let death, come for me. As soon as I closed my eyes, I was back in that apartment, the perfect decor, the perfect view, the perfect wife. All lies. A broken ankle hiding inside a boot. I felt Claude's hand on my face, stroking and cooing and speaking French words I didn't understand. I never understood.

I concentrated on the touch. The pressure of her fingers, soft at first, barely a feather brushing my skin, then harder, turning the skin white. Then the nails came out.

I woke hours later, awkward on the couch, leg hanging off, ankle a throbbing knot of torn ligament and bruise, my back a tight mess of scrapes and dried blood. More scars. More pain. When would it end?

The rain kept falling. The fire died. I had no more fuel. But at least I had food. Enough to last me until my ankle healed enough to hike out, I thought.

I limped to the kitchen and my stomach dropped.

Water. Dripping from the edge of the shelf that held the paper bags of oats and rice, down onto the shelf of cardboard items – coffee, biscuits – and collecting in a weathered depression in the countertop where I kept the packs of nuts and dried fruit. The open packs.

'No . . .' I breathed the word over and over.

The packets mushroomed with the moisture. I pushed my finger into the bag of rice. Soft, spongy, the paper gave way and my nail dug into mush. The oats were the same. The flour a solid block. On the shelf below, I hadn't properly sealed the top of the coffee can. The instant granules were fused into one black lump. The biscuit box and its contents disintegrated under the weight of my hand. The dried fruit had swollen back to something like its original shape. The peanuts were covered in a slimy mix of dust and salt.

Panic trembled my hands. That feeling of digging through your bag after a drunken night and finding your phone gone. *It must be here, I just looked away for a second.* I dug through my supplies and found bag after box after packet destroyed.

I took stock, quickly, before the gravity of my situation over-whelmed me.

Still intact – disgusting space food, but with no way to cook it. A bar of chocolate. A bottle and a half of rum.

I opened the half-empty bottle and drank until I ran out of breath. Then the gravity of my situation hit me and I drank again. As quickly as I'd taken the liquid, it came back up and out and all over the sodden countertop.

I laughed as bile ran down my chin. I laughed as I looked down at what was left of my six weeks of supplies. I laughed until I wasn't laughing any more but crying and balling my fists and trying, trying to keep breathing. But what was I breathing for?

I couldn't hike out. I couldn't get help. No heat, no food, no hope.

'What would your father do?' came her voice. Soft as a snake's hiss. Just as deadly.

'You know what he would do,' I replied, but I didn't know if I'd spoken the words out loud. My head swam. My tongue was a dead fish in my mouth. The cabin walls warped around me and only she was clear. Claude. Standing beside me, that look in her eyes. Pity. Disgust. Look at you, Iris, she'd say. You have a problem.

'Yes,' she said. 'And you know the solution.'

'I do?' Was that a question?

'Do you have rope?'

No.

'You can still jump, like he did. Step off the edge and fall into darkness.'

'I can barely walk.'

She smiled. 'You can make it.'

I didn't ask where. I knew where she meant and I could get there. It would take me a while. But I had time. I had all the time in the world.

My ripped coat was useless. I put on my last dry T-shirt. Didn't bother with a sock or a boot, neither would go over my ankle anyway. I didn't take a bag. Didn't take a water bottle. Didn't take what was left of my food.

Only my makeshift crutch and the half-bottle of rum.

Claude stayed in the cabin, waved from the doorway. I was leaving her there. Stepping out into the world one last time. It felt right. The only path I had would take me to the overhang, then it would be one more step, finally, to peace and silence and freedom from Claude. All other roads were closed to me and I'd always known, somewhere deep inside, that this was where I'd end up. I was my father's daughter, after all.

Every step I took, the pain lessened. The back of my T-shirt turned red with my blood, but it didn't matter. When they found me, they'd say the cuts on my back were from the fall. From the rocks below the overhang. They wouldn't know what led me here.

Maybe they'd think I was hiking – bootless, bagless – and took a wrong turn, an accident but it wouldn't be an accident. It's never an accident. If only I had a rope, then there would be no doubt.

Maybe they'd identify me, find Claude and she would fill in the blanks. Lies. Of course. The blank page in the notebook would remain blank. The words trapped inside me forever. Don't worry, Claude, I'll take it to my grave. I laughed.

I for Iris. But I'm not Iris. Not anymore. I am no one. I am not even Jane. I have failed in all things and now I'm left hobbling through the woods towards the end of the world.

But I wasn't alone.

The woman in red walked alongside me, some twenty feet away to my left. She matched my pace. She was dressed for the weather. A proper coat. The hood obscured her face and I don't think she knew I was there. Her rucksack was neatly, smartly packed with a rain cover and bulges that said tent and bedroll. Another phantom. What I could have been if I'd planned my escape better.

When I stopped, she stopped. She took a drink. I opened my mouth to catch the rain. She didn't notice me, but I wouldn't notice me either. When I started walking again, she started too. Mirror movements. Hand to my head to wipe water away. Hand to hers to tuck wet hair under her hood. I watched her out the corner of my eye as I made my slow, painful way through the forest. Then lost her in the rain. A phantom. Never there. Just like me.

I wanted it to be over now. I was so tired of being afraid. So tired of hurting. So tired of failing. This would be the one thing even I, Iris, could not fail at.

A fallen tree blocked my path. A week ago I'd have vaulted it and pretended to be a gymnast who had nailed the landing. Now, it was Everest and I was hiking on broken legs.

I hopped close. The bark was slick. The trunk thick and tall as my waist. I shimmied up it, onto it, thought I'd swing my legs over, slide down the other side.

I tried to swing my legs, but my foot hit something hard. I yelped at the jarring in my ankle, then lost my grip and fell, sliding at a strange angle off the tree. The bark ripped my back afresh.

I screamed. I swore. I spat rain. I struggled up, leant against the tree, pain echoing endless through my body, hunger racking my insides, my brain, my hands shaking in and out of fists, grazes and beads of blood swiped across my palms, throbbing heat radiating from my back, a lead weight where my ankle should be.

I was almost ready to give myself up, let the forest have me, let a hiker or jogger or dog walker – it's always a dog walker – find my body. I would watch, floating above it all, as a man in a beige suit with a flip pad notified Claude, then my mother. But it would be harder to explain away if they found me by a tree rather than at the base of a cliff. My mother could say I fell and live with losing a daughter to an accident. Claude could say I jumped and she knew why.

I pressed on. My ankle screamed, wanted to snap, but it wouldn't matter. I wouldn't need it for much longer.

The rain came down all the harder. I couldn't see the woman in red any more.

Cold seeped into my bones, my marrow, turned me to ice on the inside. Maybe I'd smash to pieces at the bottom of the cliff like one of those liquid nitrogen flowers – perfect on the outside then crumbling to dust with a tap.

I limped along, every step torture on my beaten body yet every step lightening me. I only had so many left. A thousand. Nine-nine-nine. Eight-twenty-three. And down and down.

My good foot hit a rock. Gravity upended. Stomach went up, head went down. I reached out to brace myself. Found a branch. The branch snapped. My head hit a root or a rock and for the briefest moment everything went black.

Then I was walking. I don't remember righting myself. I don't remember moving, deciding which way to go. Which way had I gone? I was still surrounded by trees but they became less and less familiar. Fog had drifted in between the spruces and removed any sense of distance or perspective.

I turned my head skyward. Let me see the stars, one more time. One last time. But rain hit my face, ran down my neck, my chest. The clouds didn't part or thin. They remained. A suffocating mass, burying me alive.

My head throbbed. Blood, diluted by the rain, poured in rivers down my face, staining the front of my shirt an uneven mixed-wash pink. The wind cut through me, lodged ice in my veins.

The woman was back. Flitting in and out of the fog, far away yet so close. I still couldn't see her face. I could call out to her, ask for her help, but I didn't want it. I wanted all this to be over. Keep walking, find the overhang, find peace.

The red jacket appeared ahead, beside, behind me, always too far off to see clearly through the blur of the rain.

I was dreaming. Hallucinating. My mind had snapped like the tendons in my ankle.

I limped a mostly straight line, or so I thought. I avoided trees, swerved boulders, tried to keep the woman in sight. We had been going the same direction before I fell; made sense we'd be going the same direction now.

Is she real, Jane? Is she even there? That looks like your jacket, doesn't it?

My heart slowed. The pain inside my body overtook me and I had to stop.

Was I going mad? (Yes.)

Anthony Perkins' ghost laughed inside my head. 'We're all mad!'

The woman was gone again. The forest quiet but for the gunfire rain. The fog had closed in, obscured the details. That woman could be lost too. Shouldn't I help her?

You can't even help yourself, Jane.

My mind flitted between death and duty. Be selfish, it said, because if not now of all times, when?

Keep walking.

My ankle had taken on a half-numb, half-aching quality that didn't exactly hurt but didn't exactly not hurt either. My toes had been numb for so long they might have fallen off. The ground had absorbed as much water as it could and mirrored me. Saturated. Overspilling.

I turned, tried to find a landmark, but the fog was thick and grey and erased my map. I hobbled around, didn't recognise anything. The trees were alien. The ground an unfamiliar swell and dip. I could have walked for hours in the wrong direction.

I was lost. Again. Always.

I sank down to the ground, and God, it felt good. The rain didn't matter. The wind whistling through the trees didn't touch me. The ground was soft and welcoming, the cold didn't feel so cold any more. I was lost and alone and oh so tired, and I'll just close my eyes for a moment, just rest a while here ... Like my father.

Somewhere else, another me sat on another couch with another father, watching the rover land on Mars. The lines around his eyes crinkled in a full, unrestrained smile. His hand held mine in a tight fist and he said, 'Wow, Rissy, wow!' over and over. Outside, the sun shone. Inside, he shone. A star of a man who, only in my dreams, had been allowed to grow old. I saw her face, that other Iris, hovering above me, calling my name.

Before

'Iris.' A whisper in my ear, rousing me from deep, delicious sleep. 'Rissy, wake up.'

Then his hands, freezing cold and heavy, on my shoulders. I opened my eyes.

My father, lit up with the soft orange from my nightlight, stood over me. His eyes full and glistening.

'Dad?'

'Quick, baby. Come see.'

I looked at my bedside clock: 4.08 a.m. 'Is something wrong? Is Mom okay?'

His excitement turned to agitation at mention of my mother. 'Yes, yes. She's fine. But get up, I have something to show you.'

I struggled up, wiped my gritty eyes and yawned. My room was a blur, my vision not quite awake yet. My father stood at my door, almost vibrating, his hands fidgeting at his sides, his expression cycling from wide smile to impatient scowl to fearful glance down the corridor.

I pulled on my dressing gown and tied the rope around my waist. Dad darted to my wardrobe and pulled out my heaviest winter coat. I put it on without question.

We padded through the silent house. Down the dark stairs. Through the empty living room. I was fifteen, but I'd never been in the house like this, with all the rooms dead and cold. It felt smaller, and the corners held deep, alien shadows. I huddled close to my father, breathed him in, and suddenly the sleeping house didn't seem so scary.

He led me out to the backyard. As soon as the door opened, the bitter February chill hit me and I pulled my big coat tight. He smiled down at me, his face dark but for moonlit highlights. In the middle of the lawn was one of the garden chairs and his telescope.

'Look,' he said, nodding to the eyepiece.

The sky was clear, the stars full, but no more so than normal. The dusty purple cloud of the Milky Way was close to the horizon, and directly above was endless, beautiful white-studded blackness.

I pressed my eye to the telescope. A circle of space, the glitter of stars.

'What am I looking at?' I whispered.

He knelt beside me, and that's when I noticed he wasn't wearing a coat. Just a T-shirt and an old pair of jeans with holes in the knees. But he didn't shiver. He didn't do anything but smile.

He checked the scope. 'Right there.'

I looked again, but again saw nothing of note. I pulled my coat tighter.

'See the cluster of five stars in the upper right?' he said.

I nodded without taking my eye away.

'Go south-west an inch.'

I mentally ran through the compass mnemonic Dad had taught me. Never. Ever. Stop. Wondering. Followed the directions, hit on a tiny star with the faintest blue tinge. I could only see the colour if I looked just to the side.

I couldn't hide my confusion, even in the dark.

'I found it, Rissy,' he said, breathy, voice trembling at the edges.

My teeth began to chatter. 'Found what?'

He pulled me away from the telescope and held my shoulders. His eyes were manic, his face set in a too-wide grin.

'The other earth.'

I tried to hide a sigh. 'Dad . . .'

'No, no, no. Look. Look at that little blue dot.'

He nodded to the telescope. Reluctantly, I looked again.

'There is another you right now looking through her telescope.

She's with her father and he's telling her of another little girl look-ing through a telescope. What would you say if you could talk to her?'

In the tiny circle of stars through the telescope, I see the blue dot grow and take shape. It balloons to the size of the moon and bigger. I see continents, oceans, clouds and cyclones. And closer still, to a seemingly empty area of land in North America. Closer, to a town, striped with roads and grids of houses. Then a back-yard, no bigger than my own. Then the black lens of a telescope and behind it, a young girl looks up, shocked at what she's just seen through her own telescope.

What would I say? At fifteen years old?

Beside the girl stood a man, staring at the same spot, without a coat on.

'What would you say to him?' I asked my dad, standing beside me, staring up at the blue dot.

My father looked down at me. In the telescope, the girl's father looked down at her.

'I'd say . . . where did it all go wrong? What choice did we make that led us here? Is there anything I can do to change it?'

'What would he say back?'

My father laughed quietly and shook his head. 'Oh Rissy, if only I knew.'

He'd talked this way before. So full of regret. So full of resent-ment. The last time, we'd been by a crater lake in Banff. He'd called me by my mother's name. He'd frightened me then too. Normal fathers didn't wake their children in the middle of the night to join in their delusion. Why couldn't I have a normal father? Why was he so unhappy all the time?

Ever since Banff, a question had danced about in the back of my mind. Every time he went into these dark patches, the ques-tion reared forward, but I never asked. There was never a good time. But now, in the dark, in a silent backyard, in a silent neigh-bourhood, I couldn't ignore it any longer.

'Do you wish you'd never met Mom?'

He blew air through his nose. Took a second too long to answer.

My heart sank; the cold infiltrated my bones, lodged there and wouldn't be moved.

'Course not,' he said finally but unconvincingly. 'Because then I wouldn't have you.'

He tried to smile, but I saw the truth, even in the silver moonlight. He saw my recognition too, and he fell into a strange, tense silence. I needed to break it.

'I'd ask . . .' I said, keeping my voice light, putting on a smile I didn't feel. 'I'd ask her where I put my birthday money from Grandpa. Because I know I put it somewhere safe, but I can't remember. It was a hundred dollars!'

My father laughed a little. 'Let's get you to bed.'

He put his arm around me and led me to the back door.

I stopped on the step. 'Dad.'

'Hmm?'

'I know you're not always happy, but I don't wish you were another you. If that other planet has another you on it, then he might have made different choices, in which case he wouldn't be my dad. *You're* my dad, and I love *you*.'

'Rissy . . .'

'And,' I said quickly, 'if you and Mom aren't happy, then me and Helen will understand. You don't have to stay.'

He pulled me into a hug, and I felt some warmth returning to my body. He kissed me hard on the top of my head, and I thought I heard and felt him crying.

'Go on now,' he said, releasing me and opening the door. 'Up to bed.'

After

I dreamed of stars colliding.

Supernovas exploding in the far-flung corners of space.

Stars dying and being reborn in nebulae.

I was nowhere.

I was untethered, watching helpless and awestruck as the universe rearranged itself around me, solidified into unknown shapes, new dark masses, new galaxies.

A new, different earth. And a different Iris staring up at those same stars.

I was sick. I was dying. I needed more help than this forest bolt-hole could give.

'Maybe that is why you let it go on for so long,' Claude said, and suddenly she was beside me, in the forest, in the cabin, floating in the black.

She cradled her right hand in her left, rubbed at dark purple bruises across her knuckles and fingers, wiped blood from her wedding ring.

'Maybe that's why you didn't see.'

I bolted upright. Splinters of pain shot through my ruined back, down into my ankle. Pain brought panic. I wasn't in the forest. I was on the couch, in the cabin. I was wrapped in my sleeping bag, my ankle bandaged and resting on Claude's duffel.

I didn't remember coming back. Didn't remember climbing the ladder to get my sleeping bag, tending to my ankle or . . . I lifted the sleeping bag . . . changing my T-shirt to one I didn't remember bringing with me. One I hadn't seen since my 'cosy' apartment days.

I struggled to my feet, but dizziness forced me back down onto the couch.

My daypack was propped up by the cabin door, but I was sure I'd left it up on the mezzanine. And my red jacket hung on a nail nearby. It looked different, cleaner, and from this angle, I couldn't see the rips in the back.

I sat up, twisting so I could see the window.

The rain had stopped.

The sun was shining. The birds returned. The forest was alive again.

I hopped to the door, ignoring the pain, and flung it open, smelt the warmth in the air. I limped outside and stood in a patch of sunlight.

My body woke up. My skin prickled with heat for the first time in a week. My vitamin D stores ticked back up into the black and the dark clouds that had been circling inside my head slowed their spin.

Using the cabin walls for support, I hopped around to the woodpile. Maybe some would be dry now and I could get a fire going. But as I rounded the corner, I froze.

A woman sat at the fire pit.

This time it wasn't Phantom Claude.

My stomach tightened as this new person, this new human who had invaded my solitude, sat by herself on a tree stump, jacketless, packless, drinking from a wide-necked bottle. I shrank against the cabin.

Was she a park ranger who would tell me I was squatting illegally and had to leave? A cop who'd followed my trail and wanted to take me back to Claude? I thought about hiding, but the way this woman sat, drank, each movement careful and slow, the way she looked from ground to sky, through the trees to some place I couldn't see, the way she seemed so peaceful, even at this distance, I knew she wasn't here to arrest me. She would have spotted me by now. She would have drawn a weapon or announced herself. Something about her felt familiar.

She stood up, dusted off her pants, twisted the cap back onto her water bottle and turned towards the cabin. She froze when she saw me.

And I saw her.

I did know her. And she knew me.

She looked right at me. No hood or hat. I could see her clearly. Her short blonde hair wild. Her eyes on mine.

The woman with the red jacket. The woman from the clearing. The woman from last night.

My mirror companion.

It couldn't be, but it was. Her face, her eyes, her build, her hair. I knew them all.

They were mine. Mine were hers.

She was *me*.

A different me. But unmistakably me.

I'd gone to the woods to find myself.

I found her. Literally.

Right there.

No. I didn't. This wasn't real.

I shook my head to clear it. I was sleep- and food-deprived. I was freezing cold and aching. I was limping and scraped up and ready to die. I was sick of rain and mud and that decay smell in the background. My hallucinations had levelled up and I was actually losing my mind. Things like this happened in movies, not real life. My eyes weren't trustworthy. After all, hadn't I seen Claude stride through the cabin more than once? But I'd known then that she wasn't real. And the wrong stars in the clearing? Explain that.

But this felt real. Your delusion has progressed, said my in-head shrink, so you can't tell the difference anymore.

She stared and I stared and neither of us moved.

I pressed my eyes shut. Counted to ten like I did when I wanted to rid myself of Claude. If this woman was still there when I opened my eyes, if the forest was as it had always been, I would pack up, limp out, board a bus and find help. The professional, hospital kind of help.

I wouldn't end up like my father.

One . . . two . . .

And if she is there? If she is real? My chest tightened at the thought.

Nine . . . ten . . .

I opened my eyes and the woman wearing my face opened hers at the same time.

'This is weird,' she said, and closed the gap between us.

I hobbled to the steps and sat.

She looked me up and down and wondered what she was seeing. She was dressed for hiking Everest. I was barely dressed at all – an old T-shirt, dirty jeans, unlaced boots. I was a hangover; she was a chipper girl scout. But we wore the same face. Same eyes. Same exhaustion behind them.

'Did you . . .?' I pointed to my ankle and the fat white bandage.

She nodded. 'I found you in the woods. In the rain in a T-shirt, with one boot. You know you could have died, right?'

That was the idea, I almost said.

I fought for the right words. 'It . . . Do . . . Is it just me? Do you see it too?'

'Our uncanny resemblance?'

I nodded.

'Yeah, I got nothing,' she said. 'Last night, in the dark, I didn't see it, but now . . .' She shook her head. 'It's wild.'

'What are you doing out here?'

'I was hiking up to Randall Peak. You know it?'

I'd never heard of it, but I nodded anyway. For some reason I didn't want this woman, whoever she really was, to think I was an idiot as well as a slob.

'I found you a few hundred yards past that clearing. You were muttering something about a cabin and the Mars rover.'

She smiled, and it was my smile but wasn't, and her voice was my voice but wasn't. The closeness of her story and mine unsettled me. Was she going to Randall Peak for the same reason I was going to the overhang?

'Sorry, this is strange,' I said, tried to lighten myself, pretend I was talking to a stranger or an old friend or a new friend or anyone but who I was actually talking to. 'I mean, did my parents have twins and not tell me?'

'I don't think we're twins.'

'What do you think we are?'

She shrugged. 'Genetic coincidence?'

'You really think that?'

She didn't answer for a few seconds. I knew that pause, that thought process. Knew that in three . . . two . . . one . . .

'No.'

'What's your name?' I asked.

'What's *your* name?' she said, the hint of defensiveness all too familiar.

We narrowed our eyes at the same time. Like looking in a mirror.

So. Fucking. Weird.

'You first.'

'No, you.'

Eyes narrowed further and we said it together. 'Iris.'

We both squinted at each other. Both took a deep breath.

'Birthday?'

We said the same date at the same time.

She put her hands on her hips and blew out her cheeks. 'Look, I don't know what this is or who you are, but it isn't funny.'

I raised an eyebrow. My rant. My tone. How dare she?

'Do you see me laughing?'

She sighed. 'So explain it then.'

'You explain it. I was delirious and unconscious. You found me. Why didn't you just leave me there?'

'Because you would have died!'

I looked away. 'Well I'm not dead, am I, so you can go.'

She shook her head. 'Wow. Okay. Fine. I'm going.'

'Fine.'

'Fine!'

She stormed past me into the cabin. I heard sounds of packing, gathering, the plastic rustle of her jacket.

In the trees past the fire pit, Claude watched. She held up her hand, waved, her fingers danced in the air.

Don't go. Don't leave me with her.

I almost said it. Almost grabbed the woman who was and wasn't me as she stormed out the cabin in her full hiking regalia. But I didn't. I remained silent because that's what I'd done every day for years and it's a hard habit to break.

'I'm going then,' she said.

'To Randall Peak. I heard.'

I watched the muscles of her jaw clench. 'What will you do?'

I shrugged. 'Enjoy the splendour of nature.'

She rolled her eyes. 'You don't have any food.'

'You're perceptive.'

I hated my tone. My petulance. The side of me Claude had tried to beat out.

'I'll come back,' she said, softening first. 'After my hike, I'll swing through and check on you. Then we can talk.'

'Okay.'

'I'll be a few days. Four. Five max.'

I nodded, hung my head, couldn't look at her. Would I still be here then? Now the weather had broken, I could take another run at the overhang. Surely this whole exchange had proved my madness. Proved it was time to go.

The idea fizzed inside me, burned away the anger.

She walked towards the treeline, where Claude no longer stood.

'I see it now,' she called back with half a smile. 'When people say he and I are alike. A woman at the mall last year, she said we were like mirrors, same eyes, same smile, despite his beard.'

I looked up at her. 'Who?'

'My father.'

Her father. My father. Last year?

But he died. Years ago.

Not for her.

He's alive.

But she's not real. He's not real.

But what if she is? He is?

What's going on?

Memories of him surfaced for a moment and were pulled back under. The oak, the rope, the empty tent. The stars, the lake, the telescope. Had she had all those moments with him? How many more did she get? How many 'I love yous' and bear hugs and fights and tears and laughs and evenings in front of the TV and days out in the woods and dinners with the family – the *whole* family – that I hadn't? How many had I missed because I'd been selfish? My mind swam, head ached. I wanted to throw up and cave in at once, because nothing made sense any more. Nothing felt real any more but him and her and the agony of it all.

I surged to my feet, ignored the pain. I almost called out to her, told her to stay, but when I looked for her in the trees, she was gone. As if she'd never been there.

Fuck.

My father was alive somewhere, and right then I didn't care if it was a hallucination, if my madness had kicked up a gear and I was on a spiral towards a straitjacket and padded cell. What did that matter anyway?

The sky clouded over and spots of rain hit my cheeks.

I had to last five days until she was back and we could talk. She could stay for a while, I could learn about him, discover all I'd missed or could have missed if she was real, which she wasn't, of course. But I'd need supplies. Which meant I had to go to Mennier. My ankle throbbed at the thought, but what was pain now? My father was alive.

I felt Claude's breath on my cheek, her voice in my ear. 'So how are you going to tell Iris you killed him?'

Before

'You haven't touched your drink,' Ellis said, nudging my elbow. 'What have you done with the real Iris?'

I tried to smile, but it wouldn't take. I turned the glass around in my hands, the red wine almost spilling. We were in that bar again. The steel-fronted pomposity, the place I'd first seen Claude.

'Trouble in the penthouse?'

I bristled, straightened and took a sip. 'No. No. Everything is fine.'

'Looks fine.' He put his hand on mine and tried to catch my eye, but all my attention was on the blood-red liquid in my glass. 'Iris. Come on. What's going on? Are you and Claude, like, fighting?'

Fighting. That word. Why that word? I felt the sting in my cheek all over again. It had been two months since the party, and while she acted like nothing had happened, I couldn't stop flinching when she touched me.

'No. She's just . . . It's complicated.'

Ellis raised his eyebrows, his signal for me to carry on.

I sighed. 'She didn't get this big promotion at work and it was kind of my fault. I feel like shit over it, but she hasn't forgiven me yet. She was so mad, she . . .'

I cut myself off. Couldn't say it out loud. She hit me. She hit me hard. I couldn't see Ellis for weeks after because I had to wait for the bruise and my shame to go down. I could lie to my boss, Neil, cover it with make-up, but Ellis would see through the foundation and my kitchen-cupboard-in-the-face, clumsy-old-Iris excuse in a second.

'She what?'

'We had this big fight,' I said. 'She's under a lot of stress. Her job, you know. I wasn't making things any easier.'

Ellis frowned and looked at me like I was a kitten with a broken paw, pity and confusion and what have you done to yourself?

'You and Claude have been shacked up for, what is it, four years?' I nodded.

Ellis whistled, then fell silent.

I watched my wine whirlpool in the glass. Then checked my watch: 8.30. Claude would be home. I hadn't told her I was going out. I checked my phone. Nothing. Would she be mad I hadn't left a note? Anxiety fizzed inside me.

'You're so different,' Ellis said quietly.

'Different?'

'Yeah, like, not in a bad way, just I don't know, want me to fetch your pipe and slippers?' He threw his hands up and laughed in his over-the-top Ellis way. 'Look. We've been friends forever and in all the times we've been out, I never once saw you check your watch. Until you met *her*. And what happened to your hair and the way you dress? Man, Iris. Come on. Where'd you go?'

I tugged at my shirt. One Claude had bought me. Grey and sedate but stylish and flattering. 'You will look beautiful in this,' she'd said, 'and so professional.' And my hair. Well. My hair was a compromise. I missed my Pris cut, missed the flash of it, but Claude had asked me to grow it out – 'You'll be taken more seriously, Iris, isn't that what you want?' – and then, well . . .

'I've grown up. I can't present myself like a teenager all the time. I need to be taken seriously.'

Her words. Her justifications. Parroted up my throat.

'Totally. I get it. It's not like I have any of that bullshit, and you know, fine, I'd cut my hair for the right girl, but, Iris, are you . . .' He sighed and leant close. 'Are you happy with her?'

'Of course I am.' I smiled. Can't be a lie if I'm smiling.

Ellis gave me the kitten look again.

'Ell, really. I'm fine. I'm happy. I love Claude and she loves me. Sure, we have our fights, but that's what marriage is.' My tone was harsher than I intended.

'It's not like I would know, huh?'

'I didn't mean it like that.'

'Whatever, you know. It's fine. I'm just worried about you. I guess I miss old Iris. She would be on her third glass by now, screaming for shots. She'd be downing pitchers, not sipping on a Chardonnay—'

'It's a Barolo.'

'Oh my God, do you hear yourself?'

'I'm still her.'

'Uh huh. With *that* shirt on?'

I laughed and he laughed, then we both fell into a morose silence, staring at our glasses.

'Do you ever wonder,' I said after a few minutes had passed, 'what your life would be like if you'd made difference choices?'

'Only every day. There is some alt-dimension Ellis who, when he was thirteen years old, actually got up the courage to ask Cindy Davenport to the spring formal, and since of course she said yes, he began to believe in himself, apply himself, got into MIT and is now living the dream as a tech millionaire with a harem of supermodels.'

I laughed. 'You have thought about this.'

'That girl is my forked path, for sure. Everything would be different if I'd been a little braver.'

'Think you'd be happier?'

He seemed to be weighing up the possibility, half a nod, half a head shake, then finally, 'Probably. Grass is always greener, right?'

'Sometimes I wonder what would have happened if I'd stayed with Bella. Where would we be now? Married? Kids?'

'Maybe,' he said, 'but you wouldn't be happier. Grass is still grass, no matter how green. We can't eat the stuff, so what's the point?'

I smiled and agreed out loud but not in my head. A life composed of different choices had to be better than what I was living. But thinking that way, analysing every decision I'd ever made, trying to map a new timeline, new potential branches and forks and what-ifs and maybes seemed like a quick slide into madness. I didn't have time to be mad.

When Ellis went to the bathroom, I checked my watch again, and when he came back, I told him I had to go.

He made a whip-crack sound as I grabbed my coat and told me to call him, any time, if I needed him.

Claude wasn't home and it was past nine, which meant she was either working late and would get home tense and snappish, or she was out unwinding with colleagues, in which case she would return rosy and pawing. Neither was appealing, so I went straight into the bathroom and locked the door.

I let down my hair, let the lank brown locks fall around my shoulders. I looked at my clothes. Claude's clothes. The ugly shirt. The corporate pants. The low black heels. I looked at my face. The make-up hers, subdued and sensible, not bad exactly, just not anything special.

I unbuttoned the shirt, untucked it, let it hang open. Then took it off, balled it and threw it on the floor. The bra was mine at least.

I took a clip from the drawer under the basin and twirled up my hair, clamped it on top of my head like a pineapple.

I rummaged in the cabinet for my make-up. Right at the back in a small forgotten pouch. Eyeliner and eyeshadow and thick black mascara. I went to town. Smoky eye and flick and reshape the brows and spike the hair with gel and hello Mad Max.

I stared at myself in the mirror and realised two things simultaneously. How much I'd changed in the four years of Claude. And how much I missed myself. Ellis was right. I was different.

But maybe that wasn't bad.

The longer I looked at myself, this version I used to be, the more I saw the cracks. The ones Claude had tried to fill in and paint over. It was gaudy. It was over the top. It was juvenile. That's what she'd said, and I heard her again, her words lodged deep in my chest, repeating, sending out another drip of reassurance with every beat.

Reassurance or poison?

I unclipped my hair and took a cotton swab to my face.

Plain Jane again.

★   ★   ★

I heard Claude's keys in the door at ten. She bustled in, dropped her jacket on the counter, her bag on top of it, and chucked her keys in the ceramic dish I'd bought for the purpose.

She saw me a second later, on the couch, reading.

'Good, you're here,' she said, and went to the cupboard for a wine glass. 'I need to talk to you.'

My stomach twisted into fat knots.

'Is everything okay?' Translation: did I do something?

'It will be,' she said, and came to the couch with two glasses and the bottle. She poured. I panicked, silently, inwardly. But then I remembered Ellis. Iris used to scream from the rooftops, drink until the sun came up, and run about town like she owned it. She didn't cower and shake when her wife – her *wife* – said she needed to talk.

So I straightened my back. I took the offered glass and I drank deep.

She held up her glass to me like she was saying cheers, and smiled, that deep, full smile that made my knees weak.

'I got you a job,' she said and clinked my glass.

Huh?

'I have a job. I have a job I love.'

'I realise that, but since I didn't get the promotion, we need to reassess.'

She meant since I lost her the promotion.

'What do you mean, reassess?'

She sighed, shuffled closer to me, and laid her arm along the back of the couch, her fingers just reaching my shoulder. 'This building isn't rent-controlled. They are raising the rent next year by a disgusting amount and I can't cover it alone anymore.'

A stone hit my stomach. 'We could move somewhere cheaper.'

She shook her head, gave a sad smile. 'I don't want to move. I love it here. The terrace. The views. This is our *home*, isn't it?'

I didn't want to admit that after four years, I still sometimes felt like a lodger in her apartment. But that wasn't her fault. She'd given me equal space in the closets, the dresser, the bathroom. We redecorated together.

'Maybe I can ask Neil for a raise.'

'It won't be enough.'

'It might,' I said, shuffled back, drew my knees up. 'If I explained the situation.'

'That you need to double your salary to maintain your Upper West Side lifestyle? Don't be ridiculous.'

'He might, I can ask. How much is the rent anyway?'

'It's not just the rent, it's the service charge, the maintenance costs for the building, the heritage fees. I'll take care of all of it, but I need your help. This new job, it pays very well. More than enough.'

'What is it?'

She shifted then, coughed a little. 'Lead procurement and billings administrator for Hoss.'

'Hoss?'

'Hoss Oil and Gas.'

'Let me guess, a client of yours?'

She narrowed her eyes just enough to tell me I was on dangerous ground. Then the tension fled her shoulders, her voice. She seemed to deflate.

'Please, Iris. I don't want to lose our home. It's just a job, isn't it? You can still volunteer at the Planetarium, still visit, still love the stars.'

'But . . .'

She took the wine glass from me, set it down and held both my hands. 'I wouldn't ask if I didn't need it. I got you that job you love, didn't I? I wanted you to be happy more than anything.'

A slow-rising panic bubbled up inside me, forced air from my lungs, tears from my eyes, forced my blood to tremble in my veins.

'You want me to give up my dream job.'

'I want you to help me keep our home. If I had the promotion, it would have been enough.'

She said it kindly, not a hint of reproach, but I felt the daggers in her words. The guilty stabs in my heart. She bowed her head and when she raised it again, she was crying.

'I came here from France with very little and this place isn't the most friendly to foreigners. This city can destroy a person, can take their drive and their love and rip them up,' she said, a nostalgic glow in her eyes. 'I grew up reading the American magazines my mother subscribed to. So glossy and decadent and in such bad taste most of the time, but I loved them. I would tear out the pages and stick them on a, what do you call it . . . a corkboard? The people in these magazines had such lives. They all lived in these pre-war buildings, glorious twenties and thirties architecture, exuberant and ornate, a real show of the money they had. I wanted that life. I wanted to be treated with that respect because I'd earned, literally, every cent of it. Now I have it. We have it. And I have fought it twice as hard as any man to get it. I don't want to give it up. I don't want us to give up this life. I want our life to expand and grow, not shrink. Don't you enjoy the food, the wine, the views? Don't you like our home, our life? Don't you love it here, with me?'

I held her hand, stroked her thumb with mine.

'I do love it,' I said. 'I just . . .'

Just what, Jane? Just want to make the woman you love give up her dream too?

Claude fought back tears, and for the first time in months, I saw my wife. The woman I loved. The woman I'd sworn in front of a hundred guests I would do anything for. I'd never seen her like this, so open, so pleading, wearing her hurt so brazenly upon her tailored sleeve.

'There must be another way,' I tried, a last pass across the field, but my throw, my voice, was weak and didn't carry.

'Believe me, my love, if there was another way, I would have found it.'

I knew that was true. Claude was nothing if not thorough.

She gripped my hands. 'Do you think I want you to be unhappy? What kind of monster would that make me? I did everything I could think of. God, I even asked Lloyd for my bonus early to cover for another few months.' She paused, shook her head. 'That was not well received. I expect I've done more damage to my reputation.'

I winced. More damage. I got her into this mess at the party, and now, to keep our home, she'd dug deeper to try to spare me.

'Can I think about it? Just a couple of days.'

She winced. 'They need an answer in the morning.'

I took a deep breath, felt the edges of my world collapsing, the pride in my career and my accomplishments souring. But they still existed. The Story of the Universe would run at the Planetarium for years; that was something, something I did that a new job couldn't diminish, something my father would be proud of. I looked at my wife, at the wide-eyed pleading. She'd given me my dream, at least for a while. I could give her hers.

'I'll do it.'

Her tear-streaked face broke into a smile. 'You will?'

I nodded. Felt my heart crack at the thought of resigning. The shock on Neil's face. The sadness in mine. Felt my heart rip at the thought of walking into an office, a corporate, faceless office, where I'd have to push papers again, looking to the ground this time, to oil, to gas, instead of up to the stars.

But for Claude, I'd do it.

Because for the first time in four years, Claude needed me and asked me for help, and that, at least, felt good.

She threw herself on me, covered me in kisses until we were a tangled, laughing mess on the couch.

'Thank you,' she said, with more sincerity than she'd spoken our wedding vows. '*Je t'aime*, my Iris, *je t'aime à la folie*.'

Have you ever looked in a mirror and not recognised the face staring back at you? The lines, the freckles, the hair, the skin, they belonged to someone else. Another Iris. One who was happy about this job, or at least was better at faking it.

I stood in front of the bathroom mirror and tried on a smile. Forced the edges of my mouth up. Imagined the first meeting with my new boss, the 'I'm thrilled to be here' lie, the limp handshake, the oohs and aahs at seeing my new office, new colleagues, new routine. The walkthrough, the nods, the 'pleased to meet you', the 'excited to work with you', the restrooms, the break room, the kitchenettes on every floor, the corporate generosity I had to pretend to be impressed by: 'We have fruit delivered every morning and a vending machine in the hall full of healthy snacks.' I took a deep breath. Forced the smile wider.

'Here.'

I jumped at Claude's voice. She stood in the bathroom doorway holding a skirt. Tan-coloured, pleated in the right places, knee-length, expensive.

Claude smiled and handed it to me. 'This would be perfect with a white shirt.'

'I was going to wear pants. And my red shirt, you know, the one with the white threading. I set it out on the bed.'

'I saw. But . . . really, darling, that shirt makes you look a little . . . how do you say . . . country?'

'Country?'

'Like a cowboy.'

She came close and threaded her arms through mine, around my waist.

'Besides, you can't wear a bright red shirt on your first day. That's a statement, isn't it? You need to fit in. Then you can show them a little personality.'

'But . . .'

'Please, Iris, you're not used to the corporate world. I am. Trust me, fitting in is everything.'

She kissed me, but I barely felt it. I stared past her into the mirror. Into eyes I didn't recognise. That other Iris slowly shook her head and dropped her gaze, and I felt her give in.

I pulled away from Claude and looked at the skirt. 'It's nice.'

'Of course it is,' she said. 'I had Celine at Bergdorf pick it. She has exquisite taste.'

She hadn't even found it herself. She had employed someone to dress me. Could I be angry? Did I have the energy right now when I had a whole day of small talk and forced happiness ahead of me?

Claude's manner changed. 'You don't want it. We can find something else. I just . . . I wanted you to be confident on your first day. I want all of those Hoss suits to look at you, your taste, your style, your beauty, and think, there is a future VP. There is one to watch. And in this, in the shirt I have for you, with the right make-up, they will see you as someone whose opinion matters.'

My opinion mattered at the Planetarium without all these theatrics.

It wasn't my style, but I had to admit, when I put on the costume she'd chosen for me, I looked good. Claude did my make-up, and when she was finished, she threw the eyeliner onto the floor with a flourish and said, '*Voilà! Une déesse emerge!*' A goddess emerges.

I smiled and stared at myself in the mirror. I looked sophisticated, accomplished. Not at all like I felt inside. Maybe that was the point.

I gathered my things for the office as Claude rushed to get ready herself. She would be late because she'd helped me. A tiny act of selflessness that warmed my insides.

We rode down in the elevator together, hand in hand. Dante hailed us separate cabs, and as Claude's pulled up, she kissed my cheek.

'Try smiling, will you?'

Her tone caught me off guard, a sudden stinging attack, then she was in the cab and gone with a wave and a '*bonne chance*'.

It took every ounce of strength I had not to turn and flee back into the safety of the apartment, to run to Neil and beg him for my job back. I could – it had only been a few weeks, he probably hadn't found anyone yet – but Claude . . . I didn't want to think what she might do. I didn't want to disappoint her again. So I got in the cab, rode it to the offices of Hoss Oil and Gas, a glass-fronted skyscraper just like all the others, and walked into my first day with a fake smile.

I cried in the bathroom on my lunch break.

I cried on the subway home.

I cried myself to sleep while Claude held me and whispered sweetness into my ear. 'Oh Iris, I'm sorry, my love, but look what you've given us. Our home. Our lives. Thank you, thank you.'

I cried every day until I was numb and resigned and Claude stopped holding me and starting sighing through her teeth. 'Enough, Iris. The CFO of Hoss called and said you were doing a good job, why are so you upset?' She stopped thanking me and not-so-gently told me to stop whining, 'Why, oh why, are you always complaining? You still have your telescope, you still have your stars, you can still volunteer at the Planetarium, can't you?'

I couldn't set foot in there knowing everything I'd lost, it would be like reopening a wound barely closed and expecting it to heal quicker. But I didn't tell Claude that. To Claude, I said, 'I'm sorry. I'll be better.'

Days bled into weeks, then into months, and I tried to focus on other things. I had more money now. My own money. Though of course a chunk of it went to Claude to pay the hiked rent. But I still had a lot left over. And I had vacation days. Six weeks of them – a perk like that was the only way to keep anyone in that job – and I used every single one. Claude barely took a day off and we rarely went on vacation, so I spent those six weeks, spread unevenly through the year, alone. I suddenly had time and money and no idea what to do with either.

So I explored my city. I spent more time with friends. I went to talks. I took a three-day mini course in the science of exoplanets. I took another on the basics of astrophysics. I understood less than half of it. But then I did the course a second time and understood more.

And I walked. I picked a direction, a street, and I walked until I found something new. A public garden floating between two skyscrapers, an abandoned 1900s subway stop, a museum in a freight elevator. I rode the Staten Island ferry back and forth, I crossed bridges, I went underground.

I tried to live outside of work. To think of those ten or twelve hours a day as a block of time that didn't define me but allowed me instead to be myself. It was a sort of freedom. A sort of joy. A change to my life I hadn't wanted or planned for but one I'd try to make the most of.

I played games with myself. I'd see how quickly I could get from point A to B. I'd find the most direct or the most circuitous routes. I'd see how long I could walk without stopping. I'd track my walks and map them on a huge roll-map of the city I kept hidden from Claude. For some reason, I didn't want her to see what I was doing, where I was going, how I was spending my money. Not that she ever asked. As long as the rent was paid, and I went to the occasional work function, she left me largely to myself.

One morning, about a year after I started the awful job, I left the apartment before dawn. I didn't have a plan, just let my feet and my instinct guide me. Something had woken me around 5 a.m., because I am *not* a morning person. Give me a vat of coffee and a buttery pastry and in an hour I might be able to string a sentence together, but that morning, I woke wired. Eyes bright and wide. Limbs twitching with pent-up energy, like I'd been electrified in the night, charged up to full capacity. I got up, dressed, and was outside in fifteen minutes. I didn't stop to eat or drink, because I didn't need it. Didn't want it. I was fuelled up.

I didn't know where I was going, only that I had to walk.

Half an hour later, I reached the edge of the island. Riverside Park. I strained against the railing because I wanted to keep going. Something was telling me to keep going. My legs ached for standing still, knees pressing against the cold metal bars.

Below me, the black water of the Hudson broke against the rocky banks. White foam stark in the pre-dawn light. A few runners and cyclists rushed by me. One or two paused, asked a quick are-you-okay before leaving with a nod from me.

Was I still asleep? Was this some elaborate sleepwalk or ultra-vivid dream?

My calves burned, feet tensed and cramped. Walk. You need to walk.

Further up Riverside, the railing pressed against my side. Every step was a wrench. I was going in the wrong direction. But every direction felt wrong except into the water. Across it. Up the other side. Away.

I walked back to that spot at the railing. I could jump. I could swim. The idea felt right. But when I returned to the spot, as the sun, so far behind me, was rising and lightening the overwhelming dark to bleak grey, someone stood there. Right where I wanted to be. A woman, staring into the water just as I had.

Was she my ghost? Had I left behind a shadow?

But she was real. In running gear. Blues and greens that looked glossy black in the light. She leant over the railing. Then jumped back when she saw me.

I met her eyes, she met mine, and something, some strange exchange, happened. Like I'd been on receive and her on transmit and we'd suddenly come within range of each other. The pull in my legs had gone. They were still warm with exertion and right where they should be.

Then I saw her closer. Saw the shape of her face. The colour of her hair. I knew them all and yet they were draped on another body.

Me. My face. My eyes.

Seeing angels.

I said something, but she couldn't hear it.

She spoke, but I couldn't hear either.

She reached out her hand and I reached out mine because I had to touch her. I had to connect. It was as crucial to me as breathing. And I knew, just knew, it was the same for her because I was her and she was me.

Our fingertips brushed, but no, they didn't. We didn't touch. There was something in the way.

She was gone.

A blink. A light bulb blowing. A quick cut on a movie reel. Nobody stood at the railing but me. A passing jogger gave me a strange look and I realised I still held out my hand. To no one.

My breath misted in the September air. The sun rose and lit up the world, turning the magical into the mundane. My body was heavy. Tired. As if all my energy and fuel had left with the woman.

Dream. Hallucination. Sleepwalk. Whatever. I shook it off. I tried, at least.

I made my way back home and realised I'd neglected to pick up my keys. Instead of waking Claude, I had the doorman let me into the building and sat outside our apartment until I heard her humming a tune in the kitchen, the roar of the coffee machine. Then I knocked and slipped guiltily inside.

'Where have you been?'

'Out for a walk.'

She didn't ask more.

As the weeks passed, the seasons changed, I walked the streets of my city whenever I had a spare day or hour. I only felt myself and at peace with the direction my life was taking when I was moving. Some days I felt my father walking beside me, or the woman from the riverside. Sometimes childhood friends, camp-ground pals I thought I'd forgotten, sometimes Ellis, sometimes Bella, sometimes, even, Claude. I found myself walking those same streets night and day, going further and further out, expand-ing my loop as if compelled to by an invisible guiding force. The metal in a bird's beak pulling it south.

I was walking a line the world, the universe had laid out, and though I couldn't imagine where, I knew it was taking me some-where. I only had to follow it.

After

Mennier wasn't there.

The road wasn't there.

The trail I'd followed into the forest faded in the undergrowth, disappeared among the ferns so quietly I didn't realise until I'd walked half a mile.

The forest felt different. More contained. The rain sounded different, not the soft sound of water on leaves but the hard tap-tapping on a car roof. The ridges and hillocks warped and turned in directions I didn't remember. The trees seemed to bow at the canopy, bending in on themselves like a fish-eye lens. And the light. It had a diffuse softness to it, as if the sun shone through water.

I came to the horseshoe of trees where I'd camped on my first night in the woods. Yet it wasn't a horseshoe but a circle. A full ring of mature birches. I hadn't been in the woods that long. Must be a different place, but I didn't think it was.

I kept walking, as fast as my ankle would allow. I stopped and ate a few bites, drank a few sips. Followed the path I knew was there but couldn't see.

Then it was dark. Then it was sunset or rise, I couldn't tell. Then I felt the electrical buzz that told of storms or something else. The smell of metal, a static charge I could feel in my teeth.

Strange sounds filled the air. Echoes of footsteps that weren't mine. A laugh I knew but couldn't place. The sounds of sorrow. A back racked with sobs, heaving, pumping out grief. They were everywhere. Then a smaller sound. A creak. The sound of a rope tight around bark, a dead weight swaying.

Then I saw her. Standing under an oak that looked eerily familiar, but that was impossible. It shouldn't, couldn't be there.

Claude smiled, uncrossed her arms, and in a blink she was in front of me, filling my vision. Her phantom fingers tucked my hair behind my ear. Her eyes flashed with other-worldly light. Her perfume expanded my lungs and seeped into my bloodstream like a drug.

'You haven't gone anywhere,' she said in a purr.

'I haven't?'

'You fainted.'

'No . . .' But had I?

Pain bloomed in my temples. A tight pressure above my eyes.

'You're stuck inside your own head,' she said. 'My poor Iris.'

I pushed away from her but it felt like I was pushing through sand.

I'd moved, but she was still just as close. She reached for me, brushed her thumb across my cheek. Across the scar she'd given me.

'Why is this happening to me?' I said, and a sob caught in my throat, caught the words and held them.

'You deserve it.' The words I dreaded. The ones I knew were true.

Claude smiled, too wide, a grim rictus spreading across her perfect features, turning them ghoulish.

I pressed my eyes closed. Couldn't bear to see it.

When I opened them, she was gone and I was alone in the woods. My ears had popped, and bright spots sparked in my vision. I leant against a tree and pulled in breath after breath, felt my heart slow, felt the dark clouds in my mind retreat an inch. Enough.

My hands shook. I was hungry. Blood sugar at rock bottom. That was all. Just a dizzy spell.

I was going to starve to death, taunted by Claude and a better version of myself.

I laughed. Because what else could I do?

I laughed into the strange, warped forest and wondered if Claude had been right. Was I really out cold on the cabin floor? How would I even wake myself up? Did I even want to?

I walked towards the town I knew was there, but when I crested a low ridge, I saw it. The cabin. I was back. Or maybe I'd never left.

I stumbled, too confused to pay attention to my footing. I caught myself on a sprawling tree. It had huge red flowers and branches like reaching arms. A rhododendron. I didn't remember seeing it on any hike. But I knew it. We'd had one in the garden at my parents' house. My father had loved it. Told me stories of how these trees created portals. Doorways to fantastical realms. I played on it every weekend. Every day in summer. Pretending I was finding my way to Narnia. Or to an undersea kingdom. Or to a planet full of singing aliens. Then he died, and Mother had the rhododendron cut down. He doesn't need this ugly tree anymore, she'd said, he's got a whole forest of them.

Did she miss him? Or was she angry he'd left her alone with two teenagers, a crippling mortgage and no savings?

My father's life seemed punctuated by stars and trees. He died on a night where the dusty arm of the Milky Way was overhead, when Venus was highest in the sky. Beneath the oak tree we camped under time and again. Every trip a seed of hope for his escape. Then he did escape. For good. Because of me.

I was on my hands and knees in the forest mud. The skin on my cheeks tight with dried tears. My hair plastered to my face and neck. The day later than it should be. The light faded to old gold and rising dark. The cabin just ahead. About eight steps away.

I felt Claude's presence behind me, watching me from afar, felt her terrible smile on my back, her eyes boring through my skull.

If you tell her, she'll laugh at you. If you tell her, she'll agree with you. You did deserve it. Every moment of it. You're selfish. That's why he died.

'I know,' I whispered to Claude. Felt her laugh run through me. Felt her presence, closer now, heavier.

Would he be alive if I'd gone with him into the woods that day?

I looked towards the cabin. Wondering if Other Iris had made it to Randall Peak. I imagined her alongside my father, older now but still a mountain goat on the trail. I imagined them both at the summit staring out over the quiet forest with that content, calm look on their faces. The look I'd never been able to master. The one I'd never truly felt since early childhood, before Banff and the lake, before I was sixteen and lost my father forever. Made him go. Dismissed him with the unfeeling petulance of a teenager.

She hadn't done that, or maybe she had but my father loved her more so had stayed. Was it her choice or his? Did she have a terrible life like mine as punishment? She couldn't smile like that if she did. Couldn't have that beatific look on her filled-out cheeks.

I needed to know her life so I could understand how mine had gone so wrong. Maybe then I could begin to fix it.

I just had to survive until she got back. I'd ration further, go without, stay still, not burn unnecessary calories.

I limped to the cabin, pushed open the door and nearly screamed.

Other Iris sat on the couch, arms folded, foot tapping, a look of thunder on her face. 'What did you *do*?'

Before

'I can't believe, sometimes, that I found you,' Claude said, a murmur in my ear as we lay in bed.

We'd been doing well. Claude hadn't lost her temper, I hadn't complained about the awful job she'd made me take. We had settled into a frictionless, if passionless, routine.

'Me neither,' I said.

'You're the love of my life.'

The surge of heat at her words quickly evaporated. She curled her arm around me and we stayed like that for a while. Her warm breath tickled the back of my neck, evening out as she drifted off to sleep. But I couldn't fully relax.

As much as the conflict had disappeared between us, so had almost everything else. Claude often spent nights at her office, talking of Japanese markets and time differences I didn't care enough to interrogate. Or she'd be home so late she might as well have slept at her desk. But when she was in the apartment of an evening, she was happy. Sometimes she'd come home with flowers, sometimes with nothing more than the affection I'd been sorely missing. We still had sex, but her mind was elsewhere, on currency exchanges and energy markets, and so was mine. I had a pinhole inside me. A small black dot in my centre. It had been there with Bella and it had been there all along with Claude, though I'd tried to ignore it. Since leaving the Planetarium and my career, the dark spot had grown.

I lay beside my wife and felt like I was lying beside a stranger. We led separate lives now. We barely spoke of anything below the surface – how was work, what do you want to eat, I'm going out, back later – when once we'd talked for hours. I became little more than a decoration at her work functions, forbidden to speak except in pleasantries, my alcohol intake carefully monitored, but at least the anger was gone. At least her temper wasn't provoked.

When I told Ellis all this over a line of tequila shots, he wondered if she'd found someone else to have the passionate all-nighters with.

I laughed. 'As if she has time. She works constantly.'

'So she says,' he slurred, and winked and sipped his tequila.

I shook my head and brushed it off. Claude, cheating? No. That's crazy.

The next night, I sat up and waited for her. Not with any thought of confronting her – because, frankly, it was ridiculous that she might be seeing someone else and I hated Ellis for putting the thought in my head – but more because I wanted to see her, speak to her, try to reconnect with her or at least acknowledge the yawning space between us.

Claude's key turned in the lock, and she came in with two cotton bags bulging with groceries. I got up to help, taking both bags from her and setting them on the kitchen counter.

'*Merci*,' she said, and kissed my cheek, moved past me towards the bedroom.

I put away the groceries and waited. She emerged from the bedroom in a black cocktail dress, fixing a gold hoop to her ear. My heart sank.

'Are you going out?'

She went to the kitchen, got a glass of water. 'Mmm-hmm. Drinks.'

'Can we talk?'

She set down the glass, carefully blotted a drop of water from her lipstick.

'Right now?'

I motioned to the couch. She sighed, ran her tongue along her teeth, and joined me. Eyebrows up, body tense, hands clamped in her lap. I had no idea what to say.

A minute passed. She checked her watch. A Rolex. A

twenty-grand watch I'd never seen before. I stared at the dial, ringed with two rows of diamonds. When had she got that? Could we even afford it? Or had it been a gift?

She splayed her hands, breaking my line of sight, snapping me out of the ticking hypnosis.

'Well?'

Just say it. Come right out and say it.

'Are . . .' I couldn't. The words wouldn't come.

'Iris, can this wait?' She stood up, flattened out her dress. 'I am meeting the partners in an hour.'

I looked at my hands, at a speck of dirt under my thumb-nail. I worked at it. Dislodged it. Anything not to look up at Claude.

I heard the impatience and frustration in her footsteps as she grabbed her bag, her keys, her coat, as she reached the front door and turned the handle—

'Are you having an affair?'

The words left my mouth like bullets.

She froze. Door open an inch, shoulders tense and high.

'Why would you ask me that?' she said.

She quietly closed the door and turned to face me, her expression blank.

I stood, found my bravery. 'Are you?'

'No.'

The simple force of the word made me flinch. Fine. That's the end of it. I'd asked, she'd answered, case closed. But I saw the raw fire in her eyes and knew it wouldn't be that easy.

'Why would you ask me that?' she said again.

'It doesn't matter.'

She crossed the room towards me. 'Why, Iris?'

'Nothing. No reason. Just something Ellis said, a joke—'

'Ellis?' She laughed, sneered. 'The *connard*. He would say anything, huh? A jealous little shit.'

'Hey—'

'He is in love with you, you know that? You're not blind to that, are you?'

'That's not—'

'And now he gets in your head, trying to come between us.'

Claude came over to me, took my hand in both of hers. Her fingers played over my palm, over my veins and tendons, as if looking for the weak spot. I couldn't speak for the shock, the explosion of anger towards my friend.

'Ellis doesn't feel that way about me.'

Claude shook her head. 'Oh Iris, don't be so naive. Of course he does. It's obvious, the way he looks at you. He's so defensive of you. You know he spoke to me at our engagement party?' I frowned, she nodded. 'He took me to the side and he said, "Iris is mine. You are only temporary. Soon she'll see that I am better for her than you." That is why I don't like him and won't spend time with him. He is waiting for us to fail so he can be your shining knight.'

'That's . . .' But I had seen them talking that night and Claude had been uncomfortable with him ever since. The suggestion Ellis had feelings for me was crazy, but . . .

'Iris. I love you. You know I love you, don't you?' she said, and her grip on my hand tightened. 'I always have, always will.'

'I know.'

'And yet you are thinking I am seeing someone else.'

'I don't. Not really. But . . .'

'But what?'

'You're away so much, so many nights at the office. When you come home, you're happy and relaxed, and you never used to be. You bring me flowers.'

'I sound awful.'

'What I mean is . . .' I struggled for the words. 'If this were a movie, the surest signs of a cheating spouse are a change in behaviour, a guilty conscience, and overcompensation with gifts and affection, but nothing substantial, all surface-level intimacy. It's textbook.'

Claude raised her eyebrows and took a step back. 'This isn't a movie, Iris. I bring you flowers because I know you are unhappy in your job. The job I made you take. I am affectionate because I miss you because I have to work so much harder to reclaim lost ground, and to ensure every year Sophia has no excuse to stop sponsoring my visa.'

Her visa. I'd never even considered that. Her entire life in this city was reliant on her making her company money and her bosses liking her. I'd jeopardised that at the party. No wonder she'd lashed out. How selfish are you, Iris?

'Claude, I—'

'*That* is why I stay late and overnight. And now you think I am cheating? That I am some *putain*? All I do is for *you*. For *us*.' I'd never seen her so upset.

'I'm sorry, I'm sorry.' I surged forward, needing to hold her, take it all back, reset us to five minutes ago, before I'd thrown accusations around like live grenades.

I grabbed her hand. She shook me off. She was a tight wire of rage, all directed at me and my mindless accusation.

'I need to go.'

'Wait, Claude. Don't leave like this.'

She whirled around to me. 'Like what? Angry my wife doesn't trust me?'

'I do! I trust you! It's just . . . I've just . . .'

'You let a man up here.' She stabbed at her temple. 'Next you will let him down there, and then who will be the *putain*?'

I recoiled. 'That's not fair.'

'Fair! What do you know about fair? I support you, I get you work, I pay the bills, I take care of everything. I give you a life so many women would kill for and you repay me with this? This is bullshit. If you don't love me anymore, you leave, but don't you dare accuse me of having an affair.'

She turned away, strode to the door, and I knew if I let her walk out like this, we'd never come back from it.

I rushed after her, grabbed hold of her arm.

She exploded at the touch. Her arm, body, energy whipped around, the wire unravelling.

Her fist cracked against my cheek.

The sound was alien and deafening – a dull slap of flesh – and the silence after absolute.

Beth Lewis

I blinked, not sure what had happened. Sparks filled my vision like a sky full of supernovas. Slow pain blossomed then hit me full force in a searing, bone-deep trauma.

I clutched my face and stared at Claude. Not believing and yet knowing. This. This was. I couldn't form thoughts. Sharp spikes needled through my cheek, something wet and warm spilled from my skin.

'I have to go,' she said, her breathing thick, her voice shaking. But she didn't move.

Then something happened. Her humanity returned in a way it hadn't after the party. The anger left her. I watched it drain away like old bathwater. Her shoulders dropped. She stared down at her hand, at her knuckles. Red skin swelling, smeared with blood from her rings. A newly pink diamond blinked up at her. A silver band glistened scarlet.

'Iris.' Barely a whisper. Barely a word. 'I'm sorry, my love, I'm so sorry.'

Then she was holding me, her hands on my face, prising mine away from my cheek, assessing the damage. Cooing, whispering soft, sweet words.

She kissed me. Tentative at first, then harder. As if all the passion that had been missing from our relationship suddenly came back with the force of her blow. I tried to shake her off – the pressure of her hands, her face, her kiss sent shots of pain through my cheek and neck – but she held me tight.

She pressed her lips to my forehead and repeated, in a muffled whisper, 'Why do you do this to me? Why do you do this?'

I don't know how long we stayed there, fixed in place like Renaissance marble. My head and face throbbed, felt twice their size, ready to burst. Blood dried to sticky smears on my cheek. Nothing mattered.

I felt her move, her hand twist, arm turn. The slight metallic *tink* as her watch moved on her wrist.

She stood up without a word. She went to the bathroom and I heard the tap, then the pop of her lipstick as she touched up. She came back to me, looked at me again and gave a sympathetic sigh as if I'd done this to myself while rollerblading.

'I'm not cheating on you,' she said. For a moment, I thought she was going to say something else, I saw the thought behind her eyes, the words behind her tongue, but she didn't. She just smiled and said, 'I'll see you later. I love you.'

Then she left.

Just like that.

The sound of the door slamming rang in my ears.

I walked to the bathroom on unsteady legs. I didn't recognise the woman in the mirror. A mask of tears and blood and shock.

'Who are you?' I whispered to the glass, to the woman staring back at me with a gash on her cheekbone, a fat bruise under the surface waiting to show itself.

'Who *are* you?'

'WHO ARE YOU?'

I screamed it. Cried it. I smashed my fists on the glass. I threw bottles of perfume at the floor, at the walls. I swept everything from the shelves. I cracked the mirror. Shards fell into the sink, throwing up ghoulish reflections. Upside-down me. Warped me. Pieces of the room. The door. The hallway. Fragments of a life. Like mine, but broken. My legs ached for wanting to move. To walk. To run. Anywhere but here. But I had nowhere.

I slid to the floor.

Claude would be furious if I left.

I looked at the destruction around me.

Claude would be furious I'd made such a mess.

She'd say I was acting like a child. That it had been an accident. She was angry and I'd grabbed her and she'd just reacted.

It was true, after all.

Besides, this kind of thing doesn't happen between two women, does it? That's what the cops would say: oh, you two had a cat fight? Call us next time so we can watch. And what my family would say: Oh don't be silly, Iris, it's not a *real* fight, you can work it out.

They were right. We would work it out.

It had been an accident after all. She hadn't meant to hurt me.

She'd apologised right after . . . hadn't she? I didn't remember; the moments before and after were fuzzy patches. She must have apologised. She wasn't a monster. She'd kissed me. Held me. Said she was sorry.

She didn't mean it.

I pulled myself up from the floor. I picked the shards of broken glass from the sink and laid them on a towel. I washed my hands and face and dabbed antiseptic onto the cut, hissing through my teeth, then put on a Band-Aid. I went to the kitchen, poured a large measure of whisky over ice and held it to my cheek.

I slept in the second bedroom that night. Claude brought me coffee in the morning with a kiss and a '*Bon matin, ma chérie*' as if nothing had happened, and really, what had?

It had been an accident.

After

The cabin stank of damp. The walls and floor a shade darker for being permanently soaked, a softness to every step instead of the crisp hardwood sound I'd become used to. My clothes stank just as bad and refused to dry. The stove was cold and there was a persistent dripping down the chimney.

I stood in the doorway, staring at an angry woman who wore my face and shouldn't be there.

'What did you *do*?' she said again.

'What do you mean?'

She stood, took a step towards me and pointed out the window. 'Randall Peak isn't there. The trail isn't there. I walked for two hours due north and ended up back here. How is that possible?'

'You can't read a compass?'

She laughed an angry, bitter sound. 'Fuck you. I can read a compass.'

'I don't know what you want me to say,' I said. 'You got turned around, missed a trail marker, I don't know.'

Her fist balled at her side. 'I didn't get turned around. I walked straight. I ended up here. I tried again, I watched my compass, needle steady, and again I ended up here. I tried a different fucking direction but still *I ended up here*. I got no more than five miles in any direction.'

I folded my arms. 'How is that my fault?'

She surged towards me. My instincts flared and I flinched, back slammed against the wall, sending rivers of pain through my body.

She stopped then. She saw my reaction. My fear. Immediately, her tone changed.

'I'm just saying,' she said. 'I'm happily hiking, everything is normal, then I meet *you*, a woman who looks exactly like me, has my name, my birthday, talks like me, *is me*, and everything changes. If this is Ellis playing a prank, I swear to God, that man . . .' She trailed off, shaking her head.

The name woke me from the fear. 'How do you know Ellis?'

'How do *you* know him?'

Our eyes narrowed at the same time. God, it was unsettling. A living mirror.

Out of synch but in the same tone, we said, 'He's my best friend.'

After a few minutes, I said, 'I tried to hike out too, get supplies, but I ended up back here. I thought it was my ankle, the pain confusing me, but I guess not.'

'This is ridiculous!' she said, and threw up her arms.

I limped over to the couch and took the weight off my ankle. It had swollen up again; my boot was tight and hot around it.

'Undo it,' she said.

'My boot?'

Her anger hardened like a fist. 'No! Whatever it is you did to trap us here.'

'You think *I* did this? You think I'm fucking Gandalf over here and have magicked up a force field to mess with you?'

'You're mixing your genres there, Jane,' she muttered, and my eyes widened.

'Did you just call me Jane?'

She scowled at me. Same frown lines I had. A deep one right there at the top of my nose. Her nose. 'Why would I call you Jane?'

'Because I call myself Jane!'

She paused, cocked her head to one side. 'This is bullshit. Fix it.'

If I'd had two working legs, I'd have stormed off. 'I can't. I didn't do anything. *You* fix it.'

'You must have. What other explanation is there?'

'I don't know!'

She sighed. I sighed.

'This is it,' I said, to myself, not to *myself*. 'I've gone mad. Totally mad.'

'Why would *you* have gone mad?' I – she – asked and I looked at her – me.

'What other explanation is there?' I parroted her words without thinking because they were my words too. I sighed and breathed and tried to put distance between us. 'I mean . . .' I began, but I didn't know what I meant.

'You mean that we look identical and are both called Iris and you think we're the same person so you *must* have gone mad. Right?'

I winced. 'Right.'

'And that's not to mention some time–space loop that no matter which way we go always leads us back to this point and to each other.'

'It can't be real, can it?' I said. 'Because if it's all in my head, that's one thing, but if it's real . . .'

'If it's real, then it means neither of us is crazy and something else is happening here. Something out of a movie or a book, something not real.'

I put my hands on my knees and blew out my cheeks. 'Fuck. This is weird.'

I thought of the stars, the woman in the clearing – *her* – one moment there, then gone. 'It happened out of nowhere. Maybe it'll go away just as randomly.'

'Or maybe we'll be trapped here forever.'

'Always looking on the bright side,' I said, smiling.

'That's me,' we said together.

I shook my head, couldn't wrap my mind around this. Was I alone in the middle of the woods, talking to myself – but not myself in this way, myself in my head? Was this all in my head?

'What happened to you?' she asked, and I looked up at her.

She nodded to my ankle.

'I fell the other day. Is this your shirt?'

She nodded. 'Your back was cut up. From the fall too?'

'It was a bad fall.'

We both fell silent. She leant against the counter. I ran my hands through my hair as she raised her hand to do the same. She stopped herself. Maybe I had made it to the overhang after all. Maybe I'd thrown myself off, bungee-jump style, all swan-dive grace, and *bam!* This was purgatory. Stuck in a loop, facing a better version of myself who reminded me of all the chances, the decisions, the relationships I'd destroyed. She'd got them all. I'd got a broken back and a page 10 headline: *Unidentified Woman's Body Found at Base of Cliff.*

I dug my nail into the meat of my palm. Dug it hard until I couldn't bear it. Can you feel pain in purgatory? Or hell? I looked down at my ankle, felt the tight scabs on my back. Had I gone straight to the pit?

'You can't be real,' I said, my voice low, my eyes on the floor. I couldn't look at her. If I didn't look at her, she wasn't there and I wasn't crazy or dead or both.

'The universe is fucking with us,' she said, but I still didn't look. 'I know I'm not mad. Not today, anyway. So you aren't either.'

I shook my head, kept shaking it as if it would Etch-a-Sketch away the image of her.

'Hey,' she said, suddenly kind, suddenly caring. 'Hey, look at me.'

I tried not to, but she grabbed my shoulders and I looked.

'I'm real,' she said. 'You're real. We must be here for a reason. We just have to figure out what it is.'

'And then what?'

She shrugged. 'In the movies, when the good guys win, everything goes back to normal.'

'This isn't a movie, Iris.' I remembered when Claude had said those words and felt sick.

'Are you sure? This is some science-fiction shit if you ask me.'

I tried to smile. 'That's what I was thinking.'

'Good. So let's Mulder and Scully this and figure it out.'

The black clouds inside my head dissipated, the nausea faded. My mental sky remained grey, but at least it wasn't storming.

She stretched her arms and easily reached down to her feet. I groaned inwardly. Please don't let me do yoga.

'We're both Iris,' she said slowly. 'But we're not exactly the same. Different hair, different clothes.'

'Right.' I nodded, gathering my thoughts into one coherent line, letting them coalesce into a question. 'Do you believe in parallel worlds?'

A half-smile in the corner of her mouth, a slight narrowing of one eye. An expression I didn't recognise in myself.

'I was afraid you were going to say that.'

I hobbled to the couch. She stayed at the counter.

I began to notice our differences as well as our similarities. Her cheek was free of the scar on mine, which sent a tremor through my chest. Did she have a Claude? A kind one? I hoped so. Her eyes were brighter too. Her skin a few shades paler. She had a mole on her jawline that wasn't on mine. I had a dusting of freckles under my eyes I couldn't see on her. Her hair was blonde, cut fairly short and neat. A more sedate version of my Pris cut. The kind of cut you could happily walk into a bank wearing and be confident they'd give you the loan. She had better gear than me. Her jacket – the one hanging on the nail in the cabin – and boots were well worn and high quality, suggesting she used them both regularly. She was a little plumper around the face and neck. A little softer in the hands and collarbones. She had no mania in her eyes, no fear. She looked, I realised with a pang of jealousy, content.

I coughed, snapped back to the conversation. 'There is usually a point of divergence.'

She smiled. 'Maybe if we can find that . . .'

'And solve the puzzle.'

'. . . the universe will let us go.'

We both nodded. My chest tightened. To Randall Peak? To do what? I wanted to ask, but couldn't. If she told me, I'd have to tell her, and how could I tell another version of me that I wanted to jump off a cliff?

Jump off a cliff. You can't even say it, can you? Have to make it flippant, don't you? Say it. Go on. Say it, Jane.

Kill myself.

Like my father did, half a lifetime ago.

'You know how crazy this sounds, right?' she said. Her voice startled me.

'This whole situation is crazy.'

'Good point. Okay, so how do we do this? Where do we start? I guess at the beginning? My parents always wanted kids, but when they got them decided they really didn't. How about you?'

'Similar.' The same. Identical.

'I have one older sister,' she carried on. 'Helen. She tried once to get us to call her—'

Bile rose in my throat. 'Veronica.'

Other Iris laughed, but it died quickly. 'Yeah, Veronica.'

'My mom, Josephine,' she continued, 'Josie to my dad, she had this group of real bitchy friends who used to shame us for eating Tater Tots.' She smiled but I couldn't. Then she turned serious. 'She wasn't perfect, but she tried.'

Mine didn't. I wanted to cry and throw up at the same time. My hands shook. My body wanted to get away from her, from this, from what was coming next. Sister? Check. Mother? Check.

Oh God.

'And my dad, Mit—'

'I can't do this.'

I wanted to. I wanted to hear about him, how alive he was, how happy they all were, but I wasn't ready. How could I hear that my father hadn't loved me enough to stay but had loved her?

I struggled to my feet. Other Iris frowned. I knew what she was thinking because I would have thought it. A mix of 'How rude' and 'Are you okay?' and I didn't want to respond to either.

'Iris?'

'Can you . . . leave? Just, go outside.'

'Are you serious right now?'

'Yes. Deadly. Please.'

Other Iris blew a sigh through her nose, grabbed her stuff and left. I closed the door behind her.

Sudden quiet. Closed off from the world. Closed off from myself. Literally.

Except for everything, nothing about my situation had changed. I still had no food. No dry wood to burn. No dry clothes to wear. The roof still leaked. The raccoon was still gone. I was still mad and I couldn't walk more than ten steps without fainting.

I was trapped again. By my body, by the forest, by my own mind. I'd traded a gilded cage for one strangled by ivy. I hopped to the couch, every inch of me aching, throbbing, stinging, and curled up on the worn, musty cushions.

She had to be a hallucination. A madness brought forth from my brain in an attempt to avert suicide. My neurons plotting amongst themselves. Give her a puzzle to solve, that'll buy us time.

I still wanted to do it. That hurt to admit. I wanted out. Wanted oblivion and quiet darkness. Wanted an end to the pain and guilt and fear. My life had been so full of fear and sadness for so long. Maybe this was my brain's ham-fisted way of telling me there was another way. There was hope. But I'd lived so many years without hope, it was scarier to believe in change than it was to stay in my cage and starve.

Something Other Iris had said came back to me. Five miles. She'd said she couldn't walk more than five miles in any direction before being brought back here. The overhang was three miles. I could get there if I needed to. I could end it whenever I liked. Escape from this new prison before my sorrow accepted the walls. I had time, and I was too curious to leave yet. I needed to speak to her, get past the spectre of my father's death and hear her out.

Tomorrow I would be brave. Today the ghosts had too strong a hold. In the cold, clear light of day, all the horrors and ghouls of the night would be banished to the corners.

'Oh will they, my love?' Claude's voice came from the kitchen. She leant against the countertop, hair wrapped in a scarf. She smiled at me and touched her hand to her mouth, blew a faint kiss.

I turned over on the couch and blocked her out.

Her laugh reached my ears.

I forced my eyes shut, forced the sound out of me, forced my mind to still and my breath to calm and my heart to reset its beat.

When I opened them, Claude was gone, the cabin empty. But her weight was still there, sitting on my shoulders, the yoke of my old life.

I cocooned myself in my sleeping bag and drifted into a shivering sleep, thinking of my father and how he loved another me more.

Before

I ran up the steps into our building, into the elevator, bouncing on my heels as the carriage chugged up. Then a last walk-jog down the corridor to our door. I stopped outside. Tried to push down the rising anxiety I'd felt every day of the two months since I'd accused her of cheating.

I was late. It was my fault. It was always my fault because no matter what I'm doing, I never leave enough time. For Christ's sake, Iris!

I said it all to myself before she could. Took the sting out.

I breezed in hoping I wasn't *that* late, only twenty . . . seven or so minutes, and besides, Claude always allowed contingency time because she knew me so well.

But this time, I'd fucked up.

This time, Claude's contingency had melted away in a panic of preparation, and when she said 5.30, she meant 5.25, not *eh, sometime around six.*

'Hey,' I said, all light and smiling, dropping my keys on the side table.

'*Hey?*'

Fuck.

'Where have you been?'

Claude stood behind the kitchen counter, sleeves rolled up to her elbows, apron on, patched with flour and some kind of sauce, hair tied back, smear of chocolate or similar on her jawline, surrounded by a battleground of canapés and 'small bites' and everything that could possibly go into making them.

I put the groceries she'd asked me to get on the table and set about unpacking and putting away before she could tell me to.

'Sorry, babe, I was looking everywhere for the olives you wanted. It took forever.'

'That's why I asked you to go *yesterday*.'

And I'd planned to. I'd tried to. But then Ellis called and we went for a drink and then another, and ended up at the movies and, well, shit.

'Did you get the olives?'

I braced myself. 'I tried four delis, nobody had them. I got these instead.' I held up the jar. Steeled myself.

Claude sighed, hands on the counter, chin to her chest. She stayed like that, taking long, slow breaths, while I stood awkwardly, a schoolchild outside the principal's office without a chair.

'I'm sorry,' I tried, but she shook her head.

'Will you help me with the salmon? Guests will be arriving in an hour.'

I reached out to her, but she moved away, picked up a knife, sliced the chives.

'Claude?'

She put down the knife and looked at me for the first time since I walked in the door. 'Iris. It is my birthday and my friends are coming for dinner. In an hour. I want it all to be perfect, so please, can you prepare the salmon?'

I did. Best I could. I wasn't what you'd call a natural-born chef. My mother said eating was my strongest skill. But I cut the smoked fish, layered it on tiny toast discs, dabbed on some cream cheese and a couple of perfect chives, all under Claude's eye. I felt her bristle beside me, felt the weight of her judgement, felt her hover over my movements. When a piece of salmon toppled, I heard her sigh. When the cream cheese dab was too big, I heard a sharp inhale. But she never said anything. Never tried to take over.

I laid each tiny canapé on a large slate she'd bought especially. She oversaw. Nodded.

She checked whatever was in the oven. She told me to decant the wine, polish the glasses, set the table. Properly. Set it properly, Iris. She checked every single thing. She adjusted a fork. She sighed because I'd put the wine glasses the wrong way round. She moved them without a word. She turned the plates so the design sat symmetrically. Then she went to get ready and told me to do the same.

I found a dress box waiting on the bed. I had planned on wearing pants, a nice top, I'd had it all picked out for a week. As much as I liked getting glammed up, doing it in my own home felt strange. I wanted to be comfortable.

I opened the box. Not a dress. A long blue jumpsuit, tailored, backless, thin straps, plunging neckline. Gorgeous. I put it on and looked at myself in the mirror.

'I saw it,' Claude said from the doorway as she fixed an earring, 'and I thought you would look beautiful.'

I smiled at my reflection. At this tall, chic, adult woman. Claude appeared in the mirror behind me, slid her arms around my waist.

'I was right,' she said, and kissed my exposed shoulder.

'You usually are.'

'I'm sorry for getting angry,' she said, lips against my skin.

I put my hand over hers and squeezed, then turned and kissed her.

'I'm sorry about the olives.'

She smiled, kissed me back, and held on longer than she usually would. She was nervous, not angry, and all I wanted to do was hold her, reassure her.

'It's going to be great,' I tried, but she just smiled, moved away.

I watched her hips, how the sleek black dress both hugged and didn't, a jaguar on the hunt.

The first of the guests arrived on time. Claude's friends Virgil and Anais. Then Margot and Denise a few minutes later. They brought gifts, which Claude put aside to open later. I served them all champagne while Claude played host.

Let's do this quickly, shall we? Virgil and Anais, a sweet, if dull, couple. Claude knew Virgil from her time in Montréal. He was a beautiful man, Anais a beautiful woman, icy blonde, almost transparent. Newly engaged. She worked in fashion, or was it interior design? He was a lawyer. Yawn.

Margot and Denise. Thirties, been together for about ten years, on and off. Open relationship Denise didn't enjoy any more, or so went the late-night drunken confessions. Denise worked in publishing, Margot in finance. Denise – redhead, quiet and kind. Margot – stunning, with flawless skin. That's what I always remembered about Margot, her skin. Both women fantastically successful in their own fields, a constant source of low-level envy on my part. Margot had her terse moments, but the love between them was obvious to even the most bigoted observer.

And then we came to the final guest. Gerard. Almost thirty minutes late. Claude's eyes narrowed as the doorbell chimed and Gerard swanned in, double-kissing everyone. He was the one I was least looking forward to spending an evening with. A slouchy, messy man in his early forties with the blood bloom of early alcoholism on his face. But his eyes unsettled me most. Piercing. Sharp. Alert to every tic of body language. Watching for weakness, waiting for the chance to assert his dominance over a room and become the captain of the conversation, steering the stories, the jokes, even who spoke. He was an artist living in a loft in the Meatpacking District. Paints, canvases, lots of nudes – men, women, old, young, *very* young if the rumours were true, and I believed them because with some men you can just tell. He sold plenty. The Whitney exhibited his work. He was the most important artist of the decade, so cawed the sycophants. He was also Claude's brother.

And I'd invited him. Sort of.

'*Joyeux anniversaire, ma chère soeur!*' he bellowed, and wrapped his arms around her.

'Thank you, brother,' she said and extricated herself without causing offence. She gave me a sharp *this is all your fault* look. But it wasn't. Not this time. She'd told her mother about the party. Her mother told Gerard. Gerard called, I'd answered. I couldn't exactly say no, could I?

That's what I'd said to Claude. Yet she still gave me that look.

I handed Gerard a glass of champagne, tried to smile.

'You look magnificent, Iris,' he said, kissed my cheeks for the second time. The feeling of his spit on my skin made it crawl.

'You too, Gerard,' I said, and he laughed.

'Wine and women. The healthiest diet a man can have,' he said, grabbing his paunch and giving it a shake. 'Virgil understands, don't you, friend?'

Virgil had met Gerard before. The others had not.

'Oh yes, of course,' he said, with a tight smile and a raised eyebrow from Anais.

Gerard finished his drink in one mouthful and went to the kitchen for another.

'He's looking well,' Virgil said. 'Such a card, too.'

'He does seem genial,' said Margot.

'He's your brother?' asked Denise.

Claude nodded. 'For better or worse. I didn't expect him to show up.'

Everyone smiled and conversation dwindled. Claude's eyes darted from friend to friend to her brother and finally to me. There was worry there, behind the steel and glass. They were judging her. Judging her family. The one member she couldn't control. Who was never meant to be here and wouldn't have been, if it wasn't for me.

I went to the kitchen, where Gerard had poured himself a large glass of red wine – the wine we had decanted and been saving for the main course, but whatever. I grabbed the slate of canapés.

'Claude may have prepared a perfect rack of lamb and pomme something or other and a jus with all kinds of alcohol,' I said, holding out the platter, 'but I think we'll all agree the real culinary skill in this family is mine. This exquisitely sliced salmon, the ratio of fish to cream cheese to bread. I mean, it's a masterpiece.'

Polite laughs all round. Hands reached for the canapés. Tension dissolved by full mouths and nods of over-earnest agreement.

'Anais, how are the wedding plans?' I asked, and the woman came to life.

'We've booked the Boathouse in Central Park. June next year.'

'How beautiful,' Denise said, and I watched as Margot tensed. 'Wouldn't that be just the perfect place in the city to get married?'

Margot nodded but gave nothing more.

Then Virgil joined in. 'Even I'm enjoying the planning. The flowers will be oranges, yellows and reds, to mimic the sunset. We were engaged at sunset.'

He and Anais shared a rosy-cheeked smile and a quick kiss.

'You old romantic, V,' said Claude.

She caught my eye and mouthed, *thank you*, and my heart kicked. I found her hand and squeezed it, and she held on and didn't shake me away.

Those arguments weren't important any more. There was love here, real partnership, and a fight or two didn't diminish that. If anything, it increased it. We could and would overcome anything.

They sat down for dinner as I helped Claude serve. We danced around each other in the kitchen, knowing exactly what we were doing. It was a ballet. I heaped buttered broccoli and roasted Romanesco cauliflower into bowls while Claude poured the jus into individual jugs. I pulled the gratin dauphinois from the oven – Christ, it looked good – while Claude carved the lamb at the table. A feast even Gerard couldn't spoil, despite his best efforts.

'A toast,' he cried, raising his third, maybe fourth, glass of wine. 'To my beautiful sister. May your next thirty years be as full and bounteous as your first.'

We all raised our glasses, ready to toast, but Gerard wasn't finished. I stifled a smile as Margot gave a whispered 'Oh joy.' I hoped Claude didn't hear.

'Claudette, my dear, dear sister. What a terror you were. I won't regale you all with talk of Claude's childhood missteps – there are too many for one evening.' He belched a laugh and we politely tittered while Claude seethed. '*Pardon, ma soeur*, I am in your home and I will speak kindly. I am very proud of my sister. She has grown into a beautiful woman. Very beautiful. And has found herself a wife. Iris, *belle-soeur*, you have made Claude very happy and much more fun than she used to be. Oh Claude, don't make that face. You know you were a boring child. Iris makes you human and you should keep hold of her. Because if you don't, someone else will!' He laughed again and grabbed my shoulder to illustrate his point.

Claude stood, raised her own glass to cut him off. '*Merci*, Gerard. Please, sit and eat. Thank you all for coming to celebrate with me. My true friends. A toast to you all.'

Gerard guffawed. 'True family too, despite not getting the invite until two days ago. Two days, friends, can you believe it?'

'Lost in the post, I guess,' I said, and his eyes found mine. Narrowed. Like Claude's.

'Anyway,' Virgil said, and his soft voice cut through the awkwardness. 'This looks amazing, Claude. You have outdone yourself. You too, Iris.'

I expected a quip from Gerard, but none came. A collective exhale and we began to eat.

Lots of appreciative noises, lots of compliments, from everyone but Gerard. He remained silent, watching us all, eating little, drinking more.

'Gerard,' Virgil began, 'how is the new show coming?'

Oh Virgil. You idiot.

Gerard ummed and aahed and took a drink before answering. 'I am stalled.'

'How so?' Virgil asked.

'I have no muse for my central piece. The model I had to sit for me, she ... she is like Anais here, very beautiful,' the woman reddened with the flattery, 'but with no, how do you say ... substance. No weight behind the eyes, you understand?'

Anais' expression faltered.

'What's the show about?' Denise asked, deftly changing the subject with a consoling look to Anais. Her bright eyes and sharp voice a welcome spark of normality in the evening.

'Women. Their beauty. Their weakness. Beauty as weakness. Weakness as beauty.' The more he drank, the thicker his accent. 'The way all women carry weakness within them, as do all men, but you never see until they allow it. Until you get so, so close. You must peel away their outside and see their vulnerable selves, and that truth is what I capture in my work.'

'I don't believe women are weak,' Margot said.

Gerard smiled. Claude had a smile like that. A 'challenge me' smile. He sat back in his chair and set down his glass.

'You don't?'

Margot shook her head. 'You have a male perspective of women that all they are is beauty and weakness. To be controlled and conquered. Men and women are the inverse of each other. Men project strength on the outside, but are little more than frightened children inside. Women may project weakness in their physicality, but inside, Gerard, women are iron. We are steel. You have no idea.'

He laughed and held his hands up. 'A feminist, I see.'

Margot's hackles rose. 'A misogynist, I see.'

'Dear Margaret,' he said, knowing full well her real name. 'I paint from my experience. I can only do that. The women I paint, they show me truth through their eyes, and I capture it on canvas. You cannot deny another woman's truth, can you?'

'I can deny a man's interpretation of that truth,' she said, and I smiled. Score one for Margot.

'You believe a man's perspective invalid?'

'Often.'

'A misandrist and a misogynist at the very same table.' He laughed and the trap closed. He'd equated them and Margot knew it.

'Virgil, my ally, my only man,' Gerard went on. 'What do you believe?'

Virgil gave a nervous laugh. 'Oh I'm not qualified to pass judgement, especially on art.'

'Or on women, I see,' Gerard said. 'Do you know, Virgil, when I first met you all those years ago, I thought, ah, there is a gay man.'

Virgil's eyebrows shot up.

'Gerard, enough,' Claude tried, but her brother was not hers to control.

'Is that an insult?' he gasped, feigned offence. 'In this company, surely homosexuals are welcome. Maybe that is true of women here but not of men. Equality, huh?'

He winked at Margot. She did not return the gesture.

I wished I had a pithy retort. I wished I had something other than shock at how this man was speaking. And guilt that I had brought him here, however unwittingly.

'I have had a few men,' Gerard continued. 'Not my favourite way to fuck, but I respect all orientations, Virgil. I don't judge you.'

Virgil, stunned as I was, muttered, 'I'm not gay.'

But Gerard was already zeroing in on his next target.

'*Pardonne-moi*, Claude. You have created a wonderful evening and we are all here to celebrate you. How is your work?'

Claude forced a smile. 'Fulfilling.'

'You are partner now?'

Claude's smile cracked and I felt sick. 'Not yet.'

Gerard frowned. I knew what was coming, but before I could deflect, he threw the knife.

'I thought you were promoted.'

'You were misinformed.'

'Didn't you tell me of a promotion some time ago? You didn't get it?'

Claude swallowed. This was a secret. *This* hadn't left this apartment. Claude had told one person other than me and they were not around this table. Her mother had a big mouth.

'I didn't.'

Denise and Virgil both looked at Claude with sad eyes, and the platitudes began. 'Claude, so sorry to hear that,' said Virgil. 'It's their loss, you totally deserve a promotion,' said Denise. Margot added more salt to the wound. Anais nodded and said Claude was brilliant. Then Virgil took her hand and squeezed it. The pity. The sympathy. All heartfelt and honest, but nonetheless utterly unwelcome, and Gerard knew it. Claude's steel gaze didn't waver from her brother.

'Thank you, all of you, but it was for the best,' she said, pushing back the tide, extracting her hand from Virgil's grip.

'Maman never said why,' Gerard continued, and I wanted to strangle him with his cravat. 'Was your work not up to standard?'

You fucking fuck, I almost said, but couldn't bring myself to speak.

'My work,' Claude began, jaw clenched, 'was excellent. The person who won the promotion slept with the senior partner.'

'And you didn't want to sleep with him?'

Male assumption. I rolled my eyes.

'I didn't want to sleep with *her*.'

Gerard frowned. 'But why not? Surely a fuck between women is of less consequence. Iris would forgive it, I'm sure, for a hefty pay rise. Wouldn't you, Iris?'

I started at the mention of my name. I tried to smile.

'Uh,' I tried, and Claude's gaze fell on me. The reason for her loss of the promotion. The one who had accused her of cheating. The reason for her embarrassment right now.

Gerard waved it away, drained his glass and reached for the bottle. The wine sloshed into the glass, spilling over the edges, staining the pristine tablecloth. That's what Gerard was. A stain. Indelible and vivid. Better to just throw out the whole thing.

Denise, bless her, coughed then and said in her light, bright voice, 'Marg and I have some news.'

All eyes turned to her. She wouldn't look at Gerard, unsurprisingly, but kept her attention flitting between everyone else.

'We've decided . . .' She smiled and blushed. 'Truthfully, I have finally managed to wear Margot down and she is on board with the idea. It's taken a few years, but we're here, finally, among friends . . .' A noticeable pause there. I smiled. 'Margot and I are going to start a family.'

A moment of shock, then an eruption of congratulations and 'How wonderful!' and 'You will make great parents!' while Gerard remained painfully silent. I hugged Denise and said, 'I'm so happy for you both.'

I caught Claude's eye and she smiled, wide and full, and said to me, 'Don't get any ideas.' And we all laughed.

Except Gerard. We all waited for it. The nasty, snide remark concealed inside the shell of an innocent question.

But none came.

He stood and raised his glass. 'Brava and congratulations to you both.'

We raised our glasses with him, waited for the sting in the tail.

'There is nothing more important in this world than family,' he said.

'Cheers to that,' Virgil said, and we clinked and drank, remaining firmly on edge.

The evening wound down around eleven. Dessert eaten, more wine consumed. Virgil and Anais left first. Anais had to be up especially early to work off the meal at the gym. She had a Vera Wang to fit into after all.

Denise and Margot sat on the couch with Claude, chatting happily about their future family, while I began to clear the table. Gerard stayed in his seat, watching me. Not helping. Not offering. I had to lean close to him to grab a plate. His fingers brushed my arm.

'I know it was you,' he said quietly. 'You lost Claude her big job.'

I shivered at his touch, at the closeness of his words. 'I don't know what you're talking about.'

'Hush, child. She must love you very much to forgive it. The Claude I knew . . .' He trailed off, shook his head. I didn't want to hear the rest, because I already knew it. The Claude he knew would have made me suffer. And she had.

I pulled away from him and dumped the dishes in the sink.

Then I went to the bathroom. A moment alone to clear my head. I set the water running, stared down at the swirling.

I didn't hear him come in.

But I heard the door close.

I looked up, hoping for Claude, but his bloated, alcoholic face stared at me in the mirror. He leant against the door. Blocking my only exit.

My heart thundered.

'What are you doing?' I said. 'Open the door.'

His eyes left my face, roamed down my body so slowly, so lasciviously I could almost feel it, like hands all over me.

'You're my centrepiece.'

'What?'

He took a step closer. I instinctively pushed back against the sink.

'For my collection. I see so much beauty on the outside. But I see that beauty is the shell of you, Iris. There is another you on the inside. Weak and frail, full of darkness. Like a rotten tooth. You are perfect.'

Another step closer. I couldn't move. Nowhere to run. He stood between me and the door, his bulk blocking it completely.

'You need to get out, now,' I said, but there was no strength in my voice. It was all tremble. All fear.

He smiled on one side of his face. There were bits of Claude in his expressions, in the shape of his eyes and nose. A resemblance that suddenly made me sick.

'Do you want that? Truly? Let me paint you. I will show the world the real Iris.'

He came closer and closer. His smell filled the room. Wine and meat and sweat and something else. Something I recoiled from but couldn't put a name to. A primal response.

'Get out.'

Then his hands were on my bare arms, squeezing hard and unshakeable, his grimy nails digging into the soft underside of my upper arm. He pressed his body against me. Pain flared where my back met the sink, the porcelain sharp against my spine and hips and him heavy and flat against me. I felt his excitement. Felt the aggression, his potential for violence against my thigh. Then his face was at my neck. He breathed me in. His touch was acid on my skin. His closeness brought nausea up my throat and I wanted to scream, but still some stupid part of me didn't want to embarrass Claude. Wanted to protect her from the truth about her brother.

Something wet touched my neck and he murmured, 'Beautiful,' in one long, hot sigh of a word.

Something in me snapped. All my strength gathered at once and I pushed him away.

He looked shocked. Then angry. Then his fist balled at his side, Claude's temper alive in his eyes.

The door opened.

Claude. Thank God. *Claude. Help me*, I wanted to say. I wanted to speak before he could. But I was frozen and mute.

'Denise and Margot have left. Time for you to go too, Gerard,' she said, her voice level and cold. 'The doorman will call you a cab.'

Gerard's aggression, his sneer, broke into a wide, loose smile. He turned and embraced his sister. She locked eyes with me over his shoulder. Just for a second. They were as cold as her voice.

'A wonderful evening,' he said as they both left the bathroom. Their voices, their pleasantries and goodbyes, faded with distance until finally the front door opened, closed, and the apartment fell silent.

I almost collapsed, as if the only thing keeping me standing was caught between fight and flight. The sudden pressure release made me stumble. I caught myself on the sink. Stared at the mirror. The places he'd touched me seemed to glow neon red in the glass. His spit glistened on my neck. I pulled a dozen tissues from the box and wetted them, scrubbed my neck until it turned pink and raw, but it wasn't enough. I still felt him.

'What was that?' Claude's voice made me jump.

I looked at her in the mirror. Couldn't answer. Didn't know how.

'What was that?' she asked again.

'Nothing.' Because what was it?

It was your brother trying to assault me. Why can't you say that? Same reason you make excuses for Claude. You brush off what she did as lesser than it was, as your fault, as an accident, as a moment of passion directed the wrong way. Nothing to it. Nothing to admit. Why?

Because you deserve it, came the voice. The lilting, whispering, not-there voice. My voice.

'It didn't look like nothing, Iris,' Claude said, but her tone didn't carry worry or sympathy. It was thick with accusation.

I straightened. 'What did it look like to you?'

Her knuckles whitened on the door handle. Her eyes, in one moment beautiful, in the next deadly, bored into me, down to my marrow. She held me there, impaled.

'It looked like you trying to fuck my brother.'

Shock made me laugh, but it wasn't funny and Claude wasn't joking.

'Are . . . are you serious?' I said, because how? *How* could she be serious?

She took a step into the room. 'Is that why you invited him?'

I gaped. 'I didn't! He invited himself.'

'And you just couldn't say no, could you, Iris?'

Her voice was simmering a degree under hot-boiled rage. She'd drunk too much and I couldn't help but see her brother in her eyes. The same cruelty beneath the good-looking, outwardly respectable veneer. But it was all a mistake.

'Claude.' I tried to keep my voice calm, but inside, I was shaking. Inside, I was afraid. 'I don't want to fuck your brother. I don't want anything to do with your brother. He came in here after me and he . . .'

Another step closer. I instinctively moved away. My back hit the sink. Again.

'He what?'

What good comes from telling her? It ruins an already tenuous relationship with her brother.

If she believes you . . .

'He was drunk,' I started, faltered. 'He . . . grabbed me. My arm.'

Claude closed the gap between us. Her eyes never left mine. Her breathing never changed.

She looked at my right arm, at the already fading red mark he'd left. She placed her hand over the area. Tender, soft.

'And then what?' she said, a whisper now but no less vicious.

I closed my eyes and immediately the moment replayed. The smell of him. The pressure against me. His face at my neck.

'He . . .' I felt the tears heat in my eyes. 'He said he wanted to paint me.'

'He says that about every woman he fucks.'

The simple, matter-of-fact cruelty in her words shocked me, made the tears fall, made the anger come.

'I told him to get out, but he pushed me against the sink.'

'Like this?' Claude shoved me hard. The porcelain cut into my back a second time, and I cried out. The anger rose higher.

'Claude . . .'

'What next?' When I didn't answer, she dug her nails into my arm, clenched her fist around me like I was paper to be crushed. 'What next?'

I looked up at the ceiling, tried to focus on the light fittings. 'He . . . put his face to my neck . . . and . . .'

She repeated his movement, breathed me in like he had. I felt her breath on my neck, rushing down my spine. 'And?'

Count the lights, I told myself. Count the cracks in the paint. Tell her what she wants to hear.

'He . . .' I closed my eyes against the memory, the feeling of his tongue, the burning in my skin that would never go away. 'He . . . kissed my neck.'

Claude's lips brushed my skin. Once. Then again. Her touch turned tender, her grip on my arm loosened. Her other hand moved up my body, to my chest, then rested gently on my collarbone.

'And?' she murmured. 'What did you do?'

'I pushed him away,' I said. My voice was weak, a whisper. My chest would barely move to breathe, my heart almost ceased to beat.

Her hand moved around my throat, thumb stroking my windpipe, fingers playing in the light hairs at the base of my skull. She kissed me again.

'You pushed him away?'

'Yes.' Barely a word, little more than a breath.

'I don't believe you,' she said, and her grip on my throat tightened.

My eyes sprang open. She lifted her head and our eyes met. Pure fear and pure hate locked together, neither able to look away.

Her grip tightened further. The air rushed out of me.

'Claude . . .' I tried, but she wasn't Claude any more. Some evil thing had taken her over and she wasn't seeing me.

I grabbed her hand with my free one. Scratched, pulled, dug my nails in. But her grip was iron. She pressed me hard against the sink. My eyes bulged, turned red. All the air left me. My eyes rolled. The ceiling swam. The tiny paint cracks turned to chasms and swooped down to swallow me.

She let go of my arm.

And both hands were on my throat.

Two vice grips squeezing harder and harder.

I was going to die. The words ran through my head at speed. Over and over in endless loops and swirls, and here I come darkness, here I come Father, here I come cosmic nothing, and again and again I'm going to die, I'm going to die, but it wasn't scary it wasn't dark oblivion because there were stars bursting in my eyes, stars I didn't know, stars I'd never seen, wrong stars. Wrong stars. Then the fear came. How can the stars be wrong? This is bad. No. I don't want to go there. I don't want to go where the stars aren't mine and my father's because he won't be there. Don't let me be where he isn't.

No. No. NO. NO.

I could see again.

I could feel again.

I was in my body again.

I was on the floor. The lines of the tiles made a map to the far side of the room. To a woman. Her back to the wall, her knees drawn up, her head down, hair draped over her shins.

Her hands were shaking and she was crying, and I remembered.

I tried to say her name, but needles of pain shot through my throat and I couldn't speak.

I pushed myself up and regretted it. The pain in my throat exploded up into my head and down into my chest. My eyes were too big for their sockets. My arms had no strength. My whole body trembled, as if my bones were vibrating.

I managed to sit myself up against the wall before Claude noticed. When she looked up, her eyes widened. Her face was awash with tears and black streaks of mascara. Her head began to shake side to side like a metronome, and fresh tears fell.

'I'm sorry, I'm sorry, I'm sorry,' she kept saying, sometimes in English, sometimes in French, her voice fading in and out with her breath, with each burst of tears, with each surge of guilt.

My hand went to my throat and I winced at my own touch. I swallowed glass and salt. I breathed slowly, as if too quick would close my throat again. I concentrated on my heartbeat. Still there. Still strong.

I tried to get up, pull myself up with the sink, with the wall, with the towel rack. But I was weak and I struggled and then I felt her hands on me. Like ice. Like fire.

I flinched away, fell back down.

'Iris,' she said, all whispers and tears. 'Let me . . . I can help . . .'

I don't want your help, I wanted to shout, but I couldn't speak a word.

I nodded. I let her.

Upright, the world swam. My head filled with bright spots, pulling me close to fainting then letting me go. Claude's arm around my waist, holding my wrist, felt both awful and reassuring.

She helped me to the bedroom, helped me lie down. Brought me water. I sipped it, coughed and wanted to cry.

She sat on the bed and wouldn't look at me. Red-hot rage blazed inside me. I tried to examine my throat, but it was one big bruise. I swallowed a few more times and it got easier.

'I'm sorry,' Claude said after a while. 'I don't know . . . I don't know who I am when I get angry. I don't like her.'

'Me neither,' I croaked, barely a whisper, but she heard. She looked at me for a second, then looked away.

I'd never seen her like this. Full of shame, full of guilt. A cowed, undone woman.

'I'm trying,' she said with a touch more force. 'But when I saw you with Gerard . . .' She shook her head.

'Nothing happened,' I said.

'I know.'

'Do you?'

She looked at me then but didn't answer.

'I love you, Iris. And the thought of you and him, of his hands on you. Especially after you accuse me of cheating. For me to see that . . . I lost my temper.' She bit her lip.

I didn't ask the question burning in my mind. *Did you want to kill me?* Because what answer could she give? A second's hesitation and my marriage, my life, was over. Instant denial and how could I ever be sure she meant it? Better not to ask. Better not to even put the idea in her head.

Could I leave?

I looked at Claude, the expensive dress dishevelled, strap hanging off a shoulder, and despite myself, despite my fear and the hate that had grown in me that evening, despite the pain and memory of her slap, her fist, her cutting tone, I loved her. Still and deeply.

And I hated myself for it.

'I need to sleep,' I said in my broken, weak voice.

Claude nodded. She went to pat my leg under the duvet, but I rolled away. She lingered a moment, deciding what route to take, anger or understanding. Finally she made up her mind, stood and walked to the door.

'I'll check on you later,' she said.

I heard the door close, and a few seconds later, the sound of dishes and tidying.

I clutched the pillow close to me and wept silently into the fibres.

How did I get here? Did I want to stay here? Would it get better if I did?

Before I could find answers, sleep and darkness took me. For a moment, as my consciousness hung on the precipice, I thought I was dying all over again. For a moment, I wanted to.

After

Nothing was normal.

I woke wincing against the sunlight, sweating my white T-shirt grey. The cabin steamed, cheeks red, lips dry, mouth a pit of sand, ankle throbbing and stiff but bearable. A fire burned in the stove. A fire I hadn't lit.

Other Iris was in the kitchen area, assessing my supplies, pulling out the space food, tutting and throwing it on the countertop.

I coughed and she turned.

'You sleep like the dead. I haven't exactly been quiet. That fire took the best part of two hours to get going. Had to cut the wood down to kindling before it would take, old trick my dad taught me. That axe out there? That blade's for shit, you know.'

My chest ached and I didn't want to be around her, couldn't bear to hear stories about her dad who was my dad only better. Alive. I pulled myself up, wincing at my stiff ankle.

I dressed in warm clothes, almost dry thanks to her fire, and felt close to human again. I tied up my long, boring hair and glanced enviously at hers.

I grabbed an empty water bottle and limped outside. I felt her eyes on my back. My ankle was sore and still swollen, but with the broom as a crutch, I could get around without much pain. I hopped to the stream and filled up my bottle, drank half in one long gulp. She followed, watching with her arms crossed over her chest. I tried not to look. If she was anything like me – I almost laughed – her defences would go up as soon as I started asking personal questions.

'Are you going to talk to me?' she asked.

My voice. Same annoyed tone. Same inflection.

I didn't look up. Told myself to make a plan.

God, Iris, do you hear yourself? Make a plan to talk to a hallucination and tease out information about an alternate life you maybe could have had?

I wanted to slap myself.

'You're going to have to at some point,' Iris said.

I heard her sigh. Heard her pace behind me. Knew, without looking, she'd be throwing her arms up and shaking her head, because that's what I would do.

She called out, 'You can't ignore this.'

She was right. Looking at her, at me, at a me so much healthier, happier, better prepared, was agony. The gnawing darkness that had pushed me towards the overhang, that had wished I'd had a rope so I could end it quicker, clawed at me from the inside. First it tested my edges, nudging at the chain link, pacing the perimeter. Then it began to whisper.

You know what you did.

It's your fault.

It's why you deserved what Claude did to you.

That's why you're out here, Iris. That's why you're playing woodsman, trying to please him, fulfil his dreams so he'll forgive you.

He'll never forgive you.

That's why you see Claude, not him. Because he blames you. He hates you. And you'll never have a better life.

You're going to die here.

I splashed my face because it was the only thing I could think of that might shock some sense into me. I tried to stand, and in a moment Other Iris's arms were under mine, helping me up. So strange. So foreign. And yet so completely known. It wasn't like being touched by a stranger. More like when you sleep on your arm and wake up numb. It's your hand, you can see it moving as it touches your other arm, but you can't feel it.

When I was stable, she let go and I finally met her eyes.

'Look,' she said, sighing like I sigh, 'I'm not going anywhere. I literally can't. No matter which direction I go, and I've tried them all, the path brings me right back here. To you.'

'What's your point?' I said,

'My point, is that there is a reason for it. The universe, aliens, God, whatever, has put us here for a reason. Which means we need to figure out what it is.'

'You said that before. Have you figured it out yet?'

Her eyes narrowed at my petulance but I didn't care. I found myself hating her. Her perfect skin. The hair I wanted and had to give up. The clothes I'd needed. The gear I'd forgotten.

'No. I haven't,' she said. 'It clearly takes both of us.'

'Right, right.' I felt Claude's mannerisms, her lack of patience, rise inside me. I moved my hands like she did, I felt her smirk on my mouth. 'And I'm supposed to believe you why? Because you look like me? Because you say so? Or because you're so desperate for something extraordinary to happen you're willing to believe anything? Do you really think the universe gives a shit about you?'

I was talking to myself. Shouting in the woods like a madwoman.

She recoiled. 'I don't want to fight with you.'

Everyone fights with you, Jane. Your mother, your sister, Ellis, Claude. Life is one big fight for you.

'Too bad,' I muttered.

Besides, this wasn't even real.

'What happened to you?' she said.

Everything. 'Nothing.' I crossed my arms over my chest.

Anger flared in Other Iris's cheeks. They reddened from nose to ear, just like mine.

'On my ninth birthday, my father gave me a telescope,' she said. 'I watched Carl Sagan with him, and from that moment, that exact moment, I believed in the impossible. I still do. Your father gave you a telescope too, the same one as I have. You carried a *telescope* into the woods with you.'

I hugged myself. Pushed my own memory of that night away. I couldn't answer. She knew that meant yes.

'What happened to you to make you like this?'

I killed him. The words hit me like a sledgehammer. I forced them back down into the pit, slammed the trapdoor closed.

'I grew up.'

She shook her head. 'No you didn't. If you did, that telescope wouldn't be in the cabin, set up to view Venus.' Then her eyes brightened. 'Maybe this is why we're here. Maybe you have to get the wonder back.'

'Oh fuck off.' I laughed, because if I didn't, I'd throw up. 'This isn't an after-school special or some eighties movie where everyone lives happily ever after. God, the universe has a fucked-up sense of humour putting me with you, Miss Anne-with-an-E.'

Missile on target. She took a few steps away, circled back full of anger. 'What do you suggest? Because in case you hadn't noticed, we're trapped here.'

A light bulb flashed in my head. 'There's a radio.'

'A radio?'

'An emergency one, in the cabin.'

'And you're just mentioning this now!' She pressed her fingers to the bridge of her nose. 'Where is it?'

I limped inside, dug under the kitchen counter and dragged out the green metal survival box I hadn't looked at since I'd arrived. Inside, among the flares and candles, was the two-way radio. A bulky black walkie-talkie-like thing with a telescopic antennae that reached almost to the ceiling when Iris opened it. I smiled.

She pushed some buttons, flipped some switches. It seemed intact.

'The battery's dead,' she said. 'It looks like it hasn't been used since the eighties.'

'Can we change it, or charge it?'

She sighed and threw it back in the box. 'I have no idea. Besides, what would that accomplish?'

'We could radio for help.'

'And if they get here and are trapped like us? Or can't find us at all? If we can't get out, what makes you think a search-and-rescue team could get in?'

'I don't know. It was just an idea.'

'We need better ideas.'

'You come up with one then!'

God, I was infuriating sometimes.

But if she was right and we had to solve some riddle before the forest would let us go, I had an idea of what mine might be. That blank page. Claude's name, gone over and over with thick black ink. My phantom.

'Why are you out here?' I asked.

'I told you, I'm hiking to Randall Peak.'

'Why?'

She shrugged, suddenly defensive, arms crossing her chest, suddenly that light tone.

'I like hiking.'

I smiled. 'My voice goes like that when I lie too. Or it used to. I've got better at hiding it. Tell me the truth.'

She didn't say anything for a few seconds, just looked at me. My face. The differences between us. She held my eyes and I felt a sudden yearning. I wanted to know her. I hated her but I loved her. And I wanted to connect with her but I didn't. I wanted her to go away but I wanted her to stay. She was me but she wasn't. Are you real? I wanted to ask. But the more I spoke with her, the more muddled that answer became.

She could be.

But she couldn't be.

'Tell me the truth,' I said again.

'I'm taking a vacation,' she said with a shrug. 'I haven't been hiking for a while. I had some vacation days saved up. I went hiking a lot with my father.'

'Me too,' I said, and in that moment, the anger and tension between us melted away. We were the same. We were Iris, we were Jane, and I desperately needed her to be real because that meant I wasn't alone.

'I don't know about you,' she said, 'but I need a drink.'

'It's only just noon.'

'Five somewhere, right?' She laughed, got up and left the cabin.

I followed, watched her jog to her tent while I hobbled to the fire pit. It was so good to be outside, in the air and light, after so long trapped by the rain. The sun warmed my back and the fecund scents of the forest rose from the earth, seeped from the bark of drying trees, steamed from grateful leaves. Iris returned with a bottle of good rum, her own collapsible cup and the GO TIGERS mug from the cabin. I watched her move, free and quick, unhampered by injury, and my jealousy turned green as moss.

She set a waterproof blanket on the ground on the opposite side of the fire pit and reclined against a tree stump. She poured rum into her cup and mine, and downed hers with a wince, poured another, took a sip before she began to speak.

'Are you married?' she asked.

I nodded. 'You?'

She smiled and held up her ring finger. A thin gold band caught the light. 'Four years.'

I wondered if Other Claude was better than mine. She could hardly be worse.

'Tell me about her,' I said.

Iris drained her cup, refilled it, offered me a top-up but I hadn't even taken a sip.

'She's great,' she said. 'Sweet, kind, beautiful, we share the same interests.'

Sweet? Kind? Claude? 'I'm not seeing a problem.'

'There isn't a problem. Why would you ask that?'

'Sorry, I just thought, as you're out here alone . . . She didn't come with you.'

'She's not in the best shape to be out in the wilderness.' She saw my frown and smiled. 'She's pregnant.'

Well, that was unexpected.

'Wow. Uh. Kids . . .' I had no idea what to say. How different could her Claude be? I suddenly wanted to meet her. See the Claude I'd always wanted. The woman I'd always dreamed was in there somewhere and yet I could never coax out. A sudden bubble of hope grew in my chest. I clutched at it, cradled it.

'I know,' she said with a gentle head shake. 'I didn't expect it. Never thought I'd want kids, but when Bella suggested it—'

'You married *Bella*?'

She looked at me. 'You didn't?'

I shook my head. 'I didn't even consider it.'

The defences went up. 'Maybe my Bella is better than yours.'

'I doubt it,' I said.

Sweet, kind Bella. The decision I'd often wondered over, the one I'd spoken aloud to Ellis more than once. What if I'd never let her go?

She took another sip and said, 'We met at a lecture. She was doing a thesis . . .'

'. . . on astrology in old paintings.'

'Yes! I was twenty-four and an idiot and I thought that was so hot. We moved in together about four months later, into my tiny apartment . . .'

'. . . with Hubble photos on the bedroom ceiling.' I smiled, felt a warm something bloom in my chest. 'I miss that place.' And her.

The level of rum in Iris's bottle was lower than I'd expected, I hadn't noticed her pour another.

'I'd never been so happy,' she said, eyes on the cup. 'It was great, you know. It was . . . it was good.' She smiled. 'This one time, we'd been married about a year and had just moved into a bigger place, I came home from work to find she'd made a fort out of boxes in the living room. You know, sheet over the top, pillows inside, twinkly lights. Our bed was still flat-packed, so we slept in the fort that night. We ordered pizza. We watched a movie. She made that place home . . .'

'But?' I knew the answer before she said it. I'd felt it then, the fear of that suburban life my father so detested, but now? I yearned for its simplicity.

'I didn't notice it for a few years. The routine. Bella got a job in an archive. I don't even know what she was doing there, and when she started to tell me, I zoned out because *yawn*. I was pushing papers at a supply company. I didn't even care any more that it was for NASA. I stopped saying it. I used to drop in the bragging rights, but by then, it didn't matter. We lived in the suburbs. We had our morning routine and every day it was the same. Same breakfast, same kiss goodbye, same commute, same lunch in the same Tupperware in the same bag in the same place in the refrigerator at the office. Same commute home, same faces on the subway, same clot of people on the sidewalk. Same "Hey, Ris" greeting, same kiss on the same cheek, same four meals in rotation, same shows on TV, same conversation, "how was work, fine, how was yours, fine". The same sex, the same dreams. And then it would start all over again. I was stuck in this hamster wheel. My life began to feel like an endless rerun of a boring episode of *Friends*. The One Where Iris Cracks Up.'

She rubbed her face. I thought I saw tears. But I couldn't feel sympathy for her. She was fretting over a simple, content, safe life while I had been in danger of losing mine altogether. She lived in dull harmony, while I lived on the edge of a knife.

'There were no more blanket forts or Hubble photos or spontaneous evenings in the city. We used to go to this little Italian place tucked down an alley, but I realised Bella only went there because she didn't want to try anything else. She decorated the house. A few of her favourite paintings, but otherwise it could have come straight out of a catalogue. Ready-made home! We stopped having adventures. We stopped having *personalities*. And you want to know the worst part?'

I smiled, sadly. 'She loved it.'

Iris raised her cup and nodded. 'She *loved* it. And me . . . I don't know what happened to me. So I'm here trying to figure it out.'

'Why now?'

'The baby is due in a few weeks. And then . . . I don't know who I'm going to become.'

I shook my head. Job. Home. Loving wife. Happy home. A family. A chance to undo mistakes our own parents made. And you're running away?

You have no idea, I wanted to say. You have no idea how lucky you are.

'Do you love her?' I said instead.

The question hung in the air like a bad smell.

'Of course. She's my wife.'

'Then why can't you tell her all this?'

'Because she's my wife.'

I laughed, though it wasn't funny.

'Think that did it?' she said. 'Think we're free?'

'Want to go find out?'

She made a face, drained her cup, but didn't move.

She had the perfect life and she took it for granted. But what about him?

'What's this got to do with your father?'

She frowned. The bottle was half empty now and she wasn't stopping, yet there was no slur in her words.

'Nothing. Why would you ask that?' A strange tone in her voice, high, like she was lying and angry about it. She was hiding something, I was sure of it.

'You said you came here because you used to take hikes with him,' I said.

'So what? My marriage has nothing to do with my father.'

Yes it does. Because mine does. 'My father hated living in the suburbs. Yours did too. You found yourself repeating his life, so you did what he did and ran away.'

Ran away. If only he'd just run away. My throat clenched, but I breathed through it. Did he? Did he die too? Did you kill him too?

'Fuck you.' She spat the words and I saw the parts of myself I didn't like. The drunk part. The red cheeks. The wet eyes. The parts of me Claude must have seen and hated and that's why she—

'You don't know my father,' Iris said. 'You don't know anything about him.'

'Yes I do. We went to Banff together, remember that?'

'Shut up.'

'And we went on a hike up past Lake Louise. To the mountain with the lake full of grey fish. You remember what he did?'

'He wasn't well. He's better now,' she whispered.

Present tense hit me like an avalanche. He is. IS. Over there, in her world, in her life, he's alive. Maybe they're estranged. Maybe that's why she doesn't want to talk about him. Maybe she sided with Mother and Fischer. Maybe he left and she hates him for it. But it didn't matter. I could fix it. I would fix it.

Hearing her talk about Bella, how perfect it sounded, how she had a living, breathing father, I knew what I had to do. If she didn't want that life, I would take it for myself.

I calmed my heart. Forced the redness from my cheeks and the bright tears from my eyes. I'd pushed too far, too fast, but I was desperate. I needed to be careful now. It's not like she could go anywhere, but she could clam up. She could wait me out. I didn't want to end up in a game of chicken with myself.

I swallowed hard and coughed, cleared the buzzing excitement from my throat.

'You're right,' I said slowly. 'He wasn't well. And neither are we. That's why we're here.'

'I don't want to talk about him,' she snapped, then softened with another mouthful of rum. 'I want to talk about you. I spilled my guts. Your turn.'

'I don't—'

'Yes you do. Let's start simple. If you didn't marry Bella, who did you marry?'

I wished I had more alcohol. 'Claude.'

Anger replaced by surprise.

'Who the hell is Claude?'

Isn't that the million-dollar question? You can do this, Jane. Keep her on the hook. Keep her talking. Give her enough but not too much. Make her feel sorry for you. Make her trust you.

'About two weeks before I met Bella, I was in a terrible hipster bar with Ellis and some friends. Leaving drinks.'

She flicked back through her mental catalogue, found the night, nodded.

'And there was this woman at the bar. She was knocking her foot on the metal siding.'

Her eyes widened. 'You married *her*?'

I nodded. 'I left Bella for her.'

'Fuck. She was beautiful. What happened?'

'I thought I was in love. I thought she loved me back. She didn't. At least not that much. She cheated on me,' I said, because it was the least of Claude's crimes. 'I found out a couple of weeks ago and so here I am.'

She narrowed her eyes. My eyes. 'I call bullshit.'

'What? You can't call bullshit. That's what happened.'

'But it's not everything, is it?'

'It is.'

She smiled. 'There's that tone. Come on. If you can't tell me, who can you tell?'

The words choked me. Caught in my throat like fish hooks. 'I . . .' I coughed, but they wouldn't move. 'She cheated on me. That's it.'

Iris frowned, the amusement gone now. 'Tell me.'

I shook my head. Claude's black-ink name flashed in my head. Her phantom laugh echoed through the forest.

Iris sat up, leant towards me. 'Tell me.'

I looked at her face, saw lines I didn't know, lines I'd known all my life. She was me. I was her. We were each other and I couldn't admit what happened. Not even to myself.

'Please,' Iris said, and I felt white-hot tears prick my eyes.

'It doesn't matter,' I managed. 'She did what she did and it was awful and so I came to the woods to escape her.'

'Escape?'

I closed my eyes. Tears fell. Sorrow and fear tinged with hope. *He* was alive. Somewhere. I'd find him and I'd be free of Claude. Two birds. I looked at Iris. One stone.

I felt Claude around me. Her arms draped over my shoulders, her soft, breathy voice in my ear. *You deserved it. You deserved it all. You still do.*

I leapt to my feet. Threw the phantom from my back. And regretted it. My ankle screamed and I almost fell.

She caught me.

'Iris,' my other self said, standing now too, her voice a balm on my stripped skin. 'Iris. Look at me.'

I did.

'What just happened?'

I shook my head. 'Nothing. It was nothing.'

'What aren't you telling me?'

Everything.

I pushed her away. 'What aren't you telling *me*? Why won't you talk about our father?'

Her lip curled, face turned deeper red. 'It's none of your business.'

'Fuck you. It's my business. Whatever you did has trapped us here!'

'Fine!' She threw up her hands. 'Don't tell me. Let's just be mad at each other until the food runs out and we starve to death.'

She had a point. I closed my eyes, took a breath, felt calm return.

'Tell me something. Tell me *anything*,' she pleaded. 'Like, how did you get that scar?'

She pointed to my cheek. I touched the tiny white scar from Claude's ring. Suddenly I was back there. Sitting on the floor, clutching my cheek. All because I'd lashed out like I just had. All because I'd accused someone of something unfair.

She had to trust me. I had to trust her.

'Claude hit me,' I said in a whisper. Just testing the words. How they fit my mouth. How they filled the air around me with alien sound.

'What did you say?' she asked. So close I could smell the sweet alcohol on her breath.

I looked in her eyes. Say it again. Make it real. I breathed deep, let my eyes fill with tears, didn't stop them flowing.

'Claude . . . She . . . she broke my heart.'

The words were glass on my tongue. Slicing the meat of me as I forced them out. I'd never said that to another person. Never even said it to myself.

'Tell me,' Iris said.

My breath shuddered in my chest and tears burned my eyes, wouldn't stop, wouldn't cool, and I heard her, all around me. Claude. Heard her laugh, her whispers, felt her kiss, her fist, her love, her hate, all in one terrible, painful moment.

Then Iris, Other Iris, other me, took over. She wrapped her arms around me and I was cocooned and protected and the guilt flooded me head to toe. She insulated me. I did. She did. I didn't know where I stopped and she began. Her words, her whispers drowned out Claude.

'What did she do?' she murmured into my ear, pushed Claude back into the darkness. But Claude wouldn't go.

What did she do . . .

Then I was laughing. Laughing over the tears. Laughing off her protection.

I pulled away from Iris. And there was Claude, over her shoulder, leaning against a tree in that dress. That black dress. Arms crossed, smiling at me with a conspirator's smile. It's you and me, Iris, she was saying. You can't bear to be without me.

I wiped my tears. Other Iris looked at me, frowning, cheeks red with rum, mouth open because I was laughing. I was still laughing.

'What did she do?' I said, and looked at Claude. The snake-like smile grew; she arched her eyebrow. How could this milquetoast version of me understand? How could this poor suburban wife with her vanilla life possibly comprehend our love, our passion, what we'd done to each other?

'What did she *do*?' Iris asked again.

My laugh died. I died. My voice became small and weak under Claude's gaze.

You can take her life, Claude's eyes said, but you'll never stop loving me, because you'll never stop hating yourself.

I turned to myself. 'Nothing I didn't deserve.'

Before

'What do you want to tell the office?' Claude asked the Monday morning after her birthday. 'You can't go to work. Not like this.'

I'd spent the weekend in the second bedroom. Alone. Claude would bring me tea, soups and anything I could eat through a straw.

'I don't know,' I said. Every word was an effort, the syllables dragged over broken glass.

Claude sat on the end of the bed and I drew my legs up and away from her. She noticed.

'I could ... I could say you were mugged walking home on Friday night?'

I coughed, and a spray of red-hot splinters hit the inside of my throat. 'Mugged?'

'Why not? They won't ask too many questions with that story. Lots of sympathy, not many questions. That's what we want.'

I coughed again, winced, and eased myself back down to the pillow. I glanced out the window. A story. What had my life become that I needed a story to hide what happened?

Better than admitting the truth, right, Jane?

Claude made the call.

She was in the living room but had left the bedroom door open so I could hear. I didn't have my boss's direct number written down – why would I? He was in the office next door and I tried my best to avoid him – so Claude had to go through the switchboard. She swore when the receptionist put her on hold, and after a few minutes began tapping her foot. I shrank against my pillows, drew the quilt to my chin. Just one more thing I'd done to make her angry.

'Finally,' she said as the line connected. 'Yes, this is Claude Marceau, Iris's wife. She won't be coming to work for at least a week.'

Pause. Dan, my manager, no doubt blathering about urgent invoices.

'She was attacked on her journey home on Friday evening . . . Yes, that's what I said. Attacked . . .'

Attacked. People on TV got attacked. People in horror movies got attacked. People in crime novels and sensationalist magazines got attacked. Masked strangers in alleys, knife-wielding men on dark streets, gangs of roaming thieves. People didn't get attacked in their homes, by their spouse.

But they do, Jane. All the time. And you are one of them.

Something broke in me then as I heard Claude lie and lie and do it with small talk and a joke and barely an apology. Everything else that had happened I'd brushed off, made excuses for and tried to forget, but this? She lied to protect me, to make things easier for me, to avoid intrusive questions and give me my privacy.

She's lying to protect herself. To make it seem like it never happened. You've been mugged, Iris. That's the truth now.

Claude hung up and breezed back into the bedroom with a smile. 'You have two weeks, full pay. You're welcome, my love.'

She kissed my forehead and disappeared into the bathroom to get ready. Twenty minutes later, she called out an *au revoir* and left me alone under the weight of my new reality.

That afternoon, Dante the doorman knocked with a delivery. My office had signed a card and sent a fruit basket. *Get well soon, from your friends at Hoss Oil & Gas.* I burned the card in the sink and threw the fruit in the trash.

It took a month for my throat to heal. For the bruises to go down enough to be covered by make-up. For the crescent cuts on my arm to fade. For Claude to ask if we could sleep in our bedroom again and for me to agree.

I spent those weeks after her birthday shut up in the apartment. Emerging from the bedroom when she went to work, returning there when I heard her key in the door. She'd bring me my favourite food, ignore the 'no eating in the bedroom' rule, rent movies she thought I'd like, buy me gifts – flowers, jewellery, even a NASA sweater. She was trying. But I wasn't convinced. The niceties came from her guilt. After the bruises healed and my voice returned to normal, my fear faded, along with my anger.

Claude was at work when a call came through on the building intercom. I hauled myself from my blanket cocoon on the couch and pressed the button. Dante the doorman's crackling voice came through the speakers.

'A visitor here for you, madam. A Mr Ryan, says you are expecting him.'

Ellis. I wasn't expecting him. But perhaps I should have been.

'Send him up,' I said.

I looked at the apartment. Except for a few spots, it was immaculate as always. Claude hadn't let my trauma or her mistake mess up the place. I was a different story. Hair ragged and greasy, week-old clothes. I hadn't showered in days and hadn't left these four rooms since Claude's birthday. Ellis had called, dozens of times, inviting me to bars, to his, to movie night, and I'd always found an excuse. He'd never just turned up before. In fact, I didn't think he'd ever been in my apartment. I'd always felt guilty, considering his situation – one bedroom, bathroom shared with a dozen strangers, on a street nicknamed Murder Row – but he was here now and I'd let him in and he'd see I didn't belong here either.

I could picture him riding up in the elevator. Running his fingers over the gilding, straightening his T-shirt – I imagined a black shirt printed with the poster from *The Thing* – and coming up with all kinds of quips or nicknames for me when he saw where I lived.

I opened the door, ready for when he arrived, and tidied my lair as best I could. Folded some blankets, threw away takeout cartons, washed my face, hid the state of my hair in a ponytail. Claude wouldn't want a visitor seeing this mess.

He's not a visitor, Jane. He's your best (only) friend.

Ellis's head peeked around the open door. 'Am I in the right place?'

'Very funny. Come in,' I said from the kitchen, tried to play the host as Claude would.

He closed the door behind him but didn't move. He stared at the apartment. I'd forgotten how impressive it was. He tugged at his shirt. Not *The Thing*, but *Halloween*. Right director, wrong movie.

I took two beers from the fridge and set them on the counter.

'Should I take off my shoes . . . or, like, disinfect myself?' he said, still at the door.

I smiled, popped the caps off the beers. 'There's a decon chamber in the back; make sure you use a good handful of lice powder while you're at it.'

Finally, Ellis moved, drawn by the beer. After a long drink, he seemed to relax. 'I knew Claude was in finance, but this is . . . I mean . . . This isn't a hotel? You live here?'

I nodded, ushered him to the couch, where we sat, slightly awkward.

'I live here.'

He looked around again, spotted the terrace. His eyes widened. 'Can I?'

'Go for it.'

The wind whipped his hair and shirt as he stepped outside. I watched him from behind the glass. Wondering if I'd looked like that when I first set foot in this place. Wondering why Claude had invited me back. Was I so starry-eyed, she imagined I'd be so grateful for all this that I'd never leave, no matter what she did?

I put the thought from my head and joined my friend. We sat on the terrace in the sun, drinking, always drinking, until we got through the niceties to the meat of his visit.

'Twenty-three,' he said after I sat down with another round of beers. 'That's how many times I called you. Seven is how many you answered and zero is how many times I've seen you in over a month. Explain, princess.'

Ah there, the first quip. I rolled my eyes.

'I've been . . . busy, I guess.'

'Busy Iris still washes her hair. Busy Iris returns calls. This Iris, I'm not sure who she is.'

Me neither.

Ellis leant forward. 'The mugging . . . was it just a mugging?'

The mugging. Claude's lie. I felt my insides break.

'I mean,' he continued, 'did they . . .? Were you . . .? You know?'

I shook my head. 'No, nothing like that.' And yet I felt Gerard's hands on me all over again. The violation. The stink of him.

Lie, Iris. Lie quickly and lie well and then everything can go back to normal.

'The mugging . . . it wasn't what you're thinking. They stole my wallet and phone, left some bruises, that's all. I've lived in the city for a decade and nothing like that has ever happened before. I didn't feel safe going out and then I felt stupid for thinking that so I didn't return your calls. I'm sorry, Ell. But I'm feeling good now. Better,' I said, and smiled. 'Everything is getting better.'

He regarded me for a moment, a deep frown across his brow.

'Really, Ell. I'm okay now.'

Just seeing him, just having a conversation where I wasn't worried about saying the wrong thing, upsetting Claude, where I wasn't flinching with every word, had made all the difference. I did feel better. I did feel okay. There was a world outside this apartment. I took his hand, gave it a squeeze.

'Stop being so serious,' I said.

'This is serious business.' He put his hand on top of mine, then broke into a smile. 'But hark! We have a queen here in this freakin' *palace* who needs to get out, get wasted and get home safe again. I can oblige, my lady. I'll be your knight, or queen's guard, or . . .'

'Jester?'

He laughed. 'That doorman of yours looked at me like I was a joke. I don't think he's a Carpenter fan, the philistine.'

'Dante is sweet but lacks a sense of humour.'

'God, I can't believe you have a doorman. And you live *here*.' He waved his arms around the terrace. 'You have a view! All I can see from my windows are tweakers and garbage.'

'You need to move.'

'And swap the tweakers and garbage for this? No thank you, your highness.'

I shook my head. 'You're an asshole.'

'Of the finest vintage. Chin, chin, milady,' he said with a terrible British accent and clinked his bottle on mine.

When we ran out of beers, we ventured outside. Ellis waited while I showered and dressed – in the *Escape from New York* T-shirt he'd given me one birthday, which Claude found vulgar – and out we went. Into the city, into the throng of it. I felt like I'd stepped into a raging river and forgotten how to swim. I was being jostled and nudged and every hit sent spasms of anxiety through me. I felt myself shrinking, my shoulders hunching, my back curling, until I was being forced to the edges, out of everyone's way.

But Ellis was there. His hand found mine, he gripped it tight and smiled. 'I've got you, Iris.'

With his help, I found my legs again. I found the Iris who strode around this city borough to borough, knowing every bar on the way, who would walk for miles and dodge every pedestrian like a gazelle outwitting a lion. It took a while, it took some deep breathing and slow going, but the tightness in my chest gradually eased. And by the time we got to the bar, a favourite sports bar we hadn't been to in years, I felt more like myself than I had in months.

We spent the afternoon and much of the night there, pitchers and shooters and wings and burgers, and a hangover to rival any that had come before.

That night saved me. Cracked open my self-pitying, fearful shell and let me breathe again. But the shell still surrounded me. I knew it was based on a lie, this fictitious mugging, this narrative that painted me the victim and Claude the saviour, and it broke my heart that Ellis believed it too.

But in my world, in those days at least, the happy lie was far better than the ugly truth.

After

'How long have you been here?' Other Iris asked, leaning against the kitchen countertop while I put my ankle up on the couch. She'd drunk half a bottle of rum and didn't seem in the least affected. Ellis would love her constitution.

Her presence made the cabin small and cramped and highlighted the worst of it. Memories of Claude were raw in my mind, and looking at her scarless cheek only made me angry.

'Not long enough.'

She smiled and busied herself, same as I would have done faced with an awkward silence. She checked the fire, threw on some more kindling. Then she set a kettle on the stove. A small silver camping kettle. She was so prepared. I almost rolled my eyes.

'I checked your supplies. You have a few days' worth. Along with mine, five, maybe six. With the both of us being careful, we can stretch it to a week between us. This food, by the way,' she held up one of the packets of freeze-dried crap, 'is disgusting. I didn't even think they made it any more. We'll eat mine first and hope the miracle comes before we have to crack open those.'

A week to figure this out. Plenty of time. Right, Jane?

'Whatever you say,' I said.

She was quiet for a while, tidying the shelves, adding her food to mine, separating it all out into seven roughly equal portions.

'Are you going to tell me?' she said, without looking at me.

'What?'

'What your wife did.'

'I told you. She cheated.'

'Is that all?'

I sighed. 'Why do you care?'

But I knew the answer before I asked. Because she was a good person. A version of me who had made good choices and ended up in a loving, full life with our father, instead of a volatile, dangerous one without him. Or maybe it was because she wanted to get on with that life of hers and I was standing in her way. I couldn't let her. She hated her life, I hated mine, so we would swap whether she liked it or not.

'Look,' I said, 'I don't know what you want from me. I don't want to talk about Claude. I don't want to talk about my past or my family. Same as you don't want to talk about yours.'

But I did. I wanted to know every detail of her life. But I couldn't push too hard.

'Fine, then let's talk about now,' she said, lifting my aching ankle and sitting on the couch in its place. She rested my leg over her lap and I didn't have the energy to tell her how strange it felt.

'Now?'

'Pretend I'm your therapist,' she said, smiling my smile. 'What's on your mind?'

'What do you think? I'm trapped in the woods by some weird loop and another version of me is sat on my couch thinking this is normal.'

Other Iris held my eyes and the sarcasm ebbed away.

'I don't think any of this is normal,' she said carefully, 'but . . . I think it's pretty cool, kind of like a cheap *Blair Witch*, you know?'

I went to argue, but couldn't. I'd thought it, more than once.

'We're trapped inside this bubble,' she continued. 'No matter what direction we walk, the path always leads back here. Compasses point north, but still, back to this cabin. It's not like there's some mystical wall keeping us in; rather, there just seems to be no way out.'

No bars, no walls, no escape. I thought of my apartment. I had a key, but I couldn't leave.

But you did leave, Iris, came Claude's soft whisper in my ear. *Come home.*

'So here am I,' Iris carried on, 'thinking this is a nerd dream come true and we're on the cusp of something amazing, that maybe this is just as it seems and we're from different timelines and the universe has brought us together for a reason, but you're not. You think it's all a hallucination. You think you're mad. And I'm not surprised, you know. Maybe you are talking to yourself out here and I'm just a figment of your psychosis. Newsflash, *I'm not.*' She swivelled on the couch so she was facing me. 'What I want to know is how you and me, the same person, with the same childhood, almost the same adulthood, can be looking at this so differently. What happened to you?'

I killed my father.

'I told you.'

She shook her head and gave a sad smile. 'You didn't.'

'What does that matter? Shit happens. I'm dealing with it.'

'Are you?'

I turned away.

I heard her sigh. 'Iris. I want to help you. I want you to help me.'

'I don't need help,' I muttered. I need a new life. I came here for a new life. Now there was one right in front of me.

'Are you sure? If you let me in, tell me what happened, maybe I can help.'

I closed my eyes. Flashes of my broken body at the base of the overhang strobed against the black. Images of Claude, the scarring punch in slow motion, the squeeze and dark and wrong stars, then him. The fact he was alive somewhere else. And this woman knew him and took it all for granted.

I jumped. My eyes sprang open. Iris's hand was on my shoulder.

'Where did you go?' she asked.

I threw away her touch and lifted my leg off her. 'I need to walk.'

'Limp, you mean. I'll come too.'

'No. I'm fine.'

'Yeah, and if you fall down another ravine and break your neck, I might be stuck here forever. Sorry, Jane, I'm going with you.'

I told her I fell, but had I said I fell down a ravine? Was that really important right now?

Outside, the air felt charged. A smell of minerals and metal. A soundless landscape, free of birds and insects. And dark.

When had it got dark?

We walked slowly, me leaning on the broom and my other self.

The stars shone. Bright sentinels in the black. I used to think they were watching over me. Keeping me safe. They were my comfort blanket, my connection to my father and the future. I'd come to the woods to connect with him, with them, with me – oh universe, you joker – but since the rain had washed away my sugar-coated shell, I hadn't looked up. Hadn't dared.

But there they were. The Great Bear. The Plough. Cassiopeia. The Pleiades. And the moon holding court, the pale lady, the star shepherd, keeping close watch. All right where they should be. Because he was right where he should be.

The forest was as familiar to me as the city. I knew the trees, knew the trails, and I found myself winding a slow path towards the overhang.

You could push her off, came Claude's voice from the darkness, *see what it's really like to kill yourself.*

She laughed, and for a moment, I considered it.

'My father told me a story once,' said Iris, and the idea faded. 'About Giordano Bruno. Do you know about him?'

I shook my head. My father hadn't told me about Bruno. Hers had. A sting of envy hit my chest and I was thankful for the darkness.

Iris walked beside me, staring up at the stars. She zipped her jacket to her chin and hugged herself against the cold. I could barely feel it.

'Everyone has heard of Galileo, Newton, Copernicus, but not Bruno. That really pissed Dad off.'

Another sting. Dad. *My* dad.

'Bruno didn't fit into his world, and I guess Dad felt he didn't fit into his. Bruno was a monk in sixteenth-century Italy and by all accounts a bit of an asshole. He liked space, magic and arguments. Kind of like a *Star Wars* fan, huh?' She smiled.

'This was the time of the Inquisition, banned books, strict rules set down by the Catholic Church for how to think, how to act, how the world, the universe, science should be all in relation to God. Dad related. Felt like the society we lived in was too strict; he was told how to think, what to want. The wisdom of Bruno's time was the earth was the centre of the universe and the universe is only what we can see in the heavens. One world, one God, you know. But Bruno thought there should be more. God was infinite, so the cosmos must be. He began to read banned books, have banned ideas.

'The story goes, one night he had a vision, a dream maybe, of the stars. They were a picture painted on a canvas draped horizon to horizon. In his vision, he went to the edge. He touched the canvas and the canvas moved. He was terrified. But he pushed through it to the other side and he experienced a moment of revelation. He saw an infinite cosmos. He saw that all the stars were suns like ours with their own planets, their own forms of life, their own beliefs and Gods. We were just one planet, one path, among millions. He saw the universe. With no centre, no focus. Infinity.

'He tried to spread his revelation across the world but was met with anger, hate, a flat refusal by these learned men to open their minds and listen to another point of view. They called him mad. He was excommunicated and eventually burned at the stake as a heretic. But he was right. We know it now. He was right. He saw other worlds, he saw a vast, bountiful universe spread out before us, but fear and pride made us turn away, slam the door.'

I turned to find Iris looking at me, an expression on her face I couldn't read.

'What if they'd believed him? Where would humanity be right now if those men hadn't been afraid? If they'd listened to him and Galileo and Thomas Digges and Copernicus? If they hadn't fought so hard against those new ideas?' She sighed. 'We've lost so much time to fear and arrogance. I don't want to lose more. Iris, the universe has brought us together for a reason, same as it gave Bruno that vision, same as it gave our father the urge to discover worlds beyond our own. Maybe I'm a vision to you. Maybe you're a vision to me. Either way, what it's showing us is right. Same as Bruno's vision was right.'

The stars blinked above me. A blanket, stretched taut, studded with diamonds. But not a blanket. Not a dome. Not a painted canvas.

Infinity.

I turned to the woman beside me. Tears hidden in the dark.

There was a new life waiting for me, but I was standing in my own way. Until I admitted what had happened in my previous life, I would never be able to step into my new one. The certainty settled over me like a quilt. I held it close.

'I still love her,' I said. 'And I hate myself for it.'

I felt Iris's hand in mine, fingers interlaced.

'What did she do?'

'She was violent.'

I felt her soften and tense at the same time. 'Did she hit you?'

I nodded, closed my eyes against a fresh wave of tears.

'Did she hit you more than once?'

I nodded again.

She stepped in front of me and made me look at her. Despite the dark, I saw her eyes.

'Did she do more than hit you?'

She held me. She wrapped her arms around me and let me cry into her shoulder.

Finally empty, I pulled away from her and met her eyes.

'Tell me,' she said.

And I did. From the day I saw Claude in the bar, to the stolen days between Christmas and New Year when I'd cheated on Bella – Iris shifted at mention of Bella but didn't interrupt – to moving in, marriage, the party, the first slap, the first punch, her birthday, the day I tried to go to the woods. But when I tried to tell her about the rest, what I'd found when I surprised Claude at work, what she did when I confronted her, the night in the hospital, why I'd run, why I was still running, I couldn't bring myself to talk about it. The first part had been easy, I'd said it before, but everything else was too raw, too close. The shame still clung to me.

'And so,' I said with a cough, searching for the right words, the right lie, 'after that day in the woods I . . . I knew I couldn't go back . . . so I came here.'

A flicker of a frown crossed Iris's face. 'That's . . . terrible. I'm sorry you went through that . . .' Her voice trailed off, the last word hung in the air.

'What?'

She looked away and back again. Sighed. 'I just . . . I get the sense that's not the whole story.'

I winced. Was I so transparent? Or did she just know me as well as she knew herself?

'That's everything,' I said, and even I wasn't convinced by my tone, but she didn't press.

Physical violence is one thing. People understand it. Though with two women, they scoff, you can't *really* hurt each other though? Just slap her back. Just push her away. But the other sort of violence. That is almost impossible to explain, to talk about, even to yourself.

Iris nodded slowly and didn't speak for a while.

'Did she give you those scars?' She pointed to my forehead and cheek.

'Yes.' And others she couldn't see.

'Why did you stay for so long?'

I let out a sad laugh. 'I've been asked that before, and really . . . I don't have a good answer except I was afraid. Not just of what Claude would do but of who I was, who I am, without her. I still don't know. I guess that's why I'm here, to find myself.'

Iris's eyebrows shot up. I realised what I'd said and we both cracked up.

'God,' Iris said, still laughing, wiping a tear from her eye, 'the universe really does have a fucked-up sense of humour.'

She slung her arm around my shoulders. 'Come on, let's have a drink.'

Back at the cabin, we sat on the couch together, both with one leg up on the cushions, a mirror of each other. The cabin was quiet but for the crackling fire and a gentle wind rocking a loose window pane. We'd talked for hours. Days, it felt like. My throat was sore, my head numb. It had felt good to speak it out loud. To tell someone what my life had become. But the relief I was meant to feel after confession never came. The darkness receded but didn't disappear.

She didn't speak for a long time. Probably felt relieved she'd never become obsessed with the beautiful woman in the bar, never run into her on the street, never gone to the intimate, romantic wine bar with her.

But why hadn't she? Because her father hadn't died. Because she hadn't killed him. Because she hadn't spent the next fifteen years punishing herself.

How lucky you are, I thought, and drank her rum.

'You said before,' she began, each word careful, 'you said you deserved what Claude did. Why do you think that?'

I gave a tired shrug. 'Because it's true. I knew what she was. I knew it from the first moment. When she kicked the bar harder, louder, even though she could see it annoyed me. When she bought me a drink without asking what I wanted. When she was late home on the day I moved in with her like she'd forgotten, like she was establishing who was in control right from the beginning. When she got me the job I'd always wanted then made me give it up. A hundred tiny red flags I was too infatuated and desperate to see. I knew what she was. But after what I did, I deserved it.'

'What do you mean?'

I saw his smile. That wide, easy smile he had. Saw him scratch his beard as he stood at my bedroom door and asked me to go with him. The crack in the smile when I said no. My chest tightened, my lungs and arteries in knots.

'Doesn't matter.'

'It clearly does.'

My eyes snapped to hers. 'It doesn't. That's enough for one night. You can sleep up there.' I nodded to the mezzanine. 'It'll be warmer than your tent.'

I waited for her to get off the couch, which eventually she did.

'Iris . . .'

'Stop. Please. Just . . . quit while you're ahead.'

*   *   *

I dreamed of a cage. Of a glass dome set gently over our world like a bell jar, trapping me and me inside. On the other side of the glass, in the pale grey mists, giant eyes watched us as we circled each other, fought and slept. They were his eyes. And Claude's. And Bella's. And my mother's and my sister's, and they all laughed.

Look what we've made, they said. Look at these creatures we've birthed and grown and moulded and chipped away at. Look how damaged they are. How fragile. See how they destroy each other.

Before

After that night with Ellis, I began to walk again. I told – not asked – Claude that I wanted to return to the Planetarium if Neil would have me back.

She agreed, with no argument.

She became the version of Claude I'd always wanted, the one that had always been somehow just out of reach. She smiled more. She laughed more at my jokes. She took an interest in my interests. Even took a day off work to go with me to the Natural History Museum. She suggested a trip to Florida to visit the Kennedy Space Center. Even her voice changed tone.

Was that what it took to shake this woman loose? Was that night in the bathroom the price for my happiness now?

Was it worth it?

I stood out on the terrace in bright, warm sunshine, staring down at the street, up at the sky, then back to our apartment and Claude within, singing a French song from her childhood.

Maybe it was.

That evening, as we sat opposite one another, a huge bowl of pasta between us, Claude set down her fork and fell silent.

A spike of fear ran through me, so I kept my head down, kept eating, but after a moment she took my hand and I had to look at her.

She was crying.

'What is it?' I asked, and immediately wondered if I'd done something.

'I need to talk,' she said, and my fear grew. 'This is hard for me, but I need to say it.'

I lowered my fork but didn't drop it. If she noticed, she didn't let on.

For a while, she didn't speak. I almost asked if she was all right when she said, 'I resented you.'

I raised my eyebrows and sat back. My grip on the fork tightened.

'For a long time, since the party. When you spoke to Lloyd and Sophia like that and you got so drunk.' She paused, eyes on her plate; easier to say awful things when you don't have to look your wife in the eye. 'When I didn't get the promotion, I blamed you. I hated you for it for so long, until every little thing you did enraged me. Your voice, even, began to be like nails in my ears.'

'Claude . . .' but she held up her hand.

'I need to say this.' She took a deep breath. 'The anger has been sitting inside me like a demon ever since, getting fat from me. Then you accused me of cheating and I thought, how dare you ask me that after what you cost me.' She looked at me then, a flash of rage in her eyes quickly disappeared. 'And then at my birthday, with Gerard. He brought up the promotion and he put his hands on you, and that demon in me took over. I thought you invited him to punish me and you came on to him to torture me and if I hadn't come into the bathroom you and he would have fucked in my house and I would be made the fool yet again because of you.'

She stopped, her voice trembling, tears rolling fat and unhindered down her cheeks.

I watched her, for any movement, any sharpness, any strike, but none came.

'I am sorry, Iris. I am so sorry. I don't want this for us. I don't want you to be afraid of me. It kills me inside to see you holding that fork like a weapon because of me.'

I relaxed my grip on the fork but didn't drop it.

'Since that night,' she said, 'I have been seeing a therapist. I am understanding now where my anger comes from and why I have been directing it at you. The truth is, I didn't get that promotion because Sophia is a homophobic *connasse* and nothing you did could have changed that. What you said to her at that party is what I've wanted to say for years.'

'You could have killed me.'

She pressed her hands to her face. 'I'm sorry. I'm so sorry. I'll spend my whole life making it up to you, my whole life, until you trust me again, because I love you. I loved you from the first second I saw you in that awful bar and you made this face at me that said I was annoying you, and I kicked the bar more because I wanted to annoy you because then you would look at me.'

That night. The hook she'd cast into me that night, still there, still tugging me closer to her.

'Really?'

She nodded. 'Then we met on the street and it was like fate pushed us together.'

'And you never called.'

'I was afraid.'

'Of what?

Her nail scratched at the place mat. 'Of loving you.'

'Why?'

'Because I thought love would make me weak. That it would get in the way of my career, that it would change me.'

'Has it?'

She tried to smile. 'Yes. For better and worse. But I would not give it up. I'm flawed, I have moments when I'm not myself. I see that now and I am trying to change. I *will* change. I promise. I *promise*. I can't lose you. I can't live without you.'

I felt a sudden yearning for her. The hook dug so deep it cut fresh wounds and made everything urgent, and if I didn't kiss her right now, this feeling, this overwhelming pull would rip me apart.

I stood, walked around the table to her. She looked up at me, afraid almost. I took her face in my hands and kissed her. I tasted her tears and her guilt and her fear of losing me and the hot mineral flavour of love. Pure, capital-L Love. We merged together and I saw a world torn asunder remake itself behind my closed eyes. We had been through cataclysm. We had ripped at each other and pulled strips of skin from bone, but now we were one shining being.

For a long time after that day, that conversation and confession, we had joy. One evening, Claude met me after work and we walked the dark winter streets together arm in arm. We talked for longer than we had in months, years maybe, about anything, everything – our families, past relationships, awful colleagues and embarrassing episodes.

'Remember when Virgil got so drunk – on white wine of all things – and proposed to a lamp post instead of Anais.'

'Easy mistake to make,' I said, and we laughed. Like teenagers, rosy-cheeked, falling about the streets, not drunk but giddy with new love.

Eventually we found ourselves on a familiar street, outside a familiar bar.

'Remember this place?' Claude's tone, her voice, her smile changed.

I looked up at the painted glass above the door. *Balthazar's.*

'How could I forget?'

Claude's thumb stroked mine and she spoke softly. 'Can I buy you a drink?'

The wine bar hadn't changed. The wood panelling, the bottles mounted on the walls, the glossy dark-wood furniture, the low candlelight and the smell of the wine. My senses exploded with the memory of the place. Those moments. Those feelings. The electricity in the air. The electricity between us.

Claude ordered white wine. 'I'm sorry,' she said with a wry smile. 'I think everyone drinks this.'

I couldn't help but smile and play along. 'Wasn't I meant to buy you a drink?'

'You can get the next one.'

We sat at the same table. We drank the same wine. We said the same words. And I was her again. That young, naive girl who couldn't believe a woman like this was talking to me, let alone touching me, kissing me, loving me. Claude cast a new hook into me that night, a sharper, stronger, deeper connection I couldn't shake and didn't want to.

We reset our relationship, started again, right from the beginning, but this time on the same level, same footsteps in the sand.

I never told anyone what had happened on her birthday, because, really, it had been for the best. Without that night, Claude would never have had the reason to change herself. That night was the catalyst, the new start we desperately needed. It was like we were suddenly living in a before-and-after and the before was barely spoken about. We took the trip to Florida, we took another to France – Europe! Paris! Claude started leaving work earlier, I saw her more. She would text me to tell me when she was coming home or if she was running late. She'd ask if I needed anything or wanted her to pick up takeout, or sometimes just *I love you*. I called Neil, pleaded for my job back, but sadly, regrettably, he had hired someone else, though he wouldn't tell me who and he didn't sound like himself. He suggested I try the Science Museum, he'd put in a word, but by then, my enthusiasm had dwindled and I never called them.

The awful job now didn't seem so bad because things were so good with Claude. The job meant more money, more time, more life, so I stayed.

For a long time I was happy and the sharp edges of my memories began to soften. It was like a drug, a sudden snort of high-grade coke that heightened every experience and never seemed to end. Even Ellis asked what I was on and could he get some. I'd not been *happy* since I was a child, going on those hikes with my father, seeing the life in him, seeing the exhilaration he felt every time we crested a hill or rounded a bend in the river and came upon a new vista. That had been happiness. And now here it was again. Maybe I was ready to go back, reclaim the good times from the grip of the bad. Claude didn't know what happened to my father, only that he'd died when I was sixteen. She read my tone, didn't pry.

I thought maybe now I could tell her. Maybe now we had turned the corner and become what we were meant to be, I could trust her in a way I never had before. Maybe I could finally say it out loud. Speak the words I never could, had never wanted to, because then they'd be real and I couldn't bear for them to be real.

Just like before, when Claude—

I shut down the cruel whisper before it could derail me. My very own Iago squatting toad-like inside my head, trying to crack my newly set foundation. I wouldn't let it. I would go to the woods. Take a walk between the trees and remember why I loved it. It was the last piece of me still missing, a square in the puzzle of Iris yet to be filled in, preventing me from moving forward.

I took a day, didn't tell Claude, and bought a pair of boots and a jacket. Just a walk, but I wanted to feel like I had back then, in the gear, in the environment, close to my father.

I caught the early train out of the city to one of the popular, easy trails, one I'd walked with my father a few times before, intending to be back before Claude finished work.

I took a cab from the train station to the trailhead. A small gravel parking lot surrounded by trees, with a log-cabin-style signpost and map. A cheerful cartoon bear said *No Littering*. No other cars, not at this time of year, so when the cab pulled away, I was alone, in the woods, for the first time in my life.

I felt his absence keenly, yet he was everywhere. In the air, in the leaves, in the dirt itself. I heard his laugh on the wind. But it was all ghosts. The more I sensed him, remembered him, the more alone I felt. The trees were suddenly taller, more forbidding, the spaces between the trunks darker, the sweet scent of the woodland suddenly acrid with rot.

Just ghosts.

I steeled myself. Checked my zips and laces. Checked the cap on my water bottle.

I dug the toes of my boots into the dirt. Made furrows.

Checked my zips again.

I stared into the trees. Into the empty spaces. The ground swelled into a low ridge a hundred yards along the trail. A huge boulder, out of place, the wrong rock for the region, stood on the curve of the path. An alien of granite and crystal. I imagined placing my hand on it, how cold it would be, how dead it would feel.

I clenched my fist.

'Just go,' I said to myself.

The trees swallowed my voice. The low grey clouds hit the mute button on the world.

I took a few steps. The wind rushed through high branches like a moan, like a dark laugh. It hit me, made me shiver, made my shoulders stiffen and arch. A warning. You shall not pass.

I took a few more steps. Stood at the threshold of the forest. One more step and I'd be inside it. Inside the enveloping greenness, the quiet hush that came from the trees, drowning out all other sounds – road noise, people noise, life noise. Like stepping into another world.

The boulder stood sentinel at the entrance to the wilderness. A millennia of watching, tolerating climbing children and adolescents with knives trying to carve their mark in its side. It was roughly square. I saw it as a barrel-chested man, head in hands, stuck in one place and sick of it. It wanted to be deeper. To be hidden. It wanted solitude from the hundreds of hikers who'd brush it with their fingers when they passed like it was little more than a good-luck charm.

I was beside it. I was touching it. My hand pressed flat on the granite. A spot worn smooth by a million hands. I wanted to say sorry. For being just another one of them who couldn't help. I pressed my forehead against the rock. Cold and rough and old and I felt it breathe.

Felt it move. Felt it unwind and unfurl and straighten its back.

I looked up and it loomed above me. A barrel-chested man. Granite head brushing the canopy.

Arms broke from the torso, fingers burst from the hands. Rock dust fell on me like rain, turned my hair grey.

My lungs wouldn't breathe and my heart wouldn't beat. Fear and guilt and sorrow surged like three rivers colliding in a canyon. A mess of white water and boiling confusion.

The giant towered above me, swung its head side to side, looked deeper into the woods, then towards the small town, then up at the empty blue sky, and finally down. Down to me.

Features broke from the block. A nose. Lips. A deep brow over cavernous sockets. Fathomless eyes found me.

The features refined. A sculptor chipping away at the marble. A face emerged.

I knew what it would be before it finished.

Knew the shape of the mouth and eyes and nose. Knew the line of the jaw.

His face.

The giant, stuck between civilisation and the wild, always on the threshold of the forest, never inside it, cocked his head to the side, just like my father used to. Just like he did the last day I saw him. Then the movement went too far. Became unnatural. Became wrong. When his ear touched his shoulder, I ran.

Back to the parking lot. To the gaudy signpost. A touchstone of civilisation. My lungs suddenly filled with air. My heart couldn't beat fast enough.

I looked back to the forest. But the boulder was just a boulder. Of course it was.

The boulder was always a boulder.

'Get a grip, Iris,' I said between breaths.

Eventually I could stand without wanting to collapse. My head cleared. My chest stopped hurting.

I wasn't ready.

I wasn't even close to ready. All that confidence was gone in a moment. I wasn't fixed. This new happiness hadn't fixed me.

Because it's not real happiness.

I crumpled to my knees beneath the cartoon bear – *Pick Up Your Trash!* – and wept into my hands until my palms were raw with salt and the sun had moved along its track to afternoon.

I needed to go home. I hadn't taken the taxi driver's number, and town was two miles away. A walk would be good. I needed to move. To put distance between myself and the forest and the memories of my father.

I raked my fingers through my hair. Fine grey dust collected under my nails.

After

The next three days passed in relative harmony. Other Iris would get up before me, climb down the ladder from the mezzanine and tiptoe around so as not to wake me. She'd build a fire ready for me to light, then go walking. I'd make breakfast, keep hers warm, and a few hours later she'd return to the cabin with a grim look.

'No change?' I asked on the third day.

'Nothing.' She sighed and shrugged off her jacket. 'I don't understand it.'

I sat on the couch, turning and bending my ankle, testing the limits of the injury. It was healing. I could walk now without the broom-crutch, but not far.

'We have four days of food left,' I said, though I knew she hadn't forgotten. She was regimented with the rations and controlled both our portions.

She slumped down on the couch beside me.

The strange unreality of our situation was sinking in for both of us. Three days of her food – boil-in the bag rice, three-grain oatmeal, pre-prepared ragù and curries, chocolate pudding and buttery flapjacks – meant in one more we'd be on to what was left of my stash, and we were no closer to figuring this out. Mostly we spent the days maintaining the cabin, fetching water, cleaning, resting, talking about movies we enjoyed or not really talking at all. Iris tinkered with the two-way walkie. She had brought a wind-up radio with her, which she cannibalised for parts, and a set of mini screwdrivers just in case. When I asked what circumstance would mean she'd need screwdrivers, she shrugged and said you never know, and guess what? She was right.

By the end of the first day, Iris had somehow managed to hook up the dynamo from her radio to the walkie.

'Here goes,' she'd said, blowing out her cheeks.

She wound up the handle and the Radio Shack reject came to life. Static hissed through the speaker. She tried frequency after frequency, wound it until her wrist ached, adjusted and readjusted the antenna. No reply. No one there. But Iris wouldn't give up.

My days had become punctuated by this chorus – whirring wind-up, static hiss, 'Mayday, mayday, is anyone receiving?' static hiss, groan of frustration, wind-up again and again. Until, on the third day, I heard a new sound. Iris was crying. Head in hands, back juddering with sobs. Trying to hide it.

'What's wrong?' I asked, and felt foolish. 'I mean . . . other than the obvious.'

She looked up, sniffing back tears. 'What if we never get out of this? What if I never see Bella again? Oh God, what if she's gone into labour already and I wasn't there?'

I shuffled closer, wrapped my arm around her shoulders and pulled her close to me.

'You're going to see her again,' I said, kept my voice calm and even. 'You said she was weeks away from giving birth, so I'm sure everything is fine. We will figure this out.'

'How? We have nothing. No information, no clues, no power. This stupid radio is never going to work.'

'We have each other. We created this. Or the universe did to fuck with us, but you know the thing about the universe? It's all about balance. Problems always have solutions. The unstoppable force and the immovable object can't exist together. The universe won't let them. And it won't let us die here. Whether this is real or not, there is an answer.'

Iris pulled away from me and wiped her face. 'And what is the answer?'

'No idea. But it's somewhere in us. In our pasts, in our futures. Maybe one of us lost something the other can help find.'

Like purpose. Or perspective. Or hope.

'What have you lost?' she asked.

I sat back against the couch and studied my hands. Thought about what those hands had done. What they might have done if I hadn't left.

'Iris?' she said, and I looked up at her.

'Myself,' I said. 'I lost myself a long time ago. Little pieces at first, so small I didn't notice until I was all gone and this stranger was left.'

Iris shifted, put her leg up on the couch, elbow on the backrest. My listening pose. 'Like what?'

I smiled. 'My hair.'

Her eyebrow arched. 'Your hair?'

'I had this bleached-blonde Pris cut, you know, like Daryl Hannah.'

'From *Blade Runner*! That's wild! I wanted the same for years but never got up the courage. This,' she ruffled her hair, 'was the closest I came.'

'Well, Claude hated it. She asked me to grow it out and dye it for the wedding. Then whenever I wanted to get it cut, she'd ask me not to.' I paused, huffed out a laugh. 'Who am I kidding? She *told* me not to. But I always wanted it back. After the hair came the clothes. My wardrobe was slowly replaced by her choices, and I faded. Seems stupid, right, to feel like you've lost yourself because you don't have the haircut you want?'

Iris shook her head. 'When choice is taken away, sense of identity goes with it. That's why abusers are so powerful. They strip away your personality, your confidence, make you feel like they are right and you can't make decisions without them. And when you love them, you don't even realise it's happening.' She leant close. 'But you have a choice now.'

'Do I? I'm stuck in a bubble with dwindling food supplies and no way out.'

'You still have choices.'

She cast around the cabin until her eyes came to a rest on her daypack by the door. She grinned at me and jumped off the couch. I knew that grin; that grin meant another round of tequila shots, or karaoke in a dive bar, or skinny-dipping at midnight in Lasker

Pool in Central Park. It meant something crazy was about to happen.

Iris dug into the front pocket of her bag and brought out a folded knife. A proper one, not some blunt stub that wouldn't bother a tomato. She flicked open the blade, silver, pocked with age but clearly sharp.

'I'm going to cut your hair,' she declared, still grinning.

I laughed. Then I realised she was being serious. 'No you're not.'

'Oh, I am.' She stepped closer and I pressed my back into the cushions.

'Not a chance.'

She sighed, grin faded, knife lowered. 'Look, Iris, Claude dismantled your sense of self one piece at a time and it started with your hair. You have it tied up because you hate it and can't do anything with it. You want it gone. I know you do, because I do too. This isn't a haircut, it's a reclamation. A *restoration*.'

When she put it like that . . . 'I don't know.'

Claude would hate it. I hadn't seen her phantom in days, but I felt her everywhere, heard her whispered scorn on the breeze.

'Full disclosure. I'm not a stylist and I have a knife, not a pair of scissors, so this is going to be a hack job. But it'll be your hack job. Come on.'

I ran my hands over my ponytail. Claude would hate it, I thought again, and smiled. 'All right. Let's do it.'

The grin returned and we set up a makeshift salon outside by the fire pit. Iris dragged out a chair and used the old sheet as a smock. She released my ponytail and ran her hands through my hair, teased out the knots with her comb – she'd brought a stocked-up toiletries bag along with screwdrivers, because of course she had – and flattened it against my back. It felt so strange to have someone, especially her, touch me gently, with not a hint of violence or anger. Months of tension fell away from my shoulders.

I felt her gather up my hair in one hand. 'Ready?'

I closed my eyes. 'Do it.'

Her knife was sharp. It sliced through my hair with minimal resistance and a sound like cutting cloth.

'You okay?' Iris asked.

'Uh-huh.' But I wasn't. Tears spilled down my cheeks as I felt the knife work, felt her gentle hands move over me.

Then she stopped. 'Look.'

I opened my eyes to the clump of hair hanging from Iris's hand. I took it, felt its weight, ran my fingers over the bristled ends. And laughed. It was gone. Really gone. I opened my hand and let the wind take it. It would warm a bird's nest or rot down into the understorey, feed the forest.

When my hand was empty, I saw her. Claude, standing by a tree, arms crossed, eyebrow raised. She shook her head and her expression turned sour.

'What have you done?'

She was too far away to hear and yet I did. Her voice floated inside my head, a snake's whisper at my ear. 'Look at the state of you, why would you embarrass me like this?'

I pressed my eyes shut and counted.

'Are you okay?' came my own voice from behind me.

I nodded, felt my hair tug in her grip. 'Keep going. Cut it off.'

The knife went to work and my hair fell like snow. When I opened my eyes, Claude was gone and the sun was shining and I could breathe again. Iris hummed while she worked and this absurd situation felt beautifully normal.

'Do you remember Anneka Taylor?' Iris asked.

The name immediately conjured memories of high school. The smell of the cafeteria on taco day, the squeak of gym shoes on the lacquered boards, the high-pitched laughter of the girl groups in the hallways. Anneka was the queen bee of one of those groups.

'God. I haven't thought of her in years.' But I could picture her perfectly, as if she were a still from a John Hughes movie.

'First crush?'

'Big time. You?'

'I asked her to senior prom. You can imagine how well that went down.'

I laughed and tried not to move. 'I wonder what happened to her.'

'I can't speak for yours, but my Anneka went to college in California. She's running for Congress now.'

'Good for her.' Senior class president to congresswoman. Some dreams do come true.

'What about Martin?' she asked in a conspiratorial tone.

'Martin! Jesus. He made a pass at me almost every week.'

'Me too.' She paused, the knife stopped. 'I think he died.'

'Way to kill the mood.'

We laughed together and fell into a happy silence as she tidied up my hair. When she was done, I studied it one three-inch circle at a time with Iris's compact. Short, uneven, rough around the edges, but all me and all mine. I ran my hands through it, got a feel for the length, shook out the cut pieces and couldn't stop smiling.

The rest of the day we spent talking, drinking, laughing about old times we shared and ones we didn't. Girls we'd liked. Boys who'd liked us. Over an hour on the decline of Spielberg and Cameron. Two on the politics we shared almost to the letter. Then night came and the alcohol warmed us enough to turn to family.

'Did your dad ever talk about another earth?' I asked as Iris pushed a skinny log into the stove and closed the door.

She straightened, brushed the wood dust from her hands. Her voice tensed. 'He did.'

'I've been wondering if, in light of all this, he was right.'

She sat sideways, facing me. 'He wasn't.'

'How can you say that? Look at us. You know, he got me out of bed once in the middle of the night because he thought he'd found it. What if he had?'

'He wasn't well then.'

I scratched my newly exposed neck. 'Did he get better?'

'Did yours?'

I looked away, hand dropped. That was answer enough.

'He did the same to me,' she said. 'Made me go out in the back-yard with him. Told me there was another earth and another Iris and I thought I could see her through the telescope. Maybe I was looking at you.' She smiled.

'He asked me what I would say to you. I said I'd ask where I left my birthday money from Grandpa.'

Iris laughed. 'In the false bottom of the ugly pink music box on my dresser. Last place Helen would look.'

I sat forward, ignored the twinge in my ankle. 'Yes! That's it! Damn. That was a hundred bucks.'

We high-fived and laughed and it felt so good. I realised how long it had been since I'd truly laughed. The muscles in my chest and face were stiff and sore by the end of the night. With every smile, every joke and reference and memory shared, I felt pieces of myself solidifying. I was an explosion in reverse, chaos slowly returning to a recognisable shape.

'You really hate him, don't you?' I asked in the silence between laughs.

Iris didn't look at me, just scratched at her knuckles.

'You would too,' she said, and wouldn't be pressed to say anything more.

We had four days before the food would run out. Four days to take the life I wanted, but that life, I realised, wasn't hers. This Iris had a bitterness lodged deep inside her that I'd never had. Sadness? Yes. Regret? Always. Anger? Too much. But I was never bitter. I didn't want to *Single White Female* her life any more. I wanted mine back.

Before

'Iris. You need to end it.'

Ellis's usually jovial expression was gone, his eyes were hard and ringed with worry. He looked exactly the same as when we'd first met. A layer of soft fat on his cheeks that wouldn't wrinkle and hid his true age. He was still alone, still working for the supply company where we'd met, still in the same cosy (cramped) one-bedroom (and no closet) apartment with spectacular views (of a dumpster-filled alley popular with the already fallen and those teetering on the edge looking for a chemical push). He hadn't moved in a decade. I hadn't stopped.

'You need to leave her,' he said.

He held my hand across his square Formica kitchen table. A seventies one with chrome trim and a chipped plastic surface. He'd found it in one of those dumpsters, forlorn and abandoned, and, drunk as he was, decided he and the table were kindred spirits. I ran my finger over the chips, pressed into their worn edges, couldn't take my eyes off the swirling green pattern, which might, once, have been leaves.

'*Iris.*'

He squeezed my hand. I sat back.

'It's not that simple.'

Ellis leant in, lowered his voice as if we'd be overheard. 'Iris, she hit you.'

We'd been telling scar stories – got this one from falling off my bike, got this one from wrestling a bear – and when he asked about the scar on my cheek, I didn't lie fast enough. A few beers later and my tongue was loose, I told him about the first slap, the punch, the blood on her wedding ring, and the real reason I left the

Planetarium, but I could never drink enough to let slip about Claude's birthday party, so I let the lie about the mugging stand.

'It was an accident,' I said.

His nostrils flared. 'Don't be that woman.'

'What woman?'

'The one who makes excuses. "He didn't mean it, he was drunk." "Oh I should never have interrupted him when the game was on." "He's so stressed at work and I didn't have dinner on the table for him, it's my fault really." Bullshit. This is no different. She hit you. More than once. And she'll do it again.'

Or worse, I thought with a sinking sensation in my chest. My hand went to my throat, fingers stroked the long-faded bruises.

After I went to the woods and saw what I'm sure now I didn't really see, the happy lie that was my life had broken. I had been an astronaut on a spacewalk, all around me an endless, fathomless vacuum. All I had to do was keep my head and concentrate on small, achievable tasks. Go to work. Earn a pay cheque. Play the doting wife. If I could do those things, the darkness would be kept at bay. But that day in the woods had changed it all. My tether had been cut and I was floating out into the nothing.

'You can stay here,' Ellis said. 'For as long as you want.'

I let myself smile. 'Thanks.'

'I mean it.'

'I know.'

He sat back, played with his beer bottle but didn't drink. 'Do you still love her?'

I nodded. 'And she loves me.'

'If she loved you . . .' he began, but cut himself off before the eruption. 'This is fucked up, Iris.'

'I know.'

'You have to leave her.'

I let my attention drop to my own beer bottle. My nail scraped at the label.

'You're going to, aren't you?' he said, and his tone changed. 'Like, now. Today.'

Hot tears pricked my eyes. 'It's complicated.'

'What's complicated?'

'We're married, Ell. I made a commitment. Through good and bad, sickness and health. Claude is seeing a shrink, she's getting better. It's all getting better. I can't throw away six years because of one accident.'

The lie was bitter on my tongue.

'And I wouldn't understand that, would I?'

I sighed through my nose.

Ellis sat back, crossed his arms over his chest and stuck his tongue in his cheek. 'Wow.'

'What?'

'She wasn't lying.'

'Who?'

'*Claude.*'

The name stung the air. The venom in his voice, the way he forced the word through a snarl, the taint it brought with it.

'I wouldn't understand any of this,' he said, 'because I'm just a pathetic man-baby who can't keep a relationship going more than six months, right? Isn't that what you said?'

'What? I never said that.'

I'd thought it once or twice, but had I said it?

'You know what, Iris, don't bother,' Ellis said, and stood up. 'Your wife told me what you really think of me.'

Claude. Claude said that. Of course she did. She'd thrown the shit in the pot and started stirring. I tightened my hand into a fist to stop it shaking. 'I don't know what you're talking about.'

'At your engagement party. Remember? Real sweet lady.' He turned away, poured the rest of his beer down the sink. 'I'm too stupid to understand marriage, clearly, because I *do not* under-stand yours. Your wife manipulates you, you say you love her. Your wife hits you, you say it's complicated. That doesn't make any sense!'

I shrank back against the chair.

'Love isn't logical, Ell, as much as dating sites try to make you believe it. When you fall for someone, the feeling . . .' I shook my head. 'It's like looking up at a clear night sky full of stars. That sky is a book of history and a map of the future all at once. Same as a relationship. One glance, one *kiss*, contains all that possibility. Trying to distil love down to logic is like trying to count every star in the sky. It's impossible. So you try to experience as much as you can of this person because you know, you *know*, you'll never live long enough to see all their stars, their galaxies, their suns, their infinite multitudes. Everyone is their own universe. You can't count their stars and you can't rearrange them. You have to love them all or you can't love any piece of them.'

'Is that why you're still with her?' he snapped.

'Yes, well. It turned out Claude's universe has a supermassive black hole in the middle of it.'

Ellis shook his head. 'Iris. She's an abuser. You're letting her abuse you and now you're making jokes about it? Open your eyes!'

I stood up then, anger fizzing in my lungs. 'They're open, Ellis, and they're looking at you and this place and your small life. What are you doing living here? You share a fucking bathroom with twenty strangers, for Christ's sake. No wonder no woman wants to stick with you once she's been here. You've got money, do something about it. Move. Get a fucking haircut. Go to the gym. But it's easier to whine about women not loving you when you're literally putting up a wall between you and them. Safer that way, isn't it? Easier not to fix all those outside problems because when they still reject you, you won't have anything to blame but yourself.'

Ellis's jaw clenched so hard I thought his teeth would crack.

I shouldn't have said it. I know I shouldn't. But who was he to talk about my marriage like he knew what was going on under the surface? Who was he to say end it, *right now*, because of a rough patch?

A rough patch that nearly killed you, Jane.

But Ellis didn't know that. If he did, he would call the police. Because he cared.

'Ell . . .'

'I'd like you to leave now.'

'Ell, I didn't—'

'Mind the crack addicts and winos on your way out.'

I didn't move. Couldn't leave it like this.

'Have you forgotten where the door is?' he said, eyebrows high, voice higher.

'Ellis, please . . .'

He pushed past me to the door and opened it. 'Here you go. This is the way out. Please use it.'

I grabbed my jacket, almost tried again to apologise but thought better of it. He was mad. I was mad, but not at him, at myself. I should never have told him what Claude had done. If I hadn't, none of this would have happened. My fault again.

He'd cool off in a week or so, I'd call, we'd drink, all would be right in the jungle again. I left his apartment with that thought in my head. I turned to throw out one last sorry, but the door was already closed. I'd give it a week, then call and grovel.

I left his building and walked the four blocks to the subway. Every step drilled shame and guilt deeper and deeper into me. And something else. I had said those things to Claude, and she'd told him. She'd stirred all kinds of shit between me and my best friend. It hadn't worked at the time because Ellis was made of noble stuff, but it had been a ticking bomb. A sleeper cell just waiting for the moment to activate. You won't understand, I'd said, because you're not married. Just drive that knife in, Iris, give it a twist.

I rode the subway home with a growing sense of dread in my chest. He was right. I needed to leave her. It was early evening on a Saturday, she would probably be at a gallery or a wine bar right now. I could pack a bag and find a hotel for the night, regroup. Maybe if I showed up at Ell's door with a suitcase and a sorry, he'd forget the last few hours in an instant.

I need to leave my wife.

I'm going to leave my wife.

I said it in my head first. Then again in a whisper not loud enough for the man in the seat beside me to hear.

'I'm going to leave my wife.'

Again. Louder.

The man looked up from his newspaper and frowned at me.

Again. Almost a shout. 'I'm going to leave my wife!'

'Can I have her?' came a male voice, followed by a *hurr-hurr* laugh.

At my stop, I rushed off the train into the rarefied air of the Upper West Side, then into my building, up in the golden elevator, into the apartment.

No Claude. Good.

Could I really do this?

I faltered on the threshold of our bedroom. Our beautiful bedroom. In our beautiful home.

I looked at the spot on the floor where I'd fallen the first time she hit me. The side of the couch I'd huddled against the second time. The closed bathroom door. The memory of what had happened behind it. The beautiful bed where I'd lain for weeks, unable to speak.

It wasn't a home. It was a prison and the walls were closing in.

I went to the closet and pulled out my suitcase, laid it open on the bed. It wouldn't fit everything, but it would be enough for a week or two. Enough time to clear my head, make a plan, make amends with Ellis, because I needed all the friends I could get right now. I thought about calling Margot and Denise, but quickly put that idea out of my head. They were Claude's friends. They would call her right after, and besides, they had their own worries to deal with right now. I thought about calling my mother, but then I'd have to explain, and I didn't know how to tell her in a way she'd understand. Helen? She'd say it was my fault, and I didn't need to hear that again.

A sudden fear bloomed in my chest. What would Claude do when she realised what I'd done? When she came home and saw my side of the closet empty. Saw my suitcase gone. Should I leave a note? Should I tell her why?

If she doesn't know by now, she doesn't deserve to.

I pushed aside the fear and started packing. Clothes first, fist-fuls of them, ripped from their neat folds and thrown in the case.

Halfway through emptying my T-shirt drawer, my phone buzzed. I found it under a mound of socks. A news alert pinged the screen – earthquake upstate – but below it, a text from Claude.

Margot cancelled. Denise gone into labour. Be home in twenty. C x

I checked the time. Sent almost fifteen minutes ago. I looked at the bed, strewn with clothes. Panic gripped me by the throat and squeezed. She would be home any minute. She would see this. See me. See what I'm doing.

My pulse turned heavy drumbeat, filled the room with sound. The world throbbed in and out of focus. I couldn't stop shaking.

Could I explain it away?

Could I get everything back in the closet in five minutes?

No.

Could I finish packing and run before she got here?

Try.

Try.

Go.

NOW.

My hands moved by themselves. They grabbed clothes and shoved them into the case. They unplugged chargers and twisted them into balls. They tore through the drawers. They forced a whole life into a three-foot rectangle.

'What is this?'

I hadn't heard the door. Hadn't heard her footsteps on the parquet flooring.

Claude stood in the bedroom doorway, her heels dangling from one hand. I couldn't read her expression. Couldn't see her clearly over the fear blurring my vision.

'Babe,' I said, fake smile, tone all high and pitchy. 'You're early.'

'Traffic was light. What are you doing?' Her voice was low, simmering. Her eyes swept across the messy bed, the piles of clothes, the bulging case.

'Uh . . .' Lie. Just lie. Say 'Surprise! Last-minute vacation!' But nothing came out. My words deserted me.

Claude stepped into the room. I flinched back a step. She picked up one of the discarded shirts – a grey silk one she'd bought me and I hated – then dropped it again. She came close to me, flipped open the top of the suitcase and eyed the chaos within.

'Are you going somewhere?'

She stood less than a foot from me. She smelled of wine and expensive perfume. Every muscle in my body tensed, every bone hardened.

'Are you going somewhere?' she asked again, her tone turned flint, her expression changed from confusion to something altogether more dangerous.

I knew that look in her eye.

I knew that tension in her jaw.

'I'm going . . .'

An inch closer. 'Going where?'

'I'm leaving.' My voice shook, but saying the words out loud gave me strength. 'I'm leaving you.'

I braced myself for the slap. The fist. The hands on my throat.

But none of them came.

'I see,' she said, and flipped the lid of the case closed. 'Do I get to know why?'

'You know why.'

The tiniest tremor in the nerves under her eye gave her away. 'Were you going to tell me? Or just run away and leave me to clean up the mess?'

'I'm sorry.'

'No you're not.'

Then something happened I didn't expect. She sat on the bed, head in hands. There was no anger in her. No violence bubbling under the surface ready to erupt. She seemed smaller, her shoulders narrower, rising and falling with a heavy sigh.

'I thought we were doing better,' she said in a small, bird-like voice. 'I thought we were happy.'

We were, perhaps . . . Or had it all been fake, a bright mask over the darkness?

'I love you, Iris.'

'I know.'

She looked up at me. Tears like diamonds in her eyes. 'I mean it.'

I pushed the case away and sat beside her. 'I love you too.'

'Then don't leave me.'

'I . . . I have to.'

'Why?'

Because I'm lost in my life.

Because I'm scared of you.

Because if I don't, I'll die the way my father died.

'I just need some time.'

She swivelled to face me, one leg up on the bed. Her hands took mine. 'We could go away together, a long trip. South America. Europe. Anywhere you like.'

'I need time alone.'

Her grip tightened. Her manner shifted. 'You're lying.'

'I'm not.'

She pulled away from me. 'You are. You're leaving me for another woman. Aren't you?'

'No.'

She stood up, her smallness gone, the bird-like demeanour turned lion.

'Admit it. Be honest for once in your life, Iris.'

I stood, took a few steps back, put the corner of the bed between us. 'I'm not lying. I need time away from you, from *this*.'

'From what? From being an adult? From marriage?'

'This isn't a marriage and you know it.'

The shot hit home and I regretted it instantly. She turned predator. Her lip curled, her white teeth bared.

'You are such a child,' she growled, and moved towards me.

I stepped back, around to the other side of the bed, but the wide expanse between us wasn't enough.

'You think you can go around with your head in the stars, life all rosy, skipping through the fields.' Her accent thickened, her words jumbled. 'You think love is all kisses and candy and easy-peasy all the time because all those movies you watch have happy endings? *Foutaise!* She spat the word. 'When will you grow up?'

She was at the end of the bed now. By the dresser, drawers still slung open, clothes spilling onto the floor. I found myself in the corner by the window. Trapped.

'Claude. Please stop.'

But my words only fed the fire.

'*Please stop, please stop.*' She mocked my voice. 'Stop what? Talking to my wife? Having a discussion like adults do?'

She picked up a brush from the dresser. Threw it. It hit the wall a foot from my head and clattered onto the bedside table.

'Claude!'

But she didn't hear. Didn't care.

'I come home to see my wife packing!' she shouted, picking up a handful of make-up. The compacts scattered against the curtain like a shotgun blast. 'She tells me she is leaving me for some *putain!*'

'I'm not—'

A bottle of perfume smashed on the wall beside me, showered me with glass and alcohol. The sickly scent filled the room like mustard gas.

'Then my wife, she says we don't have a real marriage. I put my heart and soul into this relationship. I love with all I have, I give all my money, I forgive mistakes she has made, and there are *so many mistakes!*' she screamed, and another bottle of perfume – the one she was wearing – shattered against the bed frame. Glass splinters stabbed into my arm.

'Fuck! Claude! Stop it!'

A can of hairspray bounced off the bedside table, smashing the lamp.

'You leave!' she screamed. 'You fucking leave!'

But I couldn't move. The missiles kept coming. Another bottle exploded an inch from my face. A sliver of glass sliced my neck. My hands, my arms were useless shields. Something hit my chest. Something else hit my shoulder, my side, my leg. I covered my face, closed my eyes, pressed my body into the corner, but it didn't stop.

Then something harder, heavier, hit the top of my forehead and my head snapped back against the wall.

Time seemed to stop. The sound went out of the world.

Blood on my face, in my eyes, in my mouth. My ears rang and my brain swelled against the inside of my skull.

I staggered. The missiles stopped.

Hands caught me and time sped up again. Sound rushed at me, too loud, too fast.

She shoved me back against the wall.

'*Putain!*' she screamed in my face. 'Fucking whore! You go! You leave!'

She slammed me against the wall a second time, and a third.

My head spun. My vision was a pinprick of light in the distance. All sounds muffled and wrong. Something was wrong.

'Claude . . .' I said, but the word was heavy and fat on my tongue. My voice didn't sound like my own.

'Stop.' I tried again. The corner of my mouth wouldn't move. Wouldn't shape the words. Felt numb like I'd had a tooth pulled.

I couldn't see.

'Stop.' The world was all slur and the taste of blood and the swirling dark and the buzzing in my ears.

Claude stopped shaking me. 'Iris?'

She let me fall. I remember my hand touching my forehead, feeling nothing but blood. No sensation at all on that side of my face.

I touched my mouth. My lip had dropped on one side.

'Claude . . .' I said, and my voice was alien to me.

My adrenaline spiked, cleared my vision enough to see Claude staring down at me, wide-eyed with terror.

'Ah-ambulance,' I managed, but she was already dialling.

I don't remember much after that. Just flashes. Paramedics shining a light in my eyes. The cold sting of antiseptic on my forehead. The lights in the hallway passing above me, neighbours or their live-in staff peeping out of their doors. Then the sirens. Then a man asking me questions, shining more lights, asking me my name and what day it was and who was president.

I woke up in a hospital bed with a headache the size of a planet and the far-off beeping of heart monitors. Blue curtains on all sides. An empty chair. No Claude. But her bag and coat were there. She was in the hospital. She must have stepped away. Panic rushed through me and my monitor began to beep quicker and quicker.

The curtain parted. A woman ducked in.

'Calm down now, ma'am,' she said, going straight for the monitor to check the levels, then to my drip to check the bag. Finally she looked at me and smiled. 'No use getting worked up, you're going to be fine.'

'Please,' I said, my voice a breathy croak, muffled from the numbness in my mouth.

The nurse reached for a cup of water, but I waved it away.

'Please help me. My wife . . .'

'The French lady? She's stepped out for a minute. She's been right here all night.'

'She did this to me.'

The nurse gave an amused frown. 'You two have a fight?'

I nodded to save my voice, but moving my head sent spikes of pain across my skull and down my neck. 'Please, help me.'

'I'll ask the doctor about upping your pain meds,' she said.

What could I do to make her understand?

'She hurt me! I'm scared!' but my stupid voice muffled the sounds, made them blurry.

'Don't you worry, ma'am. Your wife will be back soon and you're going to be just fine.'

I stared at the woman, that vacant expression, those rote answers. She wasn't listening. I couldn't make her listen.

'*Please.*' I tried once more. 'The police . . .'

'Your wife is with the police.'

My head swam, pain throbbed through me and my vision began to darken at the edge.

'What?'

'She's giving them a statement about the break-in. How she came home and found you. They'll want to speak with you too when you're ready.'

The shock cleared my head in an instant. I couldn't undo the lie she'd told. I had a head injury, I wouldn't be believed, not with Claude on the other side spinning lies like a spider spins silk.

I'd never be believed. I'd always be dismissed. You two had a fight? Oh dear, well I'm sure you'll work it out. They'd never say it to a woman with an abusive husband. They'd question every bruise, every tear, every stilted answer to a question about him. But me? Who would believe me?

Tears spilled down my cheeks. I'd missed my chance. I'd tried to leave and I'd ended up in hospital with a serious injury. Well played, Claude. You got me. I curled up on the bed and waited.

Claude came back at some point with the doctor and I pretended to be asleep. I listened as he told her the damage she'd caused.

Four stitches. A serious concussion. Nerve damage causing the numbness in my face. It would heal. I would regain feeling. But in the meantime, I would need help.

'Will you be able to take a few days off, maybe a week, to care for her? Watch how she sleeps, make sure she takes her medication?' he asked Claude.

'Of course,' she said. 'I won't leave her side for a moment.'

I forced down the tears threatening to give me away. Claude's saccharine tone made me want to vomit. Her lies burned my insides with rage. Her overblown concern, her unshakeable belief she'd done nothing wrong, it was all an accident. It was a break-in, it was a stranger, it was a thief in the night who did this to my poor Iris, not me. Not *me*. I'm her loving wife.

Oh no, Doctor, I'd have to say, Claude's an angel who saved my life. Gosh, if she hadn't found me when she did, with a head injury like this I don't know what would have happened.

'She's lucky to have you,' the doctor said, and Claude demurred and the doctor left us alone.

I felt Claude's hand in mine and her soft words of love in my ears. She spoke her lies in case a passing nurse overheard, her hopes for us getting back on track and how she'd look after me forever and ever because we were soulmates and everything would be fine when we got home. She'd be there for me always.

I wanted to rage. I wanted to tear my hair from my scalp. I wanted to scream until my lungs bled.

But I kept my eyes closed. Kept pretending.

After

I woke to strange sounds. A voice I didn't recognise, fuzzy at the edges, stuttering and jumping.

I bolted upright. The radio.

Iris stared at me, eyes wide and fixed. 'It's a transmission. On a loop, for the past hour.'

I couldn't tell if it was a man or woman on the other end of the line. 'What are they saying?'

Iris turned up the volume.

'*The National Weather Service in New York has issued an extreme thunderstorm warning for Green, Ulster, Delaware and Sullivan counties . . .*'

I looked at Iris. 'That's us.'

'*. . . Radar indicates extreme winds of over one hundred and twenty miles per hour moving north-west at fifteen miles per hour. Storm Mitchell is expected to hit the Catskills on Friday. Expect hail, heavy rain and destructive winds with a chance of flash flooding in the mountain areas. Take shelter, and if you're in the mountains, get to the safety of a large town immediately.*'

My insides turned cold. 'Can you talk back? Get help?'

'I tried. No one's listening. Or the radio isn't working right. I don't know.'

I shifted on the couch, drew my sleeping bag around me like a shield. 'It's bad, isn't it?'

'By the sounds of it, it'll make that rainstorm look like a summer shower. We have four days. Unless the storm speeds up, in which case, who knows?'

I looked around the cabin. The single pane of glass in the window, already cracked. The half-dozen leaks in the roof. The tremble in the beams in the lightest gust of wind.

'Fuck.'

'We have to get out of here,' she said, as if it was new information, and flicked off the radio as the transmission started again.

'It's not like we haven't tried.'

'We have to *do something*!'

'Getting upset won't help.'

'Yeah?' She stood over me. 'Well nothing else seems to be helping.'

'Calm down. We'll figure it out.'

Iris laughed and shook her head. 'We'll figure it out, she says. We'll *figure it out*? We have a few days until the food runs out and we still know nothing. Oh, but it doesn't actually matter how much food we have, because there is a killer storm coming our way.'

'Let's just take a breath, eat something, and have a rational conversation.'

Iris seethed in the middle of the cabin, arms tight across her stomach, nails digging into the flesh of her elbows.

The stove was lit and the camping kettle, blackened from the heat, sat on top, a wisp of steam rising from the spout.

I limped – but barely, my ankle almost healed – to the kitchen and grabbed the coffee can.

I tried to get my nail under the lid, but Other Iris had taken to closing packets properly since the rain. I looked around the kitchen for a knife, but neither Iris's flick knife nor the stubby vegetable peeler was in sight. I'd left mine right there, on the side, I was sure of it. Hadn't I seen Iris with it yesterday?

'Have you seen the knife?' I asked.

'Knife? What knife?' she said, and I paused at her tone. She knew exactly what knife.

'You haven't seen it?'

'Why do you care about a knife right now? We're *dying*.'

I lifted several of Iris's Ziploc bags – God, she was messy, was she always this messy? – but the knife was nowhere. Cursing under my breath, I settled for a former hiker's fork-spoon and levered open the tin. All the while, Iris stared daggers into my back.

I spooned coffee into mugs.

'You've got to be kidding me,' she said, and grabbed my shoulders, spun me around. My ankle twisted and pain shot up my leg. I cried out and she let me go but didn't calm down. 'What's the matter with you?' she almost shouted. 'How can you give a shit about coffee at a time like this?'

'You want me to think before coffee and I'm the crazy one?'

'That's right, make jokes. Ha-fucking-ha.'

I leant against the counter, arms folded. 'I can't stop a storm.'

'No shit, Sherlock, but you can fix this. It's all in your head, isn't it?'

'Is it?'

Iris sighed through her nose. 'We're trapped here because we've both clearly got shit to deal with. I tell you about Bella. You tell me about Claude. We shared. We connected. You started feeling like yourself again, haircut and all that, so why can't we leave?'

'Maybe because you don't want to. Maybe because for you, dying here in this shitty cabin is better than living in the suburbs with your wife and kid.'

Iris shook her head. A bitter laugh escaped her throat. 'Fuck you.'

'How about you stay here, I'll go check if we're still trapped. Maybe the transmission getting through means we can get out. If I don't come back, you'll have your answer.'

Finally the kettle began to whistle. I pushed past Iris, made the strongest, blackest coffee I could stand and went outside with my GO TIGERS mug. This time, she didn't follow.

I took in the calm of the forest because I felt anything but calm. I breathed in the early-morning warmth of the sun, listened for the distant birds greeting the day. Insects buzzed and chittered, invisible in the branches. Small creatures, mice and their predators, skittered here and there, quick and quiet, and yet it all seemed so loud. So sharp and violent and inescapable, and now even the weather, which had been kind for days, was turning on me too.

There was only one place I wanted to go. I wanted space from Iris, her anger, her fear. I had enough of my own. I wanted to sit on a high ledge and see the world, make sure it was still there and

I was still in it. The darkness squatted in me, a thick cloud of it strangling my thoughts. Hope had edged away, day by day, first with the food; and now, with news of the storm, any hope I had left was crushed. Maybe the universe was trying to kill me. It wouldn't let me jump that day, it wanted me to suffer for what I'd done to Claude, to my father, to myself.

Had I suffered enough yet?

I went slowly on my ankle and about halfway heard a familiar sound. A scurrying, chattering I'd heard for weeks then suddenly not at all. I followed the noise, calling his name, thinking it could be any raccoon, but I somehow knew it wasn't. Until there he was. Halfway up a tree, a sun-bleached candy wrapper in his paw. One of my old ones.

'Hello, Monty,' I said. It wasn't that long ago he was taking food from my hand. I hadn't realised until seeing him again how much he'd filled my days, how much I'd missed him.

I moved closer, held out my hand, made soft cooing noises.

He stared down at me like I was a stranger. Had that been real? Those days before Iris, when I'd come close to taming the wild? Was any of this real?

When it became clear Monty had forgotten me, or had never known me, I walked on. Felt those beady black eyes on me until I crested a ridge and dropped out of sight.

At the overhang, I sat on a boulder and looked at the world. There it was, stretched out before me just as it had been. There was the road, the pocket towns nestled in the trees, the storm clouds gathering over far-off peaks. There was no barrier between me and the rest of the world except the one I'd built myself. I couldn't leave here because the trail, the road, the town, a dozen buses back to the city, they weren't the way out. For either of us.

I stepped to the edge.

I stood in the liminal space between two lives. One step and both would resolve. One would go on as it should and one would end as it should.

'Why does yours have to end?' Claude said from the treeline. 'Why not hers?'

'Because of what I did.'

'How do you know she hasn't done worse?'

I turned to her, but she was gone. There was something Iris wasn't telling me. I could feel it. Hear it in her voice, in that high, lying tone when we talked about her father. Everything was just too easy for her, she was too perfect, her life had it all. So why was she really out here? Why was she running away from happiness and family?

Claude stood behind me, her voice close as a kiss. 'Why won't she talk about him?'

I went back to the cabin with an empty cup and a clear mind.

When I opened the door, my gut clenched.

No Iris.

Her pack was here. Her baggies of rations in the kitchen. Her boots were by the door.

A creak from the mezzanine. Her blonde head appeared and all the air rushed out of me.

'What are you doing?' I said.

'Nothing,' she said, too quick, too high. Then came a shuffling, rustling sound, like papers and clothes being rearranged. She'd been sleeping up there for a few nights, but our belongings were at opposites – hers down here, mine up there – until I wasn't sure whose were whose.

'Are you going through my stuff?' I said, setting the cup on the counter and making for the ladder.

'No, no, just having a rest,' she said, and smiled. Her eyes were wild. She'd been caught and she knew it.

I dashed to the ladder and pulled it away before she could climb down.

'What the hell? Put it back!'

I set it against the opposite wall. 'Not until you tell me the truth.'

'I wasn't going through your stuff. You don't even have any stuff.'

Anger flared inside me. 'You want me to trust you? You want me to tell you all my secrets so we can both go home?'

She set her jaw but didn't say anything.

'Fine,' I said, and walked over to her neatly packed rucksack. 'Let's see what you're hiding.'

I flipped open the top of her bag and pulled at the drawstring.

Iris held my eyes for a long moment. So strange to look into your own eyes but not know what lay behind them.

I pulled out clothes, more food, a waterproof, a first aid kit, dumped it all on the floor, and still she didn't stop me. No secrets in there. I turned my back to her and unzipped a side pocket, pulled out a small ring-bound notebook with a stub of pencil stuck in the rings. I flipped through pages of loose scrawl until I found a folded envelope, ragged-edged from being torn open.

I unfolded it and my insides turned cold. It was addressed to Iris. In my father's handwriting. The postmark was just a few months old. He'd touched this paper. He'd written these words.

'Stop! Please!' she said when she saw what I was holding. She hung off the edge of the mezzanine.

'What's in the letter?' I asked.

'It's private.'

'So is my bedroom.'

A moment. A beat. Playing chicken with myself. I could open this letter before she could jump down. I could limp out into the woods and read it before she caught me.

'Fine,' she said through clenched teeth. 'I was going through your stuff. I read like two pages of your notebook then I stopped because it's a bitchy thing to do and I'm not seventeen reading my friend's diary. So there. Okay. I'm sorry.'

'Why would you even look?'

She sighed. 'Because you're hiding something.'

My eyebrows shot up. Are you fucking kidding me?

'I tell you about the worst thing that's ever happened to me. About how the woman I loved . . .' My breath caught, I turned away.

'I know. I'm sorry.'

She sounded sorry. She sounded earnest. But something needled me. A splinter so small I couldn't see it, but I felt the pain. Was she lying? If she lied about this, what else?

'Please put the letter back,' she said, she pleaded, she begged. 'Please.'

'It's from our father.'

'Yes.'

If I had a letter from my father, I would guard it. I wouldn't want anyone else to read it, touch it, breathe near it.

I put the letter back in the notebook, put the notebook in her bag, then set the ladder against the mezzanine. I stood by the door as she climbed down.

We stood face to face. Same height. Same build. Same eyes and mouth and nose and hands. Same breath in our lungs, same blood in our veins, and yet we were worlds apart. Full of different memories, different loves, different secrets. And she did have secrets. I could see them in her eyes, in the way she couldn't quite hold my gaze, in the lying tone we shared.

'I guess we're still trapped here if you're back,' she said.

My stomach dropped. 'I . . . I didn't even check. I went to the overhang. You can see the storm coming from there.'

'You didn't check? Jesus Christ, Iris!' She grabbed her jacket and rushed out the door. It slammed behind her so hard a book toppled from the shelf.

'So dramatic,' came Claude's voice from the couch.

'Shut up,' I said, and set the book right.

'She might not come back,' she said.

I thought the same. What if the transmission did mean there was a way out? What if that was it, that was the last time I saw Iris? There were still so many questions unanswered, so many loose ends to tie up. That couldn't be it, could it?

I wasn't ready to return to my life. I wasn't fixed. I wasn't whole. Please don't let that be it.

A hand – my hand, not my hand – on my shoulder shaking me.

'Iris, for fuck's sake, wake up.' A harsh voice. My voice.

I opened my eyes to my face. 'Iris?'

She hadn't left me. It wasn't over. My heart lifted.

She gripped my sleeve and pulled me close. 'We're not alone.'

Her words were an ice bath after a sauna. 'What do you mean?'

She breathed heavily, eyes darting to the door, to the window, to me. She was terrified.

'I walked. I saw someone. I called out. They went towards the overhang. It was a woman. A woman in a red jacket.'

The ice set hard in my veins.

'I followed her. I saw her. She stood at the edge. I couldn't get there fast enough. She didn't hear me. Didn't want to. I tried. She . . . she jumped.'

My hand went to my mouth.

'She's still there. Down there. I ran. I ran towards town and then I was back here. We're still trapped. And that woman. Oh God.'

Her grip was iron. I pushed against her, got to my feet, put my boots on, my jacket. 'We have to help. She might still be alive.'

She stared at the floor, shaking her head.

'Come *on!*'

I dragged her up, pulled her out the cabin, through the forest until her legs took over and we ran together.

The rain began. Not heavy, but fat drops, full of ozone. The herald of the oncoming storm.

We both stopped at the treeline. The edge of the overhang was ten feet away and neither of us could move. The rain fell in soft sheets, no wind to guide it. The clouds, boiling black and colossal, filled the sky above the valley.

Iris stepped back. 'I can't.'

'You can.'

I grabbed her arm, pulled her with me to the edge.

We looked.

We saw.

A body. Still as the rock. A red jacket we both knew. Both wore. Short hair turned red with blood. It was her and me and us. But which? Which Iris was down there? What had she done to the people she loved?

Iris stumbled back, threw up in the ferns.

'Who is that?' she said, wiping her mouth.

'You know who it is.'

'That's impossible.'

'No,' I said. 'It's what happens if we don't face up to what we've done. Who we are. It's what happens if we keep our secrets.'

I stared down at the body on the rocks. I'd been a step away from that more than once. We were silent for a long time, for ever. The wind had dropped and the air was still. The rain was sluggish, slow. I watched a drop as it fell, as if gravity had loosened its grip on this place, as if the world had started to turn backwards. The birds didn't sing. The insects didn't buzz. There was nothing in the world except me and me. All the mes. Dead. Alive. Lying. Scared. Guilty. One was down there, broken, having taken the route I had wanted, the one my father took. One was beside me, full of secrets and regret and anger. But which would I become? Her, or her, or another?

'I was hiking here. To right here.'

Her voice snapped me back and I realised I was standing so close to the edge that the toe of my boot was in the air.

I moved back, my insides shaking, and gathered myself.

'This is Randall Peak?' I said, my voice weak against the rain. 'You said it was miles away.'

'I lied. My father, we came here once. He stood right there and looked down at those rocks and he said, "One more step, Rissy, and I'm a free man." He didn't jump. Didn't do it. But . . .'

'What?'

But I knew the answer. It all made sense now.

We would always end up here, her and me.

Iris dropped to her knees in the mud. She covered her mouth with her hands, stifled her sobs. 'I was going to jump. Like her. That would have been me down there.'

I looked at her, and for the first time, despite sharing the same face, I saw myself truly reflected in her. I saw my darkness and my light. I saw my past and where all my myriad decisions had led me. A comfort, really, despite the pain of it all.

She met my eyes and I wondered if she saw it too.

I went to her, wrapped myself around her. 'It would have been me too, down there. If I hadn't met you.'

I wanted to climb down the cliff, find the other Iris, hold her body to mine and say sorry.

'I wish I could say sorry to her,' Iris said into my shoulder.

She clung to me and I to her and we cried at what we'd lost. Who we'd lost. Who we'd become. Who we might still become.

'I don't want to die here.' I don't know which of us said it, but we both meant it.

We were numb, back at the cabin. Sat side by side on the couch in silence. The sight of her, of an Iris we both could – would – have been, had made this too real. The thought of a body out there, where no one knew to look, made me sick. That would have been me, rotting away on those rocks, carrion for the crows.

I couldn't let that be me.

I had to tell the truth. I had nothing to lose any more. I was sloughing off my fake skin and mask and discovering real Iris again. And Real Iris had lost her father.

'My dad died when I was sixteen,' I said.

Iris looked at me.

'He hanged himself from the oak tree at Putnam Reserve.'

She looked away. 'Jesus.'

'I want you to tell me about your father. He's the key to this. I know it.'

She opened her mouth, seemed to hesitate, as if she wasn't sure what I was really asking. 'He's happy now. Finally. It took a long time. Two divorces. Three states. A dozen career changes. We didn't see each other for years. After I married Bella, moved into the 'burbs, he got angry. He said I'd sold out, turned into my mother. That was just about the worst thing he could have said to me.'

I didn't believe it. My father would never say that. And yet . . . I remembered his words at the crater lake, his tone, his anger. *Damn it, Josie, don't you want me to be happy?* I forced it away. My father, for all his faults, wasn't cruel. She must have done something, hurt him somehow. She chose a boring life, while he'd always hoped she would reach the stars, walk on other planets, discover worlds, follow a passion to the ends of the earth. Like I had. I'd followed my passion to Claude. I'd followed it to the Planetarium. I'd followed it to a new life in the woods.

'But you made up?' I asked.

She pulled her knees up to her chest. 'Before he wrote to me, we hadn't spoken for years.'

Years. I hated her in that moment. Hate so hot it blistered my insides. But I cooled it. Heard myself hiss.

'We've both lost so much time with him,' I said.

She smiled, but it was half-hearted.

We sat in silence for a while. I had so many questions, but if I asked one, they would all flood from my lips and drown her. We had some time. At least until the food ran out or the storm ripped us apart.

'Where are we, do you think?' she asked. She didn't mean where in the state. Or where emotionally. She meant in space, in time. She was afraid. I heard it in her voice.

'Somewhere . . . in between our lives.'

'Like limbo?'

'Or purgatory.'

She looked down at her hands, rubbed at her thumb like I did when I was thinking. 'Are we dead? Like her, at the bottom of that cliff? Did we both jump and now we're in hell?'

I pinched her arm. Hard.

'Hey!'

'If you were dead, you wouldn't feel it.'

She stared at me in shock, mouth open, eyebrows in her hairline. Then she laughed. 'I can be a real bitch sometimes.'

'I'll drink to that.'

And we did, until there was no more rum and whatever time we had left suddenly seemed far too long. It was night sooner than I expected. I barely remembered the afternoon. Time seemed fluid, the daylight short, the night a blink and yet eternal.

She lay on the mezzanine, and I on the couch and neither of us spoke.

I still couldn't find Iris's knife, nor my own blunt one. One of my notebooks had disappeared too.

All I could think of was the body at the base of the overhang. But was it hers, or mine, or neither or both? Nothing made sense any more.

'Have you seen the knife?' I asked, and she didn't answer, just stared out the window or into the fire. I asked again and she snapped a no.

I didn't have the energy to fight her any more. She'd hidden the letter from her father too. She wouldn't be pressed on its contents. I went for a walk to strengthen my ankle, felt the pressure of the storm. The wind began to shake the trees.

I got back to the cabin an hour or so later. Iris was already up on the mezzanine.

In the morning, the wind had picked up. Another day and the storm would be upon us.

I heard her sneak off while she thought I was still asleep. She never fell asleep before me. Never woke up after.

She began to change in front of my eyes. Withdraw into herself and barely talk. Her skin turned ashen and her cheeks sunk.

We holed up that day, listening for every change in the weather, every gust of wind bent the trees and shook the window panes. We shared silent expressions when the rain grew heavy and loud. Then it would stop. The skies would clear. The wind would drop but we knew it wouldn't last. We chopped wood while we could. We monitored the radio but got nothing but static.

It took coaxing and round-about questions to learn about her mother. Her own Josie, the same as mine. Married to a Fischer. Happier without my father. And Helen, married to a John. Baby girl on the way. I told Iris to make sure she didn't call her Minnie. The poor child would never live it down. I tried to joke, but she didn't laugh. Her Ellis was settled down. Inspired by the success of Iris and Bella, he'd found the about-right girl and was gearing up to propose. Everyone's life was better in her world. A Utopia for everyone but Iris.

She wouldn't talk about Bella. She brushed off the topic every time we edged close. She wouldn't talk about the pregnancy or having a baby or what it would mean for them and for her. She would only say how excited Bella was, how much Bella wanted to be a mother, how happy Josie and Helen were. Never her own feelings towards it. Never our father's.

Iris wouldn't scratch below the surface, draw the blood we'd need to be free of this place. So I didn't either. The wounds I'd opened had dried to tight scabs. The sight of our death had shut her down.

I had to act, put an end to all this, but how? Fewer and fewer words passed between us, and any hope I had of getting to the truth about her father, where I was sure the key to all this lay, diminished to nothing.

'The storm is going to be here tomorrow. We should cover the windows at least, maybe take a look at the roof,' I said as I was splitting a log for kindling.

Iris stared out the window, through my telescope, at a rare moment of clear night sky.

'Did you hear me?'

Her shoulders dropped.

'We can't survive this,' she said in that listless tone I'd come to hate.

My temper broke. 'Not with you moping about like this. What are you hoping to achieve other than pissing me off?'

She pressed her eye to the telescope.

'The stars are different.'

I looked at her. 'What do you mean?'

'They're faint and in the wrong places. Sirius should be in the east, but it's in the north. Cassiopeia should be south-east, but it's not even there.'

I closed my eyes. Her tone was weak and needling and every word she spoke took another bite out of my patience.

'Did you ever want kids?' she asked out of nowhere.

The question shook me, and at first, I didn't know the answer.

'Claude and I discussed having children once,' I said.

She turned to face me. 'And?'

In the corner of the room, in the shadows of the overhanging mezzanine, a cigarette tip blazed orange in the dark and I heard Claude's laugh float to me like smoke.

'It never went anywhere,' I said, my eyes on that dark spot. 'By the end, I wouldn't have brought a child into that but at the beginning, it was on the cards. Claude wanted one of each. Then three. Then four. Then back to two. She said she'd raise them as her mother raised her. A glass of wine in one hand, a cigarillo in the other, and nanny down the hall.

'I told her if we had kids, we'd have to move out of the city, somewhere with parks and yards to play in. Good schools. She'd pretend to throw up at the idea. She said we could stay in the apartment. There was a terrace for them to play outside and Central Park was only a block away. What better park is there?'

Iris raised an eyebrow. 'You live on the Upper West Side?'

'Pre-war building. Parquet floors. A doorman. The works. Claude told me one of the Campbell's soup family lives two floors down, and there's a Baldwin in the penthouse, but I haven't met them.'

'Why didn't I know that?'

I shrugged. 'You didn't ask.'

She cocked her head as if to say *touché*, then said, 'What about work?'

'I was at the Hayden for a while. Deputy Head of Programming. I want to go back. I was good at that job. Really good at it. But Claude made me leave for an awful corporate position that paid better.'

'Wow, you really did have it all,' she said, not even trying to hide the bitterness in her voice.

In the corner, Claude stepped into the light and tapped cigarette ash onto the floorboards. 'You really did, Iris, you had everything'. I closed my eyes and counted. I got to four before Iris interrupted.

'The Hayden,' Iris said. 'I loved that place when I was a kid.'

I opened my eyes. She shook her head slowly, as if in disbelief, or sadness maybe.

'Me too,' I said. Claude waved. 'Dad took me there all the time.'

I forced a smile. Iris turned back to the window with a frown. Her – my – thinking face. A thought, a decision, swept across her eyes and she looked at me strangely, then turned away. Her hand reached around her back, and for a horrible second I thought she had the knife in her belt, but she only pressed on aching muscles.

She relaxed again and smiled at me. 'He would have liked you better.'

'I doubt it. But it doesn't matter. My dad's gone; you still have a chance with yours.'

She laughed, but nothing about our situation seemed funny.

After

'I have to leave,' Iris was saying, over and over. Her voice, soft but manic, floated down from the mezzanine to the couch. 'I have to go. I have to get out.'

She ranged from whispers to full-breath words and back, like she wasn't stopping to breathe, speaking on the inhale and exhale.

'There's no time left. I have to do it. Have to make it stop.'

Iris lay at the edge of the platform, legs drawn up into the foetal position, hands clutching something.

'I have to. I have to. The storm. The food.'

I flinched when I saw the light catch the blade. My missing knife.

I lay back on the couch, stared at the grain in the fabric, at the dirt and wear embedded in the fibres, and listened to the woman above me whisper.

'Has to be today. Can't wait any longer.'

I gripped the blanket. My pulse throbbed in my ears, tightened my chest with every beat. A boa of panic constricting every time I breathed. Today. What happens today?

Did Iris do this every night? Mutter into the early hours about how she needed to leave? Did she hold the knife like a talisman?

The old mattress springs sighed. The soft shuffle of her body positioning itself on the ladder.

My heart thundered. I couldn't move.

Terror held fast to every muscle and tendon. I knew this fear. We were old friends. A woman coming to hurt me. How had this become so familiar? At least Claude never used a knife.

Do something, Jane.

Fucking *do something*!

A cough exploded from my closed throat. Cleared the dust, released my body. The ladder fell still.

'Morning,' I said in my best calm, sleep-filled voice.

'Afternoon, more like,' she said, a jolly tease. A forced levity.

I watched Iris climb down the ladder, fully dressed in what she had worn the day before. She smiled when she saw me, as if nothing had happened. If she couldn't knife me, would she try to burn down the cabin? Bar the doors, light a match. I tried to return the smile.

'I'm going for a walk, see where the storm is,' I said, and she nodded.

I needed to be sure. Needed to know her intent. I searched for a way to ask without asking.

'Have you seen the knife? I spotted some bear tracks. Wouldn't hurt to have a bit of protection. Even if we can't leave this bubble, doesn't mean a bear can't get in. Even the blunt one would be better than nothing.'

Iris frowned, cast a quick glance around the kitchen. 'Haven't seen it. Maybe you dropped it outside? At the stream?'

There it is. My stomach clenched, turned cold, as if my insides were suddenly run through with ice water.

'Yeah. Maybe.'

I grabbed her jacket as if it was mine and went to the door.

The forest offered no solace now. It was a prison, not a sanctuary. Every day the animals and insects grew quieter and the air felt harder to breathe.

I headed past the stream, up a slope towards the clearing. The first place I'd seen my reality shift. The sky was grey and oppressive, the air crackled with the tension of the storm. The trees creaked and seemed to hunker down, turning their backs, drawing in their branches against the wind. Not far off, thunder boomed and a light slick of rain began to fall.

I looked back at the cabin, nestled in the dip of a valley, such a small structure among the giant oaks, firs and redwoods. They would sway and bend and survive, but that cabin? It didn't stand a chance.

Did I stand a chance against Iris?

I turned.

And came face to face with myself.

Not Iris. Not the one trying to kill me. The one already dead. The Iris at the bottom of the cliff.

Broken, bloody, smashed and torn Iris. Her arm was bent horribly, her chest caved in, her ankle twisted, snapped, hanging.

But her eyes. They blazed. Alive. And angry.

Her mouth moved. Teeth turned to splinters.

Blood poured and sprayed and she reached for me.

I screamed.

Stumbled, fell back, down the slope, ankle twisted. Head hit a rock.

The world turned red as my eyes filled with blood. Her blood? Mine?

The crimson clouds swirled and pulsed in and out, the trees grew and shrank, the light dimmed and I drifted away. Or I thought I did. The day was light and dark all at once, the forest silent and painfully loud, I was alone and then I wasn't. I was seeing myself. Dead me. Alive me. Past me. Future me. Eyes above me, unconcerned, appraising, deciding whether or not to finish the job. Fingers on my jugular. A knife in her hand.

'Are you . . .' *Trying to kill me?* I couldn't say it. Throat wouldn't push out the air, head wouldn't form the words. But the sound of my voice helped. Cleared the fog.

'Iris?'

Who said it? Her or me? I couldn't tell.

Her eyes, blazing, angry, rushed at me as she knelt. I felt hands under my shoulders, my neck, hoisting me up and onto her lap.

The forest swam into focus. Her fingers brushed my face, came away red and sticky. My own went to the cut on my forehead. Another scar. Another wound reopened.

'What happened?' she asked. 'You've been gone for hours.'

Her question opened a floodgate of pain. My brain was too big for my skull.

'She's there,' I managed. I pointed a dirty, bloody finger.

'Who? Where?'

'Her. Iris. The one who jumped. She's here.'

Iris looked around. 'There's no one here.'

I struggled up onto my elbows, my head finally clear, ears no longer ringing. The forest was empty. No broken me at the top of the hill. Only the lying one beside me.

The pain rose in my head like a flash flood. I closed my eyes against it, pressed my hand to my head as if to keep my brains inside.

My hand came away red. 'Fuck.'

'You're seeing things,' Iris said, disentangling herself from me, practically pushing me away from her in disgust.

'You finally clocked on to that, huh?'

'I'm not a fucking hallucination,' she spat. 'When are you going to get that through your head?'

Using a tree, I got to my feet, faced her and her anger, felt my own rising to meet it.

'Oh I don't know, maybe when you start telling me the truth.'

She threw her arms up. 'I've told you everything! Can you hear yourself? You're insane!'

'I'm insane? I'm fucking insane? Where's the knife, Iris? Huh?'

That stopped her.

'I don't know.'

'What's happening today? What can't wait any longer?'

'I don't know what you're—'

'I heard you! I heard your psycho whispering. I saw the knife in your hands.'

Lie exposed, she regrouped. 'I needed it. For protection.'

'Protection against what?'

'You!' She took a step towards me. 'I get what you're doing, you know. All those questions about my dad and Bella. You want all the details, don't you? Why is that?'

Same person. Same ideas. Idiot, Iris. But I'd had Claude to learn from. She once said to take a piece of truth and use it to build a lie.

'It was your idea!' I cried. 'You said we need to get to know each other. Talk about our lives, *share*. But you're a hypocrite.

Happy to listen but never sharing. What's in the letter? Why are you *here*?'

'I told you why I was going to Randall Peak.'

'No. You told me what you were going to do when you got there. You didn't tell me why you were going. Because you don't want a kid?' I laughed. The anger bubble swelled. 'That's bullshit and you know it. Why are you such a fucking coward?'

She clenched her jaw. I'd struck the nerve like it was a guitar string.

'I'm not a coward,' she said.

'Yes you are. Because I am too. I know you, remember, and I want to help you and help myself, and maybe, Jesus, maybe if we are honest with each other, I won't end up like my father or the Iris who did jump. I don't want to end up like that and I almost did.' My words caught but I forced them out, tears came and spilled like rain and I didn't wipe them away.

'Me neither,' she said.

I slid down the tree and sat on the ground. The anger had faded and left a bone-deep exhaustion.

'Please,' I said. 'I don't want to die here. Neither do you. You said so.'

Tears spiked her eyes and she hugged herself, staring at her shoes.

'I feel so trapped. The things I've done . . .' She trailed off.

I reached out to her, held her hand and felt her fingers tighten around mine. Me too, I wanted to say, the things I've done . . . but I still couldn't. Our eyes met and we both forced the same smile, then she helped me up and we went back to the cabin.

We sat together on the couch, fire blazing, hot mugs in hand. For a while, we listened to the thunder, the crackle and hiss of the wood, the light growls in our stomachs after five days of rations, until Iris finally spoke.

'I never wanted kids,' she said, eyes on the steam rising from her cup. 'Bella did, of course. She talked about it all the time. She said she had the job she wanted, the house she wanted, the wife she wanted . . .' She paused, shook her head. 'If only she knew, huh?'

I smiled and nodded for her to keep going.

'She had everything she wanted except a baby. And that was the one thing I didn't want. But I loved her and I'd promised her happiness till death do us part, right? So I asked Mom and Fischer for a loan for part of the treatment, and we went to the bank for the rest.

'When she got pregnant a few months later, I'd never seen her so happy, and for a while, that was enough. But the closer we got to the due date, the more the house filled up with baby stuff, the more debt we got into, the reality set in that this was happening and nothing could stop it. I stopped seeing friends. I hid myself from Bella. I started having panic attacks at work. I felt trapped, but Bella just kept asking, kept making plans, kept saying how wonderful it would be, and it became easier to agree. I didn't know what else to do.'

'So you thought throwing yourself off a mountain was the most sensible course of action?'

She tried to smile. 'It really did start off as a vacation. But then the thought of going back to that . . . I understand Dad a lot better now.'

'I don't.'

'Of course you don't,' she said, and looked me dead in the eye. 'We're both trapped in unhappy marriages. The difference? When you leave your wife, you're a hero. When I leave mine, I'm a coward. And I'm not a coward.'

'Aren't you?'

Her eyes narrowed and her defences sprang back up. 'What about you? You're running from an abusive marriage. I get that. But why only now? You said she nearly killed you. Why didn't you leave years ago? What happened?'

My top lip flinched. I felt the snarl under my skin wanting to get out. 'I told you everything.'

She laughed. Shook her head. A grotesque mirror. 'Bullshit.'

'And you're a paragon of truth too, huh? I'm sorry about Bella, I really am, but there's more you're not telling me.'

'Is there?'

'What happened between you and your dad?'

'I already told you.'

'I don't believe you.'

We held each other's gaze for too long, each urging the other to crack first, but we were evenly matched.

Finally Iris set her mug on the floor and got up. 'I'm going for a walk.'

She was never going to tell me. She was never going to tell the truth. And I couldn't bring myself to either. We were too similar. Yet I had at least come to terms with my pain, spoken it aloud, tried to exorcise some of my demons. She hadn't. She was a part of me I couldn't lever open, with a secret I couldn't access.

'We're dying in here,' I said. 'You see that, don't you?'

At the door, she turned. 'You know something, Iris? You have no idea how lucky you are. No fucking idea. You live in a beautiful apartment, you had a fantastic job and yeah, okay, a bitch of a wife, but you can leave her. Keep the rest and leave her. You didn't have to watch your dad grow old and miserable and you didn't have to watch him suffer every day until . . . fuck . . . I'd kill for your life. You hear me? I'd kill for it.'

Her tone set ice in my veins. Her stare could snap steel. She flung open the cabin door and stalked out into the trees.

Claude's heels clicked on the floorboards behind the couch. I felt her weight on the cushions behind my head and her breath tickling the hair at my neck.

'She means it.'

'I know.'

Other Iris reminded me of him. Of the time beside the lake in Banff when he'd started pulling logs into the shape of a cabin. The way he'd talked to himself, made plans, cursing the world for its mistakes, blaming everyone else. She did that. Blamed Bella for trapping her. Blamed her father for calling her a sell-out. Blamed her mother for everything else.

I only blamed myself.

'You should,' came Claude's whisper, right in my ear. That purr sent a shiver through me. 'It really is all your fault.'

'I know.'

'He died because of you. You told him he didn't have to stay, and he left. Forever.'

'I know.'

'You stuck with me despite what was happening. You don't deserve any better than me.'

I lowered my head.

Her whisper came closer. 'You should end it. Now. Before she does.'

I watched the door swing slowly shut. Our world was closing in on us. The morning would mean the last day of our food supplies. The storm would hit. We were out of time. I looked at the door, pictured the woman somewhere beyond it and what she might do to me if I didn't act first.

'She has a knife,' Claude said.

'I know.'

Before

Spring dragged itself free of a hard winter, bringing late buds and new growth. I watched the leaves form on the lemon tree we kept on the terrace. The pot was ceramic and too small and the tree never fruited. Every year I watched it grow and try. An inch here and there, a new crop of leaves, a branch striking out to a patch of sunlight only to be trimmed back into shape by Claude's shears.

I like the smell of the leaves, she'd said when I asked her why she cut it back so harshly. But she didn't like lemons.

The terrace door opened. Claude stepped out, fastening her dressing gown against the morning chill.

'Shouldn't you be packing?'

'My train isn't for two hours.'

'But you don't want to be late.'

I pressed my eyes closed. 'I won't be.'

Claude lingered beside me until I looked at her.

'How are you?' she asked in a tone packed with strained sincerity.

I shifted, suddenly uncomfortable with her attention. 'Fine.'

'I wish I had known your father.'

I'm glad he never knew you, I wanted to say, but didn't. Instead I forced a smile and said, 'Me too.'

She rested her hand on my shoulder. My body tensed at her touch and she felt it.

'You're coming back, aren't you, Iris?'

I looked up at her, put my hand on hers. 'Of course.'

She smiled, squeezed my shoulder and kissed the top of my head.

'See you on Saturday,' she said before going back inside and gently closing the door behind her.

I waited the forty or so minutes until I heard her leave for work, then started packing. Four days at home with my mother, sister and Fischer suddenly seemed like the worst idea I'd ever had. But I had to get away, get some space from Claude, take a breather from the daily dose of anxiety whenever I heard her key in the door.

It had been a few months since the last fight. I'd regained sensation in my face and my physio said I didn't need his services anymore, just keep doing the exercises. The scar on my forehead was still red and livid, but I could cover most of it with my hair. Ellis still wasn't speaking to me. I had resigned myself to my life. Accepted my prison walls and tried to decorate them as best I could.

I had to run to catch the train. I tried not to imagine Claude tutting at me, holding back an 'I told you so', but the image came nonetheless. My sister picked me up at the station at the other end. She smiled and waved when she saw me. We kissed both cheeks and I hugged her tighter than I ever had.

'It's so good to see you,' I said, and meant it.

As dreadful as the idea of spending time with them had been, that all disappeared the moment I saw her.

'I'm sorry I'm not back more often,' I said as she pulled out of the parking lot and onto the streets I'd grown up on.

'It's good you're here now. He'd have loved it.'

Helen had changed over the years, as I knew I had. She'd lost the sharp snark and vivacity, and had taken on a comforting, motherly confidence that instantly put me at ease.

'You cut your hair,' I said. 'It's nice.'

She touched the ends self-consciously. A short bob, tight to her chin. A style I'd never have imagined for her. She'd always worn her hair long and loose.

'You think?' she said, almost wincing. 'It wasn't planned. I went into the salon for the usual, but when I saw myself in the mirror, I thought, God, am I really that old? So I told the girl to cut it all off. Mom nearly fainted. You really like it?'

I smiled. At least one of us got to express herself. 'I love it. Suits you.'

'John was shocked at first, but now it's like we're newly-weds again,' she said with a blush.

I smiled and kept my eyes on the road. The familiar streets, the places I'd ridden my bike, the kerb I'd tripped over and scraped my hands, friends' houses I used to visit. A world caught in time.

'How is Claude?' Helen asked.

'Fine.'

She caught my tone. 'Are you two doing okay?'

I didn't answer. Couldn't. Felt the tiny white scar on my cheek, the other at my hairline, burn under my foundation.

'Iris? You can talk to me, you know.'

'Look, there's Mom,' I blurted out as we rounded the corner onto our street.

My mother waved from the porch and Helen swung the car into the drive without another word. She kept a worried look on her face most of the day, but didn't ask again.

It was a Wednesday, and Fischer was at work. The three of us had the house to ourselves. Mom made tea, Helen set about fixing some lunch. The pair of them moved around the kitchen like they lived in it, each knowing what the other was doing, never having to ask where the knives or plates or pickles were kept, never having awkward moments of going for the same drawer at the same time. They were in synch. My absence had left me a spectator in my own family.

'Rissy, dear,' my mother said. My father's nickname stabbed like a bee sting in my palm. 'Why don't you take your bag upstairs and get settled while we finish up down here.'

Time was I'd have made a comment about how I had as much right to be in the kitchen as them. But I didn't. I took my bag upstairs to my old room, dumped it in the corner and sat on the bed. The bed where I'd lain the last day I'd seen my father. The room where I'd last spoken to him. And now here I was, on the eve of what would have been his sixtieth birthday, understanding how he did what he did.

Whispers drifted up the stairs.

'Is she all right?' my mother asked.

'I don't know, she doesn't seem herself. She clammed up when I asked about Claude.'

'I never liked that woman.'

I know, Mom. I kicked the door shut and lay back on the bed.

I woke up to a gentle knock and Helen sneaking into the room. She told me to budge over, then climbed into the bed beside me.

'What's going on?' she whispered.

It was late, I noticed, the sun gone, the dark full. I'd slept all day.

'You woke me up is what's going on.'

'I'm worried about you.'

I sighed and rolled over. 'There's nothing to worry about.'

Helen stayed for a minute or two, then, when it was clear she'd get nothing more out of me, she stood up and went to the door.

'If you ever want to talk . . .'

I pulled a pillow over my head in an unfairly petulant manner. I did want to talk. I wanted to tell her everything Claude had done, but I couldn't. The shame was too great, the fear they'd laugh at me too real. They'd tell me to leave her, come home, and I'd say I'd rather be on the streets, and the argument would escalate to the point where I'd storm out. I didn't want a fight. I was sick of fighting. I wanted to drink to my father on his birthday then go home. And when I got home, I would have a conversation with Claude. A real one.

The thought turned my stomach cold.

I tried to put it out of my head and think of my father. Of how we would sit outside, cocooned in blankets, watching the stars move. Of how he would teach me the names of the trees when we hiked through the endless forests. Of the bear hugs and belly laughs and time. He always had time for me.

And on that one crucial day, I didn't have time for him.

I buried myself in the duvet and went back to sleep.

The morning began with breakfast, which I ignored in favour of coffee, and stilted conversation with Mother and Fischer. Helen got up an hour or so later, saying she hadn't had such a peaceful night's sleep since the children were born.

Mid morning, Fischer drove us to the cemetery and had the good sense to wait in the car.

My dad rested at the crest of a hill beneath a broad cypress tree. The wind had sculpted the branches into a green swipe, rich and full on one side, bare on the other. The canopy shaded his grave. Fitting, for the man caught between worlds.

We laid flowers and said happy birthday. We stood for a while in silence. Even Mother respected the occasion. She'd mellowed with the years, same as Helen, the waspishness gone, the need to keep up with the Joneses and Smiths and Hardcastles and everyone else on the street diminished. She was happy in herself, I could see it. And she was happy with Fischer.

Don't worry, Dad, I still hate him.

I kissed my fingers and placed them on the gravestone.

'Love you, Dad. See you soon,' I said, and clocked a glance between Helen and my mother.

The rest of the day was quiet, with a constant supply of food and drink and soft conversation. As afternoon rolled around, Fischer disappeared into his den. Helen went upstairs and came down with a framed photograph of Dad, taken on the first day of our Banff vacation. He stood on the shores of the aquamarine lake, hair ruffled, collar loose. He never looked happier.

Mother got a bottle of tequila and filled three shot glasses, saying it was eight o'clock somewhere when we protested at how early it was. We toasted him. Reminisced. Helen and I told stories, Mother told of how they met but mostly just listened. The tequila flowed. A happy buzz came over me and I felt a dull ache in my chest at how much I missed them, how I hadn't realised it until right then.

We laughed for what felt like hours. Fischer came out of his hole and kissed my mother goodnight before going upstairs. She looked at him with pure adoration and held him for a moment longer than necessary.

He wasn't so bad.

God, I was drunk. And so was my mother.

'You know, girls, Bob is such a good man,' my mother said, slurring her edges. 'Such a wonderful provider.'

'We're not here for Fischer, Mom,' I said.

But she didn't seem to hear. 'I *know* he's not your father, Rissy dear, but he *loves* you *so* much.'

'Uh huh.'

'Oh he *does*, he does. He's been around just as long as your father was, too.'

I frowned. 'What? No he hasn't.'

Mother nodded. 'Fifteen years in July, darling.'

Drunk maths was not my mother's strong suit.

'Ten years, Mom. You've been married to Fischer for ten. Dad died fourteen years ago.'

She shook her head, waving her hand as if to knock away the truth. 'No, no, no. *Fifteen*.'

I sighed, but something in the way Helen straightened and sipped her shot made me pause.

'Mom, how can you have been with Fischer for fifteen years?' I said.

She gulped down the tequila like it was water. 'Because we met at the post office. I remember, because I was mailing a package to Helen, who was at Camp Maki ... Mekky ... Where was that, Helly?'

'Camp Mikinak,' she muttered.

Helen had only been to summer camp once – too expensive to send her again, too expensive to send me at all, though I desperately wanted to go.

'But,' I said, 'that was the summer before senior year. A year before Dad ...'

The penny dropped like a stone.

'You were seeing Fischer while ... You were having an affair?'

Mother's sharp eyes found mine. 'No, darling.' The slur in her voice suddenly clear. 'My marriage to your father was long dead by then.'

I winced at the choice of words. 'Did he know? Dad. Did he find out?'

She didn't answer, just looked down at the table, turned the glass in her hands. Claude did that. That same movement. The spinning glass. As if it were a trick to hypnotise me. Sudden rage flared in my chest.

I looked at Helen. Silent, eyes down. Like mother, like daughter.

'You knew, didn't you?' I said to her, and she sighed.

'I didn't know how to tell you.'

'How long have you known?'

Silence. Telling, obvious silence.

'From the beginning?' I asked.

'I found out about two years after Dad died. We didn't see any sense in telling you. You took his death so hard.'

'Because he was *my father*! And he killed himself. *Did he know?*'

No answer. No one would look at me.

I slammed my palm on the table. The glasses shook. The photo toppled with a sharp crack.

'Tell me!'

My mother gave a weary sigh, as if I was a child having a tantrum in the supermarket. 'I told him.'

'When?' The word came out like a clenched fist.

'We . . . discussed it after Helen graduated high school. I told him I wanted a divorce.'

Helen's graduation. She was packing for college when he died. The timing fit. All of it.

I felt sick. Hollowed out and filled with bile. I clutched my stomach. Could barely breathe.

'Oh God. Oh you didn't.' It was all I could say, over and over. 'He knew. That's why he did it. That's why he went into the woods. Were you away with Fischer that weekend? Is that why you wouldn't answer my calls?'

My mother turned to flint. 'Your father was a troubled man. I will not apologise for falling in love. I raised his children and I put up with his complaints about his job and living in the awful *suburbs.* I did everything for him for twenty years. It was time for me to find happiness of my own. I'll not apologise, Iris.'

I sat back from the table. She'd cheated on my father. She'd asked for a divorce, and a month later, he'd killed himself. He'd waited until she and Helen were out of town and it was just me and him.

I looked at the two women around the table. A cruel, cold monster and her deceitful daughter. They had lied to me for half my life.

I reached across the table and picked up the photo frame. My father smiled at me from the Rocky Mountains. The only member of my family who'd never lied to me.

'I don't know who you people are any more,' I said. 'I don't think I ever did.'

I took the photo out of the frame and left the room. I went upstairs to pack. I shoved yesterday's clothes into my bag, grabbed my toothbrush from the bathroom and slipped on my shoes. When I turned to leave, Helen was standing in the doorway.

'Don't go like this.'

'Move.'

'Please, let's talk about this.'

'No,' I said. 'We're done talking. We're done being sisters.'

'Iris . . .'

'Get out of my way.'

She stepped aside and I brushed past her. For a moment I thought she would grab my arm, try again, but she didn't. My mother was still at the table when I came downstairs. She saw the bag and gave a theatrical sigh.

'Oh Iris, you're being so childish. This is exactly why we didn't tell you. We knew you'd overreact—'

But I didn't hear the rest over the slam of the front door. They didn't follow.

I walked to the station and changed my ticket to the 7.17 into Grand Central. I waited the twenty minutes in silence, staring wide-eyed at the cracks in the tiled floor, replaying every second of that conversation, every moment since Helen's high school graduation, to see if I'd missed anything. My mother had seemed happier in those months, but I'd put it down to pride in Helen going to college and finally getting one child out the house. But it was Fischer. She was seeing him and destroying our family, and she was happy about it.

I wanted to see Claude. For the first time in a long time, I wanted to see her, speak to her, have someone, at least, on my side. Better the devil I married than the ones I called family. I thought about calling Ellis, but it had been months since we'd spoken, and that particular door remained closed. Claude was all I had left. How fucked up is that?

I got back to the city around 9.30. I called her as soon as I stepped off the train.

After five or six rings, she picked up.

'*Oui?*' she said, a rush in her voice.

'Hey, I just wanted to—'

'Iris, I can't talk right now. I'm at the office.'

'This won't take long, I—'

'I'm sorry, I have to go. So much paperwork, I'll be here all night. I hope today was not too bad. I will see you Saturday, *ma chérie.*'

'Claude . . .' But she'd already hung up.

I gripped the phone. I needed to see her now, and no, it couldn't wait. I was in crisis.

I shouldn't have to wait. She was my wife, wasn't she? She should make time. After all this, she owed me that. I couldn't think straight, could barely walk straight. I needed an anchor, and despite everything, Claude was it.

I took the subway downtown, walked to her office. Despite the hour, the building was open and late-working besuited drones hurried across the lobby. I told the receptionist who I was, and he called Claude's assistant, who was probably too afraid of Claude to deny me access. I rode the elevator up to the Tillman and Gaines offices and was met by a confused-looking girl, twenty-something, dark hair, immaculate skirt-and-jacket combination. A mini Claude. I almost threw up at the sight of her.

The offices were empty except for a few haggard-looking associates.

I ignored the girl and forged ahead, straight for Claude's office. Not a corner. I'd lost her the corner. A bitter taste rose up in my mouth.

The assistant trailed behind, her voice like a shrill bird, 'We weren't expecting you . . . Can I get you a water? . . . Ms Marceau is very busy . . .'

I rounded the corner to Claude's glass-fronted office. Readied myself for her polite rage, decided to risk it.

But the lights were off.

Her office was empty.

The files neat. The desktop clear. The door closed.

It had been maybe twenty minutes since I'd called her, and she'd said she'd be here all night.

The assistant caught up with me. 'She's just stepped out. I can leave word.'

'When did she leave?'

'I'm sorry, I can't give out—'

I was done playing games. 'When?'

The girl looked at her shoes. 'I'm not meant to say.'

'Did she tell you to lie to me?'

No answer meant yes.

'When did she leave?'

Nothing.

'Look, I've had a hell of a day. I won't tell her you told me.'

The poor girl sighed. 'Six. Most days it's six thirty, but today she said she had to run errands.'

I nodded, because what else could I do? Six. She hadn't been at work when I called. She hadn't been at work when she said she was. So where was she?

'You know, I will take that water now, thank you.'

The girl perked up and rushed off saying she'd be back in a moment, just wait right there.

I went into Claude's office, straight for the desk. There had to be a date book or something. Claude liked appointments written down, she liked their permanence, always resisting an electronic planner in favour of a diary she took everywhere with her. I listened for the assistant but the floor was silent. Then I attacked her desk drawers, one at a time, nothing, nothing, nothing, noth—

A black leather diary she didn't bring home with her.

The date book I knew was red. My stomach flipped. Probably just for work appointments. To keep things separate from her personal appointments. I picked it up turned on the lamp and found today's date.

There, in black ink, in Claude's hand, was my answer.

6.30 p.m. Marie – dinner at Kaiseka

And the address of the restaurant.

She was having dinner with a woman. No big deal. She had to have dinners and drinks with a lot of clients. I flipped back a page. To a date she had stayed overnight in the office.

Celine – Four Seasons, Central Park Suite

My heart clenched. I kept turning pages. Every few weeks, another name popped up.

Isobel – Soho Grand Hotel

Valentine's Day – 'I'm so sorry, Iris, I have to work': *Nina – dinner at Chez Castillion*. I turned more pages.

My birthday – 'Lloyd has asked me to take lead with the Chinese, it's a big opportunity, Iris, don't be so selfish': *Summer – tickets to Carmen*.

Three days blocked out over a weekend. Her supposed business trip to Chicago. 'I'll come with you,' I'd said, 'it'll be like a vacation.' 'I'll be in meetings all day and night, you'll hate it. Stay here, see Ellis.' *Celine – Plaza, Edwardian Suite*. Celine ... the same Celine who worked at Bergdorf? The same Celine who picked out my clothes for me at Claude's request? I wanted to slam the book closed, throw it through her window, but I couldn't look away.

Christine – drinks
Eleanor – dinner at Parsus
Nina (again) – *theatre*

And on and on, back through the year, one or two a month, a handful of different women.

I closed the book with trembling hands. All the air and blood left me at once and I was hovering, floating, falling, with no one there to catch me.

After

The crash of broken glass.

Swearing. Raging. High-pitched keening.

My name. Shouted over and over.

I sprang up from the couch. A tree branch speared the window, glass littered the floor. The wind cut through the cabin, swept the food from the shelves, set the door rattling against ancient hinges.

Iris was on the mezzanine, shouting my name. The sun was barely up, but we were out of time. The storm was here.

'Shit. Fuck,' I breathed. Shit on the inhale, fuck on the exhale. And repeat.

Do something. *Now.* 'The mattress! Iris! Throw it down.'

A few seconds of shuffling and the mattress dropped to the floor. Iris followed it down the ladder and together we freed the branch and leant the mattress against the broken window. The wind howled through every crack in the cabin, made the floorboards dance and the roof shake. It lifted the mattress like it was paper and threw it across the room, just missing us. Leaves and branches and dirt blasted in through the broken window, scattered over the floor like buckshot.

We both took shelter behind the couch, felt the boards beneath us shake, the nails creak and lift. We covered our heads, covered each other, waited for the crack, the break, the collapse.

But as quickly as it came, the wind died back and an eerie, tense silence followed. Then an angry gust made the whole cabin shudder. And again, silence, stillness. We put the mattress back over the window. We knew it wouldn't stay, but it was something at least.

I leant against the couch. Iris paced the tiny room, hands in her hair, muttering to herself.

'Calm down,' I said.

It was the wrong thing to say.

'*Calm down?* Are you insane? The storm is going to rip this place apart. We're going to *die*.'

It was time. This was it. She was irate, unsteady, I was bedrock. I'd weathered storms before. I would survive this one too. I didn't have a weapon, but maybe I wouldn't need one. Claude had used her hands.

She narrowed her eyes. Her hand moved behind her back, stayed there.

Sudden fear bristled my spine. She has a *knife* and you don't, Jane.

'You need to tell me the truth,' I said, and the wind kicked up again. 'What's in the letter? What did Dad say to you?'

'I think we're past that, don't you?'

The air thickened around us, as if all the oxygen in a mile radius had been compressed into this one tiny cabin. The walls creaked in the wind. Outside, the trees were being thrown side to side as if they were kelp caught in a tide. The sound grew, stole our voices, made us shout.

'We don't have to be.'

'I'm sorry you made bad choices and I'm sorry that whatever they were they landed you here and you haven't been able to face them.'

'Neither have you.'

'You have the life I want!' she cried, 'You have *everything*! I'm sorry, Iris . . .'

Thunder split the sky, made the glass jars on the shelves shake. She pulled her knife from behind her back.

'Tell me,' she shouted, voice shaking. 'Tell me why you're out here. Tell me and maybe all this will end and you can have Bella and I can deal with Claude.'

The walls creaked louder and the rain came, pelting the cabin, forcing its way in as if the walls were made of paper. The wooden panels began to warp around us, and from outside came a sound like wood splitting.

'It doesn't work like that!'

'How do you know?' she screamed. 'If this was a movie—'

'This isn't a fucking movie, Iris!' I screamed back. 'This is life. This is our life! We only get one, there are no do-overs or swaps. We have to accept what we have done. Both of us.'

Tears fell, from her, from me. The wind, the rain, the thunder raged.

'*What did you do?*' she yelled.

'I . . .'

She held her knife in a tight fist. She stepped towards me, pointing the tip of the blade at my throat. 'Tell me!'

The wind whipped away the mattress. The books toppled from their shelf. The shelf twisted. The whole roof pitched violently to one side. From the far corner of the cabin, the sharp snap of a beam breaking.

The knife was at my throat. Cold, sharp metal on soft skin. My own eyes stared at me. My own mouth shaped the words, again and again. They became my heartbeat.

'Tell me.'

'Tell me.'

'Tell me.'

The blank page flashed in my mind. Her name a cruel black mark on my life, marring everything, drowning my world in indelible ink.

Closer now. Her breath my breath. Her pulse my pulse.

I opened my mouth. The words boiled up my throat but stopped on my tongue when I saw her.

Smiling Claude in the corner of my eye. Behind Iris. Her reflection in the blade.

My throat dried. My anger came hot and fast.

I grabbed Iris's hand, wrenched her wrist. She screamed, dropped the knife. I kicked the weapon away and didn't let her go. I didn't want either of us to have it. I pushed her back, my hands like vices around each wrist, pushing, pushing, until her back hit the wall.

A boom of thunder. The cabin shuddered. Rain drenched the floor. Books, food, debris floated on an inch of water. The shelves fell. The chimney twisted, lifted, was ripped from the stove with a scream of old metal. The pipe collapsed, raining soot.

'What did *you* do? What's in the letter?' I shouted above the din, above my own raging heart.

'What made you run?' she yelled back.

A section of the roof caved in, and above, the storm was revealed. A great thunderous mass of boiling black clouds, lightning slashed the dark, rain came down in torrents, and the wind, oh God, the wind! It stole my breath, my screams, my words. The support under the mezzanine gave way and the platform collapsed onto the couch.

'You'll never admit it, will you?' Iris shouted, soaked through, hair wild, clothes whipped tight by the wind.

'Fuck you. Tell me! What's in the fucking letter?'

A beam buckled, broke with a sound like thunder. The pieces smashed into the floorboards on the other side of the cabin.

She strained her neck, pushed herself closer to me, her face and my face a breath apart.

'You already know.'

'I don't!'

Her eyes changed with a blink. From mine to hers to his. I pulled away but didn't release her.

'You already know what you did,' she said. 'Because I did it too. I went with him into the woods that day when I was sixteen. We hiked through Putnam to the oak tree and he set up the tent. That afternoon he told me he'd had enough. It was all too hard for him.'

The day came back to me with the force of a freight train. The cabin grew quiet, the wind ebbed, the rain all but stopped, as if we'd entered the eye of the storm and the world was holding its breath to better hear her speak.

'He brought a rope,' she said, breathless, ragged. 'Found out how to tie a noose by reading one of Helen's sailing books. I told him how much I loved him and how much I needed him, but he kept crying and calling me Josie. He kept apologising over and over until finally I got through. I told him ... I said, somewhere else there is an Iris who loses her father today. I said think about how devastated she'll be, how scared and confused, how much she'll blame herself for the rest of her life.'

I couldn't breathe. The cold, the wind, the loss bit my skin.

'That . . .' Iris said with a snarl, '*that* stopped him from hanging himself. Not his daughter, right in front of him, asking him to live, but some imaginary other daughter, a better Iris. She stopped him. I lived with that memory. I couldn't look at him without seeing him sobbing in the woods, a noose in his hands, knowing I wasn't enough to save him. That's why we didn't speak for years. That's why I married Bella, because I had come so close to losing something precious, if imperfect. I would never let that happen.'

'So what?' I shouted. 'Make amends! You didn't lose him. You still have a chance!'

She rounded on me. 'He's dead, Iris! Okay? He's fucking dead!'

The air rushed out of me and I dropped to my knees. I'd lost him twice. The wind rocked the cabin, stripped shingles from the roof.

Iris knelt beside me. She spoke as if nothing was happening outside, as if the storm wasn't about to destroy us. So calm. So sad. Because nothing else mattered.

'He was sick,' she said. 'It was slow. It started with pain in his arms and legs. They thought it was arthritis. They said it was his age and decades of hiking catching up with him. A year later, he collapsed in the grocery store and couldn't get up. Six months after that, he was in a wheelchair and they diagnosed him with stage four bone cancer. He started chemo, had radiation, the full whack. It bankrupted him. Almost me too. If it hadn't been for Bella taking a second job, we would have lost the house. I *owe* her, you see.'

Her tone didn't alter, her eyes remained dry while mine welled. 'A week before he was due to get the all-clear, he broke his ankle walking down the stairs. The bone was dust. All his bones were. He couldn't walk any more. Couldn't go outside. All he could do was stare out the window, through my telescope.'

She hung her head. 'That letter. That fucking letter. Is him asking me to give him pills. To sit with him and make sure he never wakes up. That letter is our father asking me to kill him.'

'Did you?'

She pulled me closer. Her eyes were raw, shot through with his mania.

'*Yes.*'

I let her go, staggered to my feet, almost tripped over the toppled stove.

'You get it now? You understand why I'm here? Why this place is trapping us? No matter what world we're in, we will lose him,' she said, coming impossibly close, her voice like a blade cut to my bone. 'We will always lose him. He will always take more from us than we can give. We have to accept his death. We have to accept we couldn't save him. You think you deserve what Claude did to you because you killed your father. But you didn't. Do you hear me?'

'But . . .'

The wind kicked up again, stronger, fiercer than before. The icy rain lashed at my face like a whip. Thunder roared a deafening battle cry. The cabin shook. The board lifted under my feet. The walls bent at impossible angles. Curves where wood should never curve. The storm forced us together. Our anger, our denial, our sorrow, our guilt made solid, pressing in on us, destroying us.

'Tell me, Iris,' she said, calm as chaos reigned around us. 'Why did you run?'

The empty page in my notebook began to fill itself with black scrawl.

'I had to.' My voice was nothing. A whisper. A breath in a storm. But she heard, even above the world ending.

'Why?'

I met her eyes. And it wasn't Iris any more. It was her. It was Claude. Physical and real and here, just as Iris had been. Her black heels dangling from a manicured finger. Her eyes brimming with fear. The smell of expensive wine all around us.

'Why?' she asked again.

'Because if I hadn't . . .'

'Yes?'

The wind stripped the shingles from the roof. Another beam fell, crushing the kitchen cabinets. The wine smell grew more pungent, turned to vinegar, sour and stinging my eyes.

'If I hadn't . . .'

Say it. Look at her and say it. You have to say it.

I looked in her eyes. They were mine again, and Iris's and Claude's all at once. My phantoms.

Her face was a breath from mine. Too close, too hot, suffocating me.

Say it.

'If I hadn't,' I said, the blank page finally full, 'I would have killed us both.'

Claude smiled, and the cabin roof caved in on us.

Before

It was late, dark, the building quiet. I stood in the middle of the apartment.

Who had I let myself become?

I poured myself a drink. A full cut-glass tumbler. I emptied it and refilled it twice. Brought the bottle with me to the couch, dispensed with the glass and drank straight from the source until it was dry.

I went to the kitchen for a second bottle but the cabinet was all wine. *Wine.* Claude loved her wine, red and white and champagne, and only the finest, only French, only Grand Cru, blah blah blah. There were three bottles of red just waiting for her obnoxious *nose*, her Hannibal Lecter-like tasting, her sensuous *mmm, how delicious*. Did she make that noise with those women? Did she taste them? Compare them to fine wines like a hoary old cliché?

I pulled all three bottles from the rack and went out onto the terrace.

The cool night air struck me but didn't stick. The rum warmed all my parts, lit up my brain with good ideas and the confidence to follow them.

This was a good idea.

It was only wine. Claude drank it by the barrel-load, a few bottles wouldn't go amiss. A tiny voice in the back of my head said don't, she's been saving those bottles, they're the first of her new collection, that one there is an *investment* bottle, but that voice was another me. One not fortified with Jamaican Gold. One making a different set of decisions. Good decisions.

I looked at the label on the first bottle. Burgundy. Some posh-sounding vineyard with a floral motif. And what was inside?

Glorified grape juice. That's all Claude was, grape juice dressed up as fine wine.

An orchestra struck up in my head. Ride of the fucking Valkyries on full blast as glass and blood-red liquid exploded on the white flagstones. Apocalypse here and now.

Then the second bottle!

Dun-duh-duh-DUH-DUH! SMASH!

The third I shattered on the terrace wall, sending a rain of glass onto the street, but who gives a fuck about those down-below people? Up here, in the heavens, there are no rules. Want to beat you wife? Go for it! Want to cheat on her with a hundred whores? That's your God-given right!

The music faded.

The terrace wasn't a battlefield. It was a mess. A mess Claude would see. She'd see those fancy labels, know I'd destroyed her prized bottles. A few thousand dollars trickling through the white grouting, turning it red. Shards of green glass covered the ground, splinters dusted my arms.

The city came back into focus. Blaring sirens. Angry traffic. Shouts from below. The great darkness of the park, a black hole in the middle of the city. Not wild. Not nature. A poor imitation. A big fat lie encased in concrete. I hated it all.

Why had I even been surprised Claude cheated? If, in fact, she had. Those could be work meetings. In hotels. She'd explain it away. She'd find a lie to convince me and I'd believe her because it was safer. But I'd gone to her office. There would be talk at the water cooler of how Ms Marceau's crazy wife stormed in and stole a diary. Of how Ms Marceau and her crazy wife were clearly having problems at home. Word would filter up to Lloyd and Sophia. They would call Claude into their office and Claude would have to explain.

I put both hands on the waist-high wall. Palms down. Pressed against the smooth stone.

'What now?' I asked the universe.

As if in answer, a car horn blasted below me. I looked to the street, lit up orange, quiet at this hour. A black town car was parked up by the marquee. The driver jogged around to the passenger side, opened the door. Dante the doorman appeared from the marquee and offered a greeting to the woman climbing out of the vehicle. Even at this distance, I knew her.

Claude bent down and ducked her head back into the car. A kiss goodbye?

I could swan-dive onto that car. Three seconds and I'd be dead. Lying broken and bloody on top of Claude's lie. How would she explain that? *Ka-POW*, bitch, lie your way through that inquest.

Three seconds.

The thought coalesced inside me in a shining ball of light. It hovered in my chest, radiating warmth and comfort.

Yes, Jane, it said. Finally, you've got the right idea.

Like father, like daughter.

I climbed up onto the wall. My toes curled against the edge. The rum gave me balance, took away my fears. I spread my arms.

The wind cut through me but I barely felt it. I breathed in clear air. I looked up at the starless city sky. I let my hands ride the wind like I was in a car speeding down the highway, arm out the window catching the currents.

One step.

Three seconds of free fall.

I could end it all right now.

I should.

But then she'd win.

And no one will ever know what she did.

Everyone will think you're the crazy one. Same as everyone blames your father, thinks he was mad, thinks he was weak, thinks he was cruel to leave a wife and two kids. But they don't know the truth. They don't know what brought him that low.

Don't let Claude take that from you too.

Don't let her win.

My eyes focused on the street below. The car pulled away. Claude was coming.

If she saw me up here, on the ledge, drunk, surrounded by broken glass, she'd have me committed. Rehab, maybe? She always had a problem with my drinking. Or a psych ward. For my own safety. She'd tell people I was visiting family upstate for a few months. I had family upstate, after all. It wouldn't be a complete lie, but I'd never be credible again. Who would believe an alcoholic mental patient? She'd taken so much from me, I couldn't let her have the few remaining inches.

I climbed down from the wall, set my feet on solid ground.

Inside the apartment, the front door swung open.

She walked in, smiling. Didn't see me through the glass doors. The light inside the apartment hid me. Her smile quickly faded when she realised the lights were on and shouldn't be. Then her gaze found the empty bottle on the kitchen counter. The empty glass on the coffee table. The cabinet door wide open and her wine gone.

She transferred her keys to her right hand, clutched them in her fist like knuckledusters.

'Hello?' she called out. 'Is anyone here?'

She moved through the apartment, checking every corner. Was this Claude afraid? How novel.

Finally she flicked on the terrace lights and saw me.

She jumped, dropped her keys. 'Iris! Jesus!'

She leant back against the door frame, hand on her chest.

'Jesus,' she said again. 'You're home early, did something . . .'

Her voice trailed off as she noticed the carnage.

'What happened?'

I looked around at the smashed bottles, the stained grouting, the remnants of her prized collection.

'There was a break-in,' I said calmly.

'A break-in?'

'The second this year, in the very same apartment.' I feigned shock, shook my head at the damage. 'What are the chances?'

Her eyes narrowed. 'Are you drunk?'

'Are you fucking other women?'

Where did *that* come from, Jane? But the words were out and I couldn't claw them back in.

Claude frowned, then gave a small, unconvincing laugh. 'Of course not.'

'Tell me.'

'Iris. You're drunk. You don't know what you're saying.'

The alcohol in my system turned on me. Became my enemy. No more superhero confidence. No more unwavering certainty. My brain went into a downward spiral, pity welled up, swirling around with years of guilt, decades of blaming myself and only myself for whatever happened to me. Tears came and I couldn't stop them.

'What don't I give you?' I said, my voice a strangled plea.

Claude's shoes crushed broken glass as she came close. Took me by the shoulders.

'Iris, come inside.'

But I resisted. 'Tell me. Please just tell me! What am I doing wrong?'

Claude shushed and cooed. 'You're not doing anything wrong.'

My tear-stricken eyes focused on her mouth. My hands found her hips, my fists clutched the fabric of her dress.

'Why aren't I enough for you?'

'You are, you are,' she said over and over, but I didn't hear.

'What do they do for you that I don't?'

She sighed against my cheek. We were moving towards the door, Claude gently guiding me as I mumbled question after question.

'Why don't you love me?' I muttered, and my hands tightened around her back.

'I do love you,' she said.

I pulled away an inch to look at her eyes. 'You do?'

'Yes.'

She leant in, kissed me briefly, then smiled. I didn't see the tightness in her smile. Didn't feel the hardness in her lips. I saw only a woman I had to make love me. If I didn't, I would die right then. I'd throw myself off the terrace. I needed her to love me. I needed to feel it.

I kissed her. Forced my mouth onto hers. Hard and fierce like those early days. Those stolen hours between Christmas and New

Year when we didn't leave the bedroom. When I cheated on Bella. When I didn't know what Claude was capable of. I forced myself back to those days, to the passion we had, the love I yearned to feel again.

She laughed and let me kiss her. For a moment.

She tried to push me away, but I held her tight to me.

She tried to say something, but my mouth was on hers.

I pushed her against the glass wall. Pressed my body against hers. My hands clawed at her dress, yanked the fabric up and up. Just like those honeymoon weeks. We'd fuck for days. We'd melt into each other. Forget the world.

'Iris!'

She cried out, but I heard passion, not pain. Her hands were on my sides, pushing me away. I knew they were but I couldn't stop myself.

'I love you,' I mumbled into her neck. 'I love you so much.'

She said my name. She said other things. I didn't hear them. I chose not to.

One hand held her arm, pressed hard against the glass. My body pinned her body. My other hand reached under her dress, up to her centre. I remembered the car ride to the party. The way she'd ignored me all day until that moment when she leant in and kissed me, fierce and urgent, her hand under my dress, igniting me and leaving me breathless and unsatisfied. Then I remembered the way the party ended. The sharp slap across my cheek. The first broken promise of our love.

I pressed harder. She cried out louder.

'Iris! Stop! Stop!'

Was that fear? Was that what her fear sounded like?

My world split into two. I watched myself carry on down this road. Force myself on her. Hurt her like she hurt me. We would keep escalating pain for pain, hurt for hurt, until one of us killed the other. On this path, only one of us would survive this marriage. I saw myself descend into alcoholism. I saw myself stop caring about my appearance, my job, the apartment, and I saw Claude desperately clinging to the high life. I saw myself washing the dishes, her coming home and starting a fight about nothing, I felt the handle of the carving knife under the water, my hand tightening around it. I saw myself turn as she raged at me and bury the knife into her stomach. I saw the shock in her eyes, then the sorrow and fear as she fell, her life spilling wine-red onto the white carpets. Then police. Arrest. Prison. A noose made of bed sheets and a quiet evening.

I staggered back.

Away from Claude. Away from that future. I pressed my hand against my mouth, eyes fixed on the ground. Images of that other Iris slowly faded from my vision, but left ghosts. Residual shapes every time I blinked, like I'd stared too long at the sun.

Claude didn't move. She stood against the wall, palms flat on the glass, her chest heaving, her foundation streaked with tears. Lipstick smeared with my violence.

Neither of us spoke, but something had changed in the air between us.

For the first time in six years, we were both afraid of each other.

Claude moved first. She stepped away from the wall, wincing slightly, and straightened her dress. She wiped her face and smoothed her hair.

'I'm going to lie down,' she said. Her voice small and weak and not hers.

'Claude . . .'

She held up her index finger. 'No.'

She went inside, and a few moments later I heard the bedroom door close.

I sank to my knees.

The city screamed around me. Sirens. Horns. Traffic. Shouting. Crying. People dying. People killing. I was one of them. I was no better than a masked man on the street. Who had I become? What had this crucible of a marriage turned me into?

I knew the path that lay before me. I could still see the look in Claude's eyes as she died in front of me. Still feel the weight of the knife in my hand. If I stayed, was that my only future?

'Who are you?' I whispered into the darkness.

I'd asked myself the same question before, surrounded by broken glass, but I didn't have an answer then.

Now?

She'd asked me to stop. She'd struggled against me. She'd told me no and I hadn't listened. I'd hurt her. I'd hurt her in a way she'd never hurt me. I'd hurt her in a way I'd never thought myself capable of.

I still felt her blood coating my hands, pumping out of her stomach, felt the weight of her body in my arms. There had to be a different way.

Maybe I wasn't as bad as her yet, but I was on my way to being worse.

I watched the sunrise from the lounger on the terrace. I hadn't wanted to go inside. It felt like an invasion and I'd invaded Claude enough. I heard her leave around seven. She didn't look for me, didn't call out to me, and I was glad of it.

I knew what I had to do.

I found a bag. A Harvard duffel. Claude's favourite, even though she'd never attended. I ran my fingers over the insignia. A bag was the least she owed me. I found it in the closet in the second bedroom, along with some old hiking gear. I packed quickly and thoughtlessly, shoving random clothes into the bag. I paused when I saw the telescope. I couldn't leave that with her. I couldn't leave *him* with her. I wrapped it in a couple of sweaters and put it in the bag.

I swallowed back bile. Was I really doing this? Had all this really happened? What if she came home right now? What if she walked in saying she was sorry and we needed to talk and she couldn't go to work without clearing the air.

I heard her voice again. *Iris! Stop! Stop!* And all the other times. The hate in her when she'd thrown the ugly ornament that landed me in hospital. The venom in her tone the day I asked her if she was cheating – which she was! – and she gave me the scar on my cheek. The cold, flinty way she'd said *You embarrassed me* after her office party.

I stood in the middle of the apartment, bag over my shoulder, with only one solid idea. One remaining path that felt right. As if the universe itself was pushing me along. We had so much left unsaid, and yet I couldn't bear to hear it. I didn't want to be angry any more. I didn't want to be afraid. I was brimming with hate and fear and self-loathing, and Claude just kept topping up my tanks. I needed to be free of her.

I needed to find Iris again, and there was only one place I could think of.

The place I left her the day I found my father's body.

I left the apartment and threw my keys and wedding ring down the drain. I went to a bank and withdrew everything I had in cash. Then to an outdoor store, bought a tent and supplies. After that, I went to the bus station and plotted a long, laborious route into the wilderness. I bought single tickets, thinking it would be harder to trace. I waited on a hard plastic bench, shaking with manic adrenaline, checking over my shoulder every few minutes, expecting to see Claude raging through the station, a whole precinct of cops backing her up.

She never came. Never found me.

Afraid, excited, impulsively and idiotically and irrationally, I boarded a bus and left everything behind.

All Caught Up

I'm floating in darkness. A black river carries me along in one of those inflatable rafts. That's what it feels like to have a cabin collapse on your head. Under half a ton of wood and rotting shingles, it's a river.

I don't particularly want to get off the river. I'm comfortable, and the rocking motion of the water is putting me into a blissful state. The banks are crowded with trees, tangled shrubs, all bone-white like they're covered in stone dust.

My hand drops into the water. Not cold. Not hot. Exact body temperature, so I barely feel it, like I'm sailing on my own blood.

Ahead, the river curves and I think I see him. A figure in the far distance, standing on a sandy spit, two fishing rods in one hand, the other raised in a fixed wave. Plaid shirt. Wild hair I shouldn't be able to recognise from this distance but I can. I know it's him.

Something tugs on my fingers under the water.

I try to lift my hand, but I can't, my limbs are too heavy. Pinned by an invisible weight.

My father puts his hand to his mouth and calls my name. I don't hear it, but I know the shape of the word on his lips.

The thing under the water tugs harder. Small yanking movements on my thumb and index finger. I look into the black but see nothing.

My father's face changes. Turns stony and square and too pale. Bleached white. Above me, the sky is black and bright at the same time and I can't understand it but I'm not meant to and that's okay. But there are no stars. No pinpricks of light guiding me. No comfort blanket stretched above me.

I'm not meant to be here.

The thing tugs again. Tiny needle-like claws pierce the meat of my thumb.

The pain makes me jump, loosens the weight on my chest.

My father's face gets closer. His head leans to the left. His ear touches his shoulder, seems to keep going until he's twisted into a grotesque contortion.

He drops the fishing poles and waves one last time as dagger teeth bite down on my fingers.

I surge back to life.

The river was gone but the darkness lingered.

Small black claws pulled on my hand, scratching at my thumb and index finger. Rustling. Sniffing. The distant sound of night insects.

I tried to blink, but my eyes were gummed with dust and blood.

I tried to wipe my face, but the movement sent a shower of splinters over my head.

The claws stopped pulling. A flash of black and grey fur. The sound of skittering feet and rodent-like chirping fading into the forest.

The raccoon?

The bastard raccoon?

The thought gave me strength. If Monty had survived the storm . . .

'Iris?' The air scratched my throat as it pushed out the name. 'Iris? Are you okay?'

No answer. No movement in the ruins.

Images flashed through my head. Her face. My face. Claude's face. I thought of Bella, of getting home to her, of my father's fresh grave, of his old, overgrown one. Which life was mine. Which Iris was I?

'Iris!'

Nobody answered. The darkness was absolute when I opened my eyes, the black pressing against them, forcing its way into my lungs.

I carefully, shakily pushed aside planks and a section of what might have been the roof, and suddenly there was light. The cold air settled over me like a blanket. It smelled fresh, charged, so good I wanted to bite it. Above me, stars glittered in the expanse. My stars. Mine and my father's. Those stars were my guiding light. His face in the constellations said keep going. You're almost free.

But when I tried to move my legs, pain crashed through my left ankle, exploding from my mouth in a scream. The air fled my lungs and I couldn't get it back quick enough. Black spots flashed across my vision and my body throbbed, sickening waves of pain pulsed up and down my spine and legs, into my fingertips. I drifted in and out of darkness and light, and lost all concept of time.

When I opened my eyes, the stars had moved, or maybe it was a different night. The trees were loud, their limbs swaying in wind I couldn't feel, only see. I tried to move, but the pain came again, and along with it a spike of fear.

'Iris?' My voice was weak, throat like sandpaper. 'Iris, are you there?'

But still no reply came.

Dead? Under the rubble of the cabin, bleeding from a head wound? Or gone? Or never there?

'Iris . . .'

The pain brought clarity. All I'd been through, all I'd seen, phantoms upon phantoms, Claude and my father and her. Me. My own phantom. My biggest demon to face, and I had. And now she was gone.

Loneliness dropped on my chest and forced out sobs. I cried for a while, felt her loss as keenly as if I'd lost a limb. I could still feel it, the ghost of her, but she had never truly been there. I was alone, I always had been.

My chest tightened. I'd run away into the woods and told no one where I was going. No one knew where I was.

Injured. Trapped. Dying.

Alone.

For the first time in years, I didn't want to die. I wanted to live and change and thrive and love and be better.

I started screaming then. Shouting for help until my voice gave and the pain and exhaustion turned my world to darkness.

Daylight woke me. Warm sun on my exposed face. The chatter of a living forest, the scent of the trees in full summer bloom, wide green leaves pumping out oxygen, their fallen sisters giving life back at their roots.

I pushed planks and broken pieces of wood from my chest, managed to prop myself up on my elbows and angled myself as painlessly as I could to see what was pinning me.

My leg disappeared under a beam, my ankle stuck and crushed. Numb but not numb. There but not there.

Tears cut streaks through the dust on my face.

Fuck. Where's the superhuman strength people get when you really need it? If I was a child under a car, I'd have ten mothers throwing the damn thing in the air with one hand.

Shut up, Iris. Concentrate.

I clenched my jaw, breathed through the slowly fading agony and found a pole. The broom handle I'd used as a crutch. I stuck the end under the beam to the side of where my leg disappeared. I threw all my weight onto it, levered it an inch. Two. But my arms buckled, my grip failed, and it slammed back.

My scream made birds flee their nests.

I lay back, tried to calm my breathing, calm my heart, because what if I was cut somewhere and my panic was pumping all my blood straight out of my body? What if my ankle had been severed completely and the beam was the only thing keeping me from bleeding out? Moving it wouldn't do me any favours. Panicking wouldn't either. I told myself to remain calm. To count to a hundred. To call for help every ten.

That was a plan. A solid plan.

I stared up at the pale blue sky and counted and shouted, counted and shouted.

When the sky turned pinkish gold and my voice was hoarse, with my willpower wound down to a thread and the thought of sleep the most wonderful thought ever to enter my head, my shouts were answered.

A cry went up somewhere out of view.

Then footsteps crunching on dry leaves.

Then loud male voices giving orders.

Suddenly hands were all over me, lifting the planks and logs and sheets of cheap wood away from me, clearing a safe path. Then five pairs on the beam pinning my leg. Then I was free and being lifted away by men and women in bright orange vests. It seemed to take both forever and no time at all, and a jolly woman with a halo of pale grey hair told me I passed out soon after they arrived and they thought I was dead.

Search-and-rescue had found me. There had been a bad earthquake last night, they said, the area had been riddled with them for months, despite never registering anything above a three in a hundred years. Fracking, one of them moaned. They said two houses nearby had been damaged, and they were checking the trail for hikers when they heard me. You're a lucky, lucky woman, they said.

'Earthquake?' I said, delirious with exhaustion. 'But the storm . . . the wind.'

'There wasn't a storm last night, sugar,' said a kind woman, 'just the quake.'

No storm. No Iris?

'Is there someone else?' I asked. 'In the cabin. A woman.'

'There was only you,' they said. 'We checked twice.'

Only me.

But I knew that already. The Iris I thought I could have been was gone. Her life was never going to be mine, nor mine hers, and it only took the universe collapsing around me for me to understand that. But the storm? The storm inside my head made real?

Was any of it real? A storm that was an earthquake, a woman who was a phantom, a me that was . . . just me?

They strapped me to a stretcher and carried me out. The forest was open again, the trails led away into the trees, to the mountains, to new places. The air was fresh, the ground dry, the leaves crunched underfoot, and I was floating through it, under the thick, vibrant canopy, thinking only of her, and what if, what if, what if.

I could never look at a decision the same way again. It mattered now what I did, it affected the world, it affected *me*. All of me. It should have always mattered, but I had been too destructive, too absorbed in myself, too sad and guilty to realise. No more rush now, no more ill-prepared, idiotic, impulsive Iris. It was time to grow up. It was time to forgive myself.

But could I?

I closed my eyes. Counted.

When I opened them, we were in Mennier. I never thought I would be so glad to see that supermarket again. A section of the parking lot had been commandeered by search-and-rescue. There were tents and beds for those affected by the quake. Mostly empty. Staff of one paramedic and one lady behind a metal tea urn. They set me up on a cot and the paramedic gave me the once-over. Probable broken ankle, multiple lacerations and contusions, whatever they were. I'd be transferred to hospital when the ambulance arrived.

'Bathroom?' I asked, and the lone, harried paramedic, who was tending to an elderly gentleman, gave me a set of crutches and said don't put any weight on it.

Despite the emergency set-up, the supermarket was still a supermarket and the rest of the parking lot was full of cars, full of men and women strolling up to the door with shopping carts. Some loading bags into their trunks. Some dragging fighting children from the store. Several stopped to check on the emergency tents, offer help or a spare can of beans, but most didn't. They looked away, carried on, as if this was an everyday occurrence. Given how many people were using this emergency service, search-and-rescue appeared to have overreacted. But thank the stars they had, because otherwise I'd still be counting and shouting with only the raccoon to answer.

I hobbled painfully slowly across the parking lot, feeling my body tense up every time anyone came close. The place was buzzing with panic-buyers and preppers, families fighting over the last box of Hot Pockets, men bulk-buying bottled water, women hoarding milk. I felt their eyes on me, checking me over, grimacing and looking away like I was a human reminder of tragedy, or an omen of further disaster. I put my head down, gripped the crutches.

I'd been so long on my own, or as close as, that suddenly being surrounded by people unnerved me, made me shrink into myself and avoid contact. My personal space bubble had expanded to the size of the supermarket, and everybody was an invader.

And the noise! Car horns, shouting, the obnoxious *ding!* of the entrance, music blaring from hidden speakers, chatter. Relentless undertones of how are the kids and how is your mother and oh the cancer is back and did you catch the game and how about that earthquake, that's four now in two months, and what kind of juice do you want and construction on the highway is terrible and on and on. A drone of inanity. And so loud. Everything was so damn loud.

I limped into the restrooms, mercifully empty, and breathed in the quiet.

I looked in the mirror and a stranger stared back at me. Another Iris. The real Iris? No wonder people stared. I looked like a horror movie survivor. This was the first time I'd looked in a mirror since the morning I fled New York. Then, I had shoulder-length hair, not dark enough to be brown, not light enough to be blonde, an indefinable middle colour. My face had been plump with a constant supply of rich, buttery meals and wine. My skin had been porcelain thanks to Claude's dermatologist. My shoulders and arms had been slim, with soft curves of pale skin, a layer of happy fat surrounding my bones and muscles, smoothing out my definitions like an overcoat.

Now?

Jesus Christ.

Iris had cut my hair off a few days ago . . . No. She hadn't. I had done it.

I remembered it now, my shifting reflection in the stream, the knife in my hand. I cringed at how bad a job I'd done. It was greasy and stuck up at all angles, bleached by the sun.

And then there was my face. I could barely see it for dirt and a dozen scratches, smears of blood, flecks of wood and dust. Gone was the porcelain, replaced with tanned leather. Pronounced cheekbones, sharp jawline. Behind the scratches, tiny pockmarks. Freckles from the sun. Creases in the corners of my eyes.

Down to my collarbones, jutting out of my bruised chest. I pulled up my top. A xylophone of ribs, a concave stomach, thinner than I'd ever been. Taller than I'd ever been. I checked my back, found more cuts, old and new, more rips in my clothing, more blood, and smiled because it was nothing really. I'd survived worse.

My arms, golden brown, covered in bites and scratches, every muscle visible and flexing like cables. A crescent of needle pricks on my thumb and index finger said I hadn't imagined the raccoon. And then my eyes, bright and alive.

I washed my face and hands with soap and it bordered on a religious experience. As the grimy water, mixed with blood and tears and decades of guilt, ran down the plughole, I was reborn. I stuck my head under the tap as best I could, scraped some soap through my hair, and rinsed, all the while keeping an eye on the door and the crutch balanced under my arm. I grabbed a wad of tissues and went to town on my underarms and the back of my neck.

I gave my hair a quick blast under the drier and I'll be damned if it didn't look amazing. Except for the colossal pain in my leg, I *felt* amazing.

I hadn't been this kind of clean since I left my life. I didn't recognise myself. I hadn't become Jane, I'd become Tarzanna. Strong, fearless and ripped.

I'd shed my skin.

The world had collapsed around me and I'd emerged from the rubble a new woman.

I looked in the mirror and saw Iris – Other Iris – staring back. I hoped she'd got home. I hoped she realised what she had. I hoped she'd stopped blaming herself for our father. I hoped she was real.

The all-too-familiar stab of shame hit when I thought of my father. But now I could think of him without my chest constricting and my eyes filling and my brain overwhelming me with all the things I should have done to save him. It didn't destroy me like it used to.

I thought of that day when he'd asked me to go into the woods with him, the day he didn't come home, and where a few months ago there had been an ocean of guilt, now there was just a steady stream.

I knew now what had happened to the Iris who went with him. I knew now, after years of what-ifs, that there was no good outcome for my father and me. We were planets set on different orbits and his loop took him away far too soon.

I looked at the woman in the mirror, saw her shoulders lift and her back straighten, saw a light in her eyes she thought long extinguished. There was the Iris I went looking for. The version of me I lost long ago.

I used the toilet – a seat! A flush! – tidied after myself, then rejoined the real world.

Renewed and mostly clean, the looks stopped. I was an injured hiker now, not a hermit.

The supermarket was bigger than I remembered. There were the usual aisles, checkouts, but also a deli counter I hadn't noticed on my last visit, and a rotisserie. The smell of the chickens beckoned. The portly man behind the counter turned at the sound of a customer approaching. His jaw dropped when he saw the state of me.

'Good Lord, miss, are you all right?'

I forced a smile. 'I've been better.' I'd been worse, too.

His accent was local and he had a neatly groomed moustache. 'Got caught in the quake, did ya? It was a bad one, for sure. You see they set up the tent outside? Got hot coffee in there, I believe, and a doctor lady, if you need it.'

'She gave me the crutches. They're all out of coffee, though.'

'A shame,' he said. His gaze drifted into a wistful middle distance and hung there for a moment longer than comfortable.

He suddenly snapped back to reality. 'Oh Jeez, I'm sorry, miss. Where are my manners? What can I get you?'

I looked at the trays of roasted golden chicken, glazed with all sorts of sauces and spices and rubs, and my mouth filled with water. And then my stomach dropped. I had no money. Not even a dusty quarter at the bottom of my pocket. All those notes were just rotting paper in a ruined cabin.

'Uh . . . nothing. I must have left my wallet . . . Today's been, uh . . .' I shook my head. 'Thank you anyway.'

I turned to walk away.

'Hang on there, miss.'

When I turned back, he'd already bagged up half a chicken. 'On the house. You look like you've been to hell and back and you must be hungry after a journey like that.'

Tears of gratitude filled my eyes as I took the bag, but before I could babble my thanks, the man waved me away with a grin.

I found a bench outside the supermarket and ate every scrap of meat off the bones. I hadn't had real meat in what felt like forever. Or spices. Or someone else cooking for me.

My eyes drifted around the parking lot, sliding over cars, big, shiny, brand-new SUVs, old, rust-pitted trucks, a few runarounds not well suited to mountain life, and there – I squinted against the sun – a town car. A gleaming dark grey town car. So out of place. So distinct. So familiar. A reminder of the excess I'd once looked at as luxury, then eventually normality.

A car like that, here? Sore thumb was an understatement. I strained to see the driver, but before I could get a better look, the car drove away, oblivious to me. The sight of a car like that was cold water down my spine. A reminder of what I'd walked away from and what I still had to face. My old life waited and there were no more cabins to run to.

Out of the supermarket poured a family of five. The way they moved, the way they spoke put all thoughts of Claude out of my head except one horribly familiar one. Three kids, two crying, and the other, the eldest, stalking off in a huff, and the parents shouting. Really shouting. The man gripped the woman's upper arm and dragged her towards their car.

'What you thinking, embarrassing me like that?' he shouted right into her ear. 'In front of all those fuckin' people.'

I flinched and instinctively shrank away from him, even though I was nowhere near. I knew those words. That tone. People in the parking lot stopped and stared, and the presence of the emergency services did nothing to deter him.

'I'm sorry, babe,' the woman pleaded while her kids clung to her legs. 'I didn't mean anything by it, just a mistake.'

I'd seen these people before. That first day in Mennier, I'd seen them at the checkout, seen the way he treated her, and I'd looked away. I'd ignored the signs, the aggression. I'd minded my own business. I'd averted my eyes. All because I was afraid. I knew what it felt like to have that ire turned on me.

And I was still afraid. Deep down, in the primal part of me, the fear Claude had lodged there had stuck fast, got its hooks into my marrow and wouldn't let go. No matter what had happened in the woods, my demons still danced around me.

The man laughed, a horrible, bitter sound. 'Stupid bitch. That lot in there won't be calling me for a tow now they think I can't tell a porterhouse from a ribeye. What kind of man don't know his steaks? You done me out of business, you taken food out these kids' mouths. You think that's funny?'

He did something I couldn't see and she cried out in sharp agony. The kids whimpered and clung harder.

I was on my feet before I knew what I was doing, limping quick and awkward on my crutches, pain flaring with every step.

'You all right?' I shouted. I kept my eyes on her. Saw myself in every flinch.

'She's just fine, mind your damn business,' he snarled, a dirty dog of a man.

'Is that true?' I asked her.

He rounded on me, stopped short when he saw the crutches and my injuries. 'What the fuck do you want, dyke?'

The kids bawled. The older one stood a distance away, by a car, waiting, staring, like she'd seen it all before.

I ignored him and kept my focus on the woman, adjusting my balance so I could swing a crutch at him if I needed to.

'You don't have to put up with this,' I told her.

She looked at me then, a deep scowl across her features. 'I'm fine. Mind your business.'

Parroting his words. I'd done the same. *I'm fine, it was just an accident.* Something of a crowd had gathered, gawking, outside the supermarket. The paramedic stood at the doorway to the tent.

I took a half-step closer. 'Maybe I can help.'

That was a mistake.

His hand slashed across my cheek. My jaw locked and I staggered back, my ankle twisted horribly, and I fell. If he'd hit a stranger in broad daylight, in front of his children and half of Mennier, what would he do to her in private?

He spat on the ground. 'Fuck off!' Then he started dragging her away.

I pushed against the pain in a way I never did with Claude. She'd paralysed me. He'd given me a rush of anger. Pain was temporary, I knew that now. I would heal. Skin would knit back together. Bones would fuse. Scars would be left but they didn't mean anything. They were just memories. And memories couldn't hurt me any more.

I struggled to my feet. Then hands were under my arms, helping me. The paramedic. A woman in a checkout uniform.

'Leave her alone, you piece of shit,' I said.

The man turned, fists clenched, ready to put me down again, but now he faced an army. The woman's eyes widened, she clutched her kids close.

'You deserve better,' I said to her, because we all do. 'So do your children.'

I'd poked the bear and he roared.

'The fuck you sayin' about my kids?' He stepped towards me. 'You don't talk about my kids.'

Murmurs from the shoppers, and a particular word stuck out. Police. They were calling the police.

'I'm not afraid of you,' I said. But a part of me still was. The part that remembered the first slap, the first punch, the feeling of helplessness when Claude wouldn't stop. My heart beat a thunderous tattoo and the voice in my head screamed, *What are you doing? He'll kill you!*

He rushed at me.

The people around me stepped back, but I didn't. I'd been through hell and dragged myself out the other side. I'd broken bones, I'd drawn blood, I'd damaged nerves, I'd survived hands around my throat and concussion and humiliation and degradation. I'd nearly succumbed to it all, nearly become the monster standing in front of me, but I was stronger than him. I was stronger than her. I was stronger than every Iris before and after me because I'd chosen to live through the pain, not run from it. I'd chosen freedom from hate and violence and nothing would pull me back to that thorny existence. That gilded cage. Not Claude. Not my father. Not my mother and her lies. Not the Iris I could have been had I chosen differently. And certainly not this dickless piece of shit in a supermarket parking lot.

He knew it. He saw it in my eyes. Defiance. Strength.

His fists unclenched. His demeanour shifted. An old lion put down by new blood.

'Not worth the trouble,' he muttered, and spat again, but all the power, all the rage had gone from his voice.

And his wife saw it. I locked eyes with the woman. Her attention went from me to him and back, and there was something in her eyes, a new realisation that he could be beaten. That maybe one day *she* could beat him.

She nodded to me, the barest of movements, then went to her kids.

The family drove away and the supermarket resumed its business. The paramedic helped me back to the tent and checked my cheek. Just the latest in a long line of injuries to that cheek. It didn't even hurt.

*   *   *

The ambulance came a few hours later and I was taken to a hospital in Poughkeepsie. They took X-rays, put a cast on my leg, dosed me up with pain meds, and covered me in antiseptic. The nurses asked if I had any family they should contact. I gave them a name and number and waited.

A few hours later, he came.

'Sweet shit in a bucket, what happened to you?'

Ellis stood in the doorway to my private room. Claude had great insurance and I was going to use every penny.

'A cabin fell on me,' I said.

'I meant your hair.'

My heart lifted. I touched my shorn ends. 'You don't like it? Wilderness hobo is all the rage these days.'

He smiled and sat down in the chair beside my bed.

The smiles soon faded to awkward silence.

'I'm sorry we fought,' I said.

He dismissed the apology with a smile and wave of his hand. 'Who cares about that?'

'The things I said . . .'

'Shut up. It's forgotten.' He took my hand and squeezed it and I knew he forgave me.

Now he was here, now he was my friend again, I began to relax.

'I was worried you wouldn't come,' I said.

'You disappear for weeks and then I get a call saying you're in hospital, I'm on the next train,' he said. 'I thought you were dead.'

'I'm sorry.'

'Do you know how worried everyone has been? You literally upped sticks and fucked off. Claude had the police out looking for you, they questioned me for hours. She thought I was hiding you.'

'Did you tell Claude I'm here?'

He made a face and shook his head.

'Iris, you're not listening. The police contacted your family. Your sister set up a hotline. They thought you'd been abducted. There was an appeal on the news. But they had no leads. They found your keys in a drain.'

'That's because I threw them in a drain. Did they find my wedding ring in there too?'

He made another face and sat back in his chair.

'You're different,' he said after a few minutes. 'And I don't just mean the hack job on your head.'

'I feel different,' I said. My gaze wandered out the window, to the treetops, the clouds, the hint of a river in the distance. 'It's like I was split in half for years and now I've come back together.'

Ellis nodded. 'I've missed you. Not just for the last few months, though I should hate you for disappearing like that. Seriously, Iris, I thought you'd been abducted or murdered, especially after the mugging. Jesus.'

I winced at the lie. 'I really am sorry, Ell.'

'But what I mean is, I've missed *you*, for years.' He paused, searched a moment for the right words. 'Since you met Claude, you've been a different Iris.'

'I know.'

He rubbed his eyes. 'What are you doing out here?'

I tried to sit up, but my body was stiff and it hurt. 'I ran away.'

'Why?'

I sighed. Closed my eyes against a throb of pain in my ankle.

The blank page in my mental notebook was full now. The words out and in the universe. There was no block between me and them any more.

'I wasn't mugged, Ell.'

He frowned. 'What you do mean?'

I took a deep breath, blew out my cheeks just like Iris did. 'You remember when I told you Claude had hit me?'

His expression broke at the edges, sympathy washed over him and he leant towards me and took my hand.

'You had bruises on your neck . . . You were strangled.'

I nodded, pursing my lips against the oncoming tide. 'Claude is stronger than she looks.'

'Iris . . .' He didn't know what to say, and I couldn't blame him.

'I didn't tell you everything. I couldn't. It was too shameful, too *painful* to admit to you my marriage was broken, then we had that fight and ... How could I face you after what I'd said? God,' I almost laughed, 'if I'd told you everything, you would have called the police.'

His eyebrows rose at mention of the police. 'Did you think I would judge you?'

I nodded and he edged closer, held my hand tighter.

'You can tell me, Iris. You need to tell someone.'

'I know. That's what I learnt out there. I can't keep running away and lying to myself or I'll end up like my father. I need to tell you what she did and ... and what I did.'

A flicker of a frown passed across his face, but he nodded for me to go on.

I closed my eyes, felt myself solidifying, the explosion reversing, until I felt whole again. Then I spoke.

'Claude hit me for the first time three years ago. I told you she only did it once or twice, but I was lying. I've been lying to you, to myself, to the universe ever since. I wrote down what happened in notebooks while I was in the woods, but those are lies too.'

I tightened my hand around Ellis's palm and stared down at my cast. To say this, I couldn't look at him. Or anyone.

'Every few weeks after that first time, no matter what I did or didn't do, it would happen again. I would forget to pick up groceries, I would get home a little too late from work or from seeing you, I would be a little too drunk, I would complain about my job too much, I would speak too loudly when she had a headache or too softly and I'd be mumbling, I would wash her dresses on the wrong setting and shrink them, I would be early, I would be late, I'd try to make her laugh, I'd try to leave her in peace, I'd anticipate her needs and get them wrong. It didn't matter what I did, I understand that now. It wasn't about me, my actions, it was her.' I paused, forced myself to say the things I'd never said.

'There would be an argument or a telling-off, like I was a child. It wouldn't always be a slap, but it often was. She'd pinch, scratch, grab my arm or wrist so hard she left bruises. I started wearing long sleeves. More make-up. It wasn't just one time after a party. Wasn't just an accidental punch during a heated conversation. It was constant, but irregular. Sometimes she'd leave me be for a couple of months, sometimes it would be every few weeks. I could never predict it, so I lived for years on edge, waiting for the next time. And it was never an accident with Claude. On her birthday, she nearly killed me. She choked me until I lost consciousness. I couldn't speak for days. She told everyone I was mugged. After you and me fought, I tried to leave her, like you said I should. I went home and started packing, but she caught me. I ended up in hospital with concussion, nerve damage to my face, another scar, and a lie about a break-in.' I pushed aside my hair and revealed the raised white line.

Ellis's hand was over his mouth, his eyes wide. His other hand gripped mine for dear life.

'Iris . . .' he breathed. 'You have to tell someone, an official someone. She can't get away with this.'

'I'm telling you, and that's enough right now.'

He went to say something but thought better of it. Instead, he relaxed his grip, held my hand in both of his, tears in his eyes. 'Keep going.'

'For years, it was this constant barrage of abuse and fear every time I heard her come home. I was never sure which Claude would walk through the door. The days after, she'd be so attentive and kind, I almost thought it would be the last time, but then I always thought that after she hit me. After she apologised. After she promised to change. An abuser's checklist of responses, she ticked them all.

'Then I found out she was seeing other women. A lot of them. I got drunk, of course, and smashed up all her expensive wine.'

'Good.'

'She came home. We fought, and . . .'

That night came back to me. The sharp tannin smell of the spilt wine. The still night at the top of the world. The way the noise of the city faded into the background and Claude's screams took their place.

Iris! Stop! Stop!

I tasted her fear on my tongue. I felt it under my fingers.

'. . . and . . .'

I heard her crying under the weight of my body. I felt her trying to push me away. Heard her say it again and again.

Please. Stop. Please.

But I didn't. I didn't stop. I didn't pull away. I told myself I did for a long time but I was lying. I saw a future where that path led to destruction, but I wanted destruction. I wanted to hurt her. I wanted to hurt myself. And I didn't stop.

'Iris?'

'I . . .' Say it, you have to say it, 'I hurt her. Worse than she ever hurt me.'

He frowned. 'She must have deserved it.'

I shook my head. 'No, she didn't. Nobody deserves that. No matter what they've done. Nobody deserves it.'

Ellis's tone shifted. 'What happened?'

Don't say it, Jane. He'll never understand. Never forgive you.

I couldn't keep lying to myself anymore. This was it, the last door I had to walk through, the last inch of paper in the notebook about to be filled. But it hurt. I was scared to form the words, scared to see how Ellis would look at me after he knew. But if I didn't, I would end up at the bottom of that mountain, twisted and broken.

I took a deep breath, drew my hand from his and gripped my own together.

'We were on the terrace. I was in a . . . bad way. I almost jumped off the roof onto her car. I almost did that rather than face her because I knew that night would be the end of us. I didn't see any other way to escape her, but . . .' I tried to hold back the tears. 'I was a coward. I was so drunk, and when I saw her, when I saw the disappointment in her eyes . . .' I could barely speak, barely breathe over my sobs. 'I . . . I confronted her. She told me she wasn't cheating, told me she loved me . . .' I could smell her perfume on me, hear the clipped tones as she lied. My tears fell like rain. 'All I wanted was for her to love me. I *needed* her to love me, because then I wouldn't be broken, I wouldn't be my father. I wouldn't . . .'

I bit down hard on my bottom lip. My eyes were raw and stung with every blink.

Say it.

'What happened, Iris?'

'I kissed her, and . . . I kept kissing her, and she didn't want me to . . .' My voice broke.

Just breathe and say it.

'She tried to push me away. She told me to stop. She told me to stop more than once, and I heard her. I heard the fear in her. But I didn't. I didn't stop even though she kept asking me to. Even though she was fighting against me. I didn't stop. I raped her, Ell.' I closed my eyes, hot tears poured down my cheeks, burned like acid.

'It wasn't a mistake,' I said. 'It wasn't an accident. I could come up with a thousand excuses and brush it off, but I won't. I knew what I was doing to her. My wife. The woman I'm meant to love, and I do. I do love her. But I hurt her. And then I ran away.'

Ellis sat back and didn't speak. One hand grasped the wooden arm of the chair. The clock on the wall ticked down the minutes, and silence hung heavy between us. He wouldn't, or couldn't, look at me.

'I . . . don't know what to say,' he murmured.

I shook my head and pressed my hands over my eyes.

I couldn't stop hearing Claude asking me to stop, *begging* me to stop. My sorrow choked me and I couldn't breathe. I didn't deserve to breathe.

Then arms were around my shoulders. A soft voice in my ear telling me to calm down, saying *it's okay*, until slowly the tears stopped.

Ellis held me by the shoulders and made me look at him. 'Iris . . . I'm not about to say what you did was okay. But after what you've told me, all you've been through, what Claude did to you . . . I think I understand what drove you to it.' He paused, looking intently at me, sadness in his eyes. 'I'm starting to realise that maybe I never knew the real Iris.'

I felt the tears rise again.

'But I'd like to know her,' he said quickly. 'Good and bad. You've been going through hell and I'd never judge you for the decisions you made in hell.'

I hugged him to me like he was a life preserver and I was adrift in stormy seas.

We parted and he sat back in the chair. 'And the cabin?'

I wiped my eyes. 'After that night, I packed a bag and I ran. I used to hike with my father before he died and I wanted to be where Claude would never look for me. I knew if I stayed, we'd keep hurting each other. I'd become her, or worse. Maybe I already am worse. I didn't know what else to do.'

'I wish you'd told me sooner.'

'Me too.'

'You're my family, Iris, I've got your back,' he said, and I burst into fresh tears. 'You're coming home with me, to my shitty apartment, and you're going to stay there, whether you like it or not, until we figure this out.'

I nodded and leant back on the bed. My body relaxed, muscles unclenched and heart calmed. I'd never felt safer.

After Then But Before Now

I was discharged the next day and back in the city by nightfall. I signed the insurance paperwork, which meant Claude would get a call and find out what happened. She called Ellis immediately. He took pity and, with a nod from me, told her I was alive and with him, and don't you dare come within ten blocks. She listened. But still, every buzz of the bell or knock at the door sent a burst of anxiety through me.

Ellis slept on the couch and gave me his bed. My camping gear, what could be salvaged from the wreck and stuffed in my backpack, was hidden under the bed and out of sight. I didn't want to look at it, be reminded.

The hospital painkillers had worn off and my ankle was raging. I dosed up as much as I could and kept the weight off. I had four weeks of this cast. Then a few weeks of physio ahead of me. And I had no job. No money. And no place to live.

Ellis asked me often about what I got up to in the woods. I told him about the raccoon, the cabin, the earthquake.

'I can't believe you went through that alone,' he said.

I nodded along. 'It was tough, but . . .' I paused, smiled, 'I kept myself company.'

I couldn't bring myself to speak about Other Iris. I didn't want to be told I was crazy. I didn't want another person to dismiss her as a hallucination brought on by trauma and dehydration. I had started to believe that's what she was, but somehow it didn't matter. She was real to me and I didn't want to share her. I clutched her to me like she was a piece of my soul. I missed her, despite her trying to kill me in the end. Did Bella have the baby? Was Iris finally happy? Or did she leave and become the coward she never wanted to be? Somehow, that path didn't seem right for her. I saw her when I looked at the night sky, smiling down at a bundle in her arms, showing new eyes old stars.

During the long, pain-filled nights in Ellis's cramped apartment, I sometimes thought about going home. Back to Claude. It would be easier, she could look after me. We'd make it work. I could do that. I should do that. I couldn't stay with Ellis forever.

But just as quickly as those thoughts came, so did flashes of that night on the terrace, and the idea of facing her fizzled out like a wet candle.

I was in limbo again. With walls all around me and no obvious path.

'You should speak to her,' Ellis said one morning over breakfast.

He'd said the same thing the first time I'd seen Claude in that bar, all those years ago. What a strange road I'd travelled since that night.

I shook my head. 'Not yet.'

He left it alone, but two days later, over dinner, he brought it up again.

'She called me again,' he said. 'Asked if I had any news.'

'What did you say?'

'I said you were fine.'

'What did she say?'

'She asked if she could see you.'

My gut twisted. 'And?'

'I said that was up to you. She was real upset. Crying. How messed up is that? Claude crying down the phone to *me*.'

The thought of Claude hurting like that . . .

'Maybe you need to talk to her?' he said carefully. 'Make it clear you're not going back.'

But which Claude would be at the end of the phone? Which Claude would be waiting inside that apartment? I wasn't ready to find out.

I didn't call and Claude never turned up at the door. Neither did my phantom. During the day while Ellis was at work, I read

Beth Lewis

astronomy and physics books and popular science magazines, immersed myself in my first, best passion. I learnt more about the cosmos, about the technology NASA and private companies were developing, and devoured profiles of the people designing the future. A deep longing lodged in my chest, one I hadn't felt since those early days with my father, my telescope and the stars.

Ellis and I spent the nights in movie marathons, eating nachos and pizza, drinking too much and laughing more. Except for one blazing row about the length of his morning shower and where he should hang his underwear to dry, we were born roommates. He talked about getting a bigger place together, but my quiet non-committal quickly ended the conversation and he didn't suggest it again.

After four weeks, my ankle was mostly healed, my cast due off, and suddenly the rest of my life spilled out before me.

'What am I going to do, Ell?' I asked as we lounged on the couch watching *Alien*.

He paused the film and shifted round to face me. 'I've been wondering when you'd ask that.'

'And?'

'And I have no idea. What do you want to do?'

I'd been so long in survival mode, not just in the woods but with Claude too, that I'd forgotten how to look forward.

'I don't know.'

Ellis gave a tight smile. 'My place is hiring. They'd have you back, I'm sure of it.'

I smiled, but the thought of sitting in that soulless office again, pushing those same papers, eking out a living, hand to mouth, pay cheque to pay cheque, made my skin crawl. I couldn't go back. No matter what, I couldn't go backwards, and there was only one way forward.

'I have to speak to Claude, don't I?'

He nodded.

'As soon as I get my cast off. Then at least I can run away.'

He laughed and I laughed, but really, it wasn't funny.

★   ★   ★

A week later, a doctor sawed the cast off my leg, and exposed a pale, sensitive ankle covered in old scrapes from the cabin collapse. I could walk again, unaided. But I had no plan and no money except what Ellis had lent me.

Time to get your life in order, Jane.

No. Not Jane. Not anymore.

Iris.

First things first.

I called Claude from a payphone. She didn't answer her cell – unknown number, I wouldn't have answered either – so I called her office. Her assistant – a young man, not the poor girl I'd met that night – put me through.

'Iris?'

'Hi, Claude.'

'My God, where have you been? Are you okay? Where are you?'

Real concern. Real, heartfelt concern. I imagined her standing, pacing her office, hand on her forehead like she did when she was worried. My heart clenched.

'We should talk,' I said, trying to keep the tremor out of my voice.

'Tell me where. When. I'll clear my day.'

Claude *never* cleared her day. Meetings were her life.

'Really?'

'Of course. Iris. God.' Her voice muffled, as if she was holding the receiver closer to her mouth. 'I was so worried. I didn't know what happened . . .'

Her breath caught.

'I was so worried,' she said again, and drew in a shuddering breath.

She was crying.

Was it real?

'Tell me,' I said, 'were you seeing other women?'

'Iris . . .'

'Tell me.'

She sighed down the phone. 'It didn't mean anything. Just sex, no love. I promise. I'm so sorry, Iris, please?'

I closed my eyes. Rested my head against the top of the payphone. I hadn't been mad. Hadn't been crazy. Hadn't been imagining things.

'Before I can see you,' I said, 'I need you to admit it.'

'I cheated. It was a mistake. A terrible mistake.'

'Not that. The rest.'

The end of the line went quiet. I put another two quarters in the payphone and waited. Don't let her off the hook. Don't let her make excuses. I'd made a hundred excuses for her and I was done. Never again. I'd never lie about her and what she did to me ever again.

'Yes,' she said.

Barely a whisper, don't let anyone in your office overhear, Claude. Priorities. I bit back a sigh.

'I have a problem,' she said. 'I hurt you. We hurt each other. But when you disappeared, I felt like I had lost a piece of me. You're my wife, Iris. I love you and you love me. No matter where you go, that will always be true.'

She was right and I hated it. Even in the middle of the woods, she'd been with me. She would always be with me.

'The Italian café at Grand Central. Tomorrow. Three p.m.'

'Three? That's not good, the Korean—'

'Clear your day.'

I hung up and breathed out all my tension. So much of it. My shoulders and neck were solid muscle. My ankle ached. My body throbbed with memories of pain. But it was done. I'd spoken to her and I'd survived and now I had the beginnings of a plan.

I started walking back to Ellis's apartment and stopped outside a salon. Half-price midweek cuts. I saw my hair reflected in the window. Saw a version of myself I wasn't any more. Not demure wife. Not feral wildling. But something in between.

I went inside and, ignoring the strange looks from the other patrons at the state of my head, asked if they had a free chair.

I left two hours later. Hair cut short but not crazy. Blonde but not Peroxide Pris. Tidy but not boring. I caught glimpses of myself in shop windows, and every time, I paused, smiled, put a hand through my hair and walked on to the next.

I was the me I was supposed to be. I felt it through every inch of my body. I was the real Iris. The right Iris. And now my outside matched. No more what-ifs, only what-nows. I was slim, muscled, strong, tall, bright, beautiful. I was me.

But a haircut can't fix everything.

At three tomorrow, I'd have to face my final demon. I'd have to choose a path.

And I had no idea which.

I didn't sleep much. I missed my telescope – destroyed in the cabin – but I wouldn't have been able to see stars that night. The clouds were heavy and bloomed orange from the street lights. But they were out there somewhere, and that at least gave me comfort.

In the morning, I borrowed one of Ellis's wheeled suitcases and packed what I had and what he'd bought for me. I dragged the battered backpack from under the bed, where it had stayed, untouched, for a month. It stank of mould and woodsmoke and it was time to rid myself of it, move forward. I pulled out crumpled T-shirts, still damp from the storm, except there hadn't been a storm, yet I felt it again, the sound of the wind, the biting cold rain, the shouts, the crash of the cabin breaking.

I threw the shirts in the trash pile. Took a breath. Thought about throwing the whole bag away but made myself look through it. Think of it as therapy, desensitisation, more memories to face and move past.

I pulled out a pair of pants, torn, covered in mud, and put them to one side. Then the GO TIGERS mug, chipped, handle broken. More clothes, trinkets, two empty notebooks, a waterlogged pen. I emptied the side pockets. A bent tent peg. The useless multi tool. A head torch with dead batteries. Onto the pile they went. So little remained of a life I'd thought I wanted.

I went through the bag again and found, stuffed in the boot compartment, a crumpled ball of damp red nylon I took to be my jacket.

I was about to add it to the trash pile when something stopped me. This was the jacket I'd been wearing when I fell down the ravine, the one I'd ripped up the back along with my skin. But . . . I shook out the fabric and frowned.

No rips.

No mud.

This jacket was whole because it wasn't mine. It was hers. And hers. And hers. It belonged to the Iris who'd married Bella, the one who'd slept on the bus in my favourite seat, the one who'd stepped off the overhang. I held it to my chest, my face. Breathed it in. Breathed them in. Hugged it as if I was hugging them.

Had it been real? Or just real to me? Did that even matter now, after all this? Life isn't a movie, Iris, we don't always get the neat ending we want.

I slipped on the jacket and felt the weight of my decisions and their decisions, our what-ifs, our maybes. I was every Iris and they were me. Other Iris had been me and I her. I had jumped off the overhang and I hadn't. I had married Claude and I hadn't. I'd hurt her and I hadn't. The comfort came in waves, and all I could do was sit and hold myself. No matter if Iris had been real or not, I knew now I hadn't been alone in the woods. I didn't need to be alone again.

I wiped my eyes, zipped up the jacket and packed the rest of my world inside Ellis's suitcase.

When I emerged from the bedroom, he looked at me strangely. 'You look different. Was the raccoon hiding in the bag this whole time?'

I smiled. 'No, just . . . Never mind.' I took a deep breath, felt a weight lift, a dark cloud disperse. 'I have to go now.'

He didn't ask what I was doing, where I was going, because no answer would be good for him. But he gave me money. A lot of it. Just in case.

'I'll miss you,' he said.

'This isn't goodbye.'

'I know, but I just got used to having you around.'

'Whatever,' I laughed. 'You're going to be lost without me. Please, Ell, for the love of God, move!'

I hugged him and he bear-hugged me back, and I left his apartment.

The suitcase and I trundled down the street. I thought about getting a cab, taking the subway or a bus, anything would be quicker, but I wanted to walk. Needed to walk. My ankle was weak and the physio had said I shouldn't be afraid of putting it through its paces. An old physio joke there, he'd said with an apologetic grin.

I felt that familiar pull in my legs, guiding me along the city streets like a magnet. I let it sweep me along because I knew where it was leading me.

At a quarter to three, I walked into Grand Central. The station buzzed with activity. Tourist groups flashed their cameras. Lovers kissed on the famous steps. Commuters hurried across the concourse, dodging children and dawdlers. Travellers strode beaming from the platforms, huge packs strapped to their backs like hermit crabs, ready for adventure. The building gleamed yellow and gold in the afternoon light.

The departure boards flashed updates every few seconds, calling platform numbers and delays. I went to the ticket office and bought the ticket I'd always wanted to, clutched it in my hands like it was made of gold.

The Italian café was between me and the platform. I sat on a bench outside, hidden in a throng of tourists as the big clock ticked to three.

Would Claude have cleared her day for me? Would she really cancel on the Koreans, whoever the hell they were?

Ten minutes. I'd wait ten minutes.

My heart fluttered in my chest as the seconds ticked by.

People came in and out the door constantly but none of them were her.

Five past. No sign.

I checked the departures board. The train left in twenty-five minutes.

Ten past. She hadn't come. She hadn't cleared her day. She never would. Not for me. I wiped a tear I didn't know I'd cried, and stood.

Inside the café, a large table of travellers left. I watched them funnel out of the tightly packed café, and there, revealed, was Claude, alone at a table for two.

My heart kicked.

She had cleared her day. She had chosen me.

She kicked her foot against the table leg and her hands turned an almost empty coffee cup around in circles, while a second cup, full to the brim with white foam, waited for me on the other side of the table. A woman at the next table turned, scowled at her and nodded to her foot. I knew this moment. I held my breath, waited for the squint, the tilt of the head, the harder kick, but none came. She only raised her hand in apology and her foot fell still.

She didn't look like herself. Her hair was lank and unbrushed, her clothes crumpled. She was pale and tired and I wanted to go to her. I wanted to hold her and say sorry and hear her apologies and kiss her like we'd just met. I wanted to forgive her. Wanted her to forgive me. Despite myself. Despite my pain and sorrow and what she'd put me through and what I'd done to her and who I'd let myself become because of her. Despite it all, I loved her. She was broken and so was I, and I wanted to stay, to fix us, because when we were good, we were supernova. We were radiant and eternal and nobody else came close.

On the board, my platform number flashed against the service.

Inside the café, my wife waited to make amends. On the train, my life waited to begin afresh. I stood between two worlds. Again. I wondered what choice another me was making right now. Would she go to Claude? Or to the train? Would she regret going for the rest of her life? Would she regret not going more?

I took a step, faltered.

In that moment, as if sensing me, Claude looked up, out the window, through the throng of people, and found me. Her eyes brightened. Her face broke into a smile and she lifted her hand to wave. Here I am, she said. I'm here for you.

An announcement came over the PA. My train had started boarding.

How could I ever be sure of making the right decision? How could I turn my back on one life in favour of another?

I thought of Iris, the version of me who had a whole different set of regrets, even though she had made the 'right' choices, and I knew the answer. There was no right choice. No right life. Only the one we chose for ourselves. My father said I had to be brave enough to live the life I wanted, and not the one everyone expected of me. He told me not to make his mistakes, and I wouldn't.

I knew which life and which love I wanted. But I had to be brave.

I took a deep breath, gripped the handle of my suitcase, and started walking.

Acknowledgements

This is the hardest page of a novel to write. So many people work to turn a manuscript into a book and each one of them has my gratitude, especially in these troubled times. Thank you to my brilliant editors Kwaku Osei-Afrifa and Sara Adams, and to Kate Keehan and Alice Morley and the brilliant team at Hodder Studio for your all your enthusiasm and excitement for Iris. Thank you to my agent, Jemima Forrester and the team at David Higham for believing in this book.

Thank you to Colin Scott, for your unwavering support and your often inappropriate but much-needed humour in these dark times.

Thank you to my constant first reader, my mother, who is never shy in telling me how to do better.

Thank you to my daughter, Thea, for sleeping through the night so mummy could finish her edits.

And to my wife, Neen, my rock, my sounding board, my cheer-leader, thank you most of all.

About the Author

Beth Lewis was raised in the wilds of Cornwall and split her childhood between books and the beach. She has travelled extensively throughout the world and has had close encounters with black bears, killer whales, and Great White Sharks. She has been, at turns, a bank cashier, fire performer, juggler and now works in publishing. She lives in Oxford with her wife and daughter.

About the Author